EVERLASTIN' DESIRE

"Who are you?"

"No' a ghost or spirit or aught else your mind could choose to call me," she answered softly. "I be someone who can love ye despite your unwillingness to trust what's in your heart."

"You don't know me," he growled.

"I know everythin' abou' ye. No . . . Winston . . . tis time to put everythin' else aside and bond, ye and I."

"Bond?"

"Aye. As in bed me."

"No!" But even as the word tore from his throat, he knew he was lost.

"I love ye, Winston Ian Connery," she whispered. "Only ye can fill this ache in ma heart. Only I can fill yours."

He looked into her eyes. It struck him that he'd been looking for her—waiting just for her—his whole life.

BOOK YOUR PLACE ON OUR WEBSITE AND MAKE THE READING CONNECTION!

We've created a customized website just for our very special readers, where you can get the inside scoop on everything that's going on with Zebra, Pinnacle and Kensington books.

When you come online, you'll have the exciting opportunity to:

- View covers of upcoming books
- Read sample chapters
- Learn about our future publishing schedule (listed by publication month *and author*)
- Find out when your favorite authors will be visiting a city near you
- Search for and order backlist books from our online catalog
- Check out author bios and background information
- Send e-mail to your favorite authors
- Meet the Kensington staff online
- Join us in weekly chats with authors, readers and other guests
- Get writing guidelines
- AND MUCH MORE!

Visit our website at
http://www.pinnaclebooks.com

LOVE EVERLASTIN'

Mickee Madden

Pinnacle Books
Kensington Publishing Corp.

http://www.pinnaclebooks.com

PINNACLE BOOKS are published by

Kensington Publishing Corp.
850 Third Avenue
New York, NY 10022

First Printing: July, 1998
10 9 8 7 6 5 4 3 2 1

Printed in the United States of America

For Steve. May we see another 26 years together.
For Denise, who I dearly miss. For my critique members,
Guy, Rosella, Marsha, Sandy, Mike, and Buddy.
For my agent, Linda. And for the readers—
Thank you!

Special thanks and gratitude to everyone at Zebra and
Pinnacle, especially my editor, Carin, and Barbara in
contracts, for their patience above and beyond the call of duty.

GLOSSARY

abou'/about

afeared/afraid

afore/before

a'maist/almost

althegither/
   altogether

aneuch/enough

anither/another

aught/anything

auld/old

bahookie/buttocks

brither/brother

canna/cannot

claes/clothes

corbie/crow

couldna/couldn't

craiture/creature

daith/death

dee/die

deil/devil

didna/didn't

dinna/don't

dochter/daughter

dule/sorrow

efter/after

faither/father

haud yer wheesht/
   hold your noise

havena/haven't

hisself/himself

ither/other

ma/my

mair/more

mair'n/more than

mairrit/married

maist/most

mak/make

maself/myself

mither/mother

mon/man

na, nae/no

na canny/unnatural

no'/not

nocht/nothing

o'/of

oor/our

orra/odd

ou'/out

shouldna/shouldn't

tak/take

tha'/that

thegither/together

tis/it is

twas/it was

verra/very

wae/woe

wasna/wasn't

weel/well

wha'/what

wi'/with

willna/will not

winna/won't

wouldna/wouldn't

womon/woman

Chapter One

Milky fog emanated from the still waters of Loch Ken and rolled languidly across the night-cloaked land. The dense chilling mist blanketed three months' worth of packed snow. In a little more than two weeks it would be spring. A time of rebirth and newness. A time of revitalization. The winter had been a particularly harsh one, wrought with one storm after another. Many anxiously awaited the passing of the season, but to one man, snow, rain or sunshine, he would never again feel anything but numbness. Physical and emotional numbness.

Sitting half-frozen in his parked dark blue Audi, he vaguely acknowledged the deathlike nothingness threatening to consume him. His clenched hands lay atop his lap. Shaggy black hair and an unkempt beard and mustache framed his cadaverous-pale face. Dark circles punctuated the vacantness in his light gray-green eyes. Slouched in the front seat behind the steering wheel, his back to the door, he stared unseeingly at the frost-coated window on the passenger side. Sometime ago, ice had formed on the glass, cutting off most of his view of the house which loomed atop a hill on the opposite side of the road. He'd been staring at the place for several hours, trying to work up the courage to approach the inhabitants. It had taken him two months to get this far. The last hurdle, the actual act of forcing himself to get out of the Audi and climb the driveway and rap on the front door, seemed utterly beyond his capability. It was as if he had died shortly after parking on the shoulder of the road. His deep inner fears of further losing himself had vanished and had been replaced with numbness. His desperation to find emotional solace had dwindled beneath a suffocating shroud of numbness. His willpower had deserted him. Numbness. Even his anger was gone. After so long . . . *gone.* The numbness was all, the omnipresence of his existence. And since the cold had penetrated his meager clothing and his skin and his bones, he could no longer feel what he clutched in his right hand. The remnants had been so very important to him since last Christmas Eve. His only link to his wayward sanity.

His heavy eyelids drooped, now covering half of his bloodshot eyes. He told himself he was slowly freezing to death, but he couldn't even summon up a modicum of concern, of regret. He'd walked away from everything. Lost all he had, including not only the respect of his peers, but *his* self-respect. With the Phantom no longer a threat to society, he should feel exhilaration, *triumph,* but Rose's death had taken the heart out of him. His soul, the very essence of the man he'd been, had been wrenched from the flesh-and-bone shell that now housed his pathetic remains. There was no going back. Not to the agency, his flat, or his unsympathetic family. He now knew that his psychic gifts had been leading him to this point for many years.

Winston Ian Connery would cease to be this night.

He would be found frozen to the seat, his unbuttoned black trench coat haphazardly draped on him. Eventually, when his identity was known, it would be said that this promising young man had unfortunately succumbed to exposure after falling asleep in his car. The highlights of his career would be mentioned. His *family* would lament their grief, when in fact he knew they would secretly be grateful the black sheep had passed on without further embarrassing them.

No regrets. Except Rose.

He would have gladly sacrificed his own life to have given her the chance to return to her husband and two small sons. They had wept at her passing, and psychically imbibing their grief had been the darkest, most shattering experience of his life.

Winston's existence had been enmeshed with the lives of strangers for most of his life. He had experienced genuine emotion only through them. Loved, hated, feared and rejoiced only through others. Left on his own, he was but a shell. His lot in life had been that of a psychic conduit, but now that, too, was denied him.

He'd come to Baird House on the slim hope its magic would save him, or at least grant him the ability to feel *something* of his own. But he couldn't bring himself to intrude. The inhabitants of the mansion had been through enough. It wasn't his place to ask them for anything, to ask *anyone* to help him. Not when he couldn't help himself.

Releasing a thready breath, Winston drowsily watched vapors rise in front of his face. He tried to will his palm and curled fingers to acknowledge the texture of the rose petals against his skin, but he couldn't even feel his hand. His limbs had lost all sensation a while ago.

Rose. *Rose.*

She hadn't deserved to suffer as she had. If only he

could have brought her here, to this house, to be touched by the magic he had witnessed Christmas Eve. . . .

Or had that been a dream?

A spark of fear returned.

No! Not a dream! Not a hallucination!

When he attempted to verbalize a protest, only a croaking sound passed his lips.

I have to know! he mentally cried, panic enlarging his eyes. *It had to have been real! Laura Bennett. She should have died, but I saw. . . .*

He gulped past the agonizing rawness in his throat.

I know wha' I saw. I know wha' I saw, he silently chanted, a wild almost maniacal gleam igniting in his irises.

Roses in the snow.

Rose died. The bloody symbolism's there!

Why can't I think clearly?

Rose?

You bastard bureaucrats! You let her die rather than trust me to help her!

I found her, didn't I? It should have been up to me, you friggin' hypocrites!

Red tape.

A bitter, caustic laugh boomed inside his skull.

The world's bein' rent apart by numbers and red tape!

The time's comin' when we'll no' have names. "How good to see you Mr. 10583-67-991472. Wha' can I do for you this fine . . . bright . . . morn . . . ?"

The magic has to be real! Sweet Jesus, don't take tha' from me, too!

Anger made a miserable bid to heat his blood.

He had to know for sure if he'd only imagined last Christmas Eve when Lachlan Baird had transformed a winter's night into something from out of a fairy tale. All else in Winston's life could prove false right now, but *not* the significance of the rose he'd carried with him since the ghost's "miracle".

Determined to banish his doubts before it was too late, he turned on the seat.

Thought he had turned, when in fact, he hadn't moved at all. It suddenly struck him that he couldn't move his limbs. They were blocks of ice. Dead. Useless.

Unbidden, tears brimmed his eyes.

All the mistakes he'd made in his thirty-six years flooded to the fore of his mind. He winced. The cases he had solved, the lives he had saved, all paled in significance to the life of denial he'd led. No one had ever understood that his "gifts" had left him vulnerable. Had taught him he *couldn't* lead a normal life. Had taught him he couldn't *ever* hope of having anything more than what he already possessed. There would never be a woman with whom he could share his life. What woman would tolerate a man who would know her every thought, her every secret? And what woman could possibly love a man incapable of feeling his own emotions?

He would never experience fatherhood. Even *that* biological proclivity was something he had only experienced through the tapped-into psychic byways of existing fathers he'd encountered.

Since the age of three, he'd been little more than a breathing psychic machine—a highly evolved, intricately-designed conduit with which to decipher the human condition. His sole purpose revolved around the suffering of ordinary people. Ironically, without murderers, kidnappers, robbers and drug dealers, nature likely would have shelved him years ago—much as his parents had done for the sake of the family's reputation.

"Anonymity," his father would say, "has its price." And that price had been to sacrifice his only son.

To prevent friends and associates from learning of Winston's peculiar gifts, from the age of four to twenty-two, his parents had boarded him in one private school after another. If he hadn't happened upon the Shields Agency—a job in which his gifts were not only utilized but considered invaluable—he could almost believe he would still be in a classroom.

Now he was learning a lesson of a different kind.

A shudder coursed through him as he told himself it wasn't right to die this way. Not in this place. Not at this time.

Is this wha' it's like for someone contemplatin' suicide? Teeterin' on the brink o' uncertainty? Wonderin' if their despair could possibly amount to somethin' else? Somethin' . . . painless. Somethin' tha' perhaps even felt . . . good?

An agonized groan gurgled in his throat. It escalated into a strangled outcry when the door bracing his spine unexpectedly gave way. He pitched backward. In a blur of motion and confusion, his world went round and round, rightside up and upside down, leaving him with the impression that he'd been vacuumed into a spinning tunnel. He was vaguely conscious of someone trying to right him onto his feet, but his legs wouldn't cooperate. They dangled beneath him. Stiff. Unfeeling. Bent at the knees like plastic molded legs on baby dolls. Words tried to penetrate the layers of befuddlement blanketing his brain. None passed his raw, cracked lips. He continued to sink deeper and deeper into a void of merciful oblivion, until at last his torment and pain were released within the inky blackness of unconsciousness.

Unaware of the passage of time, sounds drew him from his safe haven. Soft voices spoken so as not to disturb him. The crackle and snap of flames rendering wood to ashes. There was also a backdrop of silence so full it seemed like a presence leaning over his shoulder, its chilling breath fanning the taut muscles in his neck and face. A sensation of pins and needles tormented his hands and feet, but the pain was not enough to equal the torment in his mind. He knew he was safe and secured within a dwelling, but he wasn't sure that he wanted to feel protected at the moment. He'd been on a direct path to self-destruction. So close, he believed he'd heard death's approach at the periphery of his mind.

Against his will, his eyelids fluttered open. A blazing hearth a short distance away first filled his vision. Waves of heat washed over him and he was surprised to realize that perspiration was trickling down his face. His gaze dropped to where his hands were clawlike upon his blanketed lap, the skin red and chafed and looking far older than his actual years.

Finally, the pain in his hands and feet grew unbearable. He locked his teeth against a protest and breathed sparingly through his nostrils.

"I don't like this, Roan," a woman whispered, just loud enough for Winston to make out her words.

In a slightly louder tone, a man replied, "Give it a while. If he doesn't come round soon, I'll fetch the doctor."

The woman sighed deeply, impatiently. Winston could feel her gaze on his back and he sensed her reluctance to have a virtual stranger within her home.

Winston lightly frowned as he studied the light blue and deep purple plaid of the lap blanket covering his legs. The MacLachlan plaid was red and blue, the clan badge, a castle. For the life of him he couldn't remember which clan blue and purple represented, and the fragment of lost memory annoyed him.

No, no' MacLachlan. No' the clan at all. Baird. Lachlan Baird . . .

"How are you feeling?"

The woman's soft tone drew his gaze to his right. He stared into vibrant green eyes which not only betrayed the extent of her concern for him, but also her wariness. When he tried to speak, he discovered his raw throat was incapable of releasing anything but a raspy croaking sound.

"Darlin', fetch him some Scotch."

The woman Winston knew to be Laura Bennett, straightened from her bent position and looked off to her left. "I think some hot tea—"

"Laura-lass," Roan Ingliss said with a hint of impatience, "a Scotsmon knows how to tak care o' his own."

"Fine. Then *you* get it."

Her stubbornness brought a hint of a smile to Winston's aching lips. From the corner of his eye, he saw Roan Ingliss—new laird of Baird House—leave the room. Laura drew up another winged-back chair and seated herself to Winston's right. He watched her askance as she stared into the flames for a time, her expression unreadable. Winston realized his presence had caused a rift between the couple. It had never been his intention to cause anyone a problem. Quite the opposite. He'd slithered away from his former life, sparing everyone who even remotely knew him, the embarrassment of seeing him retire from the world. He certainly hadn't parked across the street from Baird House to cause a problem for the residing couple. Not only hadn't he elicited their help, but he was perplexed that they had somehow rescued him from his own stupidity.

Finding Laura's gaze riveted on him, gave him a start. The heat of a guilt-based blush surged into his face and he looked away.

"Don't you think there's been enough deaths here to last us a lifetime?" she asked, an edge to her tone, which made him inwardly shrivel. After a moment, she added, "A nod will suffice, thank you," and it, too, was delivered scoldingly.

He nodded, then gulped past the rawness in his throat.

She sighed, its sound carrying a note of dismay. "I remember you. You were here Christmas Eve."

Again he nodded, but this time he forced himself to look at her. She was still watching him with an analytical glint in her eyes, a maternal look which reminded him of his grandmother, who had died nearly twenty years ago. He found himself wishing he could return to those days, if only briefly. Katherine Theresa Connery had been the only person in his life to understand him, and to accept him, strange gifts and all. The letters she'd written to him over the years were in the trunk of his car. They remained his only true treasures. Them and the rose petals.

"Here."

Roan's deep voice caused both Winston and Laura to start. While she delivered the laird an exasperated look, Winston hungrily fixed his gaze on the proffered brandy snifter. *Scotch in a brandy snifter?* It didn't matter. The golden whiskey that filled half the glass seemed to wink at him. He felt it beckon to him to experience its promised warmth, taste its promise of liquid stamina. He attempted to lift his right hand, but the maddening prickling sensations weighted all four of his appendages.

"I'll do it," Laura said. Taking the snifter from Roan, she tipped the rim to Winston's lips. He attempted to take too large a swig. The Scotch went down his throat, burning tissue and making him cough. Behind him, he heard the laird laugh low, and Winston's temper surfaced. But again when he attempted to speak, only garbled sounds emerged.

"Sip it," Laura chided. She tipped the brandy snifter again to his lips. This time, Winston took meager sips. The burning in his throat continued for several seconds, then finally the pain dulled to little more than scratchiness. He sipped and sipped while unconsciously flexing his fingers and toes. The Scotch settled poorly in his stomach but, undaunted, he stayed with it until he'd downed the last drop. By the time Laura lowered the snifter to her lap, Winston was alert and beginning to feel his blood flow through his hands and feet.

"Are you up for somethin' to eat?"

Winston shook his head, then almost immediately nodded when it occurred to him he couldn't remember when he'd last eaten. He didn't need to compound his weakness with a hangover.

"The stew's still on the stove," Laura said, rising from the chair. "Roan, you want anything?"

"Na. Thanks."

Winston stared down at his hands as the laird lowered himself onto the chair Laura had occupied. For a time, silence hung in the air between them.

Clearing his throat, Roan braced his forearms atop his knees. "I didn't mean to handle you so rough, but I bloody weel thought you were dead—frozen on the front seat o' your car!"

Winston cast the man an apologetic look.

"Look . . . Mr. Connery, I didn't recognize you at first. I rummaged through your wallet once I brought you inside." Roan's light brown eyes—amber in the firelight—narrowed broodingly. He reached out and took something from Winston's lap. A moment later, Winston was staring at the shriveled, dried petals of the rose he had plucked Christmas Eve, the petals he'd been clutching for more hours than he could recall. "O' course," Roan went on, "I recognized your name right enough, but I've got to tell you, you're a sorry sight compared to the mon I remember here a few months back. Now, if ma memory serves me correctly, didn't Lannie tell you to bring a womon here?"

A vile burning sensation rose from the pit of Winston's stomach into his throat. For a horrifying moment he thought he was going to vomit, but the burning proved to be psychological, not physical. He stiltedly nodded. Tears misted his gray-green eyes. Anger thrummed through his veins.

Roan lowered his gaze to his upturned palm and absently poked at the petals spread across it. "I couldn't help but notice tha' your gold shield was missin'." He spared his guest an unsettling, measuring look. "You returned here for a reason, Mr. Connery. I'd like to hear why."

Although his voice was but a hoarse whisper, Winston spoke his first name.

"All right," Roan said. "Winston, what's this abou'?"

"She died."

"I'm sorry, I truly am. But is tha' any reason to try to freeze yourself to death so bloody close to ma property?" Roan's voice grew deeper with frustration. "If you're so bent on killin' yourself, mon, at least have the decency to do it far away from Laura and the laddies. Or are you . . . *Winston* . . . fancyin' addin' yourself to the Baird House list o' the walkin' dead?"

"Your sarcasm is no' appreciated," Winston wheezed.

Roan clamped the palm of his free hand to his broad chest. "Beg your pardon, Mr. Detective, sir, but I'm resistin' a powerful urge to shake some sense into you! If you came for help, mon, this house welcomes you. But *I'll* no' tolerate anither suicide *on* or *near* this property. Do you understand me?"

"Roan."

Laura's gentle chiding straightened the laird in his chair. He rose to his feet and immediately stepped aside, allowing her to seat herself next to their guest. She laid the silver tray she carried, on her lap. "Roan made a batch of lamb stew this morning. It's pretty good."

"*Pretty* good?" Roan challenged indignantly.

With a roll of her eyes, she amended, "Absolutely the *best* lamb stew ever cooked on a gas stove."

Roan grinned. "Give the cook his due, I say."

A smile straining to appear on her lips, she went on, "Anyway, can you manage on your own? I don't mind spoonfeed—"

"I can manage," Winston rasped.

With a nod, Laura placed the tray on his lap, then rose and stepped back out of Winston's sight, allowing him to eat in a semblance of privacy.

Despite his aching trembling hands, he did manage to eat most of the stew and half the corn biscuit. He finished the cup of tea and, feeling full and almost human again, dabbed at his mouth with the white linen napkin. Shortly, Laura took the tray away and disappeared into the dining room to Winston's left. It was then he looked up and regarded the reticent laird, who stood ten feet back, his arms crossed against his broad chest.

"Thank you."

"Ma pleasure," Roan murmured. He came forward and lifted the chair. Once he had replaced it next to one of the pink and gold sofas arranged on a Persian carpet in the center of the room, he returned and positioned himself alongside Winston.

"A good night's sleep is wha' you need. Can you negotiate the stairs?"

A tremor of fear speared Winston, but he forced it back. He drew in a ragged breath and eased himself up onto his feet. At first he swayed. Teetered like a drunk. Seconds later, he felt steady enough to take a step. Then another. And another.

Laura returned. She went to Roan's side and linked an arm through one of his, her sympathetic gaze on Winston. "I think he should sleep in the library tonight. He doesn't look too steady to me."

"I don't want to be a burden."

Roan's previous burliness visibly evaporated. Going to Winston's side, he cupped a supporting hand beneath the man's elbow. "Ma Aunt Aggie fixed you a room on the second floor." He looked at Laura and explained, "The library sofa is too hard." To Winston, he went on, "It has a private bathroom. Ma aunt was lookin' forward to seein' to your needs, but the lads wore her ou'. I'm afraid she's in the grayness for a time."

"Grayness?"

"Don't ask," Roan said humorously.

"Thank you. Mr.—"

"Roan."

Winston nodded. "Roan, may I ask anither favor?"

"Sure."

"Ma rose. I'd like it back, please."

"Laura, it's on the coffee table."

"Okay, I'll get it," she said.

Winston momentarily closed his eyes. When he opened them, he found the laird shrewdly studying him. "It means a lot to me," he murmured.

"We'll talk in the morn, when you're rested. Have you a suitcase wi' you?"

Winston shook his head.

A mischievous gleam lit Roan's eyes, and he grinned. "Weel, now, you're o' a slighter build than me. Lannie's claes should fit you nicely, though."

"Oh, God," Laura groaned.

Winston arched a questioning brow. When Roan laughed, he decided he didn't want to know what had struck the man so funny. But by the time he'd gotten to the foot of the staircase, he remembered Lachlan Baird's mid-nineteenth century attire that Christmas Eve.

An image of himself dressed in black, snug-fitting trousers, black knee boots, and a full-sleeved shirt like those worn by pirates in the movies, prompted a guttural laugh to escape him. His spirits lifted and, for the first time in a very long while, his shoulders didn't feel quite so burdened with the problems of the world.

"I've claes to spare," Roan said good-naturedly to Winston. Then the laird offered Laura a playful wink.

The only thing Winston could think of to say, was another, "Thank you."

With Roan to his right and Laura behind, Winston began to climb. One step. Slowly, two steps. Feeling exhausted, the third step. He reached out to further balance himself with the highly polished mahogany rail. The instant his skin made contact, a blast of icy psychic waves coursed through him. He released an inordinately loud gasp, as if a great bellows were in his chest in lieu of lungs. He was oblivious to Laura shrinking back, and of Roan's face going pale. He could only focus on the freezing ignitions going off inside him, one after another, in such rapid succession, he couldn't catch his breath. His body violently shook, not unlike someone in the throes of electrocution. His palm was stuck fast to the wood. Wisps of vibrant blue psychic energy whiplashed from the hand.

"Roan!" Laura cried.

Winston tried to force an image to his mind. Never had he experienced a connection so powerful. But no image came. Again a first. He was beginning to think his heart would burst in his chest when, unexpectedly, the current came to an abrupt halt. He began to collapse, but Roan's quick reaction spared him from hitting the stairs. The larger man helped him to sit on one of the steps, and then sat beside him. His head spinning, Winston cleared his vision enough to scan Laura's taut, wan features. His heart was still thundering.

"Wha' the bloody hell?" Roan gasped.

Wetting his lower lip with the tip of his tongue, Winston allowed residual impressions to settle in his mind. What was formulating, stunned him.

"Sorry," he murmured. Weakly, he brushed the back of a hand across his perspiring brow. "It has never happened like this."

Warily eyeing Winston, Laura asked, "What happened?"

"I'm no' sure how to explain it."

"I'll mak it easy for you," said Roan. "Did the *house* zap you, or *you* the bloody house?"

"It's alive," Winston breathed, then released a brief burst of hysterical laughter.

Laura and Roan exchanged harried glances.

"As crazy as it sounds, it *is* alive!"

Roan grimaced. "I'm a'maist afraid to ask wha' this 'it' is."

Feeling strangely euphoric, Winston announced, "The house. It's alive."

"Damn me," Roan grumbled, rising to his feet. He raked his large hands through his mane of thick, light brown curly hair, then released a breath through pursed lips. "Just when things were quietin' down."

"It was incredible," Winston said. "I've never experienced such *pure* energy."

Winston's mind raced to analyze the tingling sensations coursing through his body. It was as if his every cell were being rejuvenated. Unconsciously, he uncurled the fingers of his right hand. Upon his upturned palm were the petals of the purple rose he'd plucked Christmas Eve. No longer were they shriveled and dried out. Their renewed velvety texture sparkled, as if winking up at him. Feeling like a child bestowed with his most wished-for gift, he looked up to find two sets of inquisitive eyes watching him. Their gazes lowered to the petals. Then again in unison, they looked at him. Winston knew they couldn't understand the importance, the *relevance,* of the restored rose petals. How could they when even *he* couldn't neatly put into words what his mind and heart were trying to tell him?

He'd been so desperate to find answers, to find himself, and he'd placed so much hope on this house.... And now the structure welcomed him. At least, that's what he deduced from the restoration of the petals. The house was telling him that he'd come to the right place. If fate meant for him to confront his mental demons, then it was surely at this place it needed to be done. Because, and he wasn't sure why he was so certain of this, the house would protect him from himself. It would allow the emotional backwash of wounds he'd obtained throughout his career, to finally heal.

"Are you . . . all right?" Roan hesitantly asked Winston.

Winston nodded in response. He felt an urge to vent his exhilaration, to shout his joy, but he held back. When the new laird of Baird House gripped his arm and drew him to his feet, Winston didn't protest. He reverently closed his fingers over the petals, then headed up the staircase alongside Roan. He was dimly conscious of Laura following. Vaguely aware that he was taking each step without the slightest discomfort. When he realized the three of them were going down a long hall, he reined in his attention.

He, too, had taken the Christmas Eve tour through the mansion, but there had been so many rooms, he couldn't recall this part of the house. His system still tingling, he watched Roan pick up his pace and open the last door on the right. Winston paused at the threshhold and gestured for Laura to enter ahead of him, then he followed closely at her heels. Roan had lit the wall gaslight by the door and was now crouched in front of the fireplace, preparing the hearth. Despite the freezing temperature outside, the spacious room was cozy. Or perhaps, Winston reflected, his experience on the staircase still had his blood afire.

Laura joined Roan at the hearth. While they conversed in hushed tones, Winston curiously surveyed his new sur-

roundings. He told himself that he could wander repeatedly through the house and never tire of its furnishings.
Not only was the decor from another century, but the air
itself held an ambiance of a more innocent age. Directly
across from the fireplace was a massive seventeenth century, oak, four-poster bed with a paneled canopy. From
where he stood, he could make out intricately carved
foliage and grapes on the headboard, posts and footboard.
The quilt and matching covered pillows were done in
vibrant blue, grays, and varying shades of purple, the pat-
tern depicting Grecian urns and peacocks. To each side
of the bed were matching tall chest of drawers. To his right
was an oak show-wood frame triple-back settee, undercut
with foliate ornaments. The upholstery was deep purple
velvet. Above this was a George II oak and gilt framed
landscaped mirror, under an oil panel of a garden scene
with browsing peacocks. A Persian rug of royal blue and
golds was centered on the otherwise highly polished wood
floor. Across the room were two elongated windows that
bore tied-back velvet drapes of royal blue. And between
these was a late Stuart chair, the back of which contained
panels of carved foliage.

Winston stepped further into the room, then again
stopped a short distance from the couple who was watching
him. His gaze swept over the red brick fireplace and the
brass knick-knacks meticulously arranged on the foliage-
carved oak mantel. The walls were textured plaster, soft-
gold in color. Every four feet, vertical, decorative pale gray
molding had been installed.

"I tak it you approve?" Roan asked with a crooked grin.

Winston nodded. He told himself that if anyone asked
him to describe the room in a single word, he would fail
miserably. He couldn't express his awe in a *sentence*. A
paragraph! He only knew that if he could lock himself

away in this small corner of the mansion, he would never want for anything else.

He was home.

But he could no more fathom why he felt this so strongly than he could even begin to understand the too-often cruel twists of fate.

He'd never felt at home at his family's estate. Yet here, in Baird House, it was as if he'd been born within its walls.

"Winston, can I get you anything else from the kitchen?" Laura asked.

"No. Thank you."

"Ma aunt put a toothbrush, soap, shampoo, and shavin' necessities in your bathroom," said Roan.

"Thank you."

Roan gave a single nod, then draped an arm across Laura's shoulders and urged her toward the door. As he passed Winston, he added, "Mak yourself at home. The lads are asleep on the third floor. They shouldn't bother you."

Winston dazedly nodded.

At the threshold, Roan stopped and looked at his guest. "I'll bring you clean claes in the morn. Get some sleep, mon."

Winston's head bobbed until the door had closed behind the couple, then he straightened his shoulders and drew in a deep, cleansing breath.

Although night's curtain was visible beyond the window panes, Winston was wide awake. Energy sang through his veins. He'd never felt so alive, so wired without an outside influence feeding his psychic channels.

Turning the gaslight key and dousing the flame, he went to the fireplace mantel and placed the rose petals on the polished surface. The fire in the hearth not only spilled waves of warmth against his legs, but softened the room's dimensions. Shadowed recesses surrounded him on three sides. He felt snug and secure, as though in a nurturing womb. The misery and despondency that had relentlessly stalked him since Rose's death, was but a dim memory.

Swathed in sheer contentment, he lowered himself onto the red brick hearth and sat Indian-style. He stared into the dancing flames for a time, his mind unburdened with thought and his spirit so at ease, he could have endlessly drifted off to a faraway place and lost himself. He didn't care what the morning brought. There was only now. Only the moment.

Although he wasn't the least bit sleepy, the peacefulness of the room beckoned him to surrender to its influence. His eyelids grew heavier and heavier until gradually lowering. When he was deep within himself, he unwittingly lowered his mind shields. Not since the age of eleven had he fully lowered his protective barriers, not even when investigating a case. It had always been too painful. Too traumatizing. Nature had not given him a ready-made defense through which to filter psychic static. He'd had to teach himself to shut out the unwanted and unnecessary energy particles in order to save his sanity.

An image formed in front of his mind's eye. The scene was of a fantasy garden. Bright white and deep purple roses in full bloom. Fantailed peacocks strutting among the bushes. Birds with vibrantly colored butterfly wings, and butterflies with various bird wings. The sky was neither day nor night. Like the air surrounding him, it was imbued with millions of glittering specks. In the heart of the garden was a tall white marble fountain. When his mind's eye zoomed in for a closer look at the statue cresting it, he was stunned to see that it was a nude rendition of himself. Water cascaded from a large golden unicorn horn held out in the statue's right hand.

Then it struck him that he was not just visualizing the surrealistic realm, but he was actually *there*.

For a long time he studied his stone face. The features were at peace. *Hopeful* . . . although hopeful of what, he didn't know. Gentle bird sounds caressed his hearing. Floral scents filled his nostrils. It was springtime, or something akin to spring. Again he wasn't sure.

From somewhere behind his position, something distracted him. He turned his head and glimpsed the outline of a figure. Horizontal contrails glimmered in its wake, giving testimony to the movement. Although the translucent form was comprised of the same sparkling particles, he managed to get a clear impression before it melted into the landscape.

Female.

He found himself straining to see her again. Bewitching air stirred around him, the cocooning contrails suggesting that she was circling him again and again. He heard a soft, musical laugh, then, "Winston, catch me if ye can."

He reached out this way and that, hoping to locate her, hoping to prompt her to solidify. To no avail. The air continued to frolic around him, whimsically eddying, teasing him.

"I would if I could!" he shouted merrily. "Come, lass. Give me a fair see!"

"Too soon, ma dour Scotsmon," she said in a singsong manner.

A smile youthening his face, he whirled about, his eyes feverishly scanning his surroundings. "Wha' is this place?"

"Ma home. I've never let anyone come afore. Why *ye,* ye ask?" Her trilling laugh lifted his spirits even higher. *"Because,* tha' be why. Reason aneuch?"

He nodded. "Can I return here when I choose?"

"'Tis lonely here. Do come again, Winston. I've been waitin' for ye a verra long time."

"Have you?" he asked, a mischievous gleam in his eyes.

"Aye. I knew when ye first came a while ago, ye would find your way to this place."

"You mean when I was here Christmas Eve?"

"If tha' be wha' is called the night o' Lachlan's passin', aye."

"Who are you?" he asked in an aching whisper.

"I thought ye knew."

He shook his head.

"I be the house."

Stunned, Winston stiffened out of reflex. "No. I saw an outline o' your physical shape. But for a second, aye, but I know wha' I saw."

"Wha' ye *wanted* to see," she whispered by his left ear.

He spun toward her voice and desperately looked for another glimpse of her. But there was nothing but the particles, glittering and pulsing with life, and the contrails which now crisscrossed in a maddening mesh around him.

"Your name!" he cried.

"Listen and ye will hear it on the wind."

"Then you have a name." His temper surfaced and his black eyebrows rose in a suspicious, accusatory manner. "The house has a name. Are you tellin' me you're called *Baird*?"

"Why are ye angry wi' me, Winston? I allowed ye here because I knew it would bring a moment o' peace to your soul."

Breathing heavily, Winston replied, "I demand to know who's in ma head!"

"Your head?" Again she laughed and it swirled around him, caressing and taunting, further testing his darkening mood. "How predictably *human* o' ye to assume someone else be the trespasser." She sighed and he could almost swear he felt her perfumed breath fan his face. *"Ye* wanted in, Winston. I could have stopped ye. Should have, I'm beginnin' to think. But tis been a long time since I've had the chance to talk. I'm now regrettin' ma rash decision to trust ye."

"Trust *me?*" A mirthless laugh boomed from him. "That's bloody rich comin' from a *house.*" Irritably shuffling his shoulders, he added, "I've little tolerance for a liar."

Moments of silence passed. Winston sensed a crackling, electrical disturbance in the air. It was on the tip of his tongue to apologize for his ill mood, but he wasn't a man who liked to be unnerved by anything or anyone. And she *did* unnerve him.

"Tell me, Winston, do ye wish me to be a womon for ye?"

Before he could reply, he noticed the peacocks had surrounded him. Their beady dark eyes were riveted on him and their heads were cocked as if they were anxiously awaiting his answer.

"Winston."

Her voice startled him. Casting a group of the birds a dirty look, he lifted his gaze and searched the nonexistent sky. "Why did you bring me here?"

Another long moment of silence followed, during which his heart began to hammer within his chest. Somewhere in the far distance, he could hear ominous rolls of thunder.

"I didna bring ye here," she said at last. *"Ye sought me.* Aye, and found me, ye did."

"You're no' the house," he challenged.

Again a long stretch of silence, then, "'Tis all I can be," she said softly, forlornly, her voice omnipresent. "But I be grateful to have this much. Ye must go now, Winston. There are people who need me. I canna waste ma time on someone as mistrustin' as ye. All I have ever wanted was to be needed."

While she spoke, Winston picked up on a wash of emotional particles. "How have I hurt you?" he asked, scowling as his gaze searched his surroundings.

She gasped, then fell silent for what seemed an eternity. When he could no longer bear the tension building up inside him, he demanded, "Tell me!"

When still she remained silent, his temper fully surfaced. "You expect me to believe you're the house, and you're capable o' *feelin'* human emotion? You're just another spirit, aren't you? Trapped here in this house. Perhaps pickin' up where Lachlan Baird left off?"

"I gave him his power," she said softly.

"I don't believe you. I *saw* a womon!"

"It is cruel o' ye to remind me o' a time long past. O' who I was afore the darkness came."

"You were once *human!*" he challenged.

"Nae. Wha' I was is o' nae importance, now." She sighed, its sound burdened with despair. "We are too different, I know now, and it saddens me. I can be content, for I must to survive. Ye, Winston, like Lachlan once was, are too bitter and too hardened by wha' life has brought ye. But *he* was nae one to hide from his emotions, so I helped him to remain. And Beth. She brought me much joy. But ye are no' ready to embrace the magic. May never be, I think. Ye have lived so long within yourself, ye have no' learned to accept wha' is truly needed o' ye."

"Needed of me? You don't know anythin' abou' me!"

"Alas, I know it all."

"Quite an accomplishment for a . . . house."

"Sarcasm. Ye brandish it weel, Winston. But can ye love?"

The question took him aback. "O' course I can."

"Nae. Who be the liar now? Love terrifies ye. We are wha' we are. In ma maist secret dreams, I yearn to be human. Like ye, Winston, I can only experience psychical love through ithers. Tis sadder for ye, though, I think, for ye are in their world. Tis sadder because ye *choose* to stay apart. *Choose* to deny yourself.

"Lachlan and Beth taught me so much. Roan and Laura are still strugglin' to find themselves, but they *will* because they love life and each ither so deeply."

"I'm ready to puke."

"Sarcasm again." A moment's silence, then, "Tell me your fondest wish, and I will grant it."

"Why?"

"Because I can," she said, an enigmatic lilt to her tone.

One corner of Winston's mouth twisted in a skeptical grin. "Genies give *three* wishes."

"I be no' a genie. Weel, Winston . . . your wish?"

"To *see* you."

Silence, and he cockily folded his arms against his middle. "Too tough for you, Baird?"

"Too simple," she said finally, forlornly. "Since ye have used Rose to remove yourself from the human race, I'll grant your wish, but wi' this wee challenge."

"Wha' abou' Rose?" he asked harshly.

"Ye will see me when you find a way to *touch* me."

"What abou' Rose!"

"Ye canna hide from me, Winston. Ye didna love her. Twas her time to leave her world, and ye took it personally."

"Damn you!"

"Too late, ma hot-tempered Scotsman. I was damned long ago, and by somethin' far mightier, far sorrier than *ye.*"

His chest rising and falling with each furious breath, Winston accused, "You're a coward, Baird!"

"Just wiser than ye," she laughed softly. Then somberly, "Goodbye, Winston. Just remember tha' ye canna hide your thoughts or feelings from me. If nocht else, it may teach ye humility."

"Wait! *Wait!*"

Realizing that he was fading from the garden, he sucked in a great breath. He experienced a *whoosh* of sensation, then opened his eyes and found himself staring into the dwindling flames on the iron grate in front of him. Profound sadness yawned inside him, opening a void so stark and desolate, he nearly succumbed to tears. But then the old Winston resurfaced. He clamped down on the fragmented emotions he believed had been transferred from the mysterious woman to him, and stiffly rose to his feet.

The room was chilled, the shadows looming like grim sentinels.

He suddenly felt lonelier than he ever had, but he refused to waste even a moment trying to analyze the cause.

She couldn't have been anything more than a figment of his imagination, a necessary diversion for his stressed psyche!

He was about to turn in the direction of the bed when something caught his eye. With a trembling hand, he reached for the object on the mantel.

Instead of the loose petals he had placed there earlier, there lay an intact rose. Despite the lessening light, he knew it was purple, and he knew it was the same rose, only fully restored now. As he drew it to his chest, a tiny invisible thorn pricked his finger. Liquid warmth entered the wound and rapidly passed into his veins.

"Ye are no' ready to embrace the magic," she had accused him.

Lifting the rose to his lips, he murmured, "You're wrong, Baird."

Chapter Two

A dark and sinister eel-like mass slithered along the boundaries of Winston's psychically protected subconscious, awakening him minutes before dawn peeked over the horizon. He bolted upright, his eyelids rapidly blinking, his heart seeming to throb wildly in his throat. He was first alarmed by the grayness in the room, then the silence, the latter so thick, he thought it an intruder hovering over him. When he tried to recall what had frightened him during his dream state, he met with a mental blank wall. The void was something he'd never before encountered. There had always been unsolicited images and impressions crowding the multiple realms of his psychic fields. Now there was nothing but emptiness.

By the time his heartbeat returned to normal, he had to softly chuckle at himself. Why was he afraid of the peacefulness inside his skull? Hadn't that been something he'd longed for since childhood? He ran his fingers through his disheveled black hair and worked his dry mouth. His stomach grumbled. Blinking hard to erase the remnants of sleep weighing his eyelids, he peered out the window.

It was a new day.

Yawning, he flexed the muscles in his back and shoulders, then threw back the covers and climbed out of bed. He relieved himself in the bathroom, then went to the fireplace and prepared the hearth. The chill in the room attached itself to every part of his exposed skin. He'd worn only his boxer shorts to bed. Once he had the fire on the andiron going, he hastily donned his dark gray slacks. In lieu of his shirt, which he couldn't see anywhere, he pulled the top quilt off the bed, draped it over his shoulders, and held the material closed with one hand. He returned to the hearth and crouched, shivering against the cold still nipping at him.

The absence of dreaming continued to perplex him. For as long as he could remember, his dreamworld had always been so vivid and consistent, there had been times he wasn't sure which world had been the reality. He had never experienced a personal nightmare, a manifestation of his own subconscious. Even his dreams belonged to outsiders. Their fears. Their insecurities. Their hopelessness.

Baird.

The woman's facetious name murmured in his skull.

If only he could grasp the foundation of his certainty that the purveyor of his . . . magical . . . journey into that other world, had not been the house. Perhaps it was because the absurdity of a *house* arguing with him, was more than he could accept. A spirit, yes. He'd had his share of conversing with the departed.

And what had *she* meant when she'd accused him of using Rose to withdraw from the world?

He was in the process of releasing a long sigh when an extraneous ripple of sorrow passed through his awareness.

His spine stiffened as his psychic radar instinctively activated. Before he could withdraw its probe and abandon further knowledge of the unwitting sender, he knew the source and location.

"Damn," he grumbled.

Standing, he irritably flexed his broad shoulders. He considered ignoring the psychic pull, then, begrudgingly, he stalked from his room. Halfway down the hall, he stopped at a door to his right, and lightly rapped on the dark wood. When no answer came, he opened the door just enough to peer inside. Across the room, a young boy was sitting cross-legged atop the bedcovers, and sobbing.

"May I come in?"

The boy glanced up, swiped his arm beneath his nose, then adamantly shook his head.

Winston lightly frowned. "I'm afraid I'm lost in this big house. Can you tell me where to find the kitchen?"

For several seconds the boy watched him through an unreadable expression. Then he lifted his right arm and pointed, a gesture which brought a genuine smile to Winston's mouth. Stepping beyond the threshold, Winston secured the quilt about his shoulders and approached the foot of the bed.

"A point isn't much help, lad."

"Alby," the boy sniffed.

"Alby, is it? That's a fine name. I'm Winston."

The boy cocked his head, and it struck Winston that Alby's eyes held wisdom far beyond his age. To pass the awkward moment, Winston glanced at the fireplace. A low fire burned in the hearth, sufficiently warming the room. He cleared his throat and swung his gaze back to Alby, who was still watching him, only now there was blatant curiosity behind his blue eyes.

"Mind if I sit?" Winston asked, pointing to the foot of the bed.

"Go ahead."

Winston seated himself to the left of the boy, but he found he was at a loss for words until he noticed a carved wooden horse, about two inches tall, on its side on the quilt between them. Picking it up, he studied the intricate workmanship, then arched a brow in the boy's direction. "A fine piece," he casually remarked.

"Lachlan made it for me."

Alby's despondent tone brought a frown to Winston's brow. "He did a fine job."

Reaching beneath his pillow, Alby removed three other carvings. A rearing bear, a lion and a monkey. He passed them to Winston, who carefully studied each one before setting them on the bed. "Is it Lachlan you're cryin' for?"

Alby's lower lip jutted out. " 'Cause I cry, don't mean I'm a baby!"

"O' course no', Alby. But it is a wee early to be so sad, don't you think?"

"Not sad."

"No?" Winston chuckled. "Ma mistake, then."

"You're forgiven," the three-year-old quipped, and Winston laughed outright. "What's so funny?"

Winston had to think through his words before replying, "I wasn't laughin' *at* you."

"Nobody here but us," Alby said sagely, his eyes narrowed on Winston.

"When you're right, you're right. So tell me, did you have a nightmare?"

"Don't be silly."

The reply further unnerved Winston, and he thoughtfully stroked his stubbled chin. "So you were just havin' yourself a wee cry, then?"

"My toys stopped playing," Alby informed, poking them with the tip of an isolated finger. "I don't like it when they stop being fun."

Baffled, Winston eyed the carvings.

"Maybe 'cause I told Lion he couldn't roar so loud." His lower lip again jutted out, and his chin quivered. "Now they're all mad at me."

"The lion . . . roared?" Picking up the piece, Winston carefully looked it over. "Mmm. Lions can be loud, all right. He probably would have awakened the whole household if you hadn't quieted him down."

"You don't believe he can roar," Alby accused, and snatched the carving from Winston's hand. "Grownups *never* believe. But you will when he bites you."

Winston unsuccessfully tried not to smile. "Oh . . . indeed. So tell me, Alby, would you be up to joinin' me for breakfast? I make a mean batch of bannocks."

"Breakfast is *ma* responsibility, Mr. Connery," said a feminine voice from behind him.

Turning his head, he blinked at the sight of Agnes Ingliss crossing the room. She was dressed in a wool-blend simple blue dress, three-quarter-length black sweater, black stockings and shoes. Her snow-white hair was neatly secured in a bun atop her head, and a pair of small pearl earrings adorned her earlobes. Stopping at the side of the bed, she opened her arms. Alby zealously sprang up and threw himself into her embrace, wrapping his arms about her neck and planting a wet kiss on her cheek at the same time. A smile glowed on her face as she hugged him. At that moment, Winston wanted more than ever to experience that kind of bond. A hollow ache replaced his heart. When he attempted to tap into what Agnes was feeling, her pale blue eyes flashed him a warning that she knew what he was trying to do. A flush stained Winston's cheeks. He'd forgotten that her *ghostly* powers were intact.

"Alby, love, wha' do you say Mr. Connery helps you wi' brushin' your teeth, while I tend to breakfast?"

The boy scowled at Winston, then buried his face to the

side of Agnes' wrinkled neck. She cast Winston a guarded look, then grinned.

"Now, now, Alby. You dinna want your sausage too weel done now, do you? Old Agnes is movin' slower these days, and I'm sure Mr. Connery would love to see how a big lad like you can brush his teeth sparklin' white."

"As white as a faery's tooth," Alby beamed.

"Aye, tha' white and mair. Weel, do we have a plan, now?"

Alby spared Winston a shy glance, frowned again, then halfheartedly held out his arms to him. Winston rose to his feet. His system tingled with anticipation as he hesitantly opened his arms. In the next instant, Alby was clinging to him, the small arms wrapped tightly around his neck, his legs secured about Winston's middle.

"Thank you . . . Mrs. Ingliss."

"Agnes," she corrected with a smile and a twinkle in her knowing eyes.

Alby grimaced and looked beseechingly at the woman. "He has *baaad* breath!"

With a low, raspy chuckle, Agnes headed for the door. Over her shoulder, she suggested, "Perhaps, Alby, *you* could show Mr. Connery how to brush *his* teeth."

When she disappeared into the hall, Winston ruefully eyed the boy's comical expression. "Tha' bad, eh?"

Alby nodded.

"Come along then," said Winston, heading for the hall. "We'll see who's the brushin' champ."

"I am."

Winston laughed, and he realized he couldn't remember when he'd felt this good about himself, or being alive.

Laura stretched luxuriously beneath the warm covers. With her eyes still closed and a grin of contentment on her lips, she reached out for Roan. His side of the bed was empty. Her eyelids lifted and she squinted into the morning light. When her vision adjusted a moment later, she spied Roan standing by the window in a beam of sunlight. His expression struck her as being both wistful and desolate. He was watching something beyond the panes, but she was relatively sure he wasn't actually seeing anything at all.

A shiver passed through her, its cause unknown. Now that their lives were settling into normal routine, the stress of what they all had endured should have been waning. Her nephews alone seemed to have adapted to their new lives. Laura harbored a sense of loss, but a loss of what she couldn't be sure. Perhaps, knowing that Roan wasn't as happy as he pretended had something to do with it. At times she thought herself the cause of his moodiness, but instinct told her his bouts of depression were somehow still tied to Lachlan and Beth's departure. The few times she had tried to get him to open up to her, he'd chosen to withdraw and seek solitude from his new family. She never once doubted he loved her. He had a way of looking at her, his eyes a stage for pure mischief, and conveying to her how deeply connected they were. But there were times when she feared she was losing a part of him that was growing more impossible to reach. A portion of his soul. She had even wondered if perhaps the original laird and mistress hadn't mistakenly taken part of Roan with them.

Whatever the reason, seeing him like this caused a hollow ache inside her heart.

As if sensing her watching him, he unexpectedly turned his head and looked her way. An instant smile curved up the corners of his mouth. The sunlight bathing him turned his irises a mesmerizing shade of amber, and highlighted his light brown hair with pale golden streaks.

"Good morn, darlin'," he said huskily, his gaze lazily, appreciatively, sweeping over her concealed body.

"Good morning, yourself," she grinned, then suggestively patted the mattress alongside her. He started toward her. A log crumpled in the hearth, briefly drawing her attention to the roaring fire heating the room. When she again looked at him, he was sitting on the edge of the bed, his right ankle braced atop his left knee. His shirtless state prompted a sigh to escape her. She would never tire of his muscular build, of the powerful width of his shoulders. His hair, which he hadn't so much as trimmed since she'd first met him, now hung just past his shoulders in soft curls. And although she'd never thought herself the type of woman to go for the "maned" look on a man, she dreaded the idea that he might get bored with it and have it chopped off.

With this thought in mind, she braced herself up on one elbow and reached out to run her fingers through the side of his hair. His left hand cupped her forearm and he reverently kissed the inside of her wrist, then leaned over and nuzzled the side of her neck. Absolute bliss heated her insides. Falling back on the pillow, she held out her arms. His smile deepening, he moaned deep inside his chest and lowered the side of his head to between her breasts. A moment later, he swung himself fully onto the bed, slipped an arm beneath her, and enveloped her within his arms and legs. Laura was never more content than when she was surrounded by him. Inhaling deeply of his musky scent, she stroked her fingertips along his exposed cheek.

"Did you sleep all right?"

"Mmm," he softly murmured, and nestled his face more comfortably between her breasts. "I was dreamin' o' a maist peculiar garden."

She located a lock of hair by his shoulder and wound it

about her middle and index fingers. "Tell me about it," she whispered.

"No' much to tell. It was all glittery and magiclike. I think oor guest was there, too. Wha' I remember maist was how peaceful it was. I didn't want to leave, Laura."

"Never?"

He was silent for a moment, then, "I'm no' sure. But I woke in a grim enough mood."

Kissing the top of his head, Laura stared unseeingly up at the ceiling. "Why can't you admit how much you miss Lachlan and Beth?"

"I do," he said brusquely. "But can we no' begin oor day dwellin' on them?"

They fell silent, each lost in their own thoughts. Unconsciously, Roan began to rotate his thumb along Laura's right nipple, which was rigid beneath her red and blue plaid flannel nightgown. His absentminded ministrations stoked sexual tension to blossom deep inside her. Trying to will herself to breathe normally, she closed her eyes and relished the liquid warmth building inside her veins.

"I was thinkin' we could tak a trip to Edinburgh next week," he said dreamily, as if speaking to himself. "If the weather lets up a bit." He slipped his left hand beneath her nightgown and absently massaged her naked buttock and thigh. "But wi' Connery here," he went on, "I'm no' sure we should mak any plans."

"No telling how long he's going to stay."

"Hmm. He's a strange mon, this Winston. Laura, I can't quite put ma finger on wha' it is abou' him tha' maks me want to bury ma head in the sand."

"He's supposedly psychic. Isn't that what Aggie said?"

"Aye," Roan replied in a barely audible voice. "I guess I'm uneasy wi' him because I know nothin' abou' him."

"Lachlan—" Laura gasped when Roan's fingers grazed the *V* of her loins and a spasm of wanton need ripped through her. "—wanted him to return," she finished, breathless, her eyes blinking rapidly.

"Aye, he did."

Lost deeper in his thoughts, a frown marring his brow, he palmed her breast and gently kneaded it. He wasn't aware of Laura's rapidly escalating desire, or of her raspy breaths.

"So much to do, I don't know where to begin."

Laura moaned softly. But despite her heated condition, she managed, "Just take one day at a time."

After a moment, Roan murmured an indecipherable response. Laura reached down to run her fingertips along his chest, but he unexpectedly sat up and wearily ran his hands down his face.

"You're right. One day at a time." Springing from the bed, he headed for the door. "I'm goin' to check on the lads. I'll meet you downstairs for breakfast."

Before Laura could utter a protest, Roan was gone. For a long moment she could do nothing but stare at the closed door in disbelief. Then she sat up, gave a shake of her head, and deeply sighed. "The honeymoon's over before it began." She glanced about the room and gave another shake of her head, then fixed her gaze on the portrait of Lachlan hanging over the fireplace mantel. "I wish you could tell me what's going on inside his head— What am I talking about? We have a psychic-in-residence, don't we?"

Her spirits lifting, she climbed out of the bed and padded toward the bathroom. Unbeknown to her, a shadow slipped from behind the curtains of the window Roan had been at when Laura had awakened. It moved toward the bed, paused for a time, then crossed the room and melted into and beyond the door.

Laura re-entered the bedroom after brushing her teeth and washing her face and hands. She was humming a medley while on a direct path for the wardrobe when a familiar sensation invaded her limbs. A feeling of liquid warmth passed beneath her skin, flowing with the steadiness of a mountain spring. The sensation centralized within her chest. Circled her heart, then gradually dissipated. As always when she was visited by this phenomenon, she was left with a sense of absolute serenity. It was as if a celestial haze blanketed her brain.

Laura got dressed, combed her hair, and left the bedroom. Hunger and a need for her first cup of coffee headed her in the direction of the kitchen. But the residual impressions she carried of the mysterious presence she'd encountered was urging her to seek Roan.

Winston stepped first onto the main landing, then swung Alby down the last two stairs. He was laughing at the boy's insistence that he be given another "swing down", when something slammed his awareness. A brief dark cloud passed across his mindscreen. Alarmed, he cautioned Alby to remain where he was, then ran to the double front doors. He passed through the small greenhouse and flung open one of the outer doors, then stepped out into the bright morning sunlight reflecting off the snow. Countless impressions invaded his mind, so forceful he staggered from the assault. He was stunned that his psychic powers had returned with such a vengeance, and that his mind had opened itself to every particle of information floating in the air. At a point where he was finally sorting through the mental deluge, thunder caught his attention.

A zephyrous "Too soon!" moaned in his ears, and he instantly recognized the voice as that of the mysterious woman he'd met the previous night. He sensed her alarm. Her distress. Then—

At the same instant he looked up to see a whirlpool of

black clouds lowering over the property, he sensed the woman send off a network of energy—energy he couldn't identify. The clouds lifted slightly. Thunder loudly rumbled. Lightning crackled and snapped within the ominous mass, then faded into the once again sunny sky.

Winston's mind cleared of all extraneous thought. Despite the brightness of the sunshine, a freezing wind lashed at his body. The quilt was nearly torn from his shoulders. Securing it, he tucked two of the corners into the waistband of his slacks, then was about to re-enter the house when he spied two boxes to the left of the steps. Snatching them up, he dashed into the relative warmth of the hallway and closed the doors behind him. Alby was waiting for him by the foot of the staircase.

"What's that?" the boy asked.

Stopping, Winston glanced at the labels on both packages. "For Roan Ingliss."

"Nuts. Thought maybe Santa left me something else."

Chuckling, Winston headed for the parlor. "Come along. I can smell breakfast on, can you?"

Alby attempted to sniff through his stuffy nose, shrugged, then fell into step behind Winston. "Nope. But I'm starvin' to death."

Winston, the packages tucked beneath one arm, led the boy into the parlor, and beyond to the dining room. Once inside, Alby ran ahead to where Roan and Laura were seated at the table. Two older boys sat across from them.

Agnes entered the room from the kitchen. "Have a seat," she said to Winston, one white eyebrow arched in a show of impatience as she lowered a silver tray to the table. "Nothin' worse than cold sausages and scones."

Winston approached the nearest end of the elaborate table and set the packages down before lowering himself onto one of the chairs. Agnes was immediately at his side, filling his mug with steaming coffee, then arranging some of the food-laden plates in front of him. Winston's gaze swept over the dishes. Eggs. Thick slices of ham and spicy sausage patties. Potato scones dripping with butter and homemade marmalade. Brose, steamy and inviting.

Suddenly, he felt as though he hadn't eaten in months.

He was helping himself to portions of everything offered when Roan's wry tone caught his attention. "Good morn to you, too."

Embarrassed, Winston graciously inclined his head. "Forgive me. Good mornin'."

Laura smiled and gestured to the two boys across from her. "This is Kahl and Kevin. Say good morning to Mr. Connery."

Kevin stuck out his tongue and made a rude sound, while Kahl merely spared Winston a sour glance before diving into the food on his plate.

Winston again nodded, then looked at the packages. "Ah, these were ou' by the front door. They're addressed to you, Mr. Ingliss."

Rising from his chair, Roan grimaced. "You mak me feel like an old mon. Roan, if you please. I'll be damned if I call you *Mr. Connery.*"

Briefly locking eyes with the mistress of the house, Winston again offered a perfunctory nod. Then, unable to deny his hunger a moment longer, he lifted the scone and took a large bite out of it. He was relishing the bursts of flavors on his tongue when he happened to look up at the laird. The contents in his mouth went down in a lump as Roan's stricken expression registered. Winston minutely lowered his mindshield and probed the man standing next to him. The depth of the laird's emotional pain took him aback. He glanced again at the packages, at Laura, at each of the boys, then cut his gaze back to Roan.

"What is it?" Laura asked.

When Roan remained as still as a statue, she left her chair and went to stand at his right side.

"Roan?"

He remained perfectly still. Winston retracted his probe. Laura took the top package and walked around to Winston's left. Setting the box down, she used one of the knives on the table to cut the string securing it. She was lifting the lid when Roan murmured a barely audible, "Don't." Ignoring him, she removed the cover and dropped it to the floor beside her, then spread apart the white tissue paper concealing the contents. A gasp of delight escaped her. Her hands trembling, she lifted a lace and satin beaded wedding gown from the box, stepped back, and held it up against her. Tears sprang to her eyes, blending with the sheer radiance glowing on her face.

"Roan! It's . . . it's *incredible!*"

Lowering his head, Roan closed his eyes. "It was made for Beth," he said in a hollow monotone.

"What?"

"For Beth. Lannie asked me to order it the morn we were in the library and he told me I was inheritin' this place."

All color washed from Laura's face as she clutched the gown tighter against her.

Finally, Roan looked at her, his own face drawn and pale. "He told me she dreamed o' havin' a grand weddin', and asked if I would order the gown for her. I'd forgotten abou' it. The ither box is probably the veil."

"So? Aunt Laura can wear it," Kahl piped up, his mouth full of food. "Or are you planning on not marrying her now, huh?"

Winston didn't believe it possible, but the laird grew even paler. Abruptly rising from his chair, he was about to tell Roan to sit before he fell, but Agnes intervened. Linking her arm through her nephew's, she led him toward the kitchen. She stopped at the swinging door and said to Winston, "By the way, your shirt and coat have *mysteriously* vanished." She cast the boys a scolding look before glancing at Winston again. "I'll no' say wha' I *think* happened to them, mind you, but I wouldna be holdin' ma breath waitin' for them to miraculously return."

With that, she pulled Roan into the kitchen.

"Nuts. Grownups blame us kids for everything," Kevin grumbled.

Winston swung his gaze to Laura, who looked as though she was about to break down into tears over a far less than joyous reason. "Boys," he addressed the trio, "wha' say you finish your breakfast and let me have a talk wi' your aunt."

"No skin off our noses," Kahl quipped. "We can eat without bein' watched."

"I'm sure." He rose from his chair. "Perhaps one of you will remember where ma belongings went to?" Ignoring the two older boys' dirty looks, Winston went to Laura's side and placed a hand at her elbow. Without the slightest protest, she allowed him to guide her into the front hall, where he took the wedding gown and draped it over his left arm. "Laura, I don't mean to pry, but—"

"He can't get over them passing on," she choked, then lifted her watery gaze and searched his features. "I'm jealous of a dead woman. What does that say about me?"

Winston's attempt to offer a smile, failed. Clearing his throat, he said, "Tha' you're a womon in love."

"I thought. . . ."

"He'd ordered the gown for you," Winston completed.

Her mouth twisted disparagingly. "I guess it doesn't take a psychic to figure that out, does it?"

A small smile finally appeared on Winston's mouth. "No. But . . . ahh . . . it's no' as though your relationship has been normal, has it? Laura, his bond wi' Lachlan Baird and the American womon was beyond even *ma* comprehension. I sense tha' he's still grievin'. It takes time.''

Solemnly, she nodded. ''I know it does, but it hurts me to see him get so twisted up inside. Sometimes, I'm terrified I'm going to lose him. He gets so distant—''

''Laura-lass.''

At the sound of her name, she spun around to see Roan standing in the doorway. He rushed toward her, pulled her into the muscular strength of his arms, then kissed her long and passionately. During this, Winston turned away and rolled his eyes to the heavens. He was tempted to probe their emotions, experience what they were sharing, but he couldn't bring himself to intrude. He was even tempted to psychically interface with their auras, absorb the particles to enhance his understanding of their bond, but this practice he'd used most of his life, felt somehow wrong now. An invasion of what strictly belonged to them and no one else.

When he heard, ''It's time to order *your* gown, darlin','' he turned his head and observed the glow on Laura's flushed face. She was looking at Roan in a way that made Winston shrivel inside. He wondered if a woman would ever look into *his* eyes with such profound love and devotion.

''There's no rush,'' she said softly, resting the side of her face against Roan's broad chest. ''It was foolish of me to react the way I—''

Three squealing boys bound from the room, Agnes chasing them.

''Throw food, will you!'' she scolded, while they laughed and dashed up the stairs out of sight. Agnes paused halfway up to spare the three adults a harried look. ''I feel the grayness tuggin', but I'll see them cleaned up afore I leave.''

Then she, too, vanished beyond the next landing.

Roan released a burst of laughter, then clapped Winston on the arm and gestured with his head toward the parlor. "Oor food's gettin' cold, and Aggie hates awastin' anythin'."

"Wha' abou' . . . ?" Winston asked, indicating the gown.

Roan released a sigh. "I'll put it away in the attic. Laura deserves her own gown. One designed for her and na one else."

Silently, they returned to the dining room, where the boys' food fight was evident on their chairs and part of the table. Roan put the gown back into the box and covered it, then seated himself alongside Laura. For a time they ate in silence.

Winston was grateful for the chance to relieve the ache in his stomach. He was part way into a second helping when Roan spoke.

"Wha' about Rose?"

Winston instinctively stiffened. He'd known he would eventually have to explain, but he had hoped for more time. Swallowing the food in his mouth, he took a long drink of his coffee, then flattened his palms atop the table and sat back in his chair.

"Have you read abou' the Phantom?"

Roan arched a brow. "Aye. The serial killer."

"She was one o' his victims."

Laura's eyes went wide. "How terrible!"

"I found her in a deep grave in Melrose some months ago," Winston went on, bitterness lacing his tone. "She was the first victim to be found alive, but she couldn't tell us anythin' abou' tha' elusive bastard. You see, the attack—the attempt on her life—was so brutal, it left her catatonic. She was little more than a zombie." Scowling and staring down at his plate, Winston went on, "We called her Rose after Melrose, and kept her at the Brownin' Institute under intensive medical care and guarded by four of our best men. I was able to probe her identity, and contacted her family. Her actual name was Kathleen Anne, but she will always be Rose to me.

"Meanwhile, I got back on *his* trail. It led me here."

"What?" Laura gasped. "A serial killer was here?"

"Aye, but he left before Christmas Eve. Another agent tracked him to Paris. Anyway, after wha' I'd witnessed Christmas Eve, I got this crazy idea to bring Rose here. Tha' somehow the *magic* could restore her mind. Give her back to her family. I put in the request. Red tape. The doctors didn't want to release her. January second, I was called in on a car chase. The Phantom had struck again, in St. Ives, and every law enforcement agent in the area was hot on his trail.

"To make a long story short, he attempted to drive off the quay. His car nose-dived into a boat. Both exploded. End of the sadistic bastard. A week later, Rose died in her sleep. They say her heart simply stopped. She was twenty-five. How does such a young heart simply . . . *stop?* If she could have just held on a while longer. Come here. Maybe. . . ."

He shrugged and dully eyed the couple. "I guess I took her death too personal. I left the agency. Left everythin' and walked away."

"I'm so sorry," Laura murmured, staring down at her plate. When she again looked up, she fixed her solemn, measuring gaze on Winston. "I detect a somewhat American accent mixed in with your Scottish."

Winston nodded. "Durin' my mid-twenties, I spent four years in the States, attendin' different paranormal institutes o' study."

"Were you born wi' your abilities?" asked Roan.

"Unfortunately, I was."

Winston's disheartened tone brought a frown to Roan's

brow. "I see. Weel, we all have oor crosses to bear, don't we?"

Winston studied the new laird for a time. "Aye," he said finally, his tone low, cryptic. "Tell me, Roan, how are you farin' these days?"

Roan shrugged. "You tell me."

A crooked grin appeared on Winston's face. "I don't make it a practice to deliberately invade people's minds. Sometimes I have no control over it, but for the most part—"

"I understand," Roan interjected brusquely. "To answer your question, I'm farin' weel enough."

Winston detected tension building within the laird. Laura cast him a fleeting warning not to pursue the subject, and Winston respectfully backed off. He forked the remainder of his cold eggs into his mouth. He was about to swallow when Roan's question took him aback.

"Wha' do you hope to find here?"

Winston swallowed and immediately replied, "Maself, I guess."

"You're welcome to stay as long as you like," said Roan. A lazy grin ticked at one corner of his mouth. "But I'm afraid the answers you seek will be tough to find. The magic went wi' Lannie. There are na miracles left within these walls, ma friend."

Winston stared at the couple for a long moment. "No' true," he said huskily, then sighed. "It's definitely still here."

Laura's look of surprise brought a smile to Winston's lips, and he said, "The air crackles wi' it."

Roan, a bewildered look on his face, gave himself a shake. "But Lannie and Beth—"

"Utilized it, but they were no' the *source,*" Winston informed. "It's here and I hope to learn more abou' it durin' ma stay."

"I'll be damned," Laura breathed.

Damned!

The word detonated inside Winston's head. He felt himself swiftly passing through time and space, through a dark tunnel of indecipherable voices. When his momentum came to an abrupt halt, dank, bone-invading coldness greeted him. The stench of decay and the unmistakable coppery odor of blood filled his nostrils and coated his tongue. Gagging, he tried to will himself away, but he discovered that he was frozen in this limbo. Straining to see more clearly into the foreboding grayness stretched out before him, he saw a cavernous room of stone. At the far end, a stone altar began to glow in hues of green. Red symbols covered the wall behind it.

Blood.

The information sickened Winston, and painfully quickened his heartbeat.

A figure swept into the room from an arch to the left of the altar. Waves of unbridled rage emanated from the man and crashed against Winston's awareness, nearly drowning him in the depths of its vileness.

Guttural chanting echoed within the room.

Warlock! Winston's mind cried.

"Master," the man's voice boomed, "grant me the power this night to fell ma enemies! *Eth duc chi'nith!* I offer ye the souls o' nature's children in return for ma revenge!

"*Damn* those unworthy of *your* true and loyal fold, Master! *Damn* and condemn the keepers o' the land, and grant this servant the power to bring forth the true magic o' this world!"

Winston quaked in sheer horror and helplessness. He could sense something dark and sinister attempting to breech the boundaries of his inexplicable placement. The voice of the man behind the altar droned on, but Winston could no longer make out his words. Terror consumed him. Seized every nuance of his being. His heart repeatedly slammed against the wall of his chest. The pulses at his temples threatened to burst free. His mind reached out to grab onto anything which could take him from this place.

The terror within him built until he was on the verge of surrendering to insanity. Then suddenly he was again traveling, soaring through time and space, the tunnel brightening with each passing second. His lungs threatened to explode. Panic, fear and terror all vied to dominate him, consume the human fibers of his existence.

The length of him crashed into unmerciful solidity. The air that had been trapped in his lungs, gushed out. Pain pulsated through every square inch of him.

"Go afore ye further weaken ma sanctuary!" cried a feminine voice.

"Baird," he grunted, weakly propping himself up on his elbows. He discovered he was on his front, a few feet from the fountain in the garden of his mysterious woman.

"Tis all I have," she wept low. "Leave!"

His gaze searching for a sign of her, he stated, *"You* brought me here."

"Nae. *Nae!* From whence place ye came, I care no' to know! Leave. *Leave* afore ye destroy this place!"

"Destroy?" Wincing with pain, Winston stiffly drew himself into a sitting position. "Wha' do you know of the history of the Baird land?"

"Go, I tell ye!" she cried.

Refusing to empathize with the waves of panic emanating from her, he bit out, "When I'm ready! Now answer me."

A sharp intake of breath echoed around him.

"Baird, I want to know!"

"He came from the Infernal Empire to be among humans," she said, her tone laced with pain and fear. "But he couldna tolerate the light. He begot a son wi' a human female. This son claimed this land, and for centuries, worked his dark powers within the walls o' his castle. I know nae mair.

"Now leave and never return. Your powers be drainin' me, and I have existed too long to wish to die now. But leave wi' this warnin', Winston Ian Connery."

Her voice grew weaker, shaky. "Ye selfishly seek me, and in doin' such have lost your true purpose. *He* waits, while *ye* wallow in self-pity. Tak heart, ma foolish Scotsmon. Danger closes in on Baird House. Heed the warnings or. . . ."

Her voice drifted off. Winston was seized with the knowledge that she was indeed dying, and instantly withdrew into himself. Again he traveled the tunnel of channelers, but this time he awakened at the dining room table, two pairs of eyes staring at him as though the couple were in a state of shock.

Breathing unsteadily, Winston pushed back his chair and rose to his feet. "Forgive me. I need to go to ma room."

Without another word, he ran into the hall and up the stairs, and didn't stop until he closed his bedroom door behind him. Labored breaths pumped in and out of his lungs. His head swam with alarming speed.

He?

Danger?

Had she meant his presence in the house?

No. The "he" is someone else. But who?

Staggering across the room, he sat on the edge of the bed and lowered his face into his hands.

Ma purpose here? Right. Why are warnings always so damn cryptic?

Falling back, his arms winged out across the bed, he blinkingly stared up at the ceiling.

You're no' shy abou' tellin' me ma failings, are you, Baird?

He grimaced. Sighed deeply.

Oh, we shall meet again, you and I. And I give you fair warnin', ma mysterious waif: I'll expose you for the womon I know you to be.

Back in the dining room, Roan slapped his palm to his brow and rose from his chair. "Darlin', this mon is too weird for ma blood." He pushed the chair into place and collected some of the dishes on the table. "Wha' say we tak the lads ou' and build us a snowmon?"

"Did he go into a trance?" Laura asked tremulously, her gaze riveted on the chair Winston had occupied.

"Don't know, don't care. Ma skins crawlin' and I *need* a diversion."

"The room turned so cold when he—"

"Darlin'," Roan groaned, "let it be."

"He was like a statue . . . just sitting there . . . his eyes so *vacant.*"

Roan grunted in dismissal.

Laura stood and uneasily looked about the room. "I keep thinking about that Phantom guy hanging around here." She shivered and hugged herself. "I know it sounds awful, but I'm glad he's dead."

Leaning over, Roan planted a quick kiss on her cool, pale cheek. "A snowmon will cheer you up, love."

Nodding absently, she began to help Roan clear the table.

They managed to put away the leftovers and do the dishes without bringing up the unnerving incident again. Laura, drying her hands with a dish towel, told Roan she'd go ahead and get the boys dressed for the outdoors. Roan remained behind, drying the last of the silverware. When he was done he hung the towel on a hook to the right of the deep sink, then braced his hands against its edge and dipped his head below his shoulders.

Despite his every attempt to will away the unease gnawing at him, he couldn't get past it. He straightened away from the sink. Holding out his hands, he observed the way they trembled. A day outside with the boys was exactly what he needed—

Who was he fooling?

Since Lachlan and Beth's departure, he'd been haunted by something he couldn't begin to define. He'd tried to tell himself he was simply going through a period of mourning, but he knew that wasn't exactly true. Oh, he missed them. He had resigned himself to the fact that there would always be a void in him, one akin to that of the loss of his son. Sometimes when he abruptly awakened in the middle of a night, he almost believed he knew what was troubling him. But then it would melt away, leaving him empty and puzzled and angry.

It was as though he were standing at the very edge of a high cliff, waiting for something to give him that slight nudge that would send him reeling into the unknown. No, it wasn't about death. He had no fears in that respect. Laura had been so supportive and understanding of his moods, but the unfairness of placing her in that position also bothered him. He loved her more than he ever thought possible. And yet he kept distancing himself. Why?

Wha' the hell is wrong wi' me!

He looked to the swinging door Laura had gone through. He felt as though he wanted to explode. Not even Aggie seemed to understand what was eating at him. In fact, she was more inclined to avoid him whenever possible. He knew she desperately missed her son, Borgie, and his heart went out to her. She remained because of the boys, but he knew she secretly yearned to pass on and rejoin with her only child. More times than he cared to remember, he'd thought of telling her to go on, but the thought of losing her, too, had been too painful, and he'd selfishly kept silent.

If only he could purge himself of the gloom residing inside his heart.

Chapter Three

For the remainder of the day, Winston stayed in his bedroom. In between Laura and Agnes bringing him pots of tea, sandwiches, and snacks, and Roan lending him a shirt and two woolen sweaters, he was content to embrace his solitude with the hope of soothing the perpetual tingling invading his body. The condition had manifested shortly after he'd retired to his room. And although he had endured it often enough in his life, usually when on a case, it continued to make him edgy.

Now and then he stared out one of the windows, watching Laura, Roan and the boys build a tall snowman near the snow-covered fountain. When they had finished it later that afternoon—potatoes used for eyes, a carrot poking out for the nose and stones forming a smiling mouth—Winston had laughed outright to see the redheaded boy, aided by Roan hoisting him up, place what appeared to be a frozen peacock on top of the snowman in lieu of a hat. The bright purples, blues, and greens of the bird's feathers stood out in sharp contrast to the white, compacted snow, a perfect complement to the delightful creation.

Now that daylight was waning, his solitude only served to feed his restlessness. Answers eluded him but for the locale of the surrealistic garden. The fourth dimension. His mind had often enough traipsed into that relatively unknown realm. The crossover dimension. A channeler's only means of bringing individual times and space into the reality of the third dimension. But never had Winston physically visited the realm. The countless times his mind had channeled through it, it was but a world of layers of grayness. *Psychic* energy, replete with impressions and memories of all who had lived throughout the ages in the third dimension, were libraried within the infinite region. Most psychics had only minimal channeling abilities to tap into the information. He, Winston Ian Connery, was one of a few who possessed the ability to utilize every nuance of the dimension. But if he had one hundred lifetimes, he couldn't even begin to dent the available knowledge.

As much as he thought about transferring himself to the "lady's" garden, he stopped himself. The prospect of causing her undue pain, yanked on his heartstrings. Briefly, on more than one occasion that day, he wished he could just once feel her solidity, but he'd been forced to abandon such thoughts when he surprisingly found himself aroused. Not exactly a pleasant condition for a man who only had sex with a woman twice in his life. And that had been with the same woman . . . one of his teachers . . . the night before and the day of his twentieth birthday. Although the physical experience had been enlightening and pleasant enough, the mental assault of her too-vivid fantasies during the exchange had shocked him.

Sex with *apes*? She'd imagined him to be *three* of the massive beasts, all lusty and ravishing her repeatedly.

The memory not only elicited a soft grimace, but caused his mouth to go dry.

He longingly eyed the empty teapot on the mantelpiece. Something stronger was definitely in order.

He glanced at the gold-rimmed face of his black, leather-band wristwatch. Four forty-seven.

Late enough for a nightcap.

Leaving his room, he casually ambled down the hall. The gas wall lamps were already lit, the orange glow softening the contours of the passageway. He made a left toward the staircase, then found himself opening a door. The change in placement left him disoriented. Seemingly of his own volition, his hand pushed the door inward. Before really looking beyond the threshold, he glanced behind him at the steep, narrow, descending stairwell. Then he heaved a breath and narrowed his gaze at what was before him.

His brief fear that he'd been displaced back in the past was dispelled when he viewed an attic. Soft flickering light graced the room. Stepping beyond the doorway and several paces further, he spied a figure sitting on the floor at the far end. He not only recognized Roan, but also the mood in the air as being undeniably morose. Approaching in slow steps, he made mental notes of the boxes and objects he passed, and of the lit lantern sitting to the laird's left. Roan was slouched against a stack of crates, mindlessly staring at a portrait propped atop a trunk. Winston identified the man in the portrait right away. Lachlan Baird. A blond woman with chilling blue eyes stared beyond the canvass, through Winston. Still staring into her beautiful but cold features, he crouched next to the lantern.

Although Roan's gaze did not leave the portrait, he spoke calmly and steadily. "You're lookin' at ma Laura in anither time. She was Tessa then." He wagged a finger at the portrait. "Can't say I miss this one much."

"She has a cruel look abou' her," Winston said.

"Aye. She was a cruel, desperately wanton womon. And so needy." Roan deeply sighed and closed his eyes for a moment. "Sometimes I come up here and stare at her, and try to understand how I could have loved her so blindly."

"It happens."

Roan's troubled gaze briefly swung to Winston, then returned to the portrait. "I suppose it does. Laura is verra different from Tessa. They're the same, but Laura . . . Laura has courage and heart. Tessa never had either."

Sitting on the floor, Winston bent his right leg and braced his forearm atop the knee. He noticed an emptied bottle of Scotch on its side by Roan's right foot, but chose to ignore its implications. Rather, he sought to console the fires burning within the laird's heart.

"You amaze me, Roan," Winston said in earnest. "No' many men could cope wi' the memories o' two lives, decades apart."

"I don't think abou' it . . . much. The sameness, I mean." He glanced at Winston and forced a lopsided grin. "Truth is, it feels natural now. A part o' me."

"It still takes a helluva mon to cope as you do."

"I don't know abou' tha'. We do wha' we must."

Winston chuckled. "I'll have to remember tha' the next time I feel like a miserable failure."

Roan's grin deepened. "I can't imagine you a failure at anythin'. What's it like to be psychic?"

"Busy," Winston said dryly.

Roan nodded. "I bet you are. You get to see the dark side o' people they think is locked away."

"Also the good. There's usually a balance."

"That's good to hear." Again Roan sighed, then frowned at the portrait. "Lachlan was a mon like none ither. I wish you could have known him."

"You were fond o' him, were you?"

Startled, Roan stared at his guest. "Fond? *Och!* Believe me, it is mightier than tha'! Generations o' ma family despised him. I came to banish him." He released a low, tremulous laugh. "I remember the first day he *poofed* in front o' me. I could hardly believe the mon wasn't alive and breathin'—breathin' fire, for he was in a foul mood tha' day. And Beth. Such a fine lady, and to die so young!" He exhaled a ragged breath and shook his head. "Damn me, Winston, what's wrong wi' me? It's all passed, but I can't seem to let it go!"

Reaching out, Winston took the whiskey bottle in hand. "Maybe you should lay off this stuff for a while."

Roan shrugged his massive shoulders. "There wasn't much in it. In truth, ma friend, I'm as sober as a church mouse. Perhaps that's ma problem, eh?"

With a shake of his head, Winston set the bottle down. "I watched you and Laura build the snowmon wi' the boys."

A genuine smile flashed across Roan's rugged face. "Aye. They're great lads. They never cease to amaze me wi' their cunnin' and energy."

"I thought the peacock a fittin' crown," Winston chuckled.

"Ahhh." Roan grew solemn. "Braussaw. He was one o' Lannie's favorites. I accidentally ran the bloody thing over wi' ma van. Had him stuffed in hopes Lannie wouldn't notice him missin'."

"Did he?"

Roan nodded almost wistfully. "One thing abou' Lannie Baird, Winston, *nothin'* ever got past *him!* He took it pretty good though, he did. Surprisingly good. But by then he considered me a friend. In spite o' everythin', he found it within himself to be ma friend. I guess tha' sums up the kind o' mon he was. Damn me, but I wish they were still here." Roan cleared his throat and deliberately stared at the portrait to keep Winston from seeing the tears in his eyes.

But Winston did see them, and he ached to firsthand understand the kind of bond, friendship, the ghost and man had shared.

"It's no' like they passed on o' their free will," Roan went on. "Beth left to spare us Viola Cooke's further wrath, and Lannie . . . weel, he couldn't stay withou' his love, could he? There was so much mair I wanted to learn from him. All lost. If only I knew they were happy."

"They are."

Roan's watery gaze cut to Winston's face. "Are you just sayin' tha' to please me?"

"A lie has never passed ma lips," Winston confessed. "I'm no' sayin' I'm incapable o' lyin', but I guess I've never encountered anythin' I felt was worthy o' one. They *are* indeed happy, although. . . ."

Roan arched an inquiring eyebrow.

"Restless," Winston murmured, staring off into space. "They are restless, but I don't know why." He focused on Roan's strained features. "Perhaps they sense *your* distress."

"Is tha' possible?"

Winston nodded.

Releasing a soft whistle, Roan started to get up. "Then I guess I should work on changin' ma mood."

When both men were on their feet, Roan took the lantern in hand. "Winston, how abou' joinin' me for a Scotch before supper?"

"Best offer I've had today," Winston grinned, and followed the laird out of the attic.

The house struck Winston as being overly quiet and still as he descended the last staircase alongside Roan. It was as if the place were sealed in a vacuum. Motionless. Soundless. Far removed from the world and its problems.

"Laura's nappin' wi' the lads," Roan explained, as if having read Winston's thoughts. "It's the only way the little buggers will go down durin' the day."

A hint of a smile was on Winston's mouth as he followed the laird onto the first landing, down a hall, and into a room on the right. He was delighted to see a bar, two tables, and an antique spooning chair. He strayed in the direction of the latter while Roan went behind the counter and placed the still-lit lantern atop the polished surface of the wood. After a moment, Roan muttered, "Damn me, I forgot to bring up a case. I'll—"

He stopped short when Agnes came into the room. "Roan, dear, I'm afraid one o' the gas burners is blocked up. Could you give me a hand wi' it?"

"Sure."

Winston offered the woman a pleasant smile, then said to Roan, "I'll get the Scotch, if you want."

Stopping in front of his aunt, Roan absently raked a hand through his thick hair. "If you don't mind. The cellar door's at the side o' the staircase. Tak the lantern. The steps are steep and the rooms down there are pitch dark. And watch your footfalls, mon. There's a few roots that came up through the concrete. I keep meanin' to tend to them. Anyway, at the bottom o' the stairs, you'll see a large door on the left. That's the Scotch room. Bring up one o' the cases."

Winston took the lantern and held it out in front of him. Agnes and Roan turned right in the direction of the kitchen. After a moment's pause in the hall, Winston went to the door at the side of the staircase and opened it. Cold air brushed against him. He chided himself for wishing he hadn't volunteered to enter the lower realm of the house, but he had, and forced himself to take the first step down. Holding out the lantern, he tried to penetrate the inky blackness lurking beyond the scope of the light. He'd always hated the darkness. Especially darkness encased in a confining area. Like in a coffin or a cellar. But down he went. One labored step at a time. When he finally reached the bottom, he released a hollow chuff in praise of his winning out over his phobia.

Confined spaces.

He'd spent a good portion of life suffering confinement along with the victims he'd psychically interfaced with. Closets. Coffins. Dark cellars. Attic rooms. *Graves.*

Heat rushed beneath his skin and into his head. It was a too familiar sensation, one that told him his phobia was making a strong bid to overpower him. To further combat his rising panic, he began to hum the theme music of the Wicked Witch of the West from *The Wizard Of Oz* movie. The tune came out faster and faster with each step he took. His darting gaze sliced into the darkness. Internal heat singed his face. Humming louder, he forced his pace to quicken. Finally, at the edge of the light across from him, he saw the door Roan had mentioned.

"All this for a Scotch," he said in an off-key, singsong tone. "Ah, but wha' right-minded Scotsmon wouldn't brave the monsters o' the dark for a wee libation? But it had better be *damn* good Scotch—"

A scurrying sound caused his taut nerves to go spastic. The accompanying squeak was his undoing. He whirled then staggered backward, the hand holding the lantern swinging out. The lamplight danced off the stone walls around him. Shadows and golden-orange light leapt into one another, totally disorienting him. To stop the dizzying effect, he unsteadily placed the lantern on the floor and backed away. He lifted a hand to block out the light's glow from his eyes. Deep, regulated breaths eventually eased his racing heartbeat back to normal. By the time he'd gotten his fears under control, the dark recesses no longer threatened him. The calm, cool Winston emerged, and he reflected on his childish reaction with disdain.

"Get a grip on yourself. It's a *bloody* cellar, you fool!"

He squared his shoulders determinedly. Flexing his fingers, he reached for the door and pulled on the metal handle. It opened smoothly without a sound.

His body blocking a good portion of the lamplight, he peered into the seemingly infinite darkness of the room beyond.

"The Scotch room. Quaint. Scotch . . . room. There's probably a wine room. Sherry room. Rrrum room. And all as dark as this here one."

He gulped and the sound seemed to echo around him. Trepidation shriveled the borders of his courage, enough so that he rocked from side to side for a few moments.

"A case of Scotch, Winston-you-coward, and you'll be on your merry way upstairs. Where there's light and people. Food cookin' on the stove. . . ."

Deciding the best thing to do was to just get it over with, he retrieved the lantern and entered the room. He was shocked at the vastness which greeted him. Holding out the lantern, he ambled down the fifteen-foot wide walkway, his gaze scanning the tall racks of Scotch that lined both sides. Dates stared back at him, neatly carved into fastened panels on the racks. When he reached bottles dating back to the early seventeen hundreds, he felt as giddy as a schoolboy.

Of course the actual cases the laird had referred to had to be near the door, but he couldn't stop himself from exploring the room to the end. His fingers touched the grooved numbers with deepening reverence. To the left and right of him, the racks went on and on, until he was beginning to wonder if there was no end to the room. His elation didn't stem from the fact that he was an avid Scotch drinker. Actually, he seldom imbibed. But the value of the collection staggered his mind. And the care and meticulous order in which the bottles had been displayed. . . .

"Lachlan, you have ma undyin' respect," he murmured.

He was about to cross to the right side again when his left foot snagged on something. He pitched forward. A wail rang out, so shrill he thought his eardrums had ruptured. But even more disconcerting was knowing that the wail had not come from him. Somehow he struck the cement floor on his side, the lantern held up and out of harm's way. The impact jarred his bones and made his teeth clack together. Searing pain razored through him, robbing him of breath. After several moments, he managed to place the lantern down and gingerly sit up.

Suddenly the excruciating pain in his head and the fact that every bone in his body felt broken and fractured, didn't matter. He stared at what had tripped him. The back of his left foot sat atop a section of a thick oak root which wove in and out of the cement floor. It wasn't the root itself leaving him numb and confounded, but the eerie green glow emanating from it. The luminance pulsed with the rhythm of a heartbeat. Faster and faster. Brighter and brighter. As if compelled, he reached out to touch it. *"Nae!"* boomed inside his head, staying his hand in midair.

In the distance somewhere above, he heard rolls of thunder and the repeated crack of lightning. Then cries.

The boys! his mind lamented.

Concern for the others in the household doused his stupor. He gripped the root to aid himself to his feet, but the instant his hand made contact, a chorus of shrill voices lanced his brain. The ground shook. The root rapidly grew warmer, then so hot he was forced to let it go. He made it to his feet amid a deluge of sounds. Thunder. Human cries. Lightning. Inhuman sobs. Concrete grating against concrete.

The green glow of the root became so bright he couldn't
look into it. He lifted his arms to cover his face, but before
that act had been completed, the luminance disappeared
with a hissing *snizzzzip*.

Again the ground beneath him quaked, so forcefully he
was barely able to retain his footing.

"Winston!"

The desperation in Laura's voice chilled him. Snatching
up the lantern, he dashed from the room and continued
to run until he was on the main landing. Laura was waiting
for him at the bottom of the staircase. He first noticed
that she was wringing her hands, then that her face was
the color of paste.

"I fell asleep! The boys took off! We can't find—"

A horrendous moan boomed within the walls, drowning
out Laura's scream. Again the house shook. Laura pitched
into Winston, who barely swung aside the lantern in time
to prevent her from colliding with it. He kept one arm
tightly about her waist and braced his back against the
newel post to steady himself. Laura clung to him, her eyes
seeming too large for her face.

The moan droned on. Instinct warned Winston not to
lower his mindshields, but he couldn't bear not knowing
what was happening. His mind fully opened. At first he
received Laura's terror and it took him aback, for she
didn't fear for herself, but for her nephews. Then a presence invaded his awareness. Terror. Agonizing pain. Cold
beyond description. Bewilderment and disorientation.
They all were somehow related to the *house*.

Winston extended his probe. He felt his awareness about
to lock onto something tangible when suddenly the house
stilled and all sound stopped. During the ensuing
moments, he could only hold his breath in anticipation
of another paranormal assault. His every sense was on full
alert, waiting to glimpse a hint of what was to come next.

Heavy footfalls on the stairs drew his and Laura's attention. Roan, Alby beneath one arm, Kahl the other, jogged to the first floor landing and faced the immobile couple.

"I can't find Kevin anywhere," he said tremulously.

"Put me down!" Kahl squealed.

Alby appeared satisfied just to dangle within the band of Roan's arm.

Roan placed each of the boys on their feet, then pulled Laura into his arms. Winston was only dimly conscious of the laird consoling Laura, telling her that Kevin had to be somewhere in the house. Winston was more intent on listening with his inner senses. Something was teasing the periphery of his awareness. Beckoning him, but to where he couldn't yet determine. Outside, thunder boomed and lightning cracked and snapped deafeningly. Winds pummeled the exterior walls.

"There are any number o' places the bugger could be hidin'," Roan assured Laura, who turned to the boys and dropped to her knees.

Gripping the front of their shirts, she asked, "Where did you last see him?"

Alby gave a negligent shrug, while Kahl scowled down at the placement of her hand.

"Dammit, Kahl, look at me!"

The redhead lifted wide eyes to met her imploring gaze.

"Where did he go?" she asked.

"To his room! Chee, why are you mad at *me!*"

With a heart-wrenching sob, Laura drew the boys into her arms and offered them a terse apology.

The front doors burst wide open. Wind and freezing droplets of water sluiced down the hall. Roan instantly dropped to his butt between the onslaught and Laura and the boys, using the breadth of his body to award them a semblance of safety. Winston placed the lantern to the side of the staircase, then stepped further into the hall. His right arm was braced to protect his face from the sting of the wind and rain. He sensed someone coming into the house. Gesturing for Roan to get Laura and the boys into the parlor, he braced himself to face whatever was to come. But before Roan had maneuvered his family halfway to the other room, the double doors slammed shut with echoing finality. The wind and rain immediately ceased. Unnerving calm blanketed the hallway.

Winston lit into a half-run at the sight of Agnes urging Kevin forward. Both were soaked. Winston hauled the shivering boy into his arms and walked alongside Agnes to where the others were waiting. Roan was quick to take the oldest boy into his own arms, and hugged him almost fiercely before giving him a single shake.

"Damn me, laddie!" Roan cried. "Wha' were you doin' ou'side?"

"But I—"

"Honey, we were so worried," Laura wept, cutting him off. Her hand smoothed the back of the boy's dripping-wet hair. "You know better than to go out after dark!"

"But the—"

Again Kevin was interrupted. "He was ou' by the north garden," Agnes said peevishly, then swiped an arm across her face. "Dead or alive, dinna matter, I *hate* bein' all wet—and me in ma best dress to boot!"

Winston didn't know whether to laugh or cry. Absorbed emotions rapidly churned inside him, swelling and crashing like storm-swept waves. He felt out of place among the family. A stranger.

An intruder.

Suddenly he sensed something was very wrong. Although he couldn't define it, he likened it to the daunting calm within the eye of a hurricane. He stepped back until he came to the tiled fireplace on the wall across from the staircase. Absently scanning the animal bone, wood, and copper artifacts adorning the mantel and wall, he hesitantly reached out. Crawly sensations broke out on his skin, staying the fingertips of his right hand a hairsbreadth from an unadorned part of the wall above the mantel. Seconds ticked by. Although a glance over his shoulder revealed that the others were talking, he could hear only silence.

His fingertips touched the wall.

The soundlessness shifted. Shifted again and he sensed it closing in on him. Shifted again, permeating the psychic fibers of his mind and threateningly rooting itself at the base of his brain. He was unaware of trembling, of having paled so drastically that the others were regarding him with deepening anxiety.

He tried to pull away from the wall, but found his fingertips were stuck fast.

No mental images came to him, only impressions. Fear. Abandonment. Loneliness as he'd never before experienced.

Then, from somewhere deep inside him, he found the strength to break his physical contact with the wall. The psychic link severed, he whirled to face the others and gasped, "It's gone!"

"It?" Roan asked through a grimace.

"The . . . the—" Winston gestured in unbridled frustration. "The bloody *magic!* It's *gone!* The house is . . . *empty!*"

Roan placed Kevin on his feet and took a step in Winston's direction. "Wha' are you talkie' abou'?"

"The energy tha' was in the house is *gone!*" Winston bit out, his face flushed with anger. "I don't know o' a better way to explain it to you!"

"Could it have something to do with—"

Laura's question was cut off by Kevin, who lunged between Winston and Roan, and raised his dripping arms in the air. "Let me talk!" he demanded, stamping a foot to punctuate his words. "What about the naked lady?"

"The *wha'* lady?" Winston barked.

"At the gazebo," Kevin replied, scowling up at Winston.

"I didna see anyone ou' there," stated a bewildered Agnes.

"She *was* there," Kevin fumed, searching each adult's face. "Like I wouldn't know a *naked* woman when I saw one! Chee! You guys are really bugging me now! Case you don't know, it's *cold* outside! She's probably all frozen up like a snowman by now!"

Winston locked eyes with Agnes.

"I'll go," she said, but before she could make a move, Winston was running for the doors.

"Fetch some blankets!" he called back as he dashed into the greenhouse.

Cold didn't adequately describe the weather. A mixture of rain and hail bombarded him as he blindly ran into the night, going by rote in the direction of the north gazebo. By the time he reached the structure, his lungs felt seared and his legs barely able to support him. He shuffled his frozen bare feet to the center of the planked floor, offering a mute prayer of thanks for the shelter of the domed roof. He anxiously swept the wetness from his face with his hands and narrowed his eyes in search of a body. His psychic radar swept the immediate area, and finally locked onto something by the rear of the gazebo. His pulse rate quickening, he started in that direction when another presence tripped into his awareness.

For a breath-robbing second, Winston experienced a rush of shocked-incredulity. Disbelief formed a burning knot inside his throat. His brain swelled and hammered at the confines of his skull.

Panting, his hands balled into trembling fists at his sides, he faced the house. His features turned to stonelike rage as his gaze sought to locate the target.

But he didn't need to *see* to know that the impressions

were true, as true and as real and as solid as the floor beneath his bare feet. There was no mistaking *this* "mark".

Forcing his reasoning to surface above his rage, he ran to the rear steps of the gazebo. There, curled in a fetal position on the bottom step, was a dark figure.

Kevin's lady, although not naked—

As soon as he'd gotten a closer look, he realized that what he'd first thought was a cape, was in fact incredibly long hair, soaked and clinging to her like a second skin.

"Sweet Jesus," he grumbled, then swept her up into his arms. Keeping his thoughts free of the second intruder, he laboriously ran toward the house. His burden never moved or made a sound. He sensed that, although she had no wounds, her heartbeat was dangerously weak. Little wonder. She was little more than a block of ice.

Roan and Laura were waiting for him inside the double doors. Although Winston was staggering with fatigue and cold combined, he stood fast while the couple unitedly worked to get two blankets about the stranger. Then Roan took the woman into his arms, and Laura opened a third wool blanket and draped it over Winston's shivering form.

"Aggie's runnin' a hot bath in your room," Roan told Winston as he rushed to the staircase.

"I'll make tea and heat up some soup," Laura said, beelining for the parlor door.

Winston set the bolts on the double doors, then headed down the hall.

Despite his wobbly legs and numbed feet, he somehow managed to keep up with Roan as they climbed the stairs to the second floor landing. Winston couldn't stop shivering, and he wondered if it was mainly due to the unmerciful chill in his body, the fact that the woman could very likely be dying, or that the one remaining outside was—

He refused to analyze how that could be possible. Not now. As long as the house was locked tight, he'd have a little time before having to warn the laird of the impending danger.

When Winston entered his bedroom on Roan's heels, the boys were nowhere in sight. Agnes stuck her head out of the bathroom, issuing a terse, "Hurry!"

"Give her to me," Winston rasped a moment before Roan would have stepped into the smaller room.

The laird turned a grimly quizzical look on Winston, but passed the woman into Winston's waiting arms.

"Listen carefully and don't ask me any questions right now," Winston stated, his authoritative tone further taking Roan aback. "Make sure every window and door in the house is locked tight. *Every* window and door!" He pushed past a dumbfounded Roan and barked at Agnes, "Watch the boys. *Don't* let them ou' o' your sight!"

For a split second he saw rebellion flash in her eyes. Then she hurried out of the bathroom, closing the door behind her.

Winston took a moment to get his wits about him. Meager steam rose up from the waiting bath. A glance at the half-filled porcelain tub gave him the stamina to force his stiff, weakened legs to obey him one stretch longer. He eased his right foot into the water. At first it felt scalding and he nearly abandoned his intentions. Clamping down on the pain, he hoisted himself up and over the rim of the tub, and stood for a second in the bathwater, telling himself he would not succumb to the fierce sensations of pins and needles assaulting his feet and legs.

Tears welled up in his eyes as he lowered himself into the deep, claw-foot tub. The reawakening of his circulation was excruciating, but he settled himself on the bottom, clothes, blankets and all, the woman angled lengthwise across his legs, one side of her unseen face against his chest. Tears streamed down his crimson and gray blotted face. Thoughts of the Phantom tried to intrude, but he forced himself to maintain his focus on the woman. Her heartbeat was steadier now, her breathing shallow but regular. She was no longer a block of ice, but supple flesh. The water was shoulder-high to her. Cupping his left hand, he scooped handful after handful of the warm liquid onto the top of her head. When he could no longer feel a chill emanate from her, he gingerly brushed her hair back, exposing a face so exquisite, his heart seemed to leap into his throat. Perhaps knowing that she wasn't aware of him was what gave him the courage to trace her features with his fingertips. Beneath her mane of thick dark hair was a smooth brow. Flawless, pale, almost translucent skin. Delicately winged eyebrows, expressive even in her state of unconsciousness. Long and thick dark eyelashes. A pert nose. Full pouty lips. A dimpled chin, slightly turned up.

It struck Winston that, even in her condition, she possessed an ageless beauty, a beauty which seemed to defy the laws of nature. His heart raced. His breathing was erratic. Never had he looked upon a face that so utterly captivated him. He brushed the side of his thumb along the underside of her chin. Even the texture of her skin amazed him. So soft. So unbelievably soft.

Gulping past the tightness in his throat, he wound his arms about her and settled himself more comfortably in the liquid warmth. He rested his chin atop the crown of her head and dazedly stared into nothingness.

Unable to stop himself, he began to go over the events of the past hour. What had happened in the cellar. The supernatural moaning. The disappearance of the *magic*. And the woman.

The Phantom was alive.

How, it didn't matter. A grave mistake had been made. Unimportant. The killer was on the loose. At Baird House.

Had the woman in the fourth dimension perished, taking with her the powers in the house?

The thought caused a fierce ache within his chest.

She had accused him of draining her energy during his last visit. Had the earthquake and storm been an aftermath of her passing?

And *this* woman?

He couldn't convince himself that her and the Phantom's arrival were mere coincidence. Had that *bastard* dumped his latest intended victim on the grounds to taunt Winston? To show Winston that the killer was not only alive, but capable of besting Winston's psychic powers after all?

The garden woman's words began to echo in his skull.

"He waits, while *ye* wallow in self-pity."

The Phantom was the danger she had warned him of!

A soft moan wrenched him from his stupor. He realized the stranger was squirming. His mind went blank in anticipation of her fully awakening.

Her head moved slightly against his heaving chest. She moaned again. Squirmed with more force.

"You're safe," Winston rasped, his voice sounding foreign and strained.

She stiffened. Then, for what seemed an eternity, she didn't move. She was fully consciousness, for he could sense the depths of her confusion. When he could no longer bear the silence, he stated, "As I said, you're safe. But can you tell me how you came to be naked and on Baird land?"

A long sigh escaped her. It was a curious sound, Winston reflected, his black eyebrows drawn down in a frown.

Her head dipped back. If he had thought himself prepared to look into her eyes, he discovered he was wrong. A breath caught in his throat when she boldly looked up at him. He found himself locked within the mesmerizing depths of her eyes, unable to speak or move. Unable to think. Her bright blue irises were sparingly flecked with gold, but the pinpoints seemed to hold tiny lights within them.

When she gracefully pulled away from him and sat up, Winston slipped his legs from beneath her and bent them at the knees to each side of her. She turned and braced her back against the brass spout, at the same time slipping the heavy, wet blankets off her shoulders. Her gaze never left his face, as if searching for a reaction in him. But none came. Winston's facial muscles were frozen. He could not even avert his eyes when the upper portion of her breasts became visible through clinging strands of her hair.

The bathroom door opened. Roan walked in, took one look at the scene greeting him, and swiftly turned his back to the tub.

"For the love o' Jesus, Mary and Joseph!" he wheezed.

Winston's spell was broken.

Scrambling out of the bathtub and casting off the blanket as he went, he positioned himself against the wall across from the tub, and glared at the stranger with heightening chagrin.

"I tak it she's alive!" Roan shakily bit out.

The woman slowly stood, the blankets lost beneath the murky water. In all ner glory, she stood before Winston, her penetrating gaze seemingly a permanent fixture on his face.

Winston vainly tried to produce saliva in his painfully dry mouth. He couldn't stop himself from looking her over, any more than he could force himself to stop shivering in the cold draft coming through the exposed doorway. For as far down her body as he could see—which was more than he told himself he *needed* to see—she was clinging hair, flawless skin, and dynamic curves.

"I-uh. . . ." Winston nervously ran the tip of his tongue over his lower lip. He lamely shrugged, then broke out in a ludicrous grin. "I would say she's *definitely* alive!"

Reflexly, Roan looked over his shoulder. The sight of her nakedness wrenched a grunt from him, and his face turned beet-red. Heading into the bedroom, he flung, "Let me know when she's decent!"

Decent?

Giving himself a mental shake, Winston ran into the bedroom. Roan was already heading into the hallway. Mumbling beneath his breath, Winston whipped the top quilt from the bed. When he turned to head back to the bathroom, he found the stranger standing in the doorway, watching him with curiosity and wariness combined.

He was about to assure her again that she was safe, but the words never left his mouth.

Agnes suddenly materialized a few feet away to his left. One glance at the stranger and the specter clamped a hand over her pseudo-heart. "Saints preserve us!" she squealed, then wagged a scolding finger at him. "Winston Connery, quit your gawkin' at the poor child!"

She snatched the quilt from his hands and hurriedly draped it over the young woman's shoulders. She fussed over her for a time, then leveled an indignant, maternal look on Winston.

"I'll no' have this kind o' behavior under this roof! You leave the carin' o' *this* guest to the mistress and me. And I *strongly* suggest, young mon, you keep your demons to yourself!"

With an impatient flick of Aggie's wrist, a stack of logs in the hearth became engulfed in flames.

What most disconcerted Winston was the fact that she'd accomplished this without her dissecting gaze wavering from him.

"How dare you bring him wi' you!" she continued to scold. "He's *your* problem. I'll no' stand for him abou', do you understand me?"

Flabbergasted by her verbal assault, Winston rasped a weak, "I think so." But he didn't understand her at all.

With a protective arm at the young woman's back, Agnes urged her in the direction of the hall door.

"Now dinna you fear none," Agnes consoled the stranger. "Some hot tea, a cuppy o' soup, and a warm bed, you'll be feelin' fine in na time at all."

Winston watched the women leaving the room. When they were turning left into the hall, the blue-eyed mystery looked back at him. For just a fleeting second, he noted pinpoint dimples in her cheeks, and read amusement in her eyes.

She's laughin' at me! he inwardly fumed.

Dragging himself to the bed, he plopped into a sitting position on the feather mattress.

"You're bloody right he's *ma* problem!" he blustered, then released a sound that was suspiciously like a whimper.

"How could I *no'* look at her?" he asked himself in a small voice. His hands flattened to his chest. "I'm only human!"

A silhouette image of the Phantom sauntered across the screen of his mind's eye.

His eyes darkening with a deadly gleam, Winston murmured, "I'll take you ou' maself, you bastard. Comin' here was the biggest mistake o' your miserable life."

His brain inflamed with outrage, he jumped up and hastily stripped out of his soggy, borrowed sweater, his slacks, and shorts.

The next instant, a clanging crash rang out.

Winston looked up in the direction of the door.

There stood Laura, a look of shock frozen on her face, and a tray, overturned bowl and cup scattered at her feet.

But Winston was beyond modesty at the moment. His unhurried gait carried him to the bathroom, where he closed the door and sat on the closed lid of the toilet.

"I can rise above all this," he murmured. "I can."

He shot to his feet and openhandedly slapped the wall to his right. "Friggin' right I can!"

Inexplicably, his anger drained out of him. Again sitting, he lethargically trenched the fingers of both hands through his wet hair.

The bathroom seemed unnaturally confining all of a sudden. His lungs felt weighted, his every breath labored.

"Am I losin' ma mind?"

How much more could happen?

"God, give me strength," he murmured, and rose to his feet.

Chapter Four

A case of the jitters plagued Winston all morning. What annoyed him the most was his inability to pinpoint its exact cause. It was as if a fiery thorn were imbedded at the base of his skull, every now and then prodding the sensitized nerves in that vicinity. He felt as if he were on the verge of exploding with anger, but anger for what he didn't know. At first he'd contributed this state to the knowledge that the Phantom was still alive. As incredible as that seemed, he *knew* he had picked up on the killer's psychic transmissions. He'd sensed the man's trace as clearly as if he'd looked into his own reflection in a mirror. And yet. . . .

The "buggers"—as Roan fondly called the boys—had managed to keep the laird and his lady love hopping the rest of the previous night, and all of this morning, thus far. It amazed Winston how three young boys could cause so much commotion. He didn't recall being as hyper or as creative as them when he was young, but then, his parents never tolerated a *noisy* or *active* child under their roof.

Somehow, Roan and Laura coped, although Winston was sure he wouldn't be any better a parent than his own. So, with clothing vanishing, food fights, Kahl's wails to be allowed to play in the tower, Kevin turning loose one of the peacocks inside the house, and Alby's hysterics over the fact he couldn't get his wooden animals to come to life, the Baird household was a circus. Winston had tried several times—both last night and this morning—to corner Roan and warn him about the killer's return. To no avail. Every time a chance arose for Winston to have his say, another crisis presented itself.

Agnes avoided him and refused to let him near the stranger. As far as Winston knew, no one but Agnes had seen the woman once she was escorted from his room. Winston had halfheartedly attempted a few times to probe the traces she'd left behind, in hopes of garnishing tidbits of information about her. Each time the venture met with a blank wall. It wasn't that he was interested in her as a *person,* but rather in her connection with the Phantom. Still, he should have gotten a fair reading on her.

Something was blocking his abilities.

He'd gone outside for a time and tried to psychically zoom in on the Phantom's whereabouts. Another blank wall. By the time he went to bed, he had convinced himself he was trying to juggle too much. So much had already happened, and he'd been in the house for less than forty-eight hours.

However, this morning he still found himself unable to dredge up information about the stranger and the Phantom. He was well-rested and had eaten a hearty breakfast. Had bathed and shaved. Was warmly dressed in a borrowed pair of Roan's jeans and a grey and burgundy striped pullover sweater, both of which were too big for him, but he wasn't trying to impress anyone. His paranormal capacity had returned when he'd entered the house, and he was warm and cozy and secure within the walls and better fed than he could remember being in a very long time. And yet, as he stared out his bedroom window, scanning the winter world beyond, his sixth sense was cold. He could no more sense the Phantom than he could fly, and that frustrated him.

Was he again suffering an overload? When he'd first gone mind-blind after Rose's death, he'd thought it a blessing. Now, his inability to ferret out the killer left him feeling vulnerable, something that was completely alien to his nature.

Outside movement distracted him. His gaze settled on the peacock perched atop the snowman. The colorful creature was dutifully preening, its tail fanned and appearing startlingly vibrant against the white backdrop of snow. A reflexive grin appeared at the right corner of Winston's mouth when the bird craned its neck and peered up at him. At least it seemed to be staring at him. He was relatively sure it wasn't.

The bird released a chilling cry, not unlike that of a cat being tortured. Winston's nerves went spastic for a moment. His heart thumped wildly, painfully inside his chest. He blinked. Blinked again. The peacock stood motionless, regally poised atop the snowman's head, its fantail retracted. Intently, he watched for a long time, waiting for the bird to move again, but it stood as if frozen.

Winston rapped sharply on the windowpane with the knuckle of his right index finger. He never saw whether the bird responded, for a rap on his door caused him a start and he whirled in time to see it slowly opening. Shortly, Agnes poked her head through the gap. As soon as she spied him, she calmly entered the room and closed the door behind her.

Apprehension swelled up inside Winston. She approached without haste, her blue gaze never wavering from his, her expression unreadable. Winston made a feeble attempt to offer a smile in greeting, but his facial muscles were reluctant to cooperate. When she came to a stop in front of him, he noticed her solidity was showing signs of losing its integrity. He couldn't see *through* her yet, but she was definitely in the process of fading. Her dark blue dress was gradually turning to shades of gray in places, and her blue irises intermittently became colorless.

"Mr. Connery, forgive ma intrudin' like this, but I must speak wi' you."

He nodded. "Is it abou' the girl?"

Agnes' shrewd gaze watched him for a time before she replied, "Aye, a bit. Maistly, I need to say ma mind abou' you and the gloom you brought into this place when you arrived."

Frowning, Winston gave a light shrug. "Gloom? I wasn't aware ma mood or ma company was *tha'* bad."

"Dinna talk around ma meanin'," she chided, scowling at him.

Winston was hard-pressed to understand her dislike of him. "Have I said or done somethin' to offend you?"

She seemed surprised at this, and the scowl melted into a look of comical bewilderment. "Offend me? Are we talkin' abou' the same thing, Mr. Connery?"

"Please . . . Winston, and I'm no' sure."

"I have nothin' personally against you," she said in earnest. "Actually, I think you're a verra nice young mon. Tis the darkness you carry inside you wha' bothers me. Tis leakin' into the house like a foul smoke hidin' in the shadows."

Before he could suppress it, a laugh burst from him. He turned to the window in a bid to get himself under control, but when he noticed the bird still frozen in place, he sobered and frowned. Yesterday, he'd seen one of the boys place a peacock atop the snowman and, now that he thought about it, it hadn't moved. Had the animated bird been merely his imagination playing tricks on him?

"Mr. Con—Winston," she corrected on a sigh, "I dinna have much time, and I *would* like to have ma say on this matter."

Still frowning, Winston faced her. He was given a momentary start when he saw that she was now more diaphanous than solid. Her face was pale gray mist, while her eyes were opaque and now eerily blue. "Sorry," he said lamely. "Wha' abou' this *darkness* in me?"

"Are *you* aware o' it?"

"Can't say as I am," he replied, and was a bit unnerved that the words came out sounding supercilious.

"I sensed it afore Roan brought you into the house. I didna say anythin' because it wasna ma place. But for two nights now, Mr. Connery, everyone—no' me, o' course— has shared your nightmares. Last night, even the lass. I spent maist o' the night flittin' from bedroom to bedroom, listenin' and watchin' them all go through the same tossin' and turnin', the same moanin' and groanin' as you. Yesterday *and* this morn, ma lads were sullen and listless—as I sensed *you* were afore I knocked at your door."

"I'm no' sure I understand."

She sighed deeply. The sound rippled the air around him. "This itherworld condition o' mine has given me a few abilities, and one is seein' people's auras. Yours is verra dark. As black as a moonless night. The ithers are unknowingly reactin' to this, Mr. Connery. This darkness in you is tryin' to influence them."

Winston tried not to appear skeptical, but wouldn't *he* know if he possessed such an aura—especially such a *vile* aura?

She faded such that he could barely make out her features.

"Mr. Connery, tis good you came to Baird House, but

you're no' an ordinary man. You must control your inner demons. Dinna loose them on the unsuspectin'."

"Wha' abou' the Phantom? Wha' can you tell me abou' him?"

"Phantom?"

"He's here. After Laura. I sensed him when I went ou' after the girl, last night."

"There is no one here but us, Mr. Connery."

"No, he *is* here. Outside somewhere. I think the girl may be one o' his victims. Has she said anythin'?"

"She's mute, far as I can tell. And there's no' a scratch or a bruise on her. However she came to be ou' on the gazebo, I dinna know, but I've seen na indication she was hurt by anyone."

Winston adamantly shook his head. "Look, I've been trackin' this killer for four years. Dammit, he was supposedly killed some months ago, but I *sensed* him on the property last night!"

She was nothing but a mist now, shimmering in the gentle drafts. "There is na killer here, Winston," she said kindly, sympathetically. "You carry him in your soul and, for whatever reason I canna fathom, you canna let go o' him. Tis *you* wha' is troubled. This . . . *Phantom* . . . is your mind tryin' to find the mon who is Winston Connery."

"That's no' possible."

"Na? Do you *sense* him now?"

Winston gulped past the sudden dryness in his throat. "So you're sayin' this is merely ma warped imagination at work?"

"No' warped," she said, and he heard a hint of laughter in her now wispy voice. "You came here to find yourself, dinna you?"

He weakly nodded.

"Aye, Master Winston, and you will. Given time. We'll

talk when I return. The grayness is too hard to resist now, and I'm so verra tired. Think o' wha' I've said."

The last word softly echoed on seconds after Winston was aware that Agnes Ingliss had completely passed over into another world—the "grayness" she'd called it. He stood very still for a time longer, mulling over her words and questioning the denial fermenting inside his brain. Given a choice, he would rather the Phantom be actually dead and his own mental wellness in question, than for the killer to be on the loose and testing Winston's ability to end his reign of terror.

But still, he was *sure* he'd sensed the man on the property last night.

Shards of pain throbbed at his temples. Without knowing why, he glanced out the window and saw the peacock again animated, its tail fanned and its gaze riveted on the window behind which Winston stood.

Dashing from the room, Winston ran to the first floor landing, out the doors, and into the brisk morning air. His socked feet instantly felt the bite of the cold as he trampled through snow until he reached the fountain on the north side of the house. A crusted layer of ice topped the snow, and the crunching his awkward, plodding steps made, seemed inordinately loud. He kept his gaze on the snowman, even when he sank into a thigh-high drift about three yards from his destination. Grunting, his teeth loudly clacking in uncontrollable chattering, he struggled out of the partially frozen hillock and reached the snowman. All the while, the peacock remained perfectly still, its tail retracted, its back to him.

Roan had called the bird Braussaw, and had said he'd had it stuffed after accidentally driving over it. But Winston had *seen* this bird move not once, but *twice!*

Could it be another bird—

He angrily snatched the stiff, feathered carcass from the

snowman's head and held it out with trembling hands. Indeed, the bird was stuffed. He stared into its lifeless eyes and wanted to scream. But of course he didn't. That would have been too human a reaction from Winston Ian Connery, which would have convinced him he was truly insane.

In a fit of uncharacteristic anger, he dropped the peacock and repeatedly stepped on and kicked it. Sawdust spilled onto the ground, a washed-out yellowish color against the pristine whiteness of the snow. Winston stomped and kicked, stomped and kicked, adrenaline heating him and warding off the bite of the freezing temperature.

Something moved in the left side of his peripheral vision. He glimpsed but a black shape against the snow, an elongated silhouette spread across the ground. With a guttural cry, he lunged atop the shape. He pummeled it with his fists, thrashed and kneed semi-solidity. Snow and slivers of ice flew up around his movements only to soundlessly settle back on the ground or on him. A voice in the back of his mind told him he was in the throes of rage, but he denied this. To be enraged, one had to feel deeply or strongly about someone or something.

He thrashed and cursed the Phantom until it suddenly occurred to him he was fighting his own shadow. The insight struck him sourly in the pit of his stomach and threatened to heave the contents into his throat. But then the lunacy of fighting himself struck home. He flipped onto his back and released a roar of laughter. It weakened him as seconds ticked by. His shadow! Oh God, his *shadow!*

Or was it?

He sobered and listened to the stark quiet and stillness surrounding him.

Agnes had warned him of his inner demons.

Something beckoned him to peer up at his bedroom windows. There, in the right one, he clearly saw the girl watching him. Her palms were pressed to the glass, and her expression told him she had witnessed enough to question his sanity.

Mortified, Winston got to his feet and testily brushed off some of the snow and ice clinging to him. He realized his feet were achingly cold, as were various other parts of his anatomy. He was loathe to go back inside the house. Loathe to face her.

Casting the de-innarded bird a remorseful glance, he trudged back to the front of the house and forced himself to enter. To his further chagrin, Kevin was sitting on the third from the bottom step of the staircase. He watched Winston with wry amusement, his blue eyes seeming far too shrewd for a boy who had recently turned eight.

"I'd get my butt kicked if I went out dressed like that," he grumbled.

Winston managed a strained grin. "I'm just a kid at heart."

"Did you just insult me?"

The boy's earnest question left Winston at a loss for words. Shaking his head, he patted the boy on the shoulder, then ascended the staircase to the second floor.

Damn, he was cold. Wet and cold and wishing he could melt into the floor and not have to face the girl.

Not only was she there to silently greet him, but so was the rolling warmth of a blazing fireplace. There hadn't even been a glowing ember when he'd gone outside. . . .

Avoiding her gaze, he crouched in front of the embracing heat and rubbed his hands together. He could feel her watching his every move and it unnerved him. Rivulets of water wormed down his brow from his sodden hair. He wanted to wipe away the wetness, but he realized his fingers were now tightly entwined.

Cramping in his calves prompted him to sit on the floor, cross-legged. He tried to wiggle his toes, but the cold-induced pain in his feet only brought a grimace to his ashen face.

A heavy quilt fell upon his back and shoulders. He drew it tightly about him while the stranger came around and stood to his right. Her bare feet were inches from his kneecap. Her feet and ankles were all that were visible beneath the light blue, floral print flannel nightgown she wore, and the strands of dark hair hanging just below the hemline. Her feet were small and slender, the ankles seeming almost too fragile. His gaze crept upward, slowly and reluctantly because he dreaded seeing what her expression was now. He paused at her concealed waistline and tried to scan her thoughts. A blank wall. Frowning, he tried again, pushing outward with his will to penetrate her shield. Again, he was denied access to her mind.

He found himself staring into her eyes and he gasped reflexively. Her expression wasn't one of ridicule or pity, or even fear that he had indeed lost his marbles. She was . . . *curious*. Curious about him and what had brought about his romp in the snow. He didn't glean the information from her thoughts, but rather sensed her mood. She was calm. Not the least afraid of him, as she would be had she been assaulted by the likes of the Phantom. His heart skipped a beat at the thought that Agnes could have been right. That the Phantom *was* dead, and it was his own projections contaminating his psyche.

Gracefully, like the petals of a flower unfurling to the rays of the sun, the stranger lowered herself to a sitting position, partially facing him. She, too, sat cross-legged, her delicate hands resting atop her knees. He'd never met a woman whose hair nearly touched the floor, or whose eyes were a brighter blue than the bluest sky. The silken strands framed a heart-shaped face, which bore an innocence he'd never before encountered, not even in a child. He couldn't think of an adjective that fittingly described

her. Lovely fell short. Beautiful seemed somehow harsh.
His thoughts raced through a list until a word glared across
his mindscreen.

Enchanting. Yes, she was enchanting.

"Hello."

He thought he glimpsed a ghost of a smile in her eyes,
but he wasn't sure. Perhaps he was merely being hopeful.

Sighing, he snuggled deeper into the quilt. "Thank
you."

Could she *hear* what he was saying? He decided to cast
a bit of bait to test her reaction.

"Ou' there . . . in the snow . . . I was forced to battle a
monster. It insulted ma mother and, bein' a mon o' princi-
ple, I was left no choice but to defend her honor."

Nothing. She didn't smile or blink. Just stared at him.

"Do you have a name?"

Nothing.

"How abou' if I call you Tinkerbell? Helen Of Troy?
Lassie? Tweety Bird?"

Deliah.

The name didn't come from her thoughts, but it came
to him nonetheless.

"Deliah? Is that your name?"

She remained silent and still, content to watch him.

"Deliah," he repeated, then smiled. "It suits you."

He stiffened when she unexpectedly took one corner of
the quilt and dabbed at the wetness on his brow. When
she settled back, she questioningly arched an eyebrow at
him.

"Why am I nervous?" he asked, pretending to know her
thoughts. "Well-ah, I'm no'. No' really. All right, I am.
You have me as timid as a schoolboy plunderin' through
puberty. Why is tha', Deliah?"

Silence stretched between them for what seemed a long
time. Winston was aware of his own shallow breathing. He

felt oddly at peace, as if he were in the comforting embrace of sleep. A deep sleep without nightmares, only nurturing escape from the cruel reality of his existence. He wondered what it would be like to hold her dry form in his arms and run his chin across her hair.

His eyelids grew heavy and he sighed contentedly.

He thought about the garden in the other dimension, and the woman who claimed to be the house. A sleepy smile formed on his lips, and he felt himself floating away from the fire in the hearth, floating through the air and coming to rest upon the decadent softness of the mattress. He imagined himself snuggling up to a warm and shapely form, spooning himself against softness graced with subtle scents of flower gardens.

Winston drifted deeper and deeper into healing sleep, unaware that Deliah had led him to the bed and now lay on her side in front of him, his damp arms wrapped possessively about her.

She stared off into space with a look of pure contentment on her face, her eyes mirroring a spring garden which then only existed in her mind.

Moments slipped by. Diaphanous flowers and birds and butterflies materialized. A floral-scented breeze, warmed by a psychically-projected springtime sun, passed throughout the room, causing the heavy drapes to gently flutter and sway.

When at last she closed her eyes, the room had been completely transformed into a sanctuary of peace and beauty and security. No one could intrude. Nothing could disturb them until he was ready to awaken.

Unknowingly, Winston slept wrapped around his one salvation.

*   *   *

Kevin gave another fierce tug of the navy blue sweater and finally pulled it free of Kahl's grip. He scowled at his five-year-old brother, daring the redheaded Kahl to defy his wishes again. While his two older brothers silently challenged each other's role as leader of this latest "plan", Alby was content to lean against the doorjamb and observe.

This was the fifth meeting amongst the brothers, concerning the plan. As before, they were in Kevin's room, sitting in front of the open closet, their collected *devices* hidden within the shadows. Kahl had originally thought up the plan, which concerned what he considered to be the lack of security measures. He'd impressed his older brother with the term and his idea of how to better their odds of defeating the chances of *another* boogeyman from ever getting into the house again. However, being the oldest and confident that *he* alone was adult-wise enough to organize the scheme, Kevin was quick to take over.

Alby was used to the power play between his brothers. Aunt Laura had once called him her little passivist. Whatever that meant. Probably that he was the quieter of the three, he reasoned. Let his brothers slug and shout at each other. Alby wasn't partial to being sent to his room for a nap. Aunt Laura's term of time-out was not his favorite.

Besides, Alby had more important things weighing on his mind, like . . . why wouldn't his toys play with him anymore? The only reason he was even participating in the plan was because Kevin had threatened to pour honey in his hair while he slept. That was right up there with time-out, time for bed, and what are you hiding?. Words worthy of his attention. What are you hiding? told him he looked guilty about something, which always resulted in time-out even if he hadn't done anything to deserve it.

"We gotta have at least *two* more," Kevin stated, smugly patting the sweater balled atop his lap. "Then we should have enough."

Kahl's stormy hazel-eyed glare remained riveted on Kevin's face. He was always peeved about being the middle boy. Never quite as adult as Kevin, nor as adorable as Alby. "Then you get 'em. I about got caught snatching *that* one."

With a shrug of indifference, Kevin said, "Okay. I can get two at one time."

"Fine, then *you* do just that. I'm bloody tired of sneaking around, anyway."

"Fine. I will." Kevin glanced at Alby. He was about to suggest Alby take his turn at nabbing at least one of the adult sweaters, but thought better of it. Alby was so short, it would take him *forever* to yank one off a hanger. Instead, he issued to the youngest sibling, "You can stand watch."

Alby's dark eyebrows jutted upward. "Huh?"

"You gotta do your share," Kahl said.

"Huh?"

"One more huh and I'm going to thump you," Kevin threatened, then sighed when Alby's lower lip stuck out in a pout. "Okay, so I won't thump you. You don't want us to get caught, do you?"

Alby had to think about this for a moment. "Naw."

Kevin grinned triumphantly. "Okay, so let's unravel this sucker."

"Kev?"

Kevin's gaze searched Alby's thoughtful expression.

"What if we do get caught? Aunt Laura's gonna be awful mad at us."

Kevin and Kahl exchanged a conspiratorial look, then Kevin grinned assuredly at Alby. "Think how happy she's gonna be when we trap us another boogeyman. Alby, you don't want him getting into the house, do you?"

It wasn't so much that Kevin's questions frightened Alby, but rather the eerie tone in which his brother had spoken. Alby gulped, then lightly bit into his lower lip as he shook his head. The last boogeyman had turned out to be a boogeywoman, and she had taken Beth and Lachlan away from them. At least, that's how he perceived the events of last Christmas Eve.

"Oh, lawd," Kahl groaned, casting Alby a look of disgust. "He's gonna start bawling again."

"Not," Alby sniffed.

"What's wrong *now*?" Kevin asked him.

"Dunno."

"You gotta know what's got you sulking like a squished worm!"

Kahl giggled, but Alby only became more despondent. "I miss Lannie and Beth."

Kahl immediately grew solemn, but Kevin gave an exasperated roll of his blue eyes. "There ain't nothing we can do about that, right?"

His brother nodded in unison with him. "Okay, so don't let it bug you. Hey!" Kevin's eyes lit up with devilish amusement. "How about if I share a secret with you guys? Promise not to tell?"

"Promise," Kahl said quickly, and crossed his heart.

It took Alby a moment longer to nod his agreement.

"Okay." Kevin bent over his folded legs, leaning closer to his brothers. "I saw the naked lady sneak into Winnie's room. I think they're doing the bump."

Kahl's eyes grew larger, while Alby muttered, "His name is Winston. He's nice."

"Winnie, Winston, close enough," Kevin said impatiently. "He's a fast worker, huh? She must like him a lot."

"Deliah."

"Huh?" Kevin asked.

"Her name is Deliah." Alby released a watery sigh and straightened away from the door jamb. "Maybe she's not doing the bump. Maybe they're just talking. Ever think of that?"

Kahl jiggled his head. "How come you know her name? Aunt Aggie told me she hasn't talked."

"Yeah," said Kevin, frowning at Alby, who shrugged his small shoulders.

"I just know."

"Right, and I'm gonna be the next queen," Kahl sneered.

Alby stuck out his tongue at his brothers. "Betcha her name *is* Deliah."

"Whatever," Kevin testily dismissed, and lifted the sweater into his hands. He bit onto the wool strands along the hemline and yanked until one at last broke. But when he lowered the bundle back onto his lap, he spat something into his hand and held out the leveled palm for his brothers to see.

"Oh gross!" Kahl gasped, staring at the bloodied tooth. "That's makes two, Kev!"

Awed that his brother had inadvertently yanked out another tooth, Alby leaned forward for a closer inspection. "Wow. Don't it hurt?"

Kevin worked his mouth against the metallic flavor assaulting his taste buds. "Naw, it doesn't hurt. Just tastes gross."

"Use scissors or a knife next time," Kahl said.

"Why? This means I get another visit from the Tooth Faery," Kevin beamed.

Alby shrank back, his cherubic features shadowed with fear. "What if the boogeyman comes instead?"

"He can have it if he pays for it," Kevin quipped, and laughed when Kahl released a squeal of laughter.

Alby remained sullenly quiet while his brothers unraveled the sweater Laura had gotten Roan for Christmas.

* * *

In the library, Roan settled onto the sofa with a cup of steaming black coffee in one hand, a stack of mail in the other. After taking a sip, he placed the coffee on the end table to his right, rested his right ankle atop his left knee, and started glancing through the letters, bills and advertisements. He was nearly through scanning the ads when Laura sat next to him, a coffee cup nestled between her hands.

"Anything interesting?"

"No' yet," he grinned, and paused just long enough to plant a kiss on her cheek. "Poor ol' Henry had a helluva time makin' it to the door. I've got to try to clear a path sometime today."

"It's snowing again," she sighed.

He moaned softly. "We'll all get bloody crazy if we don't get away for a wee spell." He looked into her smiling eyes and grinned. "I've a mind to go shoppin', lass."

Laura clamped her left hand over her heart. "You? Roan Ingliss of a mind to spend *money*? You *must* be getting stir crazy!"

Bobbing his head and grinning, his gaze scanning the fronts of the envelopes again, he said, "Aye, the walls are closin' in on me. I'll wager there's no' a person in all o' Crossmichael who isn't ready to kiss off *this* winter. Can't say I remember one quite so harsh. We never see *this* much snow in these parts."

Laura sipped her coffee, but lowered the cup when Roan held up a long white envelope and said, "Ah, tis from your parents."

He handed her the envelope, then took her cup and placed it next to his on the table. For a moment he observed her hesitancy to open the letter, then absently browsed through the remaining stack atop his lap. It had been nearly three weeks since the mailman had braved a delivery to Baird House.

At the same time Laura dryly announced, "Terrific, they

want to meet you," Roan came across an envelope which drained the color from his face. He held it up, studying the return address as if expecting it to prove to be a hoax. Not even Laura's moan distracted him.

"Dammit, Roan, they're planning to arrive next month for a week's visit. Nothing like *asking* us if we want them here! Oh sure, *now* they're interested in seeing their grandchildren. And my father's not happy that we're not married yet."

She looked at Roan's taut profile, then noticed the lifted, trembling hand which held a long, pale pink envelope. "What's wrong?"

It took a moment longer for him to respond. To her surprise, he buried the envelope beneath the pile on his lap.

"Nothin'," he said distractedly, pretending to show more of an interest in the other mail.

"Roan? I know you too well."

His troubled eyes, appearing more amber now in the direct gaslight across from him, met hers. He sighed, "Ma sister."

Laura blinked in confusion. "You never mentioned you had any family outside of Aggie."

"Aye, and for a good reason."

Lowering her parents' letter to her lap, she reached out with her right hand and lovingly brushed the backs of her fingers against his temple. "You're looking a little pale, big guy. Why would getting a letter from your sister upset you like this?"

"I'm no' upset. Just surprised is all."

"Oh, really. Aren't you going to read it?"

He shot her a heated look, one that took her aback, then he sighed again and separated the pink envelope from the others. As if perturbed that Laura had put him on the spot, he tore through the back of the envelope and removed two pale pink pages filled with bold print that struck Laura as being made on a laser printer. She remained silent while he quickly skimmed over the pages, but jerked back when he harshly balled the papers in his right hand and shot to his feet, the remaining mail falling to the floor.

"Roan, what the hell is going on?"

With a guttural cry of anger, he flung the wadded letter across the room. "Baird House made the news in the States," he said bitterly, turning to face Laura and trenching the fingers of his hands through his thick hair. "So, now it seems *her* parents are interested in wha' I'm up to these days, and ma little sister is plannin' to visit!"

He sucked in a great breath and placed balled hands on his hips. "Over ma dead body will any o' them set foot in *this* house!"

Shaken by the depths of his anger, Laura slowly rose to her feet. *"Her* parents?"

Roan's irises brightened with barely suppressed fury. "Aye, *her* parents!" he growled, trembling. "I disowned them when they abandoned me and Scotland for a *better* life in the States! Six letters in twenty-one years is wha' I've gotten from them!" He laughed bitterly. "Wha' few letters I've gotten from Taryn were maistly a feeble attempt to lay a serious guilt trip on me for preferrin' to remain in Scotland wi' Aggie!"

"I'm sorry," Laura murmured. She wound her arms about his middle and pressed the left side of her head against his chest.

His anger winding down, Roan wrapped his arms around her warm body and kissed the top of her head. "Na, I'm sorry, Laura. I shouldn't be takin' this ou' on you."

She laughed softly. "You weren't." She looked into his despondently masked face, then reached up and poked him in the chin with a forefinger. "We've had two surprises today. Everything comes in threes." She laughed. "I wonder what's in store for us next."

A moment's panic shadowed his handsome features, but this soon melted into a look of pure mischief. "Weel," he said, grinning almost ludicrously, "perhaps the third could be o' oor own makin', eh?" She squealed in surprise when he swooped her up into his arms and playfully nuzzled her neck. "Like some serious lovin'," he added, and carried her out of the room.

Chapter Five

It occurred to Winston that he really didn't know any-thing about nature. Sitting on the ground and casually braced against the white latticework base of the gazebo, he indulged his external senses' need to absorb everything around him. The morning was resplendent with warm sunshine and he delighted in its kiss against his skin. The sky was vivid blue and cloudless. Every so often a bird soared above him and chirped in greeting, to which he would smile and wave. Semi-circling him were the colorful petals of the rose garden. He filled his entire being with the sweet fragrance with each breath he drew in through his nostrils. Colors, sights, and sounds, and the velvety softness of the plucked purple and white petals he held atop each palm and repeatedly stroked, offered him more comfort than he'd ever known in his life. Nature alone knew the secret to taming the beast within a man. He was more at peace with himself than he could ever remember. At peace and truly happy. And content. He had never before taken the time to simply bask in a day as though he didn't have a care in the world. It was a curious thing to do, this nothing.

He wasn't sure how he'd gotten to the garden. Briefly, he was disappointed that it wasn't the one in the other dimension. He wondered about the woman—who referred to herself as the house—and somehow knew he wouldn't be returning to her world. He didn't know why and, surprisingly, he didn't care.

While whiling away an indefinite time, he discovered something else about nature. She had a name. MoNae, short for Mother Nature. He'd spent some time mentally conversing with her, not finding it at all strange that she replied, or that she even possessed the ability to hold a conversation. She was a complex presence. Gentle, yet strict. Loving, yet determined to have her way when it came to *her* world. Understanding, yet intolerant of the humans' inability and reluctance to work *with* her, and not for the mere betterment of what mankind sought. Overpopulation and architectural developments were gradually taking away her lands, narrowing the planet's vegetation beds.

Not so far in the future, she had cautioned, *gardens will be shut-ins, relegated to walls, floors and ceilings, and reduced to technological care rather than my nurturing abilities.*

Winston didn't know how to respond to that.

A fat, sassy bumblebee buzzed past his nose. He saw but a flash of yellow and black stripes before it flew out of sight somewhere behind him.

It was a glorious morning, and he closed his eyes, a smile youthening his features. The blackness and thickness of his long eyelashes stood out in stark contrast against the light coloring of his cheeks. He was aware he needed a shave, but didn't care. If he could spend more days like this feeling so utterly relaxed, he told himself he could even contemplate going back to work for the Shields Agency. He could do anything as long as he had times like this in which he could escape the realities of his life.

With his wrists atop his raised knees, the petals on his palms exposed to the sunlight, he remained blissfully appreciative of his aloneness in the garden.

He sensed intrusion and lifted his eyelids. At first he saw only a fake sea of flowers in front of him, then noticed hair the color of rich sable, gleaming in the rays of the sun. His gaze lifted until he was forced to squint. The petals dropped from his palms as he visored his eyes to better see the face of the woman standing before him.

For but a brief moment, he resented her presence, until she kneeled between his parted legs and sat back against her heels. Winston lowered his hands, this time cupping his knees with his palms, and steadily, deeply, looked into the mesmerizing blue of Deliah's eyes.

"Good morn," he said, forcing a smile to bypass his nervousness.

She didn't say a word, nod her head, or even offer a thought in greeting. But her eyes told him everything he needed to know at this particular, most peculiar time. They smiled back at him, smiled from within depths of such love and devotion, his heart beat erratically behind his chest. He couldn't breathe.

Couldn't speak. Couldn't bring himself to touch the shiny strands of hair beckoning him to lose his fingers in the promised softness. He could do nothing more than stare at her and wonder how anyone could outshine the sun. Even the garden's beauty faded in comparison. She encompassed nature. Encompassed everything beautiful and serene and right about the world.

Winston drew in a shuddering breath when she gracefully turned and sat on the ground, snuggling her spine against him and reclining the back of her head to his left shoulder. He closed his eyes and tightly gripped his knees, and inhaled her earthy, floral scent. Desire quivered through him. Liquid flames replaced the blood flowing in his veins. The sound of a thousand bees swam inside his head. When she gripped his wrists and coaxed him to cross his arms against her, he fought back a fierce notion to run from the garden before he lost all control. But he could no more jump to his feet than he could tell her to stop trying to seduce him. He wanted the closeness. *Needed* to cling to her solidity.

Her sigh of contentment diminished the buzzing. She released his wrists and squirmed closer to his chest. Reflexively, he tightened his hold, then dipped his right cheek and brushed it against the crown of her head. He closed his eyes and repeated the gesture, basking in her softness, her raw femininity. She shifted slightly and turned her head. Again he found himself staring into her eyes, and he knew he was lost to her will. She stroked beneath his chin with the tip of her nose, her left hand kneading the heated flesh beneath his sweater. Then she shifted again, drawing up her knees to her chest and cuddling against him like a child craving the closeness and security of a parent's embrace. She closed her eyes and, to Winston's bewilderment, fell fast asleep.

For a time he simply held her, staring into her face, wondering how long it would be before she awakened. His back ached after a while. Nagging cramps nipped at his arms and legs, and along his spine, but he didn't want to move for fear of waking her prematurely. He sensed this was the first real sleep she'd had since he'd found her.

When hours had seemed to pass and his butt had grown so numb he couldn't feel it anymore, he grew restless. He decided to probe her mind in hopes of uncovering her identity, but no matter how hard he tried, he could find nothing more in her mind but an image of the garden scene stretched out before him. Perplexed, rattled by her

ability to block him out, he made another attempt to
breach her secrets. Nothing but the garden. Not even the
hardest criminal had ever resisted his probing.

Briefly, he wondered if the woman in the other dimension was toying with him, demonstrating the extent of
her powers over his. It was a disturbing thought and he
dismissed it. The last thing he needed was to find himself
up against another unknown, especially one residing in a
dimension in which he had no control. *She* reigned there.
How would she fare in *his* world?

Winston was given a slight start when he realized Deliah
was looking up at him through eyelids half-mast. Another
nervous smile sprang to his mouth.

"You've abou' got ma whole body either numb or tin-
glin'," he said lightheartedly.

She blinked up at him, then disconcertedly settled her
gaze on his lips. A slight frown marred Winston's brow.
Although he couldn't read her thoughts, he was aware of
an unmistakable pull, a demand that was not spoken aloud
or telepathically projected into his mind, but rather felt.
She wanted to be kissed, and was impatient with what she
believed was his lack of interest. Now that amused him. If
he were any more interested, he would be forced to spend
most of his time submerged in a bath of cold water.

"No' until I know who you are," he said. He forced her
into a sitting position and expected her to take the hint
and get to her feet. Instead, she swiftly maneuvered to her
knees and turned to face him, somehow not touching him
with any part of her body. He laughed, but it was cut
short when she gripped the front of his sweater and, with
strength unusual in a woman—let alone one as fragile as
she appeared—she swung him away from the gazebo. The
next thing he knew, he was on his back and she was strad-
dling his hips.

"Wha' the!" he gasped. He couldn't make out her features. The sun was blinding him. For several seconds, he remained frozen, his mind trying to absorb what had just happened. It wasn't until her hands slipped beneath his sweater and her fingers eagerly pressed against the flesh below his pectorals, did he react. He snared her wrists and rolled to his right, effortlessly pinning her beneath him, her hands anchored to the ground above her head. To his amazement, she wasn't the least unnerved by this maneuver, and this irked him.

"Listen carefully, Deliah," he chided, scowling darkly. "It could prove dangerous to play this kind o' game wi' a man, do you understand?"

She smiled and he released an explosive sigh of exasperation.

He again felt the pull, but this one was stronger, more demanding.

"No, Deliah! I don't make love on a whim!"

Her smile faded.

"Listen, lass, for all I know, you could be married!"

Then he was kissing her. Hungrily. Passionately, as if the tormenting fires in his groin could not be doused until he satisfied her. He couldn't remember lowering himself, or remember the initial touching of their lips. Now, he couldn't stop. The fire was within him, burning out of control. He'd known lust, but never passion, and *this* was passion. His every sense was attuned to her reactions, and his desire to please her outweighed his own need to seek immediate gratification.

Releasing her wrists and sliding his arms protectively around her, he sweetened the kiss by forcing back the intensity of it. She clung to him with the abandon of a lifelong lover, of someone familiar with not only his body, but his mind. Her hands moved over the heated skin of his waist, back, and shoulders. Then she was willing him to remove his sweater. He complied without hesitation, pulling it over his head and tossing it aside. It fell draped across a yellow rosebush, the knitted wool weighing heavily on the already laden branches.

Winston ignored the sweater and swung his gaze back to Deliah's face. He was breathing laboriously, as if he'd been running a marathon. Heat brought high color to his cheeks. He watched her gaze drink in his naked upper torso and arms, and wondered if she didn't think him too thin. Next to the laird of Baird House, he felt puny, but he could read in her eyes that she appreciated his lean, muscular build. His chest was smooth. Only his lower arms and legs sported fine dark hair. The burning trail of her fingers told him she liked his smooth, corded skin, found him as enticing as he found her.

Bees, the wind whistling through the gazebo, and birds, serenaded them as Winston drew up her nightgown until he was able to slip it over her head and toss it in the general direction his sweater had gone. He couldn't stop himself from studying her small waist, her flat stomach, and the gradual ascent over her ribs to the firm roundness of her breasts. He felt giddy and lightheaded as he lowered himself and captured her mouth in a deep, exploring kiss. The softness of her skin, the swell of her breasts and her hardened nipples against him, all plummeted him into a sea of maddening sensations. Her fingers trenched his hair and massaged his scalp, urging him to kiss her deeper, deeper, until he was sure she intended to swallow him whole. He wanted the physical union with her more than he'd ever wanted anything. To bury himself in her softness. Lose himself inside her womb and claim rebirth once ecstasy unburdened his soul.

Images bombarded his mind. They were already joined, urging each other toward the pinnacle of physical love. Tormenting sensations targeted his loins, heart, palms, and temples. His skin was coated with perspiration. It hurt to breathe and it hurt not to, but he nonetheless drew in a deep breath to quell the intensity of the need flooding him unmercifully.

Her fingers sensuously stroked his cheeks and mouth, then her hands lowered and unbuttoned his pants. Anticipation lanced him so fiercely, he almost feared what was to come. What if he lost control too soon? It had been so long since he was with a woman, and these fledgling feelings warring inside him made him feel more like a teenager than a man.

As if reading his thoughts, she abandoned unzipping his pants and cupped his face within her hands. He lowered himself to kiss her again, but before their lips met, he heard her whisper, "Now, Roan. God, I love you!"

He jerked back and his eyes widened in horror at the sight of a naked Laura beneath him. Her eyes were laden with raw, primordial passion, her parted lips inviting and seductive.

"No!" he roared and scrambled to his feet.

Winston bolted up. Panic closed in around him and he blinked rapidly to clear the milky haze distorting his vision. He knew he was in his room, in bed, but how he got there was beyond him. It was difficult for him to accept that the garden and what had happened there were but a dream.

No, not all a dream. He had unwittingly tapped into Roan's mind, obviously while the man was making love to Laura somewhere in the house.

He shivered and realized the room was icy cold. Frowning, he spied a kneeling figure in front of an opened window. The hair pooled on the floor around her readily identified her.

Hastening off the mattress, he rushed to her side. She was leaning over the wide sill, her right hand outstretched as she tried to catch some of the large, downy snowflakes spilling from the sky.

"Deliah!" he said sharply, and pulled her to her feet. He shut and locked the window, then went to the hearth and testily built a fire. When the flames had fully engulfed the logs, he turned, standing at the same time. He wasn't surprised to find her still standing by the window, a hurt look shadowing her features. She stood with her hands primly folded in front of her, her hair a cascading mane about her slender form. Winston approached her and stopped within arm's reach. He was still peeved with her childish disregard for her health, but also chagrined with the vivid memory of the two of them in the garden.

"I'm sorry I bit your head off," he said, still frowning and shifting his weight from one socked foot to the other. He didn't care for the look of vulnerability she now wore, nor the way she kept her gaze demurely lowered to the floor. "Deliah, it's bloody freezin' ou' there," he said by way of an apology, "and you've nothin' on but a night-gown."

Her gaze slowly lifted until she was looking him in the eye. She heaved a sigh, then again looked down.

Winston fought back an impulse to pull her into his arms. He didn't need to complicate his life any more than it was. Perhaps after he unlocked the mysteries surrounding her, and if she was unattached. . . .

Swiping a hand down his face in frustration, he glanced at the door. "When did you last have somethin' to eat?"

She shook her head.

"Does tha' mean you don't know, or you're no' hungry?"

His somewhat cheerful tone lifted her gaze. The way she looked at him, reminded him of a skittish butterfly, waiting for the slightest movement to send it into flight.

"Join me for a sandwich or a cup o' soup?"

There were times, like now, when her silence sparked his nerve endings. He held out his right hand, waited, and was about to lower it when she reached out and entwined her fingers through his. Taking moderate steps, not the usual ones for his long legs, he led her to the leaf-carved armoire, where he pulled a borrowed blue robe from one of the hangers, and a pair of light gray woolen socks from one of the three lower drawers. He helped her put on the robe, then coaxed her to sit on the edge of the bed.

"There's a lot o' drafts in this house," he said, going down on one knee. "You've got to take better care o' yourself, lass." He slipped one of the socks on her left foot, glanced up and offered her a smile, then got her right foot covered. Playfully, he tugged the tops of the footwear upward, one at a time. The borders reached to just below her knees.

Still smiling, he glanced up and felt a psychological blow to his gut. Time froze in a moment of uncertainty for him. The breathlessness and the slamming of his heart returned with more force. She was looking at him as if trying to get inside his head. He could almost feel the intensity in her alluring eyes penetrating the center of his brow, burrowing into his brain, his mind, and exposing his every foul memory he'd stored over the years during his work. But then he told himself he would *know if* she were scanning his mind. He would *know* if she were able to mentally reach into those dark pools of knowledge he harbored.

Blinking, he settled his buttocks against his heels and continued to search her features. It occurred to him that perhaps that intensity he'd glimpsed was caused by a flashback of what had brought her to the gazebo. She seemed calm enough now. And he realized she should have been taken to a doctor, or one brought to the house. He didn't sense that she had suffered any physical trauma, and Agnes had said she hadn't seen so much as a bruise on the woman.

Still. . . .

"Has someone hurt you?" he asked softly.

She dipped her head a bit to one side.

"Can you write?" he asked, and pantomimed the question.

A ghost of a smile appeared on her lips and she shook her head.

Winston cleared his throat. "You're no' goin' to make this easy, are you," he stated, then chuckled when she again shook her head.

"Okay, lass, I promised you food, and food it is." He took her hand and led her through the door, into the hall. They were halfway to the staircase, and he was on the verge of asking her if she needed to use the water closet, for there were none on the first floor, when Agnes materialized a few feet in front of them. Winston nearly jumped out of his skin, but was even more unnerved by the fact that Deliah wasn't startled at all.

Her hands on her hips and a maternal eyebrow arched, Aggie, chided, "And just where do you think you're takin' her?"

A ragged breath spilled past Winston's lips. "To the kitchen."

"Tha' so? This child was in your room, was she?"

Winston released a painfully dry laugh. "She's perfectly safe wi' me." To emphasize his words, he crossed his heart and held up his right hand. "On ma word."

"Your word, eh?" A grin cracked through her stern expression. "Aye, I know you're a mon o' your word. I'm always feelin' ma oats when I leave the grayness. Couldna resist givin' you a wee fright." Her grin broadened and a mischievous glimmer appeared in her eyes. "Tis the ghostly thing to do, Master Winston."

Winston released an immense sigh of relief. It struck him funny to think of Agnes Ingliss as having a sense of humor. Since first stepping into the house, for some reason he couldn't fathom, she'd made him nervous. No! It was more than nervousness. When in her presence, he felt as if he should bow or fall to one knee. He was intimidated by her, and yet she had never done anything to qualify this reaction in him. Perhaps it was that she reminded him of his grandmother in small ways. Whatever the cause, he wasn't accustomed to reacting this way, be it person or ghost.

Unconsciously, he gripped Deliah's hand a bit tighter and drew her closer to his side. "Mrs. Ingliss—"

"*Och!*" she chortled, flagging a hand through the air. "You mak me feel *ancient!!* Aggie, please."

"Aggie." Again feeling like a boy in the presence of something he couldn't understand, he cleared his throat. "I was wonderin' if Deliah shouldn't see a doctor."

The old woman looked stricken with shock, her watery blue eyes riveting on the young woman. "Deliah? She's talkin' then?"

"Wha'? Oh. No. The name came to me."

Obviously confused, Agnes jiggled her head and searched Winston's face. "*You* gave it to her?"

Winston shook his head, glancing from Agnes to the girl and back to Agnes. "I'm sure it's her name. Why are you actin' so odd abou' this?"

"We dead do tha'," she said comically. Her visage cleared of its perplexity. "Sorry, Master Winston. Sometimes ma humor is a wee off." She frowned and intensely studied Deliah. "I've heard tha' name afore. Deliah. Seems so long ago."

Winston was anxious to question her further, but he could see Agnes was struggling to bring up the memory. After a few more seconds, her face brightened and she snapped her fingers jubilantly.

"Ah, I remember! Borgie, ma son, came home one eve efter workin' here in the gardens, and said he had the scare o' his life. Said he accidentally pruned one o' the rhododendrons too close and someone scolded him to be mair careful. He said the voice came from nowhere. At first he thought it was Lannie tryin' to scare the bejesus ou' o' him, but he said the voice was tha' o' a girl. He called her Deliah and, when I questioned him how he knew her name, he said he didna know. How verra *orra.*"

It is very odd, Winston thought.

Again Agnes flagged a hand, but this time it was to dismiss the issue. "Back to you thinkin' she need see a doctor, I think na. Maybe a *head* doctor, but the weather's no' worthy o' a drive to town."

Winston grinned. "I've been overly concerned wi' her inability to communicate."

"Aye, tis a shame, but she seems happy enough. And she clearly understands wha' we say to her."

Winston didn't agree that the younger woman understood much of anything. He was about to make that statement when Agnes unexpectedly sidestepped and placed a hand on the wall.

"Have you sensed somethin' peculiar abou' the house?" she asked in a hushed tone.

"Depends wha' you mean by peculiar."

A speculative frown further creased Agnes' brow. "There used to be a slight vibration when I touched the walls— like some kind o' energy flowin' throughou' the house. Tis too normal now." She moved away from the wall, her gaze locked with Winston's. "Right efter you came, I noticed the change."

Winston nodded. "I don't know what happened, but somethin' did change the other night. I can't explain it, though."

"You bein' psychic canna explain it," she murmured, her eyes staring off into space. "The magic's gone. How . . . verra sad."

"I don't think it's really *gone*, Agnes. More like . . . it's takin' a break."

Smiling eyes regarded him. "A wee vacation, is it?" she chuckled. "Perhaps it is. Weel, Master Winston, I best be off lookin' efter the lads. *They* never tak a vacation from mischief."

She inclined her head to Deliah. "I'm here if you need anythin', child."

Deliah neither responded with a word nor gesture of her head. When Agnes headed up the staircase, the young woman leveled a thoughtful look at Winston, then walked to the wall and placed a palm against it. Seconds ticked by and Winston watched her with deepening curiosity. Again he tried to probe her mind, and again he failed. He planted his left palm against the wall, an inch from hers. Face to face, she looked up at him and smiled whimsically. Her fingers spidered toward his, touched his, and her smile broadened. Winston chuckled, but sobered when she gripped the front of his sweater with her left hand, raised on tiptoes and brushed her lips against his. What felt like a mild electrical shock flashed across the area of contact. He jerked back, then realized where her fingers touched his, the same sensation existed. The intensity was back in her eyes, but this time he sensed that she was trying to visually tell him something, rather than probe his mind. He experienced the seductive pull again as she placed her lips to his in a feathery kiss. Testing him. Perhaps testing herself.

A stream of Gaelic boomed from the third floor, then, "You little buggers! Kevin, Kahl, Alby, *where are you?*"

Winston stepped away from Deliah when heavy footfalls thundered down the stairs. Roan burst onto the second floor landing, beet-faced and wearing only dark slacks. He stopped short upon seeing the couple warily eyeing him.

Although anger still armored him, he made a valiant bid to collect himself.

"Sorry, but the lads are up to na good again," he muttered. "We've nary a sweater left in the house. I don't even want to try to imagine wha' they're doin' wi' them!"

"I haven't seen them—the boys," Winston said.

"Aye, they're as proficient at hidin' as a verra wee mouse, and a damn sight mair destructive."

Winston couldn't suppress a low chuff of laughter. "We're on our way to fix a sandwich. Would you like anythin'?"

"Na." Still vexed, Roan raked his fingers though his disheveled hair. "There's ham or lamb stew if you've a mind to heat it up."

"You sure I can't get you anythin'?"

A wry grin turned up one corner of Roan's mouth. "A sweater or two would be nice. I'm gettin' icicles on ma nipples—" Blushing, he looked at his newest guest with a hangdog expression, then asked Roan, "Is she comfortable here?"

Winston nodded, looking at Deliah. "It appears so. She still hasn't spoken."

Roan released a terse laugh. "Put her in a room wi' the lads a spell and she'll be wailin' at them in na time at all." He glanced up the staircase and added, "I best get back to Laura."

"I'll give a yell if I see the boys."

Roan offered a bewildered shake of his head, then arched an eyebrow. "Perhaps you both should lock your doors when you're ou' o' your rooms. Na tellin' wha' the terror trio have in store for us now."

"I don't have a key."

"Ah." Roan looked helplessly about him. "Maybe Aggie knows where they are. I'll get back to you on it."

Roan disappeared up the staircase, and Winston and Deliah headed for the kitchen on the first floor.

He closed the bulkhead door and moved silently down the few steps to the basement. Compared to the biting cold of the outside air, the enclosure was warm, but it was so dark he couldn't see his hand in front of his face. By rote, he made his way to his secret room, the soles of his snow boots occasional scuffing against the cement floor. He was cold and hungry and tired of waiting, but wait he would, for by nature he was a patient man.

Most killers were. At least, those with a specific agenda.

Behind a stack of wooden crates and abandoned furniture, he opened a long-forgotten wooden door just enough to squeeze through. He closed it, and even managed with his bulky gloves on to engage the latch hook he'd installed nearly a week ago.

Wade Cuttstone liked to feel secure, especially when asleep.

Removing his gloves and dropping them to the floor, he worked his stiff fingers for a time then groped along the top of the table until he located a book of matches. He lit two of the seven candles. They were all black and secured within wax in various tins and broken cups. He thought about the antique silver candelabra he'd seen in a shop in town, and wished for the hundredth time he'd purchased it from the stocky clerk. But Cuttstone hadn't liked the way the man watched his every move while he browsed through the cramped rooms of the shop. Still, a candelabra would certainly perk up the starkness of his temporary quarters.

Sitting in the only chair at the trestle-legged table, he reopened the bag of pork rinds he purchased two days ago. He was studiously conscious of not making noise, and soaked each rind in his saliva before chewing.

A mouse skittered across the floor. Cuttstone eyed it impartially. He wasn't averse to sharing with nature's creatures. They were basically undemanding and minded their own business. They didn't judge, only struggled to survive. So unlike mankind. Especially the bearers, the begetters of destroyers. The ones who were gradually taking over the world with technologies not safe in the hands of mere people. He couldn't track down *all* those who already existed, but he could and was lessening the numbers of another generation. Thanks to the Guardian. Without the inner voice telling him which women would beget his enemies, he'd be lost and floundering in his assassinations. He believed in accuracy and justice. To kill was not enough. Without purpose, he would be remembered as a murderer of innocent women.

Laura Bennett was one of the marked, and the most elusive he'd encountered. He couldn't count all the times he nearly had her, both in Edinburgh, where he'd first seen her, and since her arrival at this house. Of course, now he understood why he was having such a hard time getting to her. She had powerful friends. *Spirits.* Expired begetters were determined the world would change. He was so sure of this, he was even convinced a child born of this woman would eventually lead to the destruction of the known human race. Androids would take over. Perhaps even *he* would be forced to exchange his vital organs and brain for computerized parts.

And now Winston Ian Connery was in the house. Apparently, staying for a spell. Cuttstone enjoyed the challenge the man's presence offered. He enjoyed mind games, especially when he was the controller. But there was also another woman in the house, and *she* really piqued his curiosity. Two nights ago, while he was hiding in the woods,

he saw her running naked toward the north gardens. Cuttstone had no idea from where she'd come, but he'd known
when the ex-agent had found her at the gazebo, Connery
suspected him of being responsible. As yet, the Guardian
hadn't told him the newcomer was one of the begetters,
but there was something about her that taunted his psychic
abilities. He couldn't surface images from her as he did
other women, only bizarre matrix patterns in brilliant colors that often left him mind-blind for a time.

Mind blindness was deadly to him. Without the *knowing*,
his capture was imminent.

He mulled over the problem of the boys. They were
obstructions to the cause. Too nosey for their own good.
But males were not begetters. Males were never a target.

There had to be an easier way to watch Laura, to move
throughout the house and gauge her habits.

The news had reported Viola Cooke used the spaces
between the walls to move about, but he hadn't yet found
a way to get inside them without forcibly tearing through
the plaster. And from what he could determine by her
photograph in the news, she was a small woman. He was
large. Even if he found a way to get inside the walls, he
couldn't be sure he could freely move through them.

"Patience," he whispered, and popped another pork
rind into his mouth.

Greatness required both patience and careful planning.

Chapter Six

The rest of the day passed in relative quiet. Winston was present when Roan questioned the boys about the sweaters. They swore they didn't know anything about them. Winston knew they were lying, but didn't press the issue. At the time, he was amused by their mischief, and his mind was occupied with other matters. Deliah, for one.

Between Laura and Agnes, Winston saw little of Deliah. The women fitted her with warmer clothing, braided her hair, then took her into the kitchen, which Winston later was told was a mistake. The young woman couldn't boil water! In fact Deliah's fascination with the effervescing liquid in the pan had Laura paranoid she would try to reach into the water.

Since Winston and Deliah polished off Roan's lamb stew for lunch, Laura and Agnes reheated the remainder of the ham in the gas oven. It was served with spicy apple stuffing, baked potatoes garnished with butter and sour cream, and homemade sourdough bread. With the exceptions of the boys exchanging dirty jokes and attempting to start another food fight across the table, and Laura telling Deliah how she and Roan had met, it was a quiet meal. Even Agnes sat at the table.

Deliah, as expected, was the center of attention. The silverware, glasses and plates delighted her as if she'd never actually touched anything like them. The boys laughed hysterically when she discovered things sprinkled out of the salt and pepper shakers. And the food. . . .

She had a curious way of eating. Winston was so fascinated in watching her facial expressions whenever she tasted something different, his meal had cooled before he'd hardly begun to eat. He questioned the possibility she was suffering some form of amnesia. How else could everything seem so *new* to her? She watched and attempted to imitate using the utensils. At lunchtime, she refused to taste the stew until Winston had started to eat, and he'd noticed how awkwardly she'd handled the soupspoon.

After dinner, Roan took the boys into the library to read them stories before their bedtime, and Winston helped the women clear the table and do the dishes. The latter resulted in a playful bubble fight amongst Winston, Deliah and Laura, while Agnes retired to the grayness.

With the kitchen cleaned, Winston hoped to get some private time with Deliah, but again Laura had other ideas. Since the soapy dishwater had proven so entertaining for Deliah, Laura wanted to introduce her to a bubble bath. The excitement in Deliah's eyes told Winston he couldn't compete with what Laura was describing to her, so he graciously excused himself and went into the hall.

Suddenly, he felt like the odd man out. Shoving his hands into his pants pockets, he glanced up the staircase, then down the hall to the library. The pocket doors were open. He couldn't hear Roan or the boys, but he headed in that direction, hoping to spend a little time with them. No one was there.

Winston particularly liked this room. It had a masculine atmosphere that appealed to him. Of all the rooms he could remember in the main part of the house, this one was the most sparsely furnished. The dark-stained, built-in shelves were filled with leather-bound books from the nineteenth and twentieth centuries. Red plaid covered the overstuffed sofa and two chairs. The coffee table and the end tables placed at each end of the sofa, were highly polished cherry wood. An enormous braided rug of black, red and dark green, covered the oak plank floor between the sofa and the red brick fireplace with its red-and-black veined mantelpiece.

The fireplace was fully stoked and the hearthlight's orange glow softened the contours of the room. He considered taking a book to read in his room, but then thought better of it. He wasn't really in the mood to sit or lie still. The restlessness stirring inside him was maddening. If he could only take a long walk in one of the gardens surrounding the house. Or just a long walk in the fresh air. . . .

He ended up standing in front of one of the windows, his arms folded against his chest, his gaze scanning the woods that separated the house and the open field where four headstones existed beneath a solitary oak. Large snowflakes continued to fall. Driving had to be hell, let alone walking in this stuff. He'd thought yesterday's rain would clear away a lot of the white stuff, but it hadn't lasted but a couple of hours. It had rained, then hailed, then frozen atop the accumulation of compacted snow. Now it was snowing again. He was beginning to think spring would never come. And if it did, would the snow *ever* go away?

"Depressin', isn't it?" Roan chuckled.

Winston was surprised to find the man standing directly behind him, also looking out the window.

"I'm gettin' claustrophobic."

"Aye, I know wha' you mean," Roan sighed. "Join me for a Scotch?"

"Are the boys in bed?"

Roan gave an exaggerated roll of his eyes. "I'll no' say for how long. C'mon, Winston, a good Scotch chases away the chill in the bones."

Winston sat next to his host on the sofa. Two glasses and a crystal decanter were set upon a sterling silver tray on the coffee table.

"I saw you come in here," Roan explained, holding out a half-filled glass to Winston.

"I didn't think the tray was on the table when I came in."

Roan took a long swallow of the Scotch and waited until the fiery liquid hit his stomach. He smacked his lips, grinned at Winston, then reclined against the back of the sofa and crossed his left ankle over his right knee. "We haven't had much chance to talk. Your room comfortable enough?"

"Better than I deserve. You know—" Winston took a sip of his drink, then cradled the glass between his hands. "—it was very generous o' you to let me stay. I know this isn't an open invitation—"

Winston quieted when Roan lifted a hand in protest. *"Och*, mon, tis opened, all right. Stay as long as you like. The house is far too large for us. Sometimes . . . weel, sometimes I find it bloody lonely here."

"Even with the boys?" Winston grinned.

Roan made a rueful face. "Ah, the lads. I know I bluster too much abou' them. But the truth is, I can't imagine ma life withou' them bein' underfoot. Now . . . is tha' bloody bonkers or wha'?"

"Actually, I envy you your life," Winston said softly, staring into the fireplace.

"Do you, now? Weel, I'm no' crazy or ungrateful. Laura and the lads are mair than I ever hoped for. But wha' abou' you? Ever been in love?"

A dry chuckle escaped Winston. "No."

Roan nodded and said sagely, "I guess a mon has to love himself before he can love anither."

"Never thought o' it tha' way," Winston murmured. He stared into the amber depths of his glass, a slight frown visible across his otherwise smooth brow.

"No' even a near hit, eh?" Roan laughed softly.

Winston looked up and smiled. "Infatuation a couple o' times. I guess I haven't met *ma* significant other, yet."

Taking a long swig of his drink, Roan again nodded. "Maybe you have. I couldn't help but notice the way you were watchin' the lass at the dinner table."

"Deliah?"

"So we have a name now. Have you learned anythin' mair abou' her?"

"Zilch," Winston sighed. He thought about taking another sip of the Scotch, but his head was already getting fuzzy. "She has an impenetrable wall surroundin' her mind."

"Do you come across tha' often?"

A sour burst of laughter ejected from Winston's throat. "Never! And I don't mind tellin' you it frustrates the bloody hell ou' o' me."

"Are you attracted to her?"

Winston's eyes narrowed upon the laird. "Wha' are you diggin' for, Roan Ingliss?"

With a chuckle, Roan finished off his drink and set the glass on the table. He sat back, placed his right ankle atop his left knee again, and stretched out his left arm along the back of the sofa. Amusement danced in his eyes, and a grin pulled at one corner of his mouth.

"I'll tell you, Winston, you're lookin' a damn sight better

than when I brought you into this house. You've got life back in your eyes. And although I don't claim to be psychic, I *know* when a mon has his fair measure o' happiness.''

A denial nearly escaped Winston, but he managed to suppress it. He was happy. Happier than in all his adult life. "You're observant."

"Sometimes," Roan grinned, then he sighed. "Ither times I'm a bonafide idiot."

Winston chuckled. "You're no idiot. Remember the first night we met?"

"At Shortby's? Aye."

"You were in your cups, babblin' abou' bein' the reincarnation o' Robert Ingliss." Winston set his glass on the table, then ran his hands down his face. "I thought you were one crazy drunk. Little did I know then how much you would change ma life. You're a generous mon, Roan. There are no' many people who would open up their home to a virtual stranger."

"The credit's no' mine to tak."

Despair carved its way into Roan's expression. Lowering his right foot to the floor, he leaned forward and braced his forearms atop his knees. "I was a bitter, unforgivin' mon no' tha' long ago. I guess, like you, Winston, I was lookin' to see ma way through each day and no' carin' a fig abou' anythin'. The first couple o' days you were here, I saw a lot o' ma old self in you, and I didn't like it much. I wanted to shake you till your teeth rattled in your head, but I knew you needed space."

Abruptly standing, Roan went to the fireplace. He gripped the mantel and peered solemnly into the flames, conscious of Winston's troubled gaze on his back. "There *is* magic in the house. In this land. Many have seen it. Felt it melt the wintery corners o' oor hearts." He turned just enough to regard his guest, his left hand remaining on the mantel. "But the *true* magic for me was—*is*—Lannie the mon. You think *me* generous?" He chuckled low and shook his head. "I'm no', really. When I discovered who you were the ither night, ma first thought was you could tell me how Lannie and Beth are farin'."

"Roan—"

"Let me finish," Roan said huskily. "Guilt is a mighty heavy burden, ma friend, and I've never been good at carryin' it on ma shoulders."

Winston nodded, and Roan sighed deeply before continuing, "This isn't *ma* house. It was handed over to me by a mon who rightfully should have incarcerated ma sorry ass in the wall in the tower. The *same* wall I entombed him in—*alive*—mair'n a century ago! Aye, aye, I know that wasn't *this* me, but Robert and I share the same soul, we do, and I remember every pathetic wrong he—*we*—did."

He sighed again, obviously agitated. He chuffed a bitter laugh and gestured his wariness with a wave of his right hand. "I tend to run off at the mouth when I'm drinkin', in case you haven't noticed."

Winston grinned in understanding.

"Winston, can I ask you somethin'?"

"O' course."

Roan took several seconds to mull over his words. "How is it a mon can feel so blessed, and yet so empty?"

Winton didn't need to scan Roan's psyche. He already knew the answer. "You're still connected to Lachlan Baird."

"Through this house, oor history, or wha'?" Roan asked, perplexed.

"Do you know what a contrail looks like?"

Roan's bafflement deepened. "You mean the vapor trail that's seen in the wake o' a plane?"

Nodding, Winston went on, "Wha' I'm talkin' abou' now is a *psychic contrail.* It's a phenomenon I've witnessed when someone loses someone they love—a link tha' remains between the livin' and the departed durin' the grievin' period. As time passes, it fades away."

"You see a vapor trail between this world and the ither?" Roan asked incredulously.

"It's more a filament o' light connected to each mourner, linkin' them to the heavens. The hotter white it is, the stronger the love."

"Do I have a psychic contrail?"

Winston nodded. "But I've never encountered one like yours. It's blue."

"Meanin' wha'?"

"I'm no' sure."

"Wha' abou' Laura? Does she have one?"

"She has come to terms wi' Lachlan and Beth's departure."

"Psychic contrails," Roan murmured, staring off into space. Then he looked at Winston through an expression of desperation. "If you ventured a guess, wha' would you say the blue means?"

"I generally work wi' facts, no' conjectures."

"Dammit, right now I'd be happy wi' even a *bad* guess!"

Roan reseated himself sideways, facing Winston, his left forearm braced on the back of the sofa. "Lannie forgave us."

To Winston's amazement, Roan switched to fluent Gaelic. For a time, too stunned to react, he listened to the man's passionate voice and observed the myriad of expressions flitting over his features. Finally, he said, cutting Roan off, "I don't understand Gaelic enough to follow wha' you're sayin'."

Roan jerked back, shocked. "Gaelic?"

"You were just speakin' it."

Paling, Roan swallowed. "Was I? Ah. Tha' was Robert. I never learned the language, maself. He comes ou' now and then, Robert does."

"How often?"

"No' verra." Roan shrugged. "Sometimes I think I'm trapped between the past and the present. Verra disconcertin', to say the least."

"Do you remember wha' you were sayin'?"

"Aye. I said I know I shouldn't be feelin' guilty, but I do. It interferes wi' how I respond to Laura and the boys. And I said . . . I keep gettin' this notion there's too much unfinished business in ma life, but wha' tha' is, I don't know."

Roan cast his guest a deeply penetrating, measuring look. "So, will you tell me wha' you believe the *blue* contrail suggests?"

Winston frowned, then nodded. "In ma opinion, it's no' a natural link between you and Lachlan."

"No' natural?" Roan made a crude sound that should have been a laugh. "Nothin' between us has ever been exactly *normal.*"

"Wha' I mean is, I believe the link was thrust upon the two o' you."

A skeptical, wary expression masked Roan's face. He arched an eyebrow and asked in a raspy voice, "So . . . *somethin'* . . . is keepin' us linked thegither?"

"I believe so."

Roan grimaced. "Any idea wha'?"

"No' a clue."

"Damn me," Roan muttered, glancing off in the direction of the fireplace.

"I've never dealt wi' an actual *ghost,*" said Winston humorously. "It could be, wha' exists between you and Lachlan is perfectly normal under the circumstances."

"Perfectly normal?" Roan parroted, his gaze cutting to Winston.

"Possibly."

"Wha' about ma Aunt Aggie? Does she have a psychic contrail connectin' her to her son, Borgie?"

"She does." Winston pondered hers for a short time. "Hers is bright white. It hasn't dimmed since I first saw her Christmas Eve."

"White, no' blue. She's a ghost."

"An unusually *alive* ghost," Winston corrected.

"Normal for Baird House."

Winston agreed, although a bit in awe of it all, himself.

Roan thoughtfully rubbed his chin. "So, even from *your* standpoint, things here are a wee different. Right?"

"Definitely different."

"And this blue psychic contrail which could have been *possibly* thrust upon me and auld Lannie, isn't anythin' I should worry abou'?"

Winston offered a look of uncertainty.

"Wha' would you say if I told you I've been dreamin' Mary Blossom Ingliss was comin' home?"

"Who is she?"

"Robert and Tessa's daughter," Roan said solemnly. "She vanished shortly efter her sixteenth birthday."

"She's dead?"

Roan laughed. "Tha' or *verra* old! In the dreams she's young, though. Abou' the age when she disappeared."

Winston sighed. "Lack of disclosure?"

A sly gleam brightened Roan's eyes. "Are you tellin' or askin'?"

"Suggestin'."

"Ah." Roan grinned, then did a brief drumroll on his chest with the undersides of his hands. "Weel, I'm so glad we had this chat, Winston. But why do I now have this notion to throw maself off the tower?"

Winston laughed and clapped Roan on the shoulder. Roan settled back against the sofa and stared whimsically up at the ceiling. "I think it's time I stop thinkin' in retrospect and get on wi' ma life. All I really need to do is no' think abou' Lannie and Beth, Robert, psychic contrails and—"

"Roan!"

Both men jumped up from the sofa when Laura burst into the room. She ran directly to Roan and gripped the front of his shirt. Gulping in air, her widened eyes cast Winston a brief glance. "It's the. . . ."

Roan gripped her upper arms and worriedly searched her flushed face. "Calm down, Laura."

"She's on the tower . . ." Laura sucked in a great breath and forced the rest of the words out. "She took her clothes off and is dancing in the snow!"

"Deliah?" Winston asked sharply.

Laura gave a rapid nod. "I couldn't get her to come back down."

"I'll handle it," Winston bit out, and lit into a run.

He ascended to the second floor and turned left, not slowing down until he reached the heavy red velvet drapes which covered the entrance to the tower. Beyond the threshold, he entered what had been the servants' quarters, and went up a steep and narrow stone staircase that hugged the wall. He was blind to the plain furnishings as he made his way to the fourth level, where he stopped and regarded the open door in the ceiling. A pale gray sky loomed above. Snowflakes drifted through the opening. The cold seemed more bone chilling than when he was outside earlier, and he shuddered before continuing. But halfway up this last stretch of steps, something popped into the opening and he nearly pitched backward. He braced his spine against the cold exterior rock wall, a hand over his thundering heart. A snow-sprinkled brown peahen peered down at him, craning its neck from side to side as if questioning his intrusion.

Angry that a bird had given him such a fright, he flagged

his right hand at it and forcefully ascended the few remaining steps. He heard a flutter of wings. As soon as his head breached the door frame, he saw peahens and peacocks flying off in all directions from the crenellations. Then he spied Deliah and his heart seemed to rise into his throat and cut off his oxygen. She was indeed naked, and dancing in circles with her arms lifted to the pale heavens. A heavy dusting of snowflakes covered her. A look of ecstasy masked her face and, at that moment, Winston thought her stark-raving mad.

He climbed onto the roof of the turret, his unwavering gaze watching her as though he expected her to fling herself over the crenellated wall at any given moment.

"Deliah!"

She didn't seem to hear him. Fear mingled with his burgeoning anger. He reached out to take her arm, but withdrew as if burned when a voice filled his mind.

Blue, I understand. I understand now! Tis wonderful! Tis so magical! Oh, Blue! If only we all could share a dance in this!

Deliah's voice, he realized, and swayed with the shock it dealt him. Then, collecting himself, he harshly gripped her arm and jerked her to a stop.

Time came to a breath-robbing stop. He found himself staring into sparkling blue eyes so filled with wonder, he told himself he had to be dreaming again. Against the bluish tinge of her cold skin, her cheeks were red and her lips the color of dark pink coral. Snowflakes whitened her dark eyebrows and eyelashes and most of the outer layer of her hair.

"Are you daft?" he cried, giving her a sound shake.

From the corner of his left eye he spied the bathrobe and nightgown she'd been wearing. Releasing her, he hastily snatched them up and gave them a shake to cast off the snow.

"Get dressed!" he barked, then glanced down at her feet. "Where are the socks?"

She held the clothing balled against her, staring at him as if questioning the reason behind his shortness with her.

Winston glanced about him, but couldn't see the socks anywhere. "Dammit woman, where are they?"

Furious, he looked at her and released a gasp of disbelief that she hadn't begun to don the clothing. He yanked the robe back and flung it across his shoulder, then, shivering from both the cold and his frustration with her, impatiently helped her into the nightgown. Something caught his attention as he tugged it down over her. Something he'd seen before but, like now, his brain couldn't accept, couldn't even begin to digest.

From above, an echoing rumble was heard.

He decided the robe could wait until they were off the tower. Again gripping her upper arm with more force than was necessary, he nudged her toward the opening in the floor. She resisted. Gone was her elation. The rumbling came again, and she lifted a troubled gaze to the grayness above them.

"Deliah!" he barked, causing her to jump. "Get below!"

She again looked upward, then met his gaze for a pregnant-filled moment before finally taking the first step into the room below. Winston retained his hold until she was standing on the fourth landing. Tossing the bathrobe into her face, he closed the roof door and jumped down the remaining steps to stand in front of her. She held the robe in her arms, cradling it against her chest. Violent shudders coursed through her, and her eyes held a pained expression his anger refused to acknowledge. She remained still when he took the robe and brusquely toweled her with it. The rumbling grew louder, seeming to come down through the roof now. An impression tried to worm its way into Winston's consciousness, but he was too angry to deal with anything except the exasperating woman in front of him.

"You're *worse* than a child," he scolded. Taking her by the hand, he led her down the stairs and eventually into the second-floor hall of the house. He kept the lead, pulling her behind him as if she were a recalcitrant child and he the parent bent on retaining his anger long enough to impress upon her the seriousness of her actions.

Laura and Roan were waiting at her open bedroom door. Winston marched her past them to the bed, where he finally released her, pulled the top quilt off the mattress and impatiently wrapped it around her still shivering form. She regarded him with the innocence of a small girl, which only infuriated him all the more. He turned to face Roan and Laura. They stood a few feet away, both seeming at a loss as to what to do next.

"I refuse to hold maself responsible for her anymore," Winston said testily, high color in his cheeks. "She hasn't an adult thought in her brain! I need to get to a phone and call the police. They'll have to figure ou' wha' to do wi' her."

Deliah placed a hand on Winston's arm, but he angrily jerked away and glared at her.

"I better light a fire," Roan said abstractedly, and went to the hearth.

"Should I make her some tea?" asked Laura, a sympathetic look leveled on the younger woman.

"I guess." Winston briefly massaged the back of his neck. To Laura, he asked, "Where is the nearest phone?"

"In town."

His stomach churned with dread. He loved to walk, but the town was a fair hike as it was, let alone what it would take to reach it in this weather.

Rumbling then a crack of what sounded like thunder, gave everyone a start, except Deliah. Her gaze lifted to the ceiling. After a moment, she murmured, "Too soon. Too soon."

Winston looked at her in a state of incredulity. Laura's mouth gaped open. Roan stopped crumpling newspaper and hastened back to Laura's side.

"She can talk," said Roan dazedly.

Deliah's gaze lowered to Winston's ashen face and she shrugged deeper into the warmth of the quilt.

"Wha' did you say?" asked Winston, anger returning some color to him. When she remained silent, he snapped, "Answer me!"

"Too soon be wha' I said," she replied in a small tone, and shamefully downcast her eyes.

"Tell me your little dance on the tower *just* returned your voice!" he shouted. "Tell me you *just* haven't been jerkin' our chains all this time!"

Deliah glanced at the three, as if searching for the chains Winston mentioned.

"Winston—" Laura clamped her mouth shut when Winston furiously flagged a hand at her.

"Tell me, Deliah!" he demanded.

The only sound she made was a gulp.

"Fine, lass," Winston fumed, his balled hands resting on his narrow hips. "Fine. I don't know who you are and, quite frankly, right now, I could give a flyin' fig how or why you showed up here. Wha' I *do* care abou' is washin' ma hands o' you! You can play your mind games wi' the police."

"Ye canna tak me from this house," she said, a note of panic in her tone.

"The hell I can't!"

"You're only scaring her," Laura chided Winston.

Winston shot Laura an incredulous look. "Scarin' *her*? Anyone who can dance naked in below freezin' weather, has a hide o' steel!'' His furious gaze retargeted Deliah's face. "Wha' are you *really* doin' here? Are you a reporter?"

"Oh, God," Roan moaned. "That's all we need."

"I be Deliah, no' a reporter."

Her quivering tone fell short of stirring any compassion in Winston. His eyes held such fury, it wounded her to look into them. She walked to the right side of the bed, overly conscious of the others' eyes watching her every move.

"Stop lyin' to us!" Winston hissed, turning and gripping the cherry-wood post at the foot of her bed. "You tellin' me you don't work for Jonathan Blussal?"

"Nae," Deliah said with a shake of her head. "Nae, I dinna know anyone by tha' name!"

"Oh come now, Deliah," Winston began with a mocking laugh. "Blussal is the senior editor at the *Lowland Gazette.*"

"Nae, I dinna know him!" she cried.

Winston's features were livid. "I picked up your thoughts while you were dancin' on the tower! I heard you *think* you wanted to dance wi' *Blue* in the snow. Blue sounds like a nickname to Blussal to me!"

"Aye," agreed Roan.

Clinging to Roan's arm, Laura nodded.

"Nae!" Deliah sucked in a breath. She shuddered uncontrollably. "Blue be married to ma brither. I swear on the mighty oaks, I be nae ither than Deliah . . . than wha' ye see afore you!"

Again, shock rocked Winston on his feet. He suddenly realized where he'd heard her archaic use of "be" and "ye".

"You," he accused in a barely audible voice.

She swallowed hard and nodded. "I couldna speak for fear ye would recognize ma voice, Winston. Aye, I be o' the garden place, but no' a reporter."

Thunder rumbled around them and her darting gaze

searched the ceiling. Then she met Winston's vacant eyes and explained, "I told ye ye could see me once ye touched me. Remember?"

He stiltedly nodded.

"I was below, in wha' ye call the cellar, when ye tripped over the root. Touched me, ye did, and I be true to ma word."

"Hold it!" Roan exclaimed almost comically. With a hand held up in a placating manner, he left Laura and stood alongside Winston. To say he looked beyond perplexed was a gross understatement. "Tell me, Winston, she's no' *anither* ghost."

"I be Deliah," she said firmly, as if that should explain everything.

"I met her in the fourth dimension the first night I spent in this house," Winston said dully.

A blank expression spread across Roan's face. *"Fourth* dimension?" Blinking, he sent Laura a dazed look. "Now we have us a *fourth dimension?* How . . . wonderful." He met Winston's gaze and blinked. "So, she's no' a ghost?"

"I don't know wha' she is," Winston grumbled, angrily regarding Deliah. "In her world, she tried to tell me she was the house."

"Her world? *This* house? She thinks she is *this* house?"

Sighing, Winston nodded.

Another boom of thunder crashed around them.

Laura fiercely hugged herself, her gaze searching the ceiling. "I better check on the boys."

"Agnes is wi' them," said Winston in a monotone. "There's a storm comin' in all right, but it doesn't feel like anythin' I've experienced before."

Deliah released a violent shudder and closed her eyes for a moment. "I couldna forestall the comin' any longer."

"The comin'?" Roan slapped his palms to his cheeks and walked around Winston. "I'll finish layin' the fire."

He stopped short, and Winston and Laura's heads shot around when a *whoosh* came from the hearth. A roaring fire engulfed the logs Roan had stacked on the firedog. Then the mesh screen eerily slid into place.

"Wha' the—" Roan gasped, turning wide eyes on Deliah.

The air in the room shifted and grew dense. Deliah tightly closed her eyes as if to shut something out, or to hold something inside her. She shuddered again. When her eyelids lifted, her irises were dull, her complexion pale.

Then Deliah became flushed. A fine sheen of perspiration broke out on her face. "They be weakenin' me. I can do nae mair"

The hairs on Winston's arm twitched against his skin. "Who's weakenin' you? Wha' are you talkin' abou'?"

A blood-curdling scream boomed throughout the house. Laura ran into Roan's opened arms. Winston stiffened, his face the color of chalk as he tried to decipher the images bombarding his fevered brain. He started toward the door to the hall, but stopped in his tracks when an omnipresent groan crescendoed into another wail of such torment, his blood turned to ice.

"Jesus, Mary and Joseph," Roan murmured, blessing himself.

Deliah ran into the hall breaking the trio's stupor. Winston gripped her arm as soon as he caught up with her on the landing of the third floor. Roan and Laura followed at his heels. Agnes and the boys stood outside Alby's bedroom door. The boys beelined for the adults and huddled close while Agnes glided toward them, her gaze fearfully casting about.

Everyone looked down the far end of the hallway when Deliah intensely fixed her gaze in that direction. Another wail came, not quite so loud, but nonetheless disturbing.

"Aggie, what's goin' on?" Roan asked in a whisper.

"I dinna know." She jerked when she became aware of a presence within the house. "Na. It canna be," she murmured.

Roan looked askance at his aunt. "Aggie, what's wrong?"

Deliah sidestepped closer to Winston and wrapped her arms about his middle. The quilt fell to the floor as she met his bewildered gaze, her own trying to convey that she wished she could have done everything differently. He was about to question her when a door at the far left of the hall banged open. A figure bound from the master suite and ran toward them, at first appearing to be but a blur. When what turned out to be a man was nearly upon them, gasps detonated from the group.

Electricity crackled in the air as the newcomer came to a jarring halt and cried, *'Fegs,* tis Beth! I think she's in *labor!"*

Chapter Seven

Time and space existed in a small, confining bubble, left adrift in infinite grayness. At least, that was Winston's initial impression when he realized who the man was standing in front of him. He couldn't move. Couldn't speak. And he was conscious of the others suffering the same condition. It was as if a spell had been cast over them. Suspended in the bubble, where movement was impossible and sound couldn't be heard because of the lack of oxygen, they were all drifting into the unknown, a realm of such surrealism, their minds couldn't begin to grasp what was happening to them.

Another crescendoing, pitiful moan came. Then Lachlan Baird—ghost extraordinaire—bellowed, "Have you all gone daft? Ma Beth is in pain! Come alive!"

"Stay wi' the lads," Winston heard Agnes say, and shortly realized she had spoken to Roan, who remained as still as a statue, staring at Lachlan through a face as pale as a marble statue.

The boys' mouths were agape. It was the longest span of silence that had ever befallen them during their awake hours. When Roan suddenly fell on the floor on his butt, his gaze dazedly riveted on the former laird of Baird House, Kevin sat to his right, Kahl to his left, and Alby perched himself atop Roan's lap. The scene struck Winston funny, but he couldn't laugh. Not even a smile was able to strain past the taut muscles in his face.

Then Deliah was tugging Winston along, trailing Laura, Agnes and Lachlan down the hall. For the life of him, Winston couldn't fathom how he was walking. He could barely feel his legs beneath him. His mind was trapped in a dimension somewhere between reality and makebelieve, trapped on a roller coaster going at a head-reeling speed on a track that had no foreseeable end. When Deliah squeezed his hand, he looked down at her through glazed eyes. He knew they were glazed, because she looked fuzzy. Out of sorts. She didn't look real to him, but he could feel her solidity pressing against his side, and her fingers spastically opening and closing on his enclasped hand.

Dimly he was conscious of voices. Heavily gauzed voices, and he was unable to make out what was being said.

Another scream, one that pierced his soul with its depths of agony, rescued him. His senses awakened. He stared at a woman atop the bed and immediately recognized her. The curly light brown hair. Blue eyes and creamy complexion. She still wore the long white gown he'd seen her wearing in her ghostly form that fateful Christmas Eve.

"Oh ... *God!*" she cried, gripping the bed quilt so fiercely her fingers were white.

Bloodless. . . .

Details crashed upon the shores of Winston's awareness. Beth Staples's pain-contorted face was coated in perspiration. Damp tendrils of hair clung to her brow, cheeks and neck. Her breathing was hoarse, labored. She was braced on her elbows, her raised knees parted. From Winston's vantage point by the wall near the head of the bed, he could see that her stomach was a mound beneath the gown. There was no disputing that she was pregnant. Pregnant and in the throes of hard labor.

"Aggie . . . Aggie," Beth panted. "What's happening to me? *God,* it hurts!"

The last she wailed, and Winston nearly ran from the room. He'd never witnessed a woman in labor, and swore he never would again. Laura and Aggie were on the opposite side of the bed, Aggie sitting and lifting Beth's gown over her knees. Bewilderment and panic masked Laura's face. Lachlan stood at the foot of the bed, his wide eyes fixed between Beth's legs. He looked about ready to faint, and nearly did when Agnes announced, "I see the head."

"Winston." Deliah's authoritative tone drew his gaze to her face. "Tak Lachlan away afore he drops," she ordered.

Beth released a long, suffering groan and Winston felt his blood plummet to his feet. His stomach became queasy and the room pitched into a maddening spin.

"Winston," Deliah said kindly, reaching up and brushing the backs of the fingers of her right hand down one of his cheeks. "Leave. Tis female matters here. Tak Lachlan and leave, Winston. Now."

"Laura, fetch me some hot water and clean towels," said Aggie. Her pale blue eyes targeted Winston after casting Lachlan a fleeting glance. "And for Pete's sake, get *him* ou' o' here!"

Nodding like an automaton out of control, Winston shuffled to Lachlan Baird's side. "It's time we checked on Roan and the boys." But Lachlan stood, immersed in shock and deepening revulsion at the sight of a baby's head emerging between Beth's thighs.

"Lachlan Ian Baird," Beth gritted out, "I'm going to castrate *you!*"

A breath whooshed from the former laird and he jerked back. Next Winston knew, he and Lachlan were hastening down the hall in the direction of the other males in the house. Roan was on his feet, leaning against the wall as if his legs couldn't support him. The boys were quiet, the two older brothers blinking at Winston, while Alby's face split into a grin and his eyes sparkled in wonderment. When Winston and Lachlan came to a stop, the three-year-old stepped up to Lachlan, craned back his head to peer into Lachlan's face, then breathed, "Lannie, you're back."

Lachlan and Roan locked gazes, both looking as though the world had dropped from beneath them.

"Lannie," Roan began, but another wail came from Beth, and the group in the hall cringed in unison.

"I-I c-canna tak hearin' her in p-pain," Lachlan stammered, his gaze casting about like a madman seeking escape.

"The library," Winston suggested. He, too, needed to escape Beth's cries and her panting, roaring breaths, which seemed to fill every molecule of the air surrounding him.

Lachlan lifted Alby and absently positioned him on his right hip, then hurried down the staircase. The older brothers followed. Winston hung back, waiting for Roan, who took several seconds longer to push himself away from the wall and head down the stairs.

Winston trailed behind, his thoughts in overdrive. He tried to concentrate on Deliah, but with the advent of the ghostly couple, the remaining mysteries behind the fourth dimension nymph seemed somehow trivial at the moment. At first recognition of Lachlan Baird, impressions had rushed at Winston. He still couldn't accept what his inner senses told him. Beth Staples was upstairs in the master suite, giving birth, and her dubious significant other was leading this all-male party to the library, still carrying Alby on his hip. These two factors should have convinced him that anything more *was* possible, and yet. . . .

Beth's cries and moans followed them into the library. Winston closed the pocket doors behind him, then stood guard with his arms folded against his chest. He was at a loss what to do, what to say, but saw that he was in better shape than Roan, who stood at the stoked fireplace with his back to the others.

Lachlan placed Alby on his feet and shakily instructed the boys to sit on the sofa. They did without hesitation, three pair of awe-filled eyes glued to Lachlan.

"Roan?" Lachlan cut Winston a glance before again staring at the back of Roan's bent head. "Roan, say somethin'. At least tell me how you brought us back."

The current laird's shoulders twitched beneath his wool shirt. After a moment, he turned. Devastation was deeply carved in his ashen face, and a mist of tears was visible in his eyes. Winston hadn't intended to link with the emotions in the room, but he found he was and unable to purge himself of their overwhelming influence. Each of the boys were experiencing different levels of elation. Their favorite ghosts were back and they weren't concerned with the hows and the whys. Lachlan was terrified, but of what Winston wasn't sure. He couldn't bring himself to delve into the man's psyche, for he already felt he knew too much. Roan perplexed him the most. He watched him with increasing concern. No thoughts came through, but Winston was sure Roan was on the verge of emotionally shutting down, withdrawing into himself. To hide away from his fear of having to grieve for his friends all over again.

"Laddie," Lachlan said softly to Roan, his hands opening and closing into fists at his sides. "I'm confused and scared and needin' confirmation tha' this is all no' ma bloody imagination havin' its way wi' me. Has ma mind dropped into the lap o' the deil hisself, or is this *real?*" Roan remained silent and Lachlan's face reddened with anger. *"Fegs,* answer me!"

"Don't yell at my uncle," Kevin said to Lachlan, his eyebrows drawn down in a scowl, and his chin quivering as he spoke.

Lachlan fondly searched each of the young faces. "Sorry, lads. Tis . . . tis all so confusin' to me."

Lachlan's head shot around when Roan abruptly walked toward him and stopped half an arm's length away. Winston gauged their building emotions. He was half convinced he should place himself between the two men, act as referee, but an inner voice told him to stay put and observe, nothing more.

Silence prevailed for a time. The air in the room grew thick and oppressive with anticipation. Lachlan's broad chest pumped beneath his full-sleeved white shirt, while Roan's broader chest revealed his breathing was shallow, overly controlled. Then Roan lifted his right hand and held it poised in the air for several seconds before placing it on Lachlan's left shoulder. Lachlan's right hand likewise settled on Roan's left shoulder. More time passed. Only the crackling fire could be heard.

Then, "How did you do it?" Lachlan whispered, a quavering element in his voice.

"You're really here," Roan said, his numb state holding fast. "You . . . you feel and look and . . . smell the same, you *auld* mon."

A grin cracked through the tension in Lachlan's face. "Aye, you, too, laddie. So how did you bring us back?"

Roan numbly shook his head and unconsciously kneaded Lachlan's shoulder. "I didn't. You just showed up. Popped in. Did one o' yer . . . materializin' acts."

"Na, laddie," said Lachlan unsteadily. "We were *brought* back as surely as the sun rises every morn." His voice cracked and he drew in a throbbing breath. "Fegs, this is too *weird*, even for me."

Roan's breathing accelerated. For a split second, Winston was prepared to lunge forward and separate the men, but his belief that his host was about to snap, proved wrong. Roan suddenly flung his arms around Lachlan and repeatedly clapped him on the back. Choked sounds emanated from both men, the boys started weeping, and Winston, much to his chagrin, was so choked up, he had to gulp air into his lungs in a bid to ward back tears. They came nonetheless, and he swiped them away before anyone could witness them.

"Lannie, Lannie," Roan said, in a voice caught between a laugh and a sob. "Damn me, I can't believe you're here! How many times—" He pulled back and almost roughly framed Lachlan's face between his large hands. "—will I have to say goodbye before you *stay* dead?"

A strange expression softened Lachlan's features as he stepped out of Roan's grasp. He looked as if Roan had emotionally wounded him. As if he wanted to crawl into a hole and hide from the world.

"I just arrived," said Lachlan in a low tone. "Dinna worry abou' yer position here. I've na inten—"

"*Och!*" Roan laughed, his hands raised in a placating gesture. "Lannie, I was jokin'!" He lowered his hands and offered a genuine grin. "We're all feelin' a *wee* tense, but I couldn't be happier to see you!"

Lachlan glanced at the boys, at Winston, then lowered his gaze to his hands as they brushed aside imaginary lint on his tight-fitting black pants. "This dinna feel right, Roan. Beth...." His troubled gaze lifted to solemnly regard Roan. "Pregnant? I dinna remember much abou' where we were, but I would think I would remember makin' a baby wi' ma woman."

Trenching the fingers of his left hand through the top

of his shoulder-length, dark auburn hair, Lachlan walked to the fireplace and picked up the wrought-iron poker. For a short time he prodded the burning logs, then turned to face his companions, his dark eyebrows drawn down in a frown. *"Poof,* we're back, and we're havin' us a wee one. And I'm feelin' na uncanny. No' maself." He glanced down at himself, then lifted the pointed end of the poker and began to rap it against his left palm. "Ma skin feels tight and there's buzzin' goin' round and round in ma head. I dinna know wha' to do." As he went on, he struck himself a little harder in the palm with each word. "I canna be a faither. What possible use could I be to a child, bein' dead as I am? *Fegs!* This shouldna be happenin'. The ither side is forever! If I dinna get answers soon—" He released a guttural cry and stared down at his left palm in horror. The poker fell from the other hand and struck the floor by his black booted feet.

"Lannie?" Roan probed, but didn't move.

Winston went to Lachlan and looked down at the leveled palm. A pool of blood filled it. Lachlan's face turned as white as a sheet.

"Kevin, fetch me a clean towel, please," Winston instructed the boy.

Roan stepped to Winston's side and, seeing the blood welling up in the injured palm, redirected, "Kevin, bring the first aid kit. And hurry."

Kahl joined his brother and they sped out of the room.

"Lannie, you're . . . bleedin'," Roan murmured sickly.

Lachlan side-stepped around the two men and walked to the back of the sofa. All the while, he held up the palm which had been cut with the poker tip, staring in stark disbelief at the vivid redness.

"It hurts," Lachlan breathed, his dark eyes searching the men as if expecting them to come up with a simple explanation. "Blood. Tis no' *ghostly* blood."

"No," said Winston.

A strangled chortle escaped Lachlan. "I canna see through it."

"No," said Winston.

"And ma hand—ma *arm*—pains me!"

Winston nodded. "You injured yourself," he said simply.

A comical almost rueful expression fell over Lachlan's face. "Injured maself, you say? *Fegs!* How can a *ghost* injure hisself?"

Winston swallowed past the growing tightness in his throat, then locked eyes with Roan. At first the man looked at him in puzzlement, then gradually with incredulity.

"You mean . . . ?" Roan croaked.

Winston nodded, and Roan turned an astonished look at Lachlan. "Ma God."

"Wha'? *Wha'!*" Lachlan shouted, angry that he couldn't grasp what was seemingly understood between the two other men.

"Roan, I think it best you let me talk to him," said Winston. "Keep the boys away for a time, okay?"

Nodding, Roan headed for the hall. "I'll be ou' here if you need me," he said to Winston, but his gaze was fixed on Lachlan.

When Roan was out of sight, Lachlan scowled at Winston. "Wha' is it you *think* you know?"

"Your hand. Wha' does the wound tell you?"

Lachlan watched several drops of blood fall between his fingers to the floor. "Fegs. Tis still bleedin'."

"Lachlan."

The former laird's head shot up and he dealt Winston a fierce look of denial. "Tis tellin' me it hurts like bloody hell!" he roared, the injured hand trembling. "*Ghosts* dinna bleed! And *ghosts* dinna feel real pain, only experience remembered pain!"

Winston sighed. "Lachlan, I don't know how, but you

and Beth have been given back your lives. The psychic contrails tha' connected you and Roan—''

"The wha'?"

"—are gone. You're alive, Lachlan Baird. You and Beth and your—''

Lachlan burst into a heated tirade in Gaelic, then concluded, "You're bughouse daft, mon!"

"No," Winston said kindly, a hint of a smile appearing on his lips. "Welcome to the twentieth century, Lachlan. Your new life begins today."

Breathing heavily, erratically, Lachlan repeatedly shook his head. "I dinna ask to be brought back. I dinna want a *new* life!" He trembled violently, tears streaming down his ashen face. "Ma life was tha' o' a ghost, a bloody spirit, and no' aught else!"

"You were once a mon."

"Na! He hasna existed for a verra long time, and I dinna want him to return! Lachlan Baird, laird of *Kist* House, is who I am!"

"When you've had time to adjust—''

Agnes materialized, giving both Winston and Lachlan a start. Her expression was surprisingly guarded, her posture stiff, almost hostile. To Lachlan, she said, "Beth is doin' just fine. You're the proud parents o' twins. A girl and a boy. Both healthy."

Winston shrewdly observed Lachlan, who stood frozen in shock and denial. The man's emotions rolled over Winston like great, dark storm waves.

"I canna be a faither," Lachlan rasped, again shaking his head.

Agnes primly folded her hands in front of her. Then her gaze fell upon the bloody hand and she abruptly closed the distance and gripped Lachlan's wrist between her cool, bony hands. Winston wasn't sure what to expect, but it wasn't the flash of rage he glimpsed in her eyes.

"Na!" she cried, releasing him as if the contact had burned her. "It canna be you're *alive* again!"

"I'm no'," Lachlan whispered. "I'm . . . no'. Canna be. Canna be."

"Wha' abou' ma Borgie?" she asked, desperation taking the heated edge from her tone. "Where is he?"

Lachlan shrugged helplessly. "I dinna know. Dinna remember much, right now."

Agnes backed away several paces. Except in the faces of killers, Winston had never seen such raw fury. "If you *and* Beth could come back, why no' ma Borgie? Eh? Why no' ma Borgie?" She quaked, her fists clenched at her sides. "Why no' ma boy, Lannie? Where is he? Wha' he did wasna so awful he shouldna get a second chance!"

"Aggie. . . ." Lachlan's throat closed off with tears, preventing him from talking.

"Damn you, Lannie," she gritted out, her eyes seeming too large for their sockets. "Damn you! You've been given it all, havena you? Your life. Your womon. Now . . . a son and dochter. All I ever really had was ma son. Where is he?"

Numbly, Lachlan shook his head.

With a wail of grief, Agnes vanished, her voice lingering eerily in the room for several seconds.

Roan lethargically entered, his shoulders slumped, his eyes bright with tears as he stared at Lachlan. "I sent the lads upstairs." He swallowed convulsively. "I heard Aggie. So, you're a faither. Congratulations, Lannie."

Lachlan briefly glanced at Winston, then stared down at his still trembling palm. A rattling wheeze escaped him. He swayed. Corrected himself and heaved a liquid sigh. Grew paler. Then his eyes rolled up into his head and he fell backward.

Spread-eagle on the hardwood floor, an unconscious Lachlan Baird found escape from reality.

Roan and Winston knelt on each side of him, Winston gesturing for Roan not to touch him. "Let him rest. We'll get his hand bandaged and try to get our wits abou' us before he comes around."

"He and Beth are *real?* Back for good?"

Winston nodded.

"Sweet Jesus," Roan murmured.

Beth felt herself sinking deeper into the mattress and pillows as she watched Laura leave with her sleeping son. It had been a strange day, a long and hectic day, and only now did she dare to think.

Beyond the open drapes, night had fallen and a valance of stars could be seen twinkling against the darkness. How many hours had passed she didn't know, but she'd breast-fed the twins three times already. She was exhausted, yet wired with energy. She was deliriously happy and excited, yet profoundly miserable.

Mostly, she was scared

The familiar coziness of the hearth-lit room helped to soothe her frayed nerves, but it also perpetuated her unspoken fear that she was caught up in a very real dream, one that would break her heart when she awakened and realized she would never see her adopted home again except while in a state of slumber, and she would certainly never be a mother.

Lachlan, where are you?

A burning sensation filled her throat and tears welled up in her eyes. She attributed these to remembrances, because of course she couldn't cry anymore. Tears were for the living.

But where was Lachlan? He was in the dream before she'd given birth. . . .

In some ways, she wished she could awaken and return to their existence in—

A shuddering breath escaped her when she realized she couldn't remember much about the afterlife. Elusive images fluttered at the perimeter of her mind.

She closed her eyes but for a moment while she relented to a yawn. When she opened them, she was startled to see a figure standing at one of the windows. For just a split second, Beth thought she was looking at Cousin It, a character from *The Addams Family*. Then Beth realized it had to be a woman with unusually long hair.

Abruptly, the figure turned and approached Beth's bedside. She was young, perhaps in her early to mid-twenties, and beautiful. As the woman gracefully seated herself to Beth's left, Beth couldn't tear her gaze from her features. *Beautiful* wasn't the right word, Beth told herself. The heart-shaped face had an angelic quality. Soft, innocent, and timeless.

"Can I fetch ye somethin' from the kitchen?" she asked, smiling at Beth. "I canna cook, but I can bring ye some fruit or some o' Laura's fine muffins wi' a slatherin' o' Aggie's jam. I fingered one jar o' strawberry empty, I did, and I can vouch tis grand, grand stuff."

Beth chuckled. "No, I don't want anything, thank you."

The stranger sighed while her vivid blue gaze boldly searched Beth's features.

"Who are you?"

"Deliah," she said without hesitation, and smiled again. "I be Deliah."

A smile glowed on Beth's face. The young woman was definitely strange, but she liked the strangeness. "Have you been here long?" When Deliah glanced about the room, Beth amended, "In Baird House."

"Verra long."

The answer perplexed Beth, then she pondered the

reality of those dreams before asking, "Have we ever met before?"

Deliah's slim, winged eyebrows jutted upward. "In wha' way met?"

Again, the response baffled Beth. Another yawn escaped her, making her eyes water. "I was just thinking what a *real* dream this is, and why someone I don't know, should be in it."

"Nae, Beth, tis no' a dream." Deliah frowned prettily, the blue of her eyes brightening despite her shadowed features. "I brought ye and Lachlan home. Tis where ye both belong."

"You?"

For several seconds, Beth held her breath. Then she realized she was kneading the bed quilt. She could *feel* the cotton and wool fibers. Real enough. She could smell the wood burning in the hearth. Again, real enough. She could feel a slight cool draft across her face. Real enough.

"Beth, I have a story to tell ye."

For nearly half an hour, Beth numbly listened to the young woman's account of her life on the Baird land, and how she came to be in the house. When she finished, Beth couldn't respond right away. Her mind was churning at a maddening speed. Doubts and belief warred inside her skull. Then, in barely a whisper, she stated, "That's impossible."

An endearing grin spread across Deliah's mouth. "Nae mair impossible than returnin' from the dead," she said, with such calm logic, Beth blinked in bewilderment. "Beth, I be truthful in all matters."

"But. . . ."

Her eyes sparkling mischievously, Deliah wagged a chiding finger. "Nae buts. We be wha' we be."

"Can't you tell me how you accomplished our return? Deliah, do you really have *that* kind of power?"

Seconds passed while Deliah thought through her response. Finally, she sighed and shrugged her small shoulders. "Tis no' power in the way ye mean.

"Beth, remember the night ye carried Viola off into the heavens?"

A chill passed through Beth and she nodded.

"Just afore tha' ye were inside the wall, tryin' to work up the courage to leave Lachlan behind. Ye were fiercely scared o' wha' the afterlife was like, but ye knew ye had nae choice but to get her away from the house. I remember wishin' at tha' time, I were ye, and had your kind o' courage."

Tearfully, Beth murmured, "I had no choice. She would have eventually killed the boys."

"Aye, and ye were scared for Lachlan's soul." Gently, Deliah clasped Beth's left hand between her own. "Ma kind canna harm a livin' thing, Beth, nor interfere wi' the spirit o' a human. MoNae has strict rules and, although I be lost from ma people, I must abide. I couldna stop Viola, and I couldna stop ye from removin' her from Baird land. But I could and *did* connect ye and Lachlan to me and Roan wi' somethin' akin to an umbilical cord. Ye were never completely in the afterlife, but in a plane atween the two worlds."

"Why?"

Deliah lowered her gaze to her hands. "I didna know wha' else to do."

"If this *is* all real, why now?"

Almost reluctantly, Deliah met Beth's troubled gaze. "The returnin' was meant to be slow, Beth. Winston—"

"The psychic cop—agent—whatever he is?"

"Aye. I couldna keep the knowin' from him too long. He has his own energy o' sorts and it worked against mine. Whenever Roan spoke sadly o' your and Lachlan's leavin', Winston unconsciously reached ou' wi' his mind to connect wi' ye." She sighed wistfully. "Each time he did, he weakened ma connection. I had nae choice but to initiate your return afore it became too late and the ither side took you."

"We were *dead*, Deliah."

"Only your shells."

Beth wearily massaged her throbbing temples for a time. "I'm confused."

"Aye. Little wonder. Nature is energy, Beth. Energy is life."

"And?"

Beth's skepticism elicited a low laugh from Deliah. "And earth magic has nae wee boundaries. Ye and Lachlan were buried by an oak, grantin' me the ability to store your essences in the precious roots."

"What about Carlene and her husband?"

"They died away from Baird land. Beth? Can I ask ye somethin'?"

"Sure."

Deliah glanced up at the door, a look of odd rapture on her face. "Wha' be it like to birth a child?" She cut her gaze back to Beth. "No' the pain, for I nearly left the room I so hurt wi' ye. But right efter, you werena hurtin', Beth. Ye were . . . I canna grasp wha' ye were feelin'."

"Exhilaration, I think."

"Exhilaration."

Beth nodded, then a flood of tears filled her eyes and spilled unchecked from the outer corners. "This is not a dream, Deliah? Lachlan and I are back? *Alive* and parents?"

"Aye," said Deliah, obviously perplexed by Beth's tears. "Are ye no' happy?"

Beth nodded. A sob caught in her throat and she squeezed her eyes shut for a moment. "Lachlan. Where is he, Deliah? Is he . . . *alive* . . . too?"

"Aye, o' course."

"Where is he?" Beth asked anxiously. "Has he seen the babies?"

Deliah sadly shook her head. "He be no' farin' as weel as ye, Beth. In his mind, he still be dead. He existed longer as a spirit than ever as a mon."

"What does that mean?"

"Tis difficult for him now, Beth. In time, he will remember the ways o' a mon—a *livin'* mon. Roan and Winston will see him through the tryin' times to come."

"You don't understand, Deliah. We *love* each other. I should be all he needs. And his children—"

"Beth," Deliah interrupted in a hushed tone, "twas no' a mon ye fell in love wi', but the energy o' wha' had been a mon. *This* Lachlan will be a wee different."

Warily, Beth asked, "How different?"

Deliah offered a shrug. "Hard to say. Males are o' a strange mind, even among ma kind. Tis why we females control the balance."

"We do?"

Deliah laughed. "Aye, but tis a never-endin' task, it is." She sobered and leaned closer to Beth. "Beth, be kind to him durin' his newness. I've been wi' Lachlan since afore his dyin'. I connected wi' him to have a sense o' bein' alive maself."

"Was he ever aware of you being here?"

"Nae. Whenever he tapped into ma energy to sustain his spirit life, he thought it to be somethin' within hisself. I didna mind, though. Through him, I was able to feel again. Too long afore him, I had nocht but darkness and despair. Ma kind have never known loneliness. Never understood the meanin' o' solitude. But I do and hope to never know it again."

Beth remained quiet for a long time, wrapped in a gauzy shroud of dreaminess she was unwilling to leave. She wasn't sure how she felt about being alive again. Unquestionably, she should be ecstatic with joy and counting her blessings. But she remained a little more than frightened. She didn't have God to thank for her present condition, but this incredible being called *Deliah*.

"Beth?"

Beth realized her mind was slipping away into a realm of escape when Deliah's voice penetrated the barriers. Sighing deeply, she sharpened her focus on the young woman and managed a somewhat wan smile.

"Thank you," she said simply, but the huskiness of her tone relayed the depths of her gratitude. And when Deliah gave a single nod, and Beth's eyes again filled with tears, she added, "Are you remaining in Baird House?"

The young woman's face shadowed further with a look akin to fear. "If I be sent away, Beth, I will die."

This time Beth reached out and clasped the smaller hand. "No one will ever force you from this house. You have my word on that."

Deliah nodded sadly and lightly bit into her lower lip. "Beth, promise me you'll no' tell anyone wha' I am."

"Why?"

Deliah adamantly shook her head. "The men will no' understand. Beth, do promise me this, and I'll never ask ye anither favor!"

Again seconds passed in silence. Both women looked at each other, a strange yet magical bond rapidly forming between them, and not one induced by magic itself. Finally, Beth scooted up in a sitting position. She ached and was suddenly tired and more than a little weary, but she was curious about this woman and didn't want to end their talk just yet.

"You know, when I first came to this house, Deliah, I had no idea just how lonely I was. I had no identity, and certainly no concept of my worth. It took this house, Lachlan, and dying to find myself.''

"I dinna understand.''

"Deliah, don't be afraid of who or what you are.''

"Tis easy for a human to belong here,'' Deliah murmured, misery throbbing in her tone. "Wha' I be is o' the earth. Tis shameful for ma kind to exist as I am now.''

"Why shameful?''

Deliah lowered her head. Her magnificent hair closed about her like a curtain of satin. "I have nae ring o' passage. Ma brither stole oor faither's to enter again and again this world and, in doin' so, caused a catastrophe tha' wiped ou' ma family, ma clan, ma kingdom althegither.''

"They're all dead?''

"Aye.'' She lifted her head and lethargically brushed her hair back from her face. "Be any alive, they would have searched for me. We dinna abandon oor people. Nae . . . they are gone and I am here because I hid so deeply in the roots, the evil ones couldna find me. Aye, I hid so deeply, I lost maself.''

"You're not alone here, Deliah. There's no reason why you can't live a normal life.''

A mist of tears brightened the blue eyes sadly searching Beth's face. "Tis no' aneuch to live. Withou' Winston. . . .''

"You're in love with him?''

Deliah nodded. "From the first he set foot on Baird land.'' She sighed and it throbbed with tears. "I've never seen a mair beautiful mon, Beth. He maks ma heart feel so achy.''

With a low chuckle, Beth nodded. "I know that feeling, believe me.''

"Aye, I know ye do.'' A delicate, almost shy smile graced Deliah's face. "But Lachlan loved ye afore ye came here, Beth. Winston, now . . . weel, he's no' a mon to love easily, and I fear, no' a mon who will accept ma differentness.

Afore I left the waitin' realm, I had a plan. Twas to mak him love me afore we met—in the flesh, so to say. But I didna have the time I thought and, since ma arrival, he's no' been verra happy wi' me."

"Why?"

"Weel, he think me childish because I love the winter so. I canna tell him how *new* this is for me. He would *never* understand tha', I can tell ye! And he has this problem wi' me removin' ma claes. Beth, there are times these garments are too bindin'. When I want to experience *cold,* I want to feel it *all* over ma body! Wouldna you?"

Beth laughed. "I can see his point, though. People don't usually strip in freezing weather."

"Why no'? It feels grand, Beth. Verra grand!"

"Humans can catch cold. Get sick. I think he was concerned for your health."

Dawning glowed on Deliah's face. "He's worried abou' me, is he? That's grand, nae? Twould mean he cares a wee, whether he chooses to admit it or no'."

Beth nodded.

"Ah, Beth, I want wi' all ma bein' for him to love me. But there be so many reasons he shouldna want me at all."

"Your differentness shouldn't matter."

A sob caught in Deliah's throat and she rolled her tear-filled eyes heavenward for a moment. "I canna give him children, and I dinna think I could ever be aneuch to fill his life."

"I'm sorry, Deliah, but there are a lot of human couples who can't have children. It's best you tell him everything. Give him the chance to decide for himself."

"I know him too weel," Deliah whispered, "and he wants a *family*. I can only offer maself."

A warm, understanding smile softened Beth's lovely features. "Don't sell yourself short. Love has its own special kind of magic."

Deliah swiped a hand beneath her moist nose and straightened back her shoulders. "Aye, so it does. Thank ye, Beth. Tis so nice to actually talk to ye."

Again Beth laughed. "Strange but definitely grand, kiddo."

Deliah stood and flipped her hair behind her. "You're lookin' a wee tired. I should go and let ye rest. But Beth, call me at any time. Twill be an honor to help ye in anyway I can, especially wi' the babies. They are maist wondrous!"

"Thanks, Deliah, and I'll need all the help I can get, believe me. I haven't exactly prepared myself for mother-hood."

"Tis true, but the babes are fortunate to have ye for a mither."

"Deliah?"

"Aye?"

"If you see Lachlan. . . ."

Deliah smiled warmly. "Aye, I'll have a talk wi' him. Just be patient. Remember, he be but a mon, and men can be a wee slow in adjustin' to wha' be strange to them."

"Hmm, how true. Especially Lachlan."

"Especially him. No' a mair complex mon in the world, I dare say."

Chapter Eight

By the end of the second week following Lachlan and Beth's return, the occupants of the house were as tightly strung as steel springs. It continued to snow. The record-breaking cold could have been responsible for the strained temperaments of all, but in truth it was the uncertainty of their futures. Winter lagging into spring and cabin fever only enhanced the sour dispositions.

On four occasions, Winston and Roan walked into town for groceries, bottles, diapers, blankets, and infant clothing. Although they had first tried to unbury Winston's car, which remained stuck on the roadside, then Roan's, both tasks proved futile. The long walks had been more exhausting than either man had imagined, but they'd sweetened the bitter-cold, grueling journeys with stops at Shortby's for well-deserved pints of ale. There were few patrons during each visit, but the two men hadn't entered the establishment to socialize. They had barely spoken to each other, and just downed enough beer to satisfy their needy taste buds and their bellies before returning to the seemingly close confines of Baird House.

Although the boys were the least edgy these days, they were tired of the indoors. They fine-tuned their plan until each were relatively certain the *next* boogeyman wouldn't escape their efforts. They were sure there was one, too. Each one reported to his siblings of someone standing over them while they slept in their beds. Of stealthy movements and rustling sounds between the walls. The boys pretty much ignored the cranky adults. On the surface it appeared they were on their best behavior, with a tantrum thrown in now and then so the adults didn't suspect what they were really up to in their rooms, and the adults remembered there were more than just the babies to take care of in the attention department.

Roan was disgruntled a good deal of the time. With Laura spending most of her days and nights helping Beth with the babies, the boys avoiding him, Lachlan seeking solitude, and Winston being too intense these days to be much company, he was feeling left out and abandoned, and was getting damned tired of sleeping alone.

Lachlan spent most of his time either in the library or in the attic, anywhere he could avoid people, especially Beth. His hand was almost healed, but every time he accidentally struck it or gripped something too tightly, he was reminded he was again capable of experiencing *real* pain. He repeatedly told himself he couldn't be alive. He'd existed dead far longer than his years prior to being walled up in the tower and left to bleed to death by Robert Ingliss and Lachlan's treacherous bride, Tessa. The spirit form was the more real to him. The grayness was the truer resting place, not slumber. Something as natural as a bowel movement was enough to distress him, enough to make him withdraw into himself ever deeper.

Encountering Agnes on three occasions had not helped

to ease his confusion. She refused to say anything to him, but then, she didn't have to. He could read her disappointment, her anger, and her burgeoning grief over her separation from her son, in her watery blue eyes. He and Agnes had not had a refined or amicable relationship during most of the years she'd taken care of the house. But toward the end, shortly before last Christmas Eve, they had grown fond of each other and united for Roan, Laura and the boys' sakes. It was all lost. Whenever she looked at him now, he wanted to hide. Wanted to scream that it wasn't *his* fault he was alive, and Borgie wasn't. So Lachlan found solace in his Scotch. Found warmth, forgetfulness and forgiveness in the amber liquid, and kept to himself until he could sort through his alternatives for the future. He couldn't bring himself to worry about Beth or his babies. Until he came to terms with his life, he was no good to anyone.

Winston also preferred solitude. Unlike the others, he didn't have the privilege of wallowing in self-pity. His psychic core had been under assault since the miraculous return of the previous laird and his American lady. He was enduring more and more extraneous levels and degrees of emotions, and it was all he could do to keep *his* self close to the surface. He remained in his room most of the time. Reading was futile. His brain was not willing to accept fiction, not when so much was happening beneath the multi-rooftops of this house. Sleeping was fatiguing. In lieu of his own dreams, he unwittingly tripped into the others' nightmares. Night after night, all but the babies spent their slumber in tormenting dreams. Laura's mostly involved varying creatures trapping her in the basement, creatures part human, part assorted animals. She would always awaken just as she was about to be ripped apart by their claws and teeth.

Roan's nightmares involved falling off high places, from

the tower to unknown cliffs. Each time, he would stand at
an edge, fighting for balance, but pitching into air, and he
would scream throughout the descent until, at the moment
before crashing, he would bolt up, awake.

Beth's dreams altered between two very different
themes. In one, her mother would be climbing out of soft
earth covering her grave, and she would be condemning
Beth for letting her suffer as long as she had. In the other,
a dark silhouette would hold her babies, one in each arm,
and the figure would be sliding backward away from her,
backward into infinite darkness, while Beth wept for her
babies to be returned. The latter distressed Winston the
most. Probably, he reasoned, because the infants were so
helpless. Helpless and unhelpable.

Lachlan often dreamt of his headstone and just that.
Intermittently, the date depicting his death would become
a wavering question mark. A winking, blinking, taunting
question mark. In the same way some feared death, Lachlan feared life. It was the greater unknown and, in a bizarre
way, Winston could identify with the man's feelings to a
certain degree. Life was fraught with uncertainty and the
knowing that eventually the end would come. But in death,
Lachlan hadn't feared an ending, only a continuance without his Beth. In death he would have forsaken anything
to be with her. In life, insecurity created a vast wall he
couldn't bring himself to scale.

Kevin mostly dreamt of snakes. Fat, huge snakes, which
covered him in his bed, and wouldn't let him go to the
bathroom. Sometimes Winston wondered why snakes. It
seemed a horrendous nightmare, especially one as repeti-
tive as this one, for a boy of eight.

Kahl dreamt of headless dolls pursuing him, and of Alby
being lost within walls of fire, in which Kahl tried to enter
to find his youngest sibling. The dolls Winston couldn't
evaluate, but the fire was understandable. The boys had

nearly been victims to Viola Cooke's diabolical plot to burn them in the house, then offer their spirits as a ready-made family for Lachlan. Something Beth couldn't give him at the time.

Alby's nightmares were the most benign, although still scary to him. He would be sitting in a small clearing in a jungle, where animated toy animals threatened to bite him. Often Alby wept in his sleep, as did the other boys. Sometimes, Winston went to them and remained sitting on their beds until the nightmares passed.

But of them all, Deliah's were the most disturbing. She was always alone and always in darkness. Sometimes weeping. Sometimes silent. Sometimes calling out his name. He couldn't sense anything threatening her. Not extraneous, anyway. Her true terror came from within herself, a void she couldn't fill, an emptiness that grew ever wider with every dream. Each dawn, he told himself he needed to delve more into her mysteries. He knew without doubt she was the nymph from the fourth dimension. She was *not* the house, but she *was* somehow connected to it. However, day after day passed, and he found it easier to avoid her. His subconscious knew why, but his consciousness wasn't ready to open that door yet.

Winston was relatively certain the weather and the endless confinement were mostly responsible for the frayed nerves in Baird House. Little did he know that the turbulent emotions of the others blocked out another's dreams. Dreams of stalking women and ending their lives. Dreams of ending the world of its *begetters*.

The peafowls' shrill advent of a new dawn, again awakened Winston. Groggily, he slipped from the bed and padded barefoot across the cold floor. He relieved himself in the bathroom, washed up, brushed his teeth, shaved and combed his hair. More awake now, he donned a pair of

Roan's jeans, dark woolen socks, and a heavy blue jersey. His stomach growled as he re-entered the bedroom. Another squall rent the air and he muttered a curse at the birds. If he lived in this house the rest of his life, he would never get used to the bone-chilling cries of those pests.

As he stacked logs and scrunched newspaper on the irondog in the hearth, he thought about his decision to leave Baird House once the weather permitted. Last night, while lying awake, he realized there was nothing for him here. He wasn't even sure anymore what he'd been looking for and why he'd thought he could find it in this house. He no longer morbidly dwelled on Rose's fate, and he no longer was opposed to returning to work at the Shields Agency. All he'd really needed was a vacation.

Deliah.

She bound into his thoughts like a great wave crashing on the shores of his awareness. He scowled as he struck a match along one of the bricks. For a moment he stared into the flickering flame, then lowered it to the paper. He remained hunkered and absently watched as flames gradually engulfed the wood. Rolls of warmth swept over him. He'd always liked the smell and sounds of a roaring fire. As a child in his parents' palatial home, he often curled up in front of one of the hearths to read or daydream.

Deliah.

His scowl returned and he straightened and walked to the foot of the bed. Impatiently, he raked his fingers through his hair. He was determined not to think of *her*. Not to succumb to the memories of their meeting in the dream-garden, where he'd nearly made love to her.

Against his will, his body tensed. An all-too-familiar tightening in his groin sparked his temper. He wanted her more than he'd ever wanted anything in his life, and it irked him that he couldn't exorcize her from his thoughts. But what his body so readily demanded, his mind refused

to accept. For all he knew, she was one of the solidly dead.
Like Lachlan and Beth had been. Like Agnes remained.
The fourth dimension couldn't sustain a corporeal existence. Only the mind could visit, and that had its limita-
tions. He was now convinced that he hadn't physically
transported to her garden the first two times he had
encountered her. It was all dreams. Somehow, she possessed abilities he couldn't yet fathom. But he would before
he left the estate. He would know everything about her
and prayed the knowledge would free him from her hold
over him. If not, once he returned to work, she would
become just another memory locked away in the vast storage of anomalies his mind sheltered. Just one more anomaly. Just . . . one . . . more. . . .

His stomach growled with more ferocity. He was about
to head out of the room when he felt a strong compulsion
to look out the window. Beyond the panes, he could see
nothing but a curtain of thick, downy snowflakes. Goose
bumps rose up on his arms, but it was not cold-induced.
Something was beckoning to him from within that falling
whiteness. His mind detected soft weeping, so full of sorrow, his heart skipped a beat. He was on the verge of tears,
himself, and he didn't know why, but he experienced a
maddening compelling urge to soothe the person's pain.

Without understanding what motivated him, he quickly
donned his shoes and tore out of the room. He ran down
the stairs to the first floor, turned left and soon headed
out the front doors. Winter's embrace shocked him, but
he went on, snow in areas knee-deep and slowing his prog-
ress. By the time he reached the rhododendrons bordering
one side of the driveway, he was so cold his teeth harshly,
uncontrollably, chattered. He hugged himself, but there
was no warmth to be had in the gesture. His chill-burned
eyes, squinted against the white glare, searched the land
beyond the driveway. For long seconds, he could see noth-

ing to warrant the beckoning, but still he could not bring himself to return to the house. The deepening sorrow *was* out here. It filled the air as thoroughly as did the great flakes.

And then he knew whose sorrow had reached him.

"Deliah!" he bellowed, his hands cupped around his mouth. "Deliah, where are you?"

Panic gripped him. Fear yawned within his heart like a black hole opening in space.

He trudged across the road, the effort to hurry his gait in the deep snow, causing his leg muscles to cramp in protest. When he came to the edge of the ravine, he wildly scanned the infuriating whiteness for her. She was here. Somewhere. He could hear soft, choking sobs. Then he saw her. How, he wasn't sure, for she was as snow-clad as everything else. But there she was. Sitting on the ground. Her arms about the trunk of an oak and one side of her face pressed against the rough bark.

Angry, worried and fearful, Winston started down the slope. Twice he slipped and twice his temper surfaced as he struggled back onto his feet. By the time he reached her side, he was breathing hard and his heart was hammering painfully against his chest. He didn't touch her right away. Didn't dare to. She was hugging the tree, tears spilling down her face, sobs shuddering through her. He was in part relieved that she wasn't naked this time. She was covered with a wool blanket, but that, what he could see of her nightgown, and the fur-lined slippers loaned to her by Laura, were soaked.

"Deliah?"

"I thought I heard them call to me," she wept, hugging the tree more fiercely.

"Deliah, let me help you back into the house."

He was reaching out for her when her next words gave him pause.

"I canna bear the hurtin', Winston. Ye know wha' I mean. The emptiness. The grievin' for wha' canna be. Let me die here. I beg o' ye to leave me to die."

He was angered and appalled at the same time. "So life's a little tough, sometimes," he bit out sarcastically, forcefully removing her arms from about the trunk. "Quitters never find peace, Deliah, and I'll be bloody damned if I let you lay this on my conscience!"

"Nae, Winston, *please!*" she cried when he jerked her to her feet. "I belong wi' the oak!"

"You *belong* wi' me!" he shouted, then flinched when he realized the truth had surfaced, launched from the depths of his subconscious where he'd kept it hidden.

She continued to weep as he led her to the road and beyond the rhododendrons. His grip on her hand was unyielding, and he held the lead at the maximum distance their outstretched arms would permit. He dragged her beyond one of the large, double, dark-stained oak doors and into the glass greenhouse. Before venturing past the bird's-eye maple doors, he pulled the blanket from her shivering body and shook the snow off it. Just beyond the second set of doors, he hung the blanket on a coatrack to his left, then testily pulled her toward the staircase.

A grim-faced Agnes came from the dining room. Her hands were folded in front of her navy blue, white polka-dot dress, and her mouth was set in a fine line of disapproval. But to Winston's chagrin, the disapproval was of his impatience with Deliah, and he offered the ghost a scowl.

"Agnes, would you be kind enough to bring a pot o' tea and two cups to ma room. If you're no' o' a mind, then I'll do it maself, but it'll mean the lass will be waitin' on me as wet as she is."

His gruff tone caused Agnes to stiffen defiantly, but she gave a curt nod and headed down the hall in the direction of the kitchen. It was then that Deliah tugged to free her hand of his hold. Winston turned to face her, anger heightening the color in his cheeks and brightening the green of his irises.

"You've pushed enough o' ma buttons this mornin'," he growled low, determined not to wake the others in the house. "Give me anymore trouble, and I promise you'll find yourself across ma knee and receivin' the spankin' o' your life!"

Before she could respond, he swept her up into his arms and began the grueling chore of negotiating the stairs to the second floor. His feet and legs were numb, giving the illusion he was precariously walking on hills of cotton. He grunted and winced throughout the journey to his room, where he eagerly placed Deliah on her feet beside his bed. He hastened to the hearth and danced from foot to foot, as if doing this somehow warmed him quicker.

"Get ou' o' your wet things and wrap yourself in one of the quilts," he ordered over his shoulder, his tone still laden with vexation. He kicked off his shoes and wiggled his toes in the warmth emanating from the hearth. "Dammit, Deliah, be quick abou' it!"

He heard sounds behind him and knew she was complying. Shortly, she came to stand alongside him, a heavy quilt snuggled about her. Winston studied her profile for a moment, his pique with her simmering just beneath the surface of his control.

"Have you anythin' to say to me?"

She flinched and frowned, but continued staring into the lapping flames in the hearth.

"Deliah," he issued scoldingly. "Have you anythin' to say about *this* mornin's jaunt into the cold?"

She sighed resignedly, then asked, "Wha' be a spankin'?"

Winston's jaw dropped, then he clamped his mouth shut

and deepened his scowl. "Are you playin' wi' me, lass? Because if you are. . . ."

"Nae, Winston." Her dulled blue gaze met his. "I be curious to know wha' be a spankin'."

"Never mind," he grumbled, still hopping from one foot to the other. "Suffice it to say, it's no' pleasant."

"I see. But neither is your constant displeasure wi' me."

"Act your age and I wouldn't be so frustrated wi' you!"

Her eyebrows arched. "Ma age, ye say? Tell me, Winston Ian Connery, how does someone *act* once passin' their third century?" Her tone became more flippant. "This spring, I be three-hundred and forty-seven. No' exactly ancient, but tis a fair livin' I've had."

Winston, stunned, gave in to the weakness in his legs and sat hard on the floor. He watched Deliah sit beside him. Her hair, which had been beneath the blanket she'd worn outside, was dry. The sheen on the strands cascading down her front, captured the golden glow of the fire. She stared into the blaze, her expression somber, her thick, dark eyelashes dipping now and then when she blinked. A hundred questions vied to spill past his lips, but he couldn't bring himself to speak yet. Absently, he rubbed his icy feet, only dimly aware that the ache in them was finally ebbing.

"And for your information, Winston Ian Connery," she said in a monotone, "I dinna feel the cold the way ye do. I used the blanket and Laura's boots to please *ye*, no' because I needed them. And wi' tha' said, I be expectin' ye to stop naggin' me on the issue."

"How old did you say you are?" he asked on a rushed breath.

Deliah's gaze swerved to regard him through a frown. "Are ye deaf, Winston Ian Connery, or just o' a mind to pestin' me?"

A grin quivered on his lips. "Lass, it's a fair bet there is no such word as *pestin'*." He laughed outright, although briefly. "But I like the word. *Pestin'*."

"I ask ye to let me die, and ye laugh at me!"

He sobered abruptly, turned slightly on his bottom in order to face her, and leaned toward her. Capturing her chin between a thumb and forefinger, he gave it a gentle squeeze. "I don't recall laughin' at you when you made tha' ridiculous plea. I don't recall findin' it at *all* amusin'."

She jerked back, breaking the physical contact between them. Winston cocked an arrogant eyebrow, further baiting her. "So, *now* you don't want me to touch you." He sighed with exaggeration. "Seems you can't make up your mind as to wha' you want."

"I know wha' I want, ye smug, *pestin'* mon, but I'll no' forsake ma pride to have it."

Her haughty response caused him to grin again. "Let me get this straight, Deliah, lass. First, you were the house. Then merely someone from the fourth dimension. You like snow and talk to someone named Blue. You're three hundred forty-seven years old, but don't look a day over twenty-one—and that's no' centuries. You want me and you want to die, but you have too much pride to pursue me, but no' enough pride no' to quit on life." He shook his head and chuckled. "If you're no' a case shy o' your marbles, I'll eat ma big toe."

"Start chewin'," she fumed.

A sharp rap came at the door. As Winston rose to his feet, Agnes entered, carrying a silver tray. He met her halfway and took the tray.

"Thank you, Agnes. I'm sorry I was so short wi' you downstairs."

"Cold and wet as you were, I'm surprised you didna bark louder, Master Winston."

Although her words were kind and her understanding

4 BESTSELLING HISTORICAL ROMANCES BY YOUR FAVORITE AUTHORS CAN BE YOURS, FREE!

Kensington Choice brings you historical romances by your favorite bestselling authors including Janelle Taylor, Shannon Drake, Rosanne Bittner, Jo Beverley, and Georgina Gentry, just to name a few! Each book is filled with passion, adventure and the excitement of bygone times!

To introduce you to this great club which is part of Zebra Home Subscription Service, we'd like to send you your first 4 bestselling historical romances, absolutely free! And once you get these 4 free books to savor at home, we'll rush you the next 4 brand-new books at the lowest prices available, as soon as they are published.

The way the club works is that after your initial FREE shipment, you will get our 4 newest bestselling historical romances delivered to your doorstep each month at the preferred subscriber's rate of only $4.20 per book, a savings of up to $8.16 per month (since these titles sell in bookstores for $4.99-$6.99)! All books are sent on a 10-day free examination basis and there is no minimum number of books to buy. (A postage and handling charge of $1.50 is added to each shipment.) Plus as a regular subscriber, you'll receive our FREE monthly newsletter, *Zebra/Pinnacle Romance News*, which features author profiles, subscriber benefits, book previews and more!

So start today by returning the FREE BOOK CERTIFICATE provided. We'll send you 4 FREE BOOKS with no further obligation: A FREE gift offering you hours of reading pleasure with no obligation...how can you lose?

*We have 4 FREE BOOKS for you
as your introduction to
KENSINGTON CHOICE!
To get your FREE BOOKS, worth
up to $24.96, mail the card below.*

FREE BOOK CERTIFICATE

Yes! Please send me 4 Kensington Choice (the best of Zebra and Pinnacle Books) Historical Romances without cost or obligation (worth up to $24.96). As a Kensington Choice subscriber, I will then receive 4 brand-new romances to preview each month for 10 days FREE. I can return any books I decide not to keep and owe nothing. The publisher's prices for Kensington Choice romances range from $4.99-$6.99, but as a preferred subscriber I will get these books for only $4.20 per book or $16.80 for all four titles. There is no minimum number of books to buy and I may cancel my subscription at any time. A $1.50 postage and handling charge is added to each shipment. No matter what I decide to do, my first 4 books are mine to keep, absolutely FREE!

Name _____

Address _____ Apt. _____

City _____ State _____ Zip _____

Telephone (___) _____

Signature _____
(If under 18, parent or guardian must sign)

Subscription subject to acceptance. Terms and prices subject to change.

KC0798

4 FREE
Historical Romances
*are waiting
for you to
claim them!*

(worth up to
$24.96)

*See details
inside....*

KENSINGTON CHOICE
Zebra Home Subscription Service, Inc.
120 Brighton Road
P.O. Box 5214
Clifton, NJ 07015-5214

of his mood genuine, she looked troubled and wearier than anyone, alive or dead, deserved to be.

"Agnes, is there anythin' I can do for you?" he asked gently.

The faded blue eyes flicked to regard Deliah, who had turned her head and was watching the exchange with renewed solemnity.

"Deliah, I'd like a word wi' you, child," Agnes said, her posture rigid and her tone chilly.

"Nae, Aggie. I've nocht to say."

"What's goin' on?" asked Winston.

Agnes passed him and positioned herself next to Deliah. "You promised you would consider ma request."

"Aye, Aggie," Deliah said wearily, and lowered her gaze to the fire. "I canna give ye wha' ye want, for I havena the heart to see ye go."

"Wha' right have you to deny me this?"

Winston joined the women, his eyebrows drawn down in a frown. "What request, Agnes?"

"Tha' she release me to enter the *Light.*"

Winston placed the tray on the floor, then straightened. "How can Deliah release you?"

"Stay ou' o' it, Winston."

"No, I won't, Deliah. I want to know what's goin' on."

"I need to join ma son," Agnes said, a quaver in her tone. "Seein' Lannie and Miss Beth has only worsened ma achin' for ma boy. I dinna belong here. You know tha', Master Winston, but she—" She pointed to Deliah's bent head. "—knows it mair'n maist. *She* keeps me here. *She* can free me."

"Is this true, Deliah?"

"Nocht is *tha'* simple," Deliah murmured.

Walking around the tray, Winston crouched in front of Deliah and propped up her chin with a crooked finger.

He looked deeply into her eyes, which were filling with tears. "Do you have the power to let her pass on?"

After a moment, she blinked and tears coursed down her pale cheeks. "Aye," she rasped, "but I dinna want to see her go. I beg ye, Winston, dinna push me to do this. If I die, ma energy returns to the earth. Where she wants to go is so verra far away. We would lose all o' her, and tis a waste ma heart canna bear."

Winston positioned himself on his knees, then rested his buttocks on his heels. He stared up at Agnes, scanning, reading her with the extent of his ability, then sadly lowered his gaze to Deliah's face. She looked so pitiful, he nearly pulled her into his arms. Nearly kissed away her pain. Nearly told her he would side with whatever decision she made. But for Agnes' sake, he couldn't do anything but speak from the core of his logic.

"It's cruel to force her to remain if she doesn't want to, Deliah."

Her tears came faster and her chin quivered. The misery ravaging her features brought a mist of tears to his own eyes, but he fought them back.

"Is it true you're the one keepin' her here?" he asked. Using his thumbs, he wiped aside the wetness on her cheeks. "Is it, Deliah?"

A choked sob escaped her and she nodded.

Winston looked up at Agnes. She was no longer hostile, but caught up in the emotional moment. "Agnes, do you *really* want to cross over?"

She nodded. "I'm no' needed here." She knelt to Deliah's other side and placed a shaky hand on the young woman's right shoulder. "Child, perhaps I'm selfish wantin' to be wi' ma son, but I wasna a verra good mither durin' his life. I canna be wi' the lads withou' rememberin' ma Borgie at their ages, and the ache I've carried in ma heart will no' ease these days."

Deliah swiftly turned and buried her face in Agnes' bossom. She wept hard, repeating, "Aggie, Aggie," while Agnes wrapped one thin arm about the quilt-clad quivering form, and stroked the back of Deliah's head.

"Hush, lass," Agnes soothed, her tone laced with tears. "Tis good I will be missed. I'll live on in your memories. It's oor way."

After a moment, Deliah's weeping diminished. With her face still against Agnes, she managed, "I'll grant ye your wish, but I tell ye now, I'll miss ye mair'n words can say."

A smile glowed on Agnes' wrinkled face as she passed Winston a look of profound gratitude. To Deliah, she asked, "When can I leave?"

Drawing in a ragged breath, Deliah pulled away from Agnes and searched the beloved visage. "This eve, Aggie, when the moon is governin' Baird land. Twill be the proper time, and time aneuch for ye to tell the ithers o' your decision." When skepticism shadowed the wrinkled features, Deliah added, "Ye have ma word I willna change ma mind."

Agnes planted a brief kiss on Deliah's brow then, offering Winston a nod, she stood and left the room, closing the door behind her. No sooner was she out of sight than Deliah buried her face in her hands and wept from the depths of her sorrow. At first, Winston didn't know what to do, then he settled on the floor at her back, placed his bent legs to each side of her, and eased her against him. His arms folded across her front as her head reclined to his left shoulder, and he absently kissed her crown, then nestled one cheek against its softness.

For a time they gazed into the fire. Forgotten was the tea. When at last the last tear and the last shudder left Deliah, she snuggled closer to him and released a long, woeful sigh.

"You're doin' the right thing," he told her.

"Am I?" She sighed again, this one possessing hitches. "Then why do I feel so empty?

"Would you feel better watchin' her suffer?"

"Nae."

For a time they sat in silence, watching flames curtain the remains of the logs in their lapping ascent up the chimney. No extraneous thoughts intruded Winston's mind. He felt oddly serene and at peace in his surroundings. His stomach growled now and then, but he couldn't bring himself to release Deliah. It felt too natural to hold her. His arms were at home encircling her. It was as if they were long time lovers who had shared more than an embrace, cuddling.

A door to his subconscious he would have preferred remained locked, opened, and caused him to scowl as a vivid memory surfaced. At first, he tried to will it back into the dark recesses of his mind, but it grew persistently brighter on his mindscreen.

"You took me to another place, besides your gardens," he said. No rancor colored his tone, although he still cringed at the thought of that stonish hell. He was merely curious, now, why she would have transported him to such a dark, menacing chamber.

"Anither place?" she repeated drowsily. "Wha' be tha'?"

"Dungeonlike. There was a mon standin' at an altar—"

She stiffened against him. "Twas no' ma doin'."

"How did I get there, then?"

Seconds passed before she said, "Tell me mair abou' this place. All ye can remember."

He started with how he'd been sitting at the dining room table with Roan, Laura and the boys. As he was nearing the end of his story, he was highly sensitized to the tension throbbing through her body.

". . . then I returned. I thought perhaps I'd nodded off, but it was too real to be a dream."

"Somehow ye went to the past," she murmured, and shivered.

He cuddled her closer to him. "I've been in the cellar. What I saw—"

"'Twas afore Baird House was built."

"Tha' was . . . wha'? . . . a century and a half ago?"

She nodded. "1843."

"When was this other place supposed to have existed?"

Again she was silent for a time, a longer time than before, and Winston knew she was trying to convince herself that he didn't need to know.

"Deliah?" he whispered against her left ear, then brushed his lips against her temple. "Why are you afraid to tell me?"

"No' afraid. Just. . . ."

"Just wha'?"

"'Twas a painful time, Winston. I dinna think I can talk abou' it right now."

"You can if you try."

This time when she fell silent, he fully scanned everything but her mind, which he felt would be pushing the invasion a bit too far. Her body temperature was 97.3. Lower than standard, but he sensed it was normal for her. Her pulse rate was high. His psychic audio could hear her heart and it reminded him of a jackhammer pounding into pavement. Her breathing was somewhat unsteady.

"Durin' the twelfth century, there was a monastery built exactly where this house now stands. The monks were teachers from lands near and far, and they worked hard day and night to farm the acres surroundin' their home. For centuries they coexisted wi' ma clan, learnin' all they could from us, respectin' us and oor ways, and we them and theirs. They survived wars and plagues, and as their numbers grew, the monastery was made larger. We were grateful for them, we were, for they were kind to one anither and honored nature above all else.

"Then ... in 1690, an unnatural night fell across the land. It lasted a fortnight and, when it passed, all the monks were dead. There was nocht ma clan could do for them, and they were ordered no' to approach the structure for fear wha' had taken the monks, could somehow spread among ma clan. So ma clan could do but nocht again, but watch the monks' precious home to fall to ruin ... stone by stone.

"Nae one even crossed the land till 1696. Lord Sutherland and his wife, Lady Lindsay, came and took over the remains o' the monastery. They brought many workers wi' them, and soon a castle replaced the monks' home."

Her voice hollow, she continued, "Back then, maist o' this area was pine and grand oaks, some o' which Lord Sutherland had cleared afore the castle was finished. I remember thinkin' how bare the land looked when maist o' the trees were gone. The pines I didna mind gone so much, but the oaks ... such grand, grand oaks ... were left but a few. Within a few short months, this land barely resembled oor home, but there was nocht we could do to stop him.

"You see, Winston, he was nae ordinary mon. He and his wife were witches, and practiced their black art they did. Ma parents forbade all the clan contact wi' them, but my brither had a powerful need to know mair abou' them. Some o' ma clan already feared he was bewitched when he started meetin' wi' Lord Sutherland's wife. Lady Lindsay encouraged him to lie wi' her. Ma brither was always stubborn and had a mind 'o his own, but this joinin' wi' her consumed him. He would return to us wi' stories of their magic, and their callin' on the deil, hisself, to empower them.

"The end o' ma parents' reign grew near and they

decided it was time ma brither took a bride o' his own. They chose Blue.''

Winston interrupted, ''That's an odd name.''

''No' really,'' she said wistfully. ''It suited her. She had always loved ma brither, she did, and marrait him, knowin' full weel he would be cruel to her. And cruel he was. He wasna happy unless she was miserable, and miserable she was from dusk till dawn, especially knowin' he was wi' Lady Lindsay at every chance he could.

''One night, he went to Lady Lindsay and Blue followed him. The clan waited and . . . I remember we were all afeared o' wha' was happenin' at the castle. We heard arguin' and a struggle. Then came such heinous sounds fillin' the air, we thought oor world would shatter from the vibrations. Everyone started to run for cover, but I had to know wha' had happened to ma brither and Blue. I went to the castle and saw Blue, ma brither and Lady Lindsay dead by a gazebo. And I saw this craiture—''

She gulped and shuddered. ''Twas no' human, wha' I saw. Twas no' anythin' I will ever forget. I was too afeard to return to ma clan, so I hid in an oak close to the castle. Even when this craiture went inside it, I couldna move. I couldna do aught but hide in shame and fear.

''Just afore dawn, a red cloud emerged from the castle. It seeped ou' from the stone walls and spread across the land like a giant, foul-smellin' mist. Men and women ran from the castle and began cuttin' down every tree and uprootin' every plant. They worked so quickly, Winston, like warrior ants convergin' on everythin' in their path. Then they were haulin' the felled oaks into the castle, and the castle . . . the castle . . . began to fade away.''

''Vanish?''

''Aye, vanish, it did. Wi' every mon and womon, includin' ma brither and Blue, and the rest o' ma clan. Then the ground turned as black as a starless sky, and I found maself trapped, and soon fallin' into a deep sleep.''

"Like Princess Aurora in *Sleeping Beauty?*"

After a moment, Deliah wormed out of Winston's embrace and turned on her bottom to face him. Her expression was blank, her eyes devoid of their usual sparkle.

"I know no' this person," she said flatly.

"She's a character from a faery tale."

Her eyebrows shot up and she fell into ruminative silence. It amused Winston to watch her and a grin remained on his handsome face until the ponderous glaze left her eyes and she soberly regarded him as one might regard a problem to be solved.

"Do ye now believe Blue is ma brither's wife?"

The question took him aback and he laughed a bit nervously. "It's no' important."

"It is to me."

Winston sighed. "I believe you, but there's a few dozen questions I need to ask you."

She nodded.

"Okay, Deliah, where have you been all this time?"

"Been?"

"Been," he parroted. "You said you hid in one of the oaks, and fell into a deep sleep."

"I did."

"Are you a ghost?"

A dubious smile curved up the corners of her lovely mouth. "I be as alive as ye, Winston."

"So. . . ." He faltered as he vied to collect his thoughts. "Magic kept you here?"

"Where else would I go?"

Winston sighed with a hint of annoyance. "You're evadin' direct answers."

"Nae. Ye ask strange questions."

"No' so strange from ma point o' reference."

"Let me ask ye one."

He arched his right eyebrow and considered denying her request, then shrugged that she should go ahead and ask him anything.

'Wha' are ye afraid o', Winston Ian Connery?"

"Failure."

"And?"

"Failure," he repeated in the same dull tone.

"And?"

"Why don't *you* tell *me?*"

"Ah." She sighed, and it bespoke of her fatigue and discouragement. "I *know* you're afraid o' me. O' wha' I mak ye feel."

"Deliah—"

"If ye would be honest wi' yourself, ye would know wha' I say be true. Ye are verra unlike Lachlan and Roan. When they were nervous, I urged them to speak poetry. Especially works by Robert Burns. He was a fine poet. But I can nae mair bring the urge upon ye, as I can wipe away your past. Even when I gave ye the rose—"

"Wha'?"

"The rose," she murmured. "'Twas symbolic. Ma way o' tellin' ye she would come to know peace."

"She died."

"Aye, and I can see her death still bothers ye. But why, I wonder? Nocht can hurt her now."

"You performed the Christmas Eve miracle?"

She shrugged noncommittally. "Some o' it was ma doin'. Some, Lachlan's. The rose was meant to ease your soul, Winston, and return ye to me. Ye returned, but no' in the way I'd hoped. Ye came here to die, ye did, and I resented ye at first for wantin' to deny me your company."

A shadow of hostility passed across his face. "Who are you?"

"No' a ghost or spirit. No' a witch or gypsy wench, or

aught else your mind could chose to call me. I be Deliah. I be someone who fell in love wi' ye the instant ye first came upon Baird ground. And I be someone who can love ye despite your abilities, despite your past, and despite your unwillingness to trust what's in your heart.''

Suddenly, Winston felt as if the room were closing in around him. His body temperature rose and panic robbed him of breath. Getting to his feet and patting his sweating brow with the back of a hand, he walked to the bed and kept his back to her.

"It's time you left. Change into some warm clothes and get somethin' in your stomach."

"Winston."

His name fell on his ears like a whisper both caressing and startling him at the same time.

"Winston," she repeated, but this time her hands came to rest on his shoulders. "I love ye, and I be no' ashamed to admit it.''

"You don't know me!" he growled, glaring at nothingness.

"I know everythin' abou' ye, and I glory in every detail, even in wha' ye call your darker side.

"Winston, I have seen evil and suffered from its backlash. I have known loneliness, but always knew someone would come to free me. And ye did. Now, Winston, tis time to put everythin' else aside and bond, ye and I.''

He whirled around, an incredulous look on his face. "Bond?"

"Aye. As in bed me."

"You're insane!"

She shook her head. "Share the intimacies wi' me, Winston.''

"Back off!"

"Winston . . . mak love to me."

"No!" But even as the word tore from his throat, he knew he was lost.

Chapter Nine

In an attempt to resist her enticingly pouty lips, the desire glowing in her eyes, and the maddening thrill of her fingertips tracing his jawline, Winston lifted his protective mental shields and tried to probe her mind. Deep in his subconscious, he knew there was a reason why he should avoid her, why he shouldn't give in to his body's treacherous need of what she offered. But her own shields were stronger. He couldn't penetrate even the thinnest layer of her mind. It was as if her mind belonged to infinity in its vastness. A vastness so great, to glimpse a thought or an image would only be by sheer luck. His inability to read her, to touch upon anything that would aid him in turning off his libido, left him feeling as helpless as a baby.

The soft pads of her thumbs trailed beneath his eyebrows. When he closed his eyes, she repeated the gesture over the lids. Delicious chills swept through him and he sucked in a breath. For but a second, he thought he could see sprinkles of golden, glittering dust falling on the insides of his eyelids. With the illusion, he felt himself relax. Felt oddly serene and at peace with himself.

"I love ye, Winston Ian Connery," she whispered. "Only ye can fill this ache in ma heart. Only I can fill yours."

He opened his eyes and stared into hers. It struck him that he'd been looking for her—waiting just for her—his whole life. Every botched relationship, every thought he'd ever given to settling down, had merely been ways to bide his time until he found *her*. He wondered why he'd dreaded coming to this point in his life. What was more natural than falling in love with someone as delicate and as beautiful as was Deliah? More natural than wanting to share the physical intimacies with such a vibrant lifeforce as she possessed?

In her eyes, he could see a garden filled with flowers, their brilliant colors, shapes and sizes so real, he thought himself back in that dream realm, basking beneath the rays of the sun, insects buzzing with life all around him. She radiated eternal spring. Newness. Rebirth. As long as he was with her, the dark recesses of his soul held no power over him. There was no past. Only today. This moment.

His insecurities fled on wings of contentment as he bent his head and kissed her. Her lips were warm and soft and eager to please him. He kept his hands at his sides until she dropped the quilt, then he drew her nakedness against him and wrapped her within his tender embrace. His fingers explored the glorious silken strands of her hair, while he deepened the kiss, probed the sensual perimeter of her mouth. There was no sense of unfamiliarity in kissing or holding her. None of the awkwardness he thought about during the brief times he'd allowed himself to fantasize about a moment just like this.

Floral scents filled the air. Birds chirped. Bees buzzed. A gentle breeze rustled branches in the corners of his mind.

With a low moan, he slipped his hands through her hair

and found the smooth, soft skin of her lower back and buttocks. He drew her against him more tightly, pressing her into the erection straining at the front of his slacks. Her arms slid around his waist as she stood on tiptoe, straining to mold herself against every part of him. An almost purring sound escaped her when he abandoned her mouth and trailed kisses along her neck and nibbled at her left earlobe. Desire chipped away at his resolve to go slowly, to savor each second as if it would be the last time he could see, hear, smell, touch and taste her.

"I canna wait," she whispered, her tone raspy with passion. Framing his face with her hands, her gaze adoringly flitted over his features. "May I undress ye?"

Her question caused a blush to stain his cheeks. Why her boldness took him aback, he didn't know, but a large measure of his male ego thrilled at the prospect.

Swallowing hard, he nodded. She didn't hesitate. Her hands slipped beneath his T-shirt and the fingertips trenched across his muscle-tight stomach. Then she was pulling the wool sweater over his head and tossing it aside, and next, the T-shirt. Her gaze never leaving his eyes, she unbuttoned and unzipped his pants, and Winston felt his heart racing at an almost painful pace. He held his breath when she planted her hands at his waist and slowly, sensually, lowered them, sliding both his pants and briefs down his hips. Her hands continued to glide onto his outer thighs, her palms and fingers causing electrical sensations to burst along his sensitized nerve endings. He realized he was standing too taut, too inflexible, but he felt as if he would shatter or somehow burst apart the illusion that this was actually happening to him.

Again he gulped past the tightness in his throat when she lowered herself to her knees. She urged him to step out of the garments first with his right foot, then the left. At this point, he expected her to stand and fall back into his arms. Instead, her hands caressed the back of his thighs, she nestled her face against the black curls of his pubic hair, her cheek and hair brushing against the side of his erection. For a horrifying moment he thought she would take him into her mouth and, although he'd fantasized about it, he knew he would lose all control. But she didn't. Her hands cupping his rounded buttocks, she seemed deliriously content to brush her brow and cheek against the soft skin of his abdomen. It was maddeningly thrilling, hardening him until he thought he would burst, but he managed to hold tight to his control, although he trembled with the effort.

When he was sure he couldn't take much more, he rasped, "Deliah," like a man being tortured. He scooped her up into his arms and swung her onto what appeared to be a bed of white rose petals. Lowering himself atop her and positioning himself between the porcelain whiteness of her parted thighs, he hungrily kissed her. Warm, bright sunlight bathed his nakedness. He was barely conscious of her arms circling his neck. Of her urging him to enter her warmth. His outer and internal senses gloried beyond anything he had ever experienced. He was free of every emotional shackle. Free of mere human boundaries.

"I love ye," she whispered, her breathing labored, her fingers flexing in his hair. "I love ye so, I ache from within the core o' ma existence, and tis an ache I honor above all else."

Winston's senses soared higher and higher. He kissed her eyelids, the tip of her nose, her chin, then luxuriously explored the graceful lines of her throat. The tip of his tongue grazed her collarbones, then swept between her breasts. She groaned again, longer and with such passion, he quivered in anticipation of pleasuring her beyond anything she'd ever experienced. He sought first her left nipple, his lips and tongue paying homage to the rigid peak, then the right, where he suckled in sweet, lingering bliss, one hand kneading the firm mound. She arched against him, relaying her readiness, but he wanted to relish every moment, climb the vast mountain of pleasures with her before they triumphed atop the apex in absolute gratification.

His hands roamed and explored her body. Twice, something disturbing tried to surface through the layers of his passion. Twice he ignored the warning from his subconscious. Instead, he looked into the vivid blue pools of her eyes and found himself gratefully drowning within the love she radiated. She was all he ever needed to fill his life, to fulfill the emotional emptiness he'd harbored for as long as he could remember.

His mouth sought her parted lips as he slowly entered her. Her breath filled his mouth and he kissed her more hungrily as he moved deeper inside her. An instinctual cadence gripped them. Thrust upon thrust, stroke after stroke, they carried each other into the heavens, where sensation became something so precious and yet so easily given, they became lost within its power.

For the first time in his life, Winston didn't need to rely on an outsider's influx of borrowed sensations to experience all the pleasure she awarded him. And he realized he was just as capable of giving her pleasure. He was conscious of perspiration coating their bodies, and how their slick skin enhanced their joining. The salty scent and taste of her was ambrosia. He was aware of their muscles straining to take them higher and higher, to fly them ever higher on an instinctual current of need to reach full gratification. They were a pair of perfect white doves, soaring toward a radiance of harmony and love so sublime, he could no more hope to analyze it than he could analyze the components of a miracle.

As one, their arms wrapped about each other, their bodies poetry in motion, they reached the pinnacle. Ecstasy filled the radiance now as shudder after shudder coursed through them. Their descent back to earth was deliciously gradual, like two united feathers loosed in the heavens and lazily making their way to the ground.

They clung to each other for a long time after, basking in the afterglow of residual sensations. But when the heat from their bodies began to cool to the chill in the room, Winston reluctantly rolled onto his side and drew Deliah against him, spooning the back length of her.

Exhausted, neither spoke.

Winston became wryly amused when he realized they were in his bedroom and not in the garden realm. They were atop the bed, exposed to the drafts. He noticed Deliah was dozing off. Gently easing his arm from beneath her, he rolled over and reached down for the quilt she'd dropped to the floor. He pulled it over them, wormed his left arm beneath her again, and smiled with sheer contentment when she snuggled close. Within seconds, they were both fast asleep.

Beth had just placed her sleeping daughter next to her son in the antique crib when Laura entered the nursery. Turning, Beth met the woman's tear-filled gaze and felt her own eyes misting. She walked to where Laura stood just inside the threshold. Folding her arms beneath her milk-laden breasts, she heaved a hitching sigh.

"Aggie told you?" she asked Laura, who nodded.

Laura's chin quivered as she struggled to hold back the extent of her despondency. "I don't want her to leave, Beth."

"Neither do I." A tear escaped down Beth's pale cheek. "How's Roan taking it?"

"Not too good. He-umm . . . well, he was cranky before Aggie's announcement."

"Because of—"

"No, Beth. His mood has nothing to do with your return." Laura released a watery sigh. "I think he's peeved because I've spent so much time here in the nursery."

Beth glanced back at the crib and smiled wanly, then searched Laura's gaunt features. "You've been a godsend, but you are neglecting him."

"I know, but it's hard to resist spending time with the babies. I'll make it up to Roan."

Beth was about to say something when Laura broke down in silent tears. Without hesitation, Beth drew her into her arms. "As much as we want Aggie to stay, we have to think about her happiness."

"I know," Laura sobbed.

Beth drew back and wiped away Laura's tears with her thumbs. "Do the boys know?"

Laura nodded. "They're in Kahl's room and refuse to talk to me or Roan. They're angry with Aggie. You know how Kevin can be. He was pretty harsh with her."

Beth glanced back at the crib, then looked at Laura. "I'll try to talk to them, okay?"

"It might help. Has-um, Lachlan been to see you yet?"

"No, and I'm getting beyond hurt and angry."

A tremulous grin broke through Laura's sorrow. "Men."

"Why don't you spend some time with Aggie and Roan. The babies will sleep for a couple of hours, and I'll see if I can get through to the boys."

"I'll bring you up some lunch in a little while."

"Actually, I think I'll bring the babies downstairs. I'm getting stir-crazy up here."

A genuine smile graced Laura's face. "Beth . . . I'm so glad you're back. We never had the time to really get to be friends. It's nice having a female my age around."

"If you see Lachlan. . . ."

"I'll talk to him," Laura assured.

"I was going to suggest you give him a kick in the *bahookie*," Beth said wryly.

"That could be arranged." Laura turned and left the room.

Beth checked on the babies before heading down the hall to Kahl's room. She knocked on the door and didn't wait for a response before entering the room. The brothers were sitting on the large bed. Three pairs of eyes solemnly watched her approach. Kevin's gaze possessed an edge of resentment at her intrusion, but she ignored it.

Sitting at the foot of the bed, she sadly regarded them, then stated, "Change is seldom pleasant, but we have to respect Aggie's wishes."

"Why?" Kahl asked bitterly. "Why should *we* care what she wants? She's always saying she loves us, but she wants to go now."

"Everybody leaves us," Kevin said, a quaver in his tone.

"Beth and Lannie came back," said Alby softly, his somber blue eyes brimming with tears. He flung himself into Beth's open arms and buried his face in her shoulder.

Beth lovingly smoothed a hand over the back of his head.

"We all love you," she choked, her gaze searching each boy's face. "Don't ever think that will change. But sometimes we can't help what happens . . . what changes come into our lives. We just have to make the most of what we have."

"This a pep talk?" Kevin asked sarcastically.

Alby scowled at his brother. "Leave her alone."

"Shut up, twerp."

"Enough," Beth chided the oldest brother, and he sulkily lowered his gaze to his crossed legs.

"You got your own brats to worry about," said Kahl

softly. "Don't worry about us. We're used to taking care of ourselves."

Beth allowed a moment to pass in silence, then, "The twins are fortunate to have you three."

Alby looked up into Beth's face. "Yeah?"

"Of course," Beth chuckled, and kissed him on the brow. "In a way, you'll be their cousins. Their *big* cousins, and I know they're going to rely on all three of you to teach them all the things kids need to know."

"Like what?" Kevin asked suspiciously.

"Well, like how to play safely. How to rely on one another when the adults seem too busy to pay attention." She lovingly smiled at them collectively. "I don't think I've ever told you boys how much I admire your courage and your street smarts." She was pleased to see the boys' moods were perking up. "Last Christmas was a scary time, but you were all so brave. You've proven you can accept change and roll with the punches. Better than most. Boys, I couldn't be prouder of you. I couldn't—" Her voice cracked and her eyes teared. "—love you more if you were my own children."

Suddenly, Beth was besieged with hugs. When finally the boys sat back on the bed, Alby joining his brothers, wet cheeks were brusquely dried with hands.

"Aunt Beth?"

"What Kevin?"

"Is Aggie really leaving 'cause we've been bad so much?"

Beth released a chortle. "No, hon. Whatever gave you that idea?"

He shrugged. " 'Cause we have been bad, sometimes. We make her spend her energy too fast."

"Aggie adores you three. She stayed this long because of you."

"Then why is she leaving?" Alby sobbed.

"She didn't tell you?"

All three shook their heads, then Kevin shamefacedly said, "She tried to explain, but I wouldn't let her. I didn't mean to be so mean to her."

"I'm sure she understands," Beth assured. "She's leaving because she misses her son."

"Bogus Borgie?" Kahl grimaced.

"Be nice," Beth chided, but a grin slipped past her control. "Okay, so he wasn't a nice man, but he *was* Aggie's son and she loves him. I think she imagines him alone in Heaven, and that saddens her. She knows you have all of us, but Borgie only has her. And it's not fair that she feel sad all the time, is it?"

"No," Kevin sighed. "She should be happy."

"Yeah," Kahl agreed, and Alby nodded.

"So, don't you think, boys, we should be spending these last few hours with her? Making her feel good about her decision? We don't want her to leave feeling guilty about us, do we?"

"No," all three said in unison. Then Kevin said, "She could come back when she wants. Like you and Lannie."

"No, hon. Aggie won't be back."

"Why not?" asked Kahl. "Won't the Heaven highway let her?"

Beth laughed out loud, then sobered. "No, I'm afraid she's leaving for good. Her place is with her son."

"Okay," murmured Kevin. "But maybe she won't want to see us again. I was really mean."

"Aggie loves you. I'm sure she's hoping—"

"Aye," said a voice from the doorway. All eyes turned to see Roan standing there. He wore a broad grin. Only Beth could see the sorrow hidden behind it. "Aunt Aggie was just sayin' she wished we could have a party. A proper send off wi' the whole family." He graciously bowed his head to Beth. "And extended family, as weel. So, ma fine lads, care to join me in the kitchen for some serious bakin'?"

"Baking?" asked Kevin skeptically.

"Cookies and wee cakes. Laura's plannin' to mak flavored snow cones—cold, for sure, but nonetheless appetizin', if the gleam in your eyes is any indication. So, laddies, tis up to we males to handle the bakin'. Are you wi' me?"

The boys looked at Beth, again at Roan, then scrambled from the bed with whoops of hilarity. Roan passed Beth a grateful look then, reminding the boys not to awaken the twins, ushered them toward the staircase. Before he descended with them, Beth ran into the hall and breathlessly asked, "Roan, have you seen Lachlan?"

"Last I saw him, he was headed to the carriage house."

"Thanks. I need to talk to him."

"Beth?" Roan gestured for the boys to meet him downstairs, then turned to Beth when they were out of earshot. "He's shut himself off from everyone. Are you really determined to confront him right now?"

"He hasn't come near me since we arrived. And as far as I know, he hasn't even *seen* the twins. I'm damn angry with him, Roan. I need to get this off my chest."

To her surprise, Roan leaned forward and kissed her on the cheek. He straightened back with a shy grin and a sparkle in his eyes. "Then give him hell, lass. But help yourself to one o' Laura's coats and her spare set o' boots. She won't mind. They're by the front doors on the coatrack."

"Thank you, I will. I won't be gone long. The babies should sleep until I get back."

Ten minutes later, after she'd again checked in on the twins and found them still asleep, Beth went downstairs, donned Laura's fur-lined boots which were a tad too large, and a blue, down-filled three-quarter length coat. As soon as she stepped through the outer set of doors, a freezing gust of wind slammed against her and robbed her of breath. She almost relented to an urge to dash back inside the house. But she didn't. She looked at the carriage house a short distance away and felt a lump rise into her throat.

If Lachlan meant to be cruel, then he couldn't have chosen a better way. In death he had wooed, pursued and won her heart. Now, *alive,* it was as if she were a leper. Angry? *No!* She was fuming mad and determined to make him smart just a little—if she could. From what she'd been told by Aggie, Deliah and Laura, he was *distraught* over being one of the living again. *Distraught!* Had he lost his mind?

The way to the carriage house proved slippery and, by the time she made it to the door, the cold had worked through the dark tan slacks she wore and bitten her knees. Without preamble, she opened the door and walked in. The interior was lit by two lanterns. Sitting on a cot across the spacious room to her left was Lachlan. Elbows resting on his knees and his chin atop his entwined fingers, he was deep in thought and not aware of her approach. At that moment Beth felt torn with emotions. On one hand, she wanted to throw herself into his arms. On the other—

Instinct chose the latter and she whacked him on the top of his head.

"Och!" he bellowed, jumping to his feet. The instant he realized she was the one who had hit him, he shrank back, his dark eyes seeming too large for his pale features.

Beth also recoiled at the sight of his face covered with a thick, bright red mustache and beard. They made his skin appear paler and his eyes even blacker than usual.

"Beth," he managed, her name coming out more of a croak.

"At least your memory's intact," she said flippantly, glaring at him. "Which is more than I can say for your heart, you miserable sonofabitch!"

"Dinna disparage ma mither," he muttered, looking aside to spare himself the accusation in her eyes.

"You're a coward, Lachlan Baird."

His gaze cut to her face and he scowled. "I need time to *think,* womon!"

"You need time to think? Poor baby." She sucked in a breath in an attempt to lessen another urge to whack him. Her hands clenched and unclenched. Her heart pounded wildly behind her breasts. "Have you even looked at the twins?" He glanced away and she barked, "Have you?"

He shook his head, then gestured his sense of helplessness. "I canna see them yet, Beth. I'm no' fit to be around anyone."

"Oh, you're not *fit,* all right." Tears stung her eyes. "How can you do this to them? To *me?* Was loving me only under the condition you remained *dead?"*

He looked at her as if she had punched him in the gut. "I have na future in this time, Beth! I canna offer you and the babes anythin'!"

Beth couldn't see the anguish ravaging his features, or hear the desperation in his tone. Something inside her died at that moment, and she knew it was something more precious than had been her life. Leaning toward him, tears falling unchecked down her face, she said, "If you were even half a man, your first concern would be for your family, and *not* for yourself. So wallow in self-pity. Go crawl to your grave and remember the good ol' days, mister, because you're right. You *don't* belong here. You certainly have no place in *my* future. And you look like death warmed over. Nothing like the man I thought I loved."

She fled the carriage house, leaving the door open behind her.

Lachlan sat hard on the cot. Sat like the rag-doll of a man he'd become. Tears burned at the back of his eyes but he refused to release them.

His Beth was right. Crawling back to his former resting place was his only recourse.

The Phantom's nostrils flared as he stared down at the infants in the crib. They'd been stirring for about a minute now and he realized he would soon have to leave. Dressed entirely in black, a steel gray, three-days' growth shadowing his lower face, his cold gray eyes regarded the babies with disdain. Now and then he flicked a glance at the embroidered, lace-trimmed pillow angled on the antique rocker next to the crib. It wouldn't take much to permanently silence the twins. Since he'd found the wall entrance in the library and had been exploring the narrow thruways, he'd heard the babies crying more often than not. And each time their wails cut into his ears or sparked his nerve endings, he thought about silencing them.

He had no way of determining if they would become part of the technological destruction of the planet. His Guardian only granted him foresight with the mothers, the begetters. Or perhaps, he reasoned, the fact that the infants' cries so irritated him, was indeed a sign that they, too, were the enemy.

A sob caught his notice. With the agility of a cat, he opened the secret passage at the back of the closet and slipped inside the darkness. He kept the door slightly ajar and listened. Soon, he heard, "Mommy loves you," and knew the babies' mother had returned. It struck him that her voice held an element of sorrow. . . .

Soundlessly closing the door, he stood for a time in the darkness, pondering the reason behind her despondency. Did she know her babies were destined to destroy the world?

He locked his teeth so tightly, pain shot along his jawline. Being a mother, she wouldn't have the strength to end what shouldn't have been bred. But he wasn't emotionally involved. When the right time came. . . .

Hunger wrestled Winston from his deep sleep. He felt deliciously good and reluctant to move, especially spooned as he was to the back of the warm body sharing his bed. His stomach growled, more pesteringly this time and he grimaced. Then he grinned and snugged closer, and inhaled the slight floral scent of her hair. She remained fast asleep, not even stirring when he palmed her left breast. The nipple was soft and pliable. For a moment he considered rolling her onto her back so he could feel the textured nub between his lips, but decided, instead, to content himself with caressing her. The fingertips of his left hand trailed over the breast and beneath it. Tenderly moved down her ribs and made a path across her flat abdomen. His hand was traveling upward when he came across something that made him frown. Doubting his touch perception, he retraced the area.

Where a belly button should have been, was a flat, smooth surface.

Still doubting, he scooted back and eased her onto her back. She stirred slightly, but quickly became still and lost within the depths of slumber.

Winston wasn't aware he was holding his breath as he cautiously drew back the quilt. He saw for but a second her naked torso before she turned back onto her right side and partly drew up her knees in a semi-fetal position. Realizing the cold had nearly awakened her, he lowered the quilt on them, then lay on his back staring up at the ceiling.

His eyes had confirmed what his touch had relayed to his brain. And it dawned on him that he'd *seen* the anomaly before. On the tower. When she'd been dancing nude in the moonlight.

All human beings had navels. Yet, Deliah didn't.

No longer hungry but sick to his stomach, he eased himself from the bed and lethargically donned his briefs, slacks, T-shirt and sweater. His mind was a battlefield of questions as he took a clean pair of socks from the drawer in the armoire and sat on the edge of the bed to put them on. Forgotten was that she was in the room, and that he was even sitting on the very bed where they'd made love.

No navel.

What did it mean?

He'd first encountered her in the fourth dimension.

Was she a being from that world?

She'd talked about a monastery that once stood on Baird land, and the evil that had swept over the place.

She'd hidden in the tree. Hidden? How had she fallen asleep in a tree?

He rocketed to his feet when something touched his back. He whirled and looked down to see Deliah smiling up at him sleepily.

"Ye are dressed. And here I was dreamin' o' us pleasurin' each ither again." Lowering the quilt just enough to expose her breasts, she patted the mattress. "Come, Winston."

His panic fled. So did everything else he thought he'd felt for her. His expression deadpan, he asked dully, "Wha' are you?"

She frowned prettily at first, then realized he was serious. A bleak look crept into her eyes. She sat up, drawing the quilt to her chin. Her gaze crept to the vicinity of her torso. "I thought the magic would last till this eve."

"What magic?" he asked caustically.

"The forgetfulness I sprinkled on your face," she murmured.

Winston thought of the golden sparkles he'd seen on his inner eyelids just prior to their lovemaking. Anger simmered in his blood and he took several breaths through his nostrils.

"You're a witch."

Her head shot up and her eyes widened in disbelief. "Nae. Bite your tongue! I be nae witch, good or bad. Wha' I be, ye will never understand."

"Try me."

She adamantly shook her head and cringed back against the decorative headboard. "I thought freein' ye o' your inhibitions would simplify the knowin', but I can see ye canna accept me. Ye *winna* accept wha' ye canna dissect in your mind and rationalize.

"Weel, Winston, either ye come to terms wi' the worst o' wha' you can imagine o' me or remain ignorant o' wha' be the truth." A sob gave her pause, and she visibly braced herself to go on. "I love ye wi' all your faults. Your ups and downs. Your goodness and your darkness. I accept ye. I deserve nae less. I will accept nae less."

His features darkened with contempt. "You're no' human."

"Nae? I know I have a heart, because ye are breakin' it, Winston Ian Connery. I must have a soul, because I can feel it shrivelin' inside ma breast. I bleed and I cry. And I love wi' the same passion as—"

"A *human* female?" he mocked.

She flinched as if he had struck her. Gulping back the tears rising in her throat, she slipped from the bed on the opposite side, drawing the quilt around her as she got to her feet. Her back to him, she said, "I'll no' ask forgiveness for I've done nocht wrong to ye."

Winston watched her walk out of the room, his chest rising and falling with each great breath that roared in and out of his lungs. He wanted to cry. Scream. Smash something! Anything to vent the betrayal coiling ever-tighter in his gut.

Witch. Dimensional nymph. What did it matter. She'd been somehow blinding him to truths, and he inwardly berated his stupidity to have allowed it to happen.

A feeling of being watched triggered his awareness. His head shot around and he saw a peacock perched on one of the window sills. Its beady dark eyes were staring at him. He knew it was ludicrous, but he could almost swear he read intelligence in the bird's colorful face. And he could almost swear this feathered Peeping Tom was *Braussaw*.

The bird released a spine-chilling cry, then rapped its beak twice on the window pane. Winston stepped toward the windows, but jerked back when the bird melted into thin air. For a moment he couldn't think. Couldn't move. He'd encountered more than his share of strange occurrences in his life, but Baird House was proving to be the biggest challenge of all.

Finally, he went to the left side window and looked down at the snowman. Crowning it was an intact bird. Motionless, but turned now in the direction of his side of the house. He was beginning to question if he'd actually knocked the stuffing out of the damn thing when he spied Roan trudging through the snow in the direction of the carriage house. Winston didn't need his psychic abilities to tell him that the current laird was fuming about something.

His stomach grumbled loudly, reminding him that he hadn't eaten yet today. He watched Roan enter the carriage house then, shoving his hands into his pockets, left the bedroom and headed for the staircase.

Lachlan lifted his head from his hands when he heard footfalls approaching. A weary frown masked his features as Roan approached, the livid expression on the man's face warning him he was in for another tongue lashing. He sat up straighter, his hands resting on his knees, and braced himself for Roan's anger.

No sooner did Roan come to a stop, he reached down and, gripping the front of Lachlan's shirt, harshly yanked him to his feet. The heavy wool blanket which had cloaked Lachlan's shoulders, fell on the cot. Lachlan's head whipped back with the force of Roan's action. To his further surprise, Roan shook him, then abruptly shoved him onto the cot and backed off two paces.

Lachlan was breathing heavily when he shakily got to his feet. He couldn't avert his gaze from the fury in Roan's eyes.

"Wha' did you do to Beth?" Roan shouted, his balled hands trembling at his sides. "'Tis bad enough you've been sulkin' ou' here like some wounded rodent, and avoidin' everyone like *we're* to blame for your bloody resurrection! But I draw the line when it comes to Beth, you *paughty* auld mon!" He angrily raked his fingers though his mane of light brown hair, as if the action might help to calm him a bit. It didn't, and he began gesturing wildly as he continued, "She has stood by you through it all! Stood by you when the rest o' Crossmichael wanted you damned to hell! Now she has given you two grand babies, and wha' does she get for her troubles, eh? Mair pain!"

Roan jabbed the air in front of Lachlan's face as he went on, "You were always a self-servin' bastard, weren't you, auld mon?" he charged bitterly. "Weel let me tell you this, and it best sink in verra deeply in tha' thick skull o' yours, cause I swear on ma soul, Lannie, I'll no' stand by and watch you hurt tha' womon again! You have never appreci-ated how lucky you were. *Aye!*" He spat this out contemp-tuously. "Robert and Tessa cut short your miserable life, but you had mair in death than maist in life! Mak na mistake I love Laura, and I thank God every day for bringin'

her and I back thegither, but Beth. . . . Any mon blessed
enough to have her love, should kiss the ground she walks
on! *She* is the best part o' you, you stupid auld mon! *She*
is the heart o' this place!''

Breathing heavily, Roan stepped up to Lachlan. "I saw
her come into the house a few minutes ago, lookin' as if
the life had been knocked ou' o' her. Didn't tak a genius
to figure ou' you'd hurt her again. I won't have it, Lannie.
Get a grip and start actin' like the mon you're supposed
to be!''

Several seconds ticked by in silence, enough time to
refuel Roan's anger.

"Haven't you anythin' to say for yourself?''

His gaze never wavering from Roan's, Lachlan said in a
monotone, "Dinna call me *auld.*''

Roan jerked back as if Lachlan had dealt him a stunning
blow. He stepped back, incredulity washing the color from
his face. Then, as though he didn't have it within him to
stop himself, he sailed his right fist through the air and
landed it on Lachlan's jaw. The impact knocked the former
laird onto the cot where, too stunned to move, the sounds
of his hoarse breathing filled the room. Roan, too, was
breathing heavily as he stared down at his smarting hand
as if shocked he'd actually struck out with it. His anger
became overwhelmed by guilt and shame. A temper he
had, but he wasn't a man who condoned physical violence.
Lachlan had always possessed the ability to provoke him,
but he couldn't remember ever wanting to hurt him as
much as he did moments ago.

"Damn me,'' he murmured, staggering back three
paces, and staring at the raw desolation on Lachlan's face
as if that in itself were a deadly weapon. "Soon as the
weather breaks, I'm takin' Laura and the lads away from

here. Keep your house and your bloody possessions. May it all comfort you throughou' the rest o' your pathetic existence.''

Roan headed for the door, while Lachlan sat up and gingerly touched the painful, throbbing area on his left jaw. At the threshold, Roan suddenly stopped and looked Lachlan's way.

"Aggie's passin' over right efter dinner. We're havin' a party for her and you're no' invited. You've brought us enough misery. So I'm askin' you, Lannie, stay away till she's gone. Come morn, tak back your bloody house. Tak back everythin' you've fought so hard to keep all these years."

Roan closed the door behind him, leaving Lachlan cocooned in silence so loud, it closed in around him.

"Aggie's leavin'?" he murmured, misery making taut his face. "Oh, Aggie. Dinna go."

He broke down in great, shuddering sobs. Manly or not, he couldn't stop the tears. He couldn't stop anguish from consuming him. He was desperately frightened and lonely, but had no idea how to overcome these dark forces.

His Beth. . . . He would never forget the hurt he'd read in her eyes, for he knew she would never forgive him his weaknesses. And Roan, the only friend he'd ever had, hated him. Now Aggie was leaving, and he knew it was because of him. They all belonged at Baird House. *They* were the magic, the heart of the Baird estate.

He was vaguely aware of someone sitting next to him, but was given a start when arms went around him and his head was pressed to something warm and solid.

"Lachlan," a feminine voice sighed, tender chiding lacing the tone. "You certainly have a way of bringing out the worst in some people."

Confused and trembling violently, Lachlan drew away

and forced himself to look into the face of the woman. The visage, which appeared to shimmer as he squinted through his tears, belonged to—

"Laura?"

Chapter Ten

A somewhat shy smile turned up the corners of Laura's mouth. "At least you didn't call me Tessa. I thought for sure you would want to add me to your list of admirers."

Despite his inner and external pain, he managed what sounded like a chuckle. "Wha' are you doin' ou' here? Tis cold."

"I noticed," she said wryly then, gently cupping his chin with the fingers of her right hand, inspected the left side of his face. "Did Roan do this?"

"Na." He inwardly shriveled with she cocked a challenging eyebrow. "Aye," he amended begrudgingly, "but I provoked him. Dinna blame him."

"When he came tearing into the house, I knew something had happened." She lowered her hands to her lap and regarded him solemnly. "Lachlan, you're a mess. Not to mention facial hair definitely does not become you. Why are you doing this to yourself?"

Lachlan lowered his gaze. "I dinna know *why*. Roan told

me to get a grip." He looked into the beautiful green eyes, and shrugged. "But that's the problem, Laura. I dinna know who or wha' I am, anymair. I'm displaced. Tis like I'm in the middle o' two opposin' forces pullin' me this way and tha', and I've no' a clue which is the right side." Renewed tears burned his eyes and added to his frustration. "I dinna want to hurt anyone, Laura. Na matter wha' I do, though, I'm responsible for someone's pain."

Laura was thoughtfully quiet for a time, her gaze studying him with unnerving calm.

"Okay, Lachlan, I want you to listen very carefully to me. Granted, being dead then coming back to life, can be—shall we say—unsettling?"

He nodded grimly.

"Probably as unsettling as discovering you're the reincarnation of a murdering bitch with the hots for wealth, right?"

Lachlan was taken aback by not only her words, but the humor in which they were spoken. A tenuous grin appeared on his mouth before he said, "Possibly."

"Second chances are scary, Lachlan, because we have so much to make up for from the first time around." She sighed deeply, her gaze staring off into space. Then she looked him in the eye with a more serious air about her. "You are Lachlan Baird, a man who broke away from his family to find his own path in life. A man who built an incredible house and through tragedy, created a legacy that will live on in the minds of people for generations to come. You are Lachlan Baird, whose love for a woman brought her to Baird House to die, so she wouldn't be as lonely in death as she had been in life. And you are Lachlan Baird, who not only forgave his murderers, but opened his heart and home to them."

A mist of tears appeared in her eyes as she lovingly tapped him beneath the chin. "How can you doubt who and what you are, Lachlan? You began as flesh and blood, and have miraculously been given back to those who love and need you in their lives."

"Laura," he choked, "I canna believe you're bestowin' this kindness on me."

"For the most part, you and I share a terrible past, Lachlan. Sometimes my shame for Tessa's actions comes back to haunt me, but I get past it. Do you know how?"

He shook his head.

"I remember last Christmas Eve, when I was lying on the ground with that awful knife in my chest, and you leaned over me. I remember the look in your eyes. They told me you would forgive me anything." She reached out and clasped his hands within hers. "They told me you would take my pain if you could."

"The dirk was intended for me, no' you."

"That isn't the point, Lachlan." Releasing his left hand, she placed her right palm over his hammering heart. "Long ago, you were my—Tessa's—husband. I can't count the times I've wondered how different our lives would have been if I had loved you and not Robert. If I would have had half the heart I have now. But wondering doesn't change our destinies. Nope. We're all where we should be. Together. Striving to *live* our lives to the best of our abilities.

"I *know* you're afraid, Lachlan. Maybe the reason why I understand what you're going through more than the others, is because I'm *still* frightened of Tessa. I know that era isn't mine, but I'm nonetheless connected to it through her memories, just like you'll always be connected to the eighteen hundreds. But that doesn't mean the past should rule us now."

"Aye," said Lachlan dreamily, his eyes now staring off into space. "I was a fair businessmon back then. Na reason I couldna mak ma mark in this time."

Laura's smile glowed on her face. "I can hear the wheels in your brain finally turning."

"Aye. Aye."

"You still have Baird House. And your wealth—"

"Na," he cut her off, lifting a hand in the air to emphasize the word. "Tis all yours and Roan's."

"Lachlan—"

"Laura, I'll no' tak back—"

"What is rightfully yours?" she laughed mockingly, hoping to impress upon him how ridiculous it was to refuse what already belonged to him.

Lachlan steepled his fingers in front of his chin. "Roan once talked abou' turnin' Baird House into a retreat. Does he still think abou' tha'?"

She nodded.

"Maist o' the rooms aren't in use."

She nodded again. "There are lots of empty rooms. Some I haven't even seen yet."

"Aneuch for *two* growin' families alone on the third floor. The second floor could be opened to the public. Even this carriage house would mak a grand getaway cottage."

"Personally, I think you and Roan would make hellaciously dynamic partners."

His features scrinched up. "Is *hellaciously* really a word?"

She laughed. "If not, it should be."

"Aye. *Hellaciously.* Feels good on the tongue."

Again Laura laughed, and for the first time since his return, Lachlan beamed with hope.

"Here I was afeared o' the future," he said almost breathlessly, "and the future's been starin' me square in the face. *Och,* Laura, I *can* be an *auld* fool."

"Maybe a *wee* stubborn now and then, but I think you're entitled. However, I also think it's time you groveled at Beth's feet for forgiveness."

Lachlan released a breath through pursed lips. "Fegs. She was fair ready to slay ma heart when she left."

"She was here?"

He nodded. "Roan saw her when she returned to the house. Tis why he came ou' to put me straight. *Fegs*, Laura, I've made a fine mess o' things. I haven't so-much-as looked at the twins. I've been afraid o' seein' ma failure in their wee faces."

"Well take a good look at them, Lachlan, and I can promise you won't see failure. They're beautiful, healthy babies."

"Has she named them?"

"No. I think she's been hoping you would participate in choosing the names."

"Roan said Aggie's leavin' today."

"After dinner." Laura frowned bemusedly. "She said the strangest thing, Lachlan. Said *Deliah* had finally agreed to release her."

"Deliah?"

"The young woman Winston found at the gazebo. She was naked and half frozen. We still don't know much about her, but she claims to belong to the house."

"Deliah," Lachlan murmured, his brow creased in deep thought. "The name is familiar, but a distant kind o' memory. There but no' quite. Do you know wha' I mean?"

"Is she someone from your past?"

"Na. Perhaps." Lachlan shook his head. "I just know I've heard the name. I can almost hear it now, whisperin' in ma mind."

Laura cleared her throat. "I-ah saved the best part. She thinks she's the magic in the house."

Lachlan pondered this for a time, too, then rose to his feet. A dull ache was manifesting at his temples. He felt a bit unsteady and light in the head, but Laura's words continued to echo through his mind.

"Lachlan, what's wrong? You like look you're going to faint."

He made an absent gesture with a hand. "Tis just your words are ringin' true in ma mind. Deliah. Deliah." He walked four paces away, then returned to stand by the cot. "Sometimes when I was in the grayness, I thought there was someone in there wi' me. A presence. Nocht I could see, but rather somethin' there to watch over me. To tell you the truth, I never gave it much thought."

Laura rose and faced Lachlan. "Are you sayin' you believe she's from the grayness?"

"I dinna know." Lachlan sighed wearily. "I canna think straight." He looked across the open space of the carriage house. "Tis bloody cold in here. Every time I move, I swear I can hear ma skin crinklin' wi' ice."

"Why didn't you light the wood stove?"

Lachlan's gaze followed to where she pointed. He could just make out a small potbellied stove by the wall on the opposite side of the door.

"I didna see it."

"Roan installed it. Look, Lachlan, come back to the house. It's a lot warmer, and it's where you belong."

"Aye, I've got to go back, but maistly to do the grovelin' you mentioned. No' only to Beth, but Roan. And Aggie. Laura, I canna let her leave withou' sayin' goodbye to her. But I know she doesna want to see me."

"I know you care about her," Laura said kindly. "Between you and me, I think it would sadden her if you *didn't* show up for her party." Laura grinned mischievously. "However, before making your grand entrance, *you* need a bath and a change of clothes."

Grimacing, Lachlan looked down at his shirt. "What's wrong wi' ma claes?"

"Besides being stinky and outdated?" she teased.

Lifting his right arm, Lachlan took a whiff. *"Och,* I do

smell ripe. All right, a bath it is. But I dinna know abou' wearin' a modern mon's claes. Were mine tossed away?''

"No, they're in a trunk in the attic."

He comically lifted his eyebrows.

"Lachlan, they probably smell . . . musty."

"I like musty. Tis ma middle name."

Laura laughed and raised her hands in a gesture of defeat. "Okay. At least you agreed to the bath and changing out of these clothes. And shave this mess off your face." She gave his beard a playful tug. "I'll loan you one of Roan's razors. We'll just sneak you back into the house. When I left, Beth and the babies were in the dining room with Aggie, and Roan was planning to bake with the boys. While you take a bath in the master suite, I'll get you a change of clothes from the attic."

"Roan was adamant he didna want me at the party."

Laura nodded. "He's hurt more than angry."

Nodding, Lachlan sighed, then a gleam of mischief came alive in his eyes. "I could bring him a fine bottle o' Scotch. We did oor best bondin' over a flute or two."

Laura rolled her eyes. "If you must. Just don't get drunk."

"Na. Laura?"

"What?"

"I canna thank you aneuch for this."

"You don't owe me anything, Lachlan. We're family and always will be."

With a husky moan of appreciation, Lachlan drew her into his arms and hugged her. "You're a grand lass, Laura." He released her and playfully clipped her beneath the chin. "Scotch it is."

"I mean it about not getting drunk. Beth might break the bottle over your head."

"Ouch," he chuckled, "and tha' she would." He crossed

his heart with his right hand. "You have ma word I'll be on ma best behavior."

"Welcome back, Lannie," she smiled and, taking him by the hand, led him out of the carriage house.

Kevin let loose with a fistful of flour toward Winston, who was sitting at the small table in the kitchen, trying to finish his cup of coffee. Winston closed his eyes and sputtered, while Roan, Kevin and Kahl roared with laughter. Winston was making a poor effort to wipe the flour off his face when he heard Roan scold, albeit through laughter, "Kevin! No' only isn't it nice to wreck the kitchen anymair than it is, but I'm sure Mr. Connery doesn't appreciate flour in his face!"

Placing his flour-splattered cup on the table, Winston stood and began to brush off some of the white stuff from the front of his shirt and slacks.

"Roan, I appreciate you puttin' the kitchen before me," Winston chuckled, then turned his head and narrowed his eyes at Kevin, who was doubled over with laughter. "As for you. . . ." Before Kevin could react, Winston scooped him up into his arms, rolled him forward and rubbed his chin against the boy's belly. Kevin squealed in glee and kicked wildly. Winston repeated the gesture, then lowered Kevin to his feet and rustled the top of his hair. "Next time, laddie," he grinned, "it'll be toss for toss. Understand?"

Kevin could only point to Winston's flour-speckled face and laugh, tears coursing down his youthful face.

Winston turned to Roan and shrugged. Still chuckling, Roan removed the apron he had tied at his waist, and tossed it to Winston.

"You're a sorry sight," said Roan, laughter gleaming in his eyes. He braced his rib cage with an arm. "Ma side aches, I laughed so hard."

By the time Winston had wiped off and shaken loose most of the flour from his clothing, face and hair, Kevin's mirth had wound down and he was sniffing heartily at the oven door.

"Kevin, Kahl," Roan began in his best authoritative tone, "get cleaned up."

Kahl scowled. "Hey! Don't we get to do the icing?"

"Yeah," Kevin added, standing next to his brother, his arms folded against his small chest. "That's the best part!"

"Okay. But I want you cleaned up, first. Now scat."

The boys charged out of the kitchen, whooping it up like wild Indians on a raid.

Sighing, Roan jerked a thumb in the direction of the swinging door. "I'd like to know where they get their energy."

"Me, too," Winston grinned. "They're good boys. You're a lucky mon."

Roan nodded. "Tha' I am." A shrewd gleam crept into his eyes. "Speakin' o' lucky, how are you and Deliah farin'?"

Winston abruptly turned away to place the apron on the table, then dallied with folding it while he willed away the heated flush which had risen into his face. "She remains a mystery," he said, in what he hoped sounded like a casual reply.

"Tell me, Winston, do you believe in love at first sight?"

This brought Winston around. He felt as though his blood had plummeted to his feet. "No, I don't. Why do you ask?"

"Deliah." The measuring intensity in Roan's eyes deepened. "The way she looks at you, I'll wager it's mair than just a crush."

"It's the house," Winston said, speaking through a taut grin.

Roan gave a nod, but Winston was willing to wager he wasn't fooling his host one bit.

Surveying the mess in the kitchen, Roan said, "Guess I better get to work."

Laura came through the swinging door, flashed Winston a smile, then threw her arms around Roan's neck and planted a kiss on his mouth.

"Hey, gorgeous," she grinned, leaning back her head and searching Roan's flushed face. "Care to help me gather snow for the snow cones?"

"I'd rather gather you up in ma arms and carry you to—" Roan cut his gaze to Winston and blushed. "Ah, Winston. Did you say you had somethin' to do *elsewhere?*"

"I can take a hint."

Grinning, Winston went into the dining room, where, immediately seeing Deliah, his expression turned to one of chagrin. In her arms, she held one of the babies. The glow on her face and the cooing sounds she made to the infant, caused a bottomless ache to form behind his chest. As usual, her hair was loose. She wore a three-quarter length, royal blue dress which accentuated the color of her eyes. The garment had a rolled collar, long sleeves, no waistline, and a skirt with soft folds. Red and black argyle socks covered her feet, and he found himself wanting to laugh at the bizarre contrast. But he didn't. When she looked up and her own smile faded, he nervously nibbled on his lower lip and headed for the door to the main hall. Halfway, he heard Beth exclaim, "Oh, damn!" He stopped and looked in her direction. She was standing at the table, where the other infant was atop a blanket. She finished securing the diaper, then cast Winston a pleading look.

"Aggie went upstairs with the boys. I just got christened." She smiled at her son. "He has perfect aim. Winston, would you mind holding him while I change my top?"

A breath gushed from Winston and he made a feeble gesture with his hands. "I'm no' good wi' babies."

"Nonsense." Beth swaddled the boy in the blanket and carried him to Winston. "He won't break. Deliah can't handle them both at once. I promise I won't be long."

Before he could convince her he seriously didn't want this responsibility, he found himself holding the squirming bundle. He stood frozen, staring down into a perfect pink face wreathed in the white folds of the blanket.

"He willna bite you," Deliah said softly.

Winston met her gaze and swallowed against the tightness forming in his throat.

"Ye are too rigid. Rock him gently. He'll soon fall back to sleep."

It took Winston several attempts to rock from side to side without jerking. Then, "He smiled at me."

"Gas, I'm told," she said with a light laugh. "Although, why gas would mak anyone smile is beyond me."

"He's so small."

Deliah got up and stood in front of him, the babies between them. "She's even mair tiny. Look at her fingers. Have you ever seen aught so precious?"

"No," he murmured happily, then met Deliah's eyes and sobered.

There was no need for further words to be exchanged. Winston seated himself on one of the chairs at the table, while Deliah positioned herself near the hearth, her back to him.

Meanwhile, Beth ran into the master bedroom, unbuttoning her sweater as she made her way to the bathroom. She was out of it by the time she crossed the threshold, and stopped short when she spied a wet towel on the floor in front of the tub, and heard water going down the drain. Blinking, her breaths coming in spurts, she clutched the sweater against her and slowly turned to face the bedroom.

There, not more than fifteen feet away, Lachlan sat on a footstool in front of the hearth, his back to her. He was combing his wet hair and unaware that she was in the room.

Beth's gaze swung to the portrait above the fireplace. Unbidden, she remembered when she'd thought the painting was of one of his ancestors, of the original Lachlan Baird who had built the house. How soon after that had she discovered *he* was that man, and a man who had been dead more than a century before making love with her in that very bed across from her?

Suddenly, the damp sweater didn't matter. She knew if she didn't get out of the room soon, she would either pass out or go for his jugular. She wasn't sure which she dreaded most. Her legs inordinately leaden, her knees stiff, she headed in the direction of the hall door. In her state of mind, it seemed to shift away, extending the distance she had to traverse to make her escape. When it was within a few feet, she dared to release a thready breath of relief, which she sucked back in when a blur passed her, the door slammed shut, and she found herself staring into Lachlan's dark, brooding eyes.

"Beth," he said in a hoarse whisper.

She couldn't respond.

Rivulets of water escaped the hairline along his brow and trickled down his face. When wet, the dark auburn strands had a tendency to wave and hang a good two inches past his broad shoulders. He had shaven off the beard and mustache. The cleft in his chin and the deep grooves in his cheeks filled her vision.

Beth's world shrank to within a space that could only occupy the two of them. How many tears had she spilled crying over his absence, his cruel determination to ignore her and the twins? How many times had she felt her heart break during the lonely hours she'd lain awake in the dark, longing for him to comfort her.

After all they'd been through together. . . .

She'd thought about her reaction when she next encountered him. Slug him or walk away had been her choice alternatives. Yet neither was a viable possibility at the moment. Her arms were leaden things hanging at her sides, and her legs felt like Jell-O. Her ears filled with a sound akin to rushing water, and psychological weights formed in her chest, making it hard to breathe. She could only stare at him.

He now wore a dark green, full-sleeved shirt which was opened down the front, exposing most of his powerful chest. Black snug-fitting pants and knee-high black boots, gave him the appearance of a pirate. He didn't need a sword. His selfish desire to keep himself away was weapon enough. Sharp enough to cut to the quick her belief their love could conquer all obstacles.

"Say somethin'," he said, his eyes pleading with her to snap out of her stupor. "Even a slap would be preferable to this silence, lass."

Still Beth couldn't respond. She knew if she attempted to move or speak, the dam of her control would let loose, and she wasn't sure what would happen. Crying, screaming, even hitting him wouldn't compensate for the emptiness inside her.

Tears filled her eyes, gushing from a well deep within her when his hands hesitantly framed her face. She wanted to pull away. Thrust him away. But her treacherous heart leapt with joy at his touch. The warmth of his soft palms and fingers melted into the marrow of her bones. Lightheaded suddenly, it took all her willpower not to lean into him and forget what had transpired since their return. But the emotional wound remained, and she needed it to keep herself in one piece. Needed it to retain her own fair measure of pride. When it came to Lachlan, to give in to him was to forsake everything. She'd learned shortly into their relationship that she had to hold her ground, no matter the initial pain it brought her or him. Her youth had waned during the years she'd spent taking care of her ill mother. Coming to Scotland to visit her childhood best friend, Carlene, had been the beginning of what she'd thought was her life. Instead, she'd found Lachlan Baird, ghost of Baird "Kist" House, and learned that Carlene, too, had been dead for some time. Carlene's invite had been instigated by Lachlan, who, knowing Beth was dying, coerced Carlene into bringing Beth to Scotland. She had unknowingly come to this house to die. She'd never had a chance at a new *life,* only a new *existence,* one in which Lachlan was a vital part. And it all had come about because of the portrait Carlene had done of Beth in their hometown of Kennewick in Washington State. The same portrait that hung over the fireplace in the parlor. Lachlan had somehow connected with her through that painting, connected with her through the miles, and had decided she was *his* woman. His to share eternity. And eternity they would have had together if not for their return to the living.

And if not for his abandoning her when she needed him most.

Words boiled up from within her gut, traveled upward into her throat, but never reached her lips. Before a sound could escape her, he pulled her into his arms and kissed her passionately. At first, her senses riveted on him. The musky, all-male scent of him, mingled with traces of soap from his bath. The muscular solidity of him. The height and breadth of him. The sound of his low moans as he kissed her deeper, deeper. His arms blanketed her and she was conscious of hard biceps and sinewed forearms.

Of his heart hammering behind the glorious contours of his chest.

Too soon, the kiss ended and she found herself staring into his eyes through a rush of tears. He had to know he couldn't wipe away the past two weeks with a kiss! Did he really think she was *that* weak? That *gullible?*

For several seconds he stared into her eyes as if questioning her mood, her thoughts. Then a grin twitched on his generous mouth and he said, "I knew you couldna stay angry for long, ma Beth."

Her temper flared, overwhelming her completely as she stepped back and swiped the back of an arm across her still-tingling lips. "You *bastard!* How *dare* you strut in here like you have any rights where *I'm* concerned!"

"I do."

Beth sucked in a furious breath. Tears dropped onto her flushed cheeks with each blink. "The hell you do, you *ass!*"

A flare of anger flashed in his eyes as he placed his hands on his hips and leaned a bit forward. "I swear, lass, I'll wash your mouth ou' wi' soap if—"

"And I'll knee your testicles up into your nostrils if you even try!" she threatened, and lifted her chin in triumph when he recoiled in shock at her words. "We're *not* married and I'm *not* your possession."

Lachlan recovered as best he could and eyed her narrowly, heatedly. "I'm the mon in oor family—"

"You're a useless piece of . . . of . . . *shit!*" she hissed, too angry to care about her language. The dignified Beth, the soft-spoken, ladylike, mousey Beth, was long gone.

"Och!" he cried, running his hands down his face. "I was *wrong* to care mair abou' me than you and the babes. Okay? Is tha' wha' you want to hear, Beth? This mon afore you, was *wrong!* Dinna you think I know tha'? Sweet Jesus, I'm tryin' ma best to mak amends!"

Beth adamantly shook her head. "My guess is, you're horny, Lannie *old* boy, and figured a kiss would buy you some time in my bed!"

His face took on a look of stark incredulity, then he released a strangled laugh. "Horny, you say? First o' all, ma darlin', you've never been tha' easy in the lovin' department. Secondly, ma . . . sweet . . . fire, tis *ma* bed I'm bein' denied."

"Fine. I'll move into the nursery."

Beth attempted to push past him, but his anger now matched her own. Roughly, he gripped her upper arms and yanked her against him, and kissed her punishingly, determined to weaken her determination to resist him. For his trouble, she sank her teeth into his lower lip. He wailed, released her and jumped back. He dabbed at the bleeding wound with the fingers of his right hand, then stared at the blood-smeared digits as if on the verge of passing out.

"Don't you *ever* handle me like that again, Lachlan Baird!"

Beth tore out of the room, into the hall and toward the stairs. She slowed her flight as she descended, allowing for her blurred vision, benefit of the tears she couldn't hold back.

"We're no' through," growled a voice behind her.

Her heart slammed against her chest wall. Lachlan was following her, intending to pursue the argument to what end, she didn't know. There was nothing left to be said between them. He could kiss her, hold her, spout off his words of love until he was blue in the face, and none of it would change the fact that he cared more about his sorry carcass than he did for the twins or her. She was better emotionally equipped to handle her future without him. Without trust, love didn't have a foundation.

She burst into the dining room, hoping with the others

present, Lachlan would crawl back to the carriage house and leave her alone. Startled expressions swam in front of her. Roan and Laura. Winston and Deliah. Agnes. Alby was sitting at the table, bent over a coloring book, an orange crayon poised above one of the pages.

"Beth, what's wrong?" asked Agnes.

"Damn you, Beth—"

Lachlan came to an abrupt halt behind Beth when he saw the others in the room. His chest heaved on a sigh of vexation, and he was about to offer an apology when his gaze fell on the bundles held in Agnes and Winston's arms. Roaring filled his ears. His vision blurred. His heart dropped into his stomach, then shot up and lodged in his throat.

Laura screamed. The unexpectedness and shrillness of it shocked everyone. The babies began to wail, while the adults watched in perplexity as Laura sprang atop the seat of the chair at the head of the table.

"A rat!" she squealed hysterically, pointing to the ornate sideboard. "A *huge* rat!"

Roan and Winston sprang into action, Roan removing his left shoe from his foot, and Winston passing Beth her son, then snatching one of the candelabrums from the table. The white candles spilled from their sterling silver beds as the men headed for the sideboard.

"Stop!" Deliah shouted.

Both men turned questioning looks on her.

While Beth and Agnes huddled together with the babies near the fireplace, Lachlan stayed in front of the door. Alby remained on his knees on one of the chairs, and Laura, pale and jumping from foot to foot on the seat, hugged herself.

Only Deliah seemed in command of her senses. "Shame on ye both," she scolded, her vibrant blue eyes raking the men over. "The wee craiture canna hurt ye!"

She dropped to her haunches and made a sound that resembled that of a mouse. After a moment, a small gray critter shot from beneath the sideboard and beelined in her direction. It jumped onto her extended palm and quivering in fear, twitched its tiny nose in the air.

Deliah stood and placed the side of her upturned palm to her breast, her gaze searching the others who were watching her as though she were something alien. The babies had quieted. Deliah tenderly stroked the back of the mouse's head and back until it, too, settled comfortably on her hand.

"Tis too cold ou' there for this poor craiture," she said, her demeanor challenging anyone to defy her wishes regarding the mouse. "We must give it shelter till winter passes."

"It's a r-rat," Laura stammered.

"Tis a verra wee mouse," said Deliah. "A verra *young* wee mouse."

"How . . ." Winston closed half the distance between himself and Deliah. ". . . did you get it to go to you like tha'?"

"It knows I canna hurt it," she said with a hint of impatience. "Alby, have ye somethin' we could mak a home for the poor thing. For a time, at least."

"Yeah!" Alby said gleefully, and ran from the room.

"It's not a pet!" Laura cried, looking more horror-stricken than ever.

"Laura, look at it," Deliah insisted. She walked to the chair so Laura could see it better. "It willna bite ye. It be but a baby and all alone in this big house."

"That's comforting—it being alone, I mean," Laura muttered.

"Its parents be dead, and it doesna know wha' to do." Deliah made a cooing sound to the mouse, then lifted pleading eyes to Laura. "It be hungry and frightened. Have ye nae heart for it?"

Unsteadily, Laura climbed down from the chair and reluctantly stared at the nestled rodent atop Deliah's palm. Her features contorted in a grimace and she shrugged. "I guess it is kind of . . . cute. Not crazy about its tail, though."

Deliah smiled. "If ye name him, Laura, he'll seem less fearful to ye."

"Name him?' Laura asked blankly.

"Aye."

Laura offered a genuine grimace of disgust. "Name a rodent?"

"Havena ye ever had a pet?" Deliah asked her.

Laura nodded. "When I was a little girl. A cat."

"Weel?"

"Okay, okay." Laura gulped and warily eyed the mouse. Then a semblance of a grin lessened the strain in her features. "He is kind of cute, isn't he? I like the way his nose wiggles." She glanced at Roan. "Any suggestions?"

With a dubious arching of his eyebrows, Roan stepped next to Laura and regarded the mouse. "How abou' . . . Spot? We could pretend he's the family dog. But I don't expect he'll fetch the newspaper for us."

Laura playfully elbowed him in the midriff and Roan laughed.

"Wiggles," she said finally. She straightened her shoulders as if proud to have named something that moments ago had filled her with terror. "Wiggles. It's cute and wiggly."

Deliah held the mouse up closer to her face. "Wha' say ye, Wiggles?" Then she laughed and nodded to Laura. "Tis a fine name for him, it is."

"You've all gone daft," Lachlan grumbled by the doorway.

Deliah stiffened as her gaze cut to Lachlan. "This be

Agnes' last few hours wi' us. I willna have ye spoil them for any o' us.''

Lachlan scowled at Beth, who glared at him from Agnes' side. Agnes on the other hand, was looking at him with motherly compassion.

"Lannie," she said, stepping toward him, his daughter in her arms. "I would like you to be here for ma passin'."

Lachlan ran his tongue over the smarting wound on the inside of his lower lip, then shook his head. He could feel hot tears pressing behind his eyes as his gaze repeatedly moved between Agnes' face and the cherubic profile of his daughter. Brown curls were visible beneath her pink bonnet. He wanted to have a closer look at his children. Wanted to hold them. But something dark and suffocating swirled around his insides, terrifying him, creating an emotional wall between him and the people he loved in the room.

"Lannie?" Agnes took another step in his direction. "I didna mean wha' I said."

"Aye, Aggie," he choked, backing through the doorway. "I'll miss you, you auld corbie."

"Don't go," Beth choked. "Lachlan, please."

Lachlan met her pleading gaze and stiltedly shook his head. "I canna do this. Fegs, Beth, I canna face ma mortality yet!"

He ran down the hall in the direction of the front doors, leaving Beth staring bleakly after him, her face damp with tears.

Chapter Eleven

During the celebration, laughter companioned Agnes' favorite stories of her life. Her accounts of her childhood with eight siblings in Edinburgh, and her single motherhood experiences raising her son, held the others a captive audience. All but Lachlan was present. Even Wiggles attended, although he remained in a small birdcage Kevin had found in the attic, which was now perched on the sideboard. He feasted on bread and cheese, occasionally dipping into the tiny bowl of water that had been given him.

As dusk came and went, the mood of everyone around the dining room table grew progressively more somber. The boys were uncharacteristically quiet, now and then casting Agnes woeful glances. Laura remained tearful during most of the gathering. A wistful yet sad expression seemed a permanent fixture on Roan's rugged face. Beth held her son and was often lost in thought while studying his face—a face she could already see Lachlan's once-cherished visage in. Dark hair and eyebrows, dark eyes, chiseled lips and cleft chin, all like his father. Her daughter looked more like Beth's mother. Pert nose and blue eyes, with dark brown hair, curly like Beth's.

Winston, although enjoying Agnes' stories, found himself, most of the time, watching Deliah from the corner of his eye. Before and since the cakes and snow cone treats, she held Beth and Lachlan's daughter. Not once had she looked at him. She acted as if he wasn't in the room, or that his being there didn't faze her in the least. He wasn't sure which irked him more. And he wasn't sure how he felt about the fact that, being a woman with no navel, her obvious love of babies bore an unmistakable maternal inclination.

Deliah glanced up at him as if divining his thoughts. He looked away and felt heat surge into his face. If he started thinking too much about her or dwelled too much on the maddening perplexities of her physical abnormality. . . . How could he not? How many times had he racked his brain trying to recall other discrepancies she might have? No others came to mind, but he wasn't convinced that she wasn't hiding something more from him. Something other than her origin.

"Tis time," Agnes announced.

A hush fell over the room. Winston's gaze crept to Deliah. He didn't need to be psychic to pick up on her sorrow. Despite her outward bravado, her eyes betrayed the depths of her despair. At that moment, he couldn't deny his love for her. He was determined to keep its existence to himself, but he could no longer deny it within the confines of his mind. Watching her and not caring that she was aware of his transgression, he marveled at her ability to appear so ethereal and innocent, especially in light of her fevered lovemaking the previous night.

No navel.

The thought brought a frown to his smooth brow. Animal, vegetable, mineral? Was her packaging an illusion?

Agnes rose to her feet. Winston sat back in his chair and observed the farewells with the same detachment he used when on the job. The boys collectively hugged her when she crouched and opened her arms to them. Winston absorbed wafting segments of their sadness. It was impossible not to take in some, but he decided to brace himself against too much of an influx. He liked and admired Agnes Ingliss, but he didn't know her well enough to show an outward display of emotion—contrived as it would have to be. And it wouldn't do if he absorbed too much of the others' morbidity and burst into tears like a silly old goose.

Laura was next. Sniffling but making a valiant effort to keep a firm rein on her emotions, she waited for the boys to group a few feet away, then put her arms around Agnes' thin shoulders. During the exchange, through which Laura broke into sobs while listing all the reasons Agnes shouldn't leave, Roan slowly rose to his feet. One merely looking at him would have noticed nothing more than a calm demeanor with a tad of sorrow visible in his eyes. But Winston could see beyond the veneer. See deeply into the man's soul, and it disturbed him to trespass into that vast territory. He hadn't intended to scan his host, but it had come about as naturally as a breath.

Agnes' pending separation from her friends and living family, was a festering sore within Roan's emotional center. He'd lost his wife and young son to a fire. His parents and younger sister had left him to seek their fortune in the United States, and they *had* from what little Winston had learned from Roan. Roan was a man who expected little from life, and even less from relationships. Agnes had been his family lifeline since he was eleven years old, and now she, too, was leaving. Winston detected panic in Roan. Panic and doubt regarding his ability to measure up to family life without her guidance. This surprised Winston. Of all the men he'd known, including Lachlan Baird, he admired Roan the most. Unlike most men, Roan was outgoing and dirt honest, but inside, he was complex. Scanning Roan was equivalent to riding a roller coaster in the dark. Motion in the fast lane with no end in sight. He had no goals beyond securing Laura and the boys' futures, and no preconceived notions as to what the world owed him. Roan was the best mankind had to offer. A man of honor. A man of devotion. A man of heart to even a stranger such as Winton had been.

Winston glanced away when Roan embraced Aggie. The emotions in the room were closing in around him and he didn't want to react to their infusion in his psychic matrix. He felt a little queasy all of a sudden. Lightheaded. He forced breaths through his nostrils while he pinched his lips into a fine line. His vision went hazy. Dimly, he was aware of Deliah staring at him. He thought he saw something floating through the air, then realized something was heading for his brow. It was a bright blue fiber worming toward him. As it got closer, he felt gentle waves of psychic energy emanate from it. His eyes crossed as he tried to watch it pass through his forehead. When the last of it vanished from his sight, he experienced a wash of heat. His queasiness and lightheadedness disappeared. It was as if he'd gotten a pure shot of adrenaline. His blood sang through his veins and he gratefully offered Deliah a lopsided grin.

Why? he mused, puzzled by her gift.

Because ye were abou' to succumb, she replied nonchalantly, stunning him with the clarity of her telepathic projection.

He stared into eyes as blue as the Mediterranean. Eyes which bespoke of timeless knowledge and fathomless secrets. He swallowed hard and straightened in his seat. The air stirred about him and he looked away from Deliah to find Agnes standing to his right. Her lined face was soft and maternal, her eyes glittering with hope, excitement, and expectation. She was eager to begin her journey.

Feeling awkward, Winston rose to his feet. At first he could only stare down into her wizened features. The last person he'd hugged who hadn't been or was soon to become his lover, had been his grandmother. He could not recall his parents ever touching him, and he hadn't been allowed to embrace them. And for the first time in his life, that cold wall they'd created between themselves and him, angered him. He resented the way they had physically and emotionally ostracized him. He resented having become only a portion of the man he should have been. An emotionally *whole* man, not just a man only capable of living through the emotions of others.

"I've only known you a short time, Master Winston, but I do know this abou' you," Agnes began in a soft tone. "You're a kind mon wi' a big heart, and wha' you do in the name o' justice is na wee wonder." Smiling faintly, she rested a wrinkled hand over his heart. "But life *is* short, young mon, and withou' love, tis damn lonely. So I tell you this, and you'll pay me heed because I've lived a verra long life, and I've learned a lesson or two to pass on.

"Open your eyes afore you get too lost in the darkness. Accept wha' your heart tells you is true, and follow your heart wherever its path leads you."

She stood on tiptoe and planted cool lips to his cheek in a kiss. Settling back on the heels of her flat, navy shoes, she broadened her smile. "You tak care o' ma Deliah. She's a precious resource oor world is sadly losin'. Promise me, Master Winston. I canna leave her fate to the outsiders. Promise me you'll tak good care o' her."

Her entreaty had speared him with panic, yet he heard himself say, "I will. You have ma promise."

Agnes walked around to Beth, whose head was bent over

her sleeping son in her arms. Winston felt his chest grow tight. He could hear Beth softly weeping and it rocked him. Agnes stroked the back of Beth's head, her hand trembling and her chin quivering.

"I will miss you, child," said Agnes, emotion nearly strangling her words. "If I could have had a daughter—"

Beth shot to her feet. Angling the infant to prevent it from getting scrunched between their bodies, she threw her left arm around Agnes and clung dearly to her. Now, Beth's crying came in great sobs, seeming to echo in the room. Kahl leading the way, the boys ran to the parlor, and from there, to the hall and staircase. Roan sat in one of the chairs as if his legs could no longer support him. Laura seated herself on his lap and, also weeping, laid her cheek atop his left shoulder.

"Dammit, Aggie, it hurts to let you go!" Beth wept bitterly.

Agnes pulled back and tenderly ran the backs of her fingers down Beth's wet cheeks. "Ooh, I know, Beth. If I wasna so sure I was doin' the right thing. . . ."

"No. Forgive me, Aggie," said Beth tremulously. "You have every right to go to your son. I remember seeing him, now. They're only fragments of memory, but I *do* remember seeing him."

"One day, we'll be thegither again." Agnes bobbed her head. "Aye, we'll all be thegither. Meanwhile, you and Lannie—weel, you tamed tha' deil once." She laughed, then drew in a pseudo breath and glanced at Deliah. "I feel the *Light* openin'."

Deliah nodded and stood. Walking around the table, she passed the infant she carried to Laura, then stepped back. Her face pale and taut, her eyes dull, she said, "I must ask ye all to leave. Tis no' ma place to let ye witness the *Light.*"

Roan was about to protest when he read the plea in

Agnes' eyes to do as Deliah instructed. One by one, they filed out of the room, Beth lagging behind Winston. When there was only Deliah and Agnes left, Deliah numbly unfastened the back of her dress and let it fall to the floor. She stepped clear of the material, then initiated her transformation.

Agnes watched in awe as the young woman became a vision of wonder. Deliah began her clan's dance of passage, and soon a white effulgence came through the ceiling and encompassed Agnes.

The dance continued until the *Light* had vanished, taking with it the soul, the spirit, of a woman who had brought her own kind of magic to Baird House.

Not even death had been as cold as was this night. Cloaked in two wool, full-size blankets, sitting atop his grave with his back braced against the headstone bearing his name, Lachlan stared with devastation into the dark gray sky. It was no longer snowing, but the temperature had to be well below freezing. Still, it didn't compare to the arctic cold residing where his heart should be.

He'd glimpsed a flicker of light shoot down from the sky and pierce the house. He knew what it was. While he had sat out here, freezing his ass clear to his tailbone, struggling with indecision, Heaven had decided for him. Now there was no chance to say a proper good bye to Aggie. No chance to tell her how much she'd come to mean to him. He'd let the opportunity slip away because of his asinine inability to come to grips with himself. *What* was wrong with him? How could he fear fatherhood? A new beginning with Beth? *Life?*

With a garbled cry of raw anguish, he buried his face in his hands.

"Aggie! Aggie, forgive me!"

He wept for some time to come. Wept until his body could no longer bear the cold, nor his conscience bear his ability to think.

Lachlan staggered toward the house, thoughts of his store of Scotch giving him the stamina to go on.

10:00 P.M.

Winston couldn't sleep and he couldn't stand the silence in the house. He was still in the clothes he'd worn earlier, but had put on a bathrobe over them and haphazardly knotted the tie at his waist. Staring bleakly into the night, he stood on the tower with his forearms braced on a high section of the crenellations. He wasn't looking at anything in particular. Rather, he sought the solitude and the cold to better clear his mind. He needed to analyze what was going on inside him. Grieving for Agnes Ingliss didn't make sense. He'd hardly known her. She'd *wanted* to pass over. What puzzled him the most was, he was relatively sure what he was feeling stemmed from himself, but that would mean he had an emotional core. Which was preposterous.

Sighing deeply, he looked off into the distance to his right. A few lights could be seen in some of the buildings in the town of Crossmichael. So, perhaps others were as restless as he. Why did he find that comforting? Loch Ken was barely visible, striking him as resembling a wide dark ribbon laid across the landscape. He tried to imagine how the lake would look on a spring or summer night, with moonlight dappling the water. Spring had arrived, but the weather mocked the official advent of the season. He promised himself he would do something completely out of character to celebrate the warming season when it arrived. Perhaps plant a tree. An oak tree.

A chill of awareness slued up his spine and he cut his

gaze to the grounds in front of him. In the distance was the oak tree near the main road. He sensed movement and it raised his psychic hackles. His nostrils flared. His eyes narrowed and his features pinched with tension. Soon, he spied a figure walking around the rhododendron hedge and approaching the house. From his position five stories high, she appeared tiny and but a silhouette against the stark whiteness of the ground. But he knew it was Deliah.

Communin' wi' nature, no doubt, he thought bitterly.

Twenty or so yards from the house, she stopped and looked up at him. He couldn't make out the details of her face, but he didn't have to. He had long memorized her features and the set of each emotion they displayed.

Despite his resolve to purge her from his system, a familiar ache manifested behind his breast. His pulse quickened.

She entered the house and Winston straightened, his hands remaining on the cold stones of the higher level of the crenellations in front of him. If he stood on the roof hatch, she couldn't push it open and intrude on his temporary space. If he used his weight to bar her entry to the tower, he wouldn't have to look into her eyes and wonder how many seconds it would take before she weakened his resistance to touch her.

He turned abruptly and gasped when he saw her standing on the opposite side of the closed hatchway. His heart seemed to raise into his throat and cut off his oxygen. It wasn't possible she could have climbed to the tower in less than a minute. Not possible that she could have opened and closed the hatch without him hearing the faint creak of the hinges on the cold-stressed wood planks.

Other bizarre factors penetrated the haze gauzing his mind. The tower roof was bathed in silver-blue moonlight—only the tower roof. Gazing upward, he saw a portal in the cloud-clad sky, a portal through which he could see velvet darkness bejeweled with stars. And the air surrounding him was warm, caressing his exposed skin with the tenderness of a lover's touch. Fragrances awakened his smelling sense. Spring scents of flowers and trees and rich earth.

Clenching his teeth so hard pain shot up his jawline, he turned his back to her and stared blindly in the direction of the massive oak near the main road. Feverishly, he wondered, *How does she do this? Get inside ma head and create such illusions, I can't tell them from reality?*

Gulping down the psychological solidity wedged in his throat, he heard himself asking, "Wha' do you want?"

"Companionship."

Her dulcet tone tingled in his ears, and he resented her for having such power over him.

"I came up here to be alone," he said, his vexation heightening.

"Aye, *alone* be wha' ye do best."

Although her words were a jab, her tone held no animosity, which was another facet of her that irked him. She had the maddening ability to remain calm when his insides were afire. An occasional glower or a chiding seemed to be the extent of her temper. That wasn't normal. Hell, when he was in the mood for an argument, he wanted a *fair* return. Word for word. Anger for anger. Blow for blow if it came to it, although he couldn't imagine ever raising a hand to a woman or child. He wasn't in the mood to deal with passivity or sweetness. Shouting might purge the tension viciously knotting his insides.

"Up to your jaunts again?" he asked sarcastically, determined to bait her into either an argument, or leaving him alone.

"Nae. I was up here earlier and thought I saw the glow o' a faery ring down by the oak. Alas, twas only ma saddened heart havin' a wee bit o' fun wi' me."

Turning his head, he cast her a petulant glare. "A faery ring? I suppose you believe in Santa, too?"

"I believe in all things good and natural. Unlike *ye*, Winston Ian Connery."

Ah, he thought, *she is lookin' for a fight. Whenever she uses ma whole name, wha' little temper she has is near the surface. Fine, lass. I'm game.*

But he realized he had stared at her too long, for the moonlight served to enhance her loveliness, and the sight of her pierced him to his soul. Her eyes were like fiery sapphires in a sea of porcelain skin. Dark, pouty lips slightly parted in what he construed to be an open invitation to be kissed. Button nose and soft dimples in her cheeks. The graceful lines of her throat swept into proudly held shoulders. A full-length dark blue robe was tied at her waist, the Vee in the front revealing a small portion of her nightgown and just enough of the swell of her breasts to make his blood sing with need. As usual, her hair was unbound, the glossy strands reflecting the moonlight in such a way, he could almost believe the light shone from within her.

Turning his head, he lowered his chin to his chest and closed his eyes. This was not going as he'd hoped. She was beating him without a fight. Getting inside him without effort and winning the battle before it had really begun.

He realized she was standing next to him when she said, "We should be comfortin' each ither, no' tryin' to compound oor woes."

Lifting his head, he looked askance at her profile. She was staring off into the distance, her chin lifted as if she were braced for whatever he could verbally toss her way.

"'Tis empty here withou' Aggie," she said on a sigh. "So long be she a part o' this house, I canna imagine never hearin' her voice again."

"She's where she should be," he said dismissively.

After a moment, Deliah turned and rested her right forearm on the tower wall. "Is this how ye manage no' to feel pain, Winston? Pretend nocht bothers ye?"

"I believe I told you I wanted to be alone." He looked into her eyes, his own hard and unyielding. "Shall I leave, or will you?"

She studied his face for a time, her expression unreadable.

"Ye enjoy bein' cruel, dinna ye? It must be comfortin' to know ye have the power to hurt ithers wi' a word, a glance. Does it mak ye feel protected, Winston? Does hidin' behind your mental walls help ye to ignore the tragedies and joys o' life? I dinna think so."

Turning and placing his left forearm atop the wall, he scowled at her. "Little Miss Saint, are we?"

"No' *ye*," she chuckled without mirth. "There be nocht saintly abou' ye, Winston Ian Connery. And I wouldna be testin' the waters for a fight, if I were ye. Ye be ou' o' your element wi' me."

His black eyebrows arched in a challenge. A warm breeze tousled his hair and his outgrown bangs fell across his face. Swiping them aside, he countered, "Is tha' so?"

She nodded.

"Deliah, may your delusions comfort you."

A hint of a smile glimmered in her eyes. "When ye be in a snit, your Scottish tongue awakens. It pleases ma ears."

"Oh, I aim to please," he said, his tone heavily laced with sarcasm. He continued, now affecting a thicker Scottish burr and some of her speech mannerisms. "Tell me, Deliah-lass, wha' be the *real* reason ye didna permit we sorry mortals the privilege o' seein' the *Light*? Be it ye have mair to hide than even *ma* futile imagination can conjure up?"

"Ye are mockin' me," she said with a sigh.

"Ye be bloody right, lass. Short o' conkin' ye on the head, wha' will it tak to get ye to leave me alone?"

"Truth, spoken from your heart."

Her softly spoken words hung in the air like a rain cloud about to burst. Winston turned sideways to her, his jawline taut, short gusts of air channeling through his nostrils.

"Ye be so perplexin'," she said in a tone of resignation. "I dinna grasp hostility. Ma clan knew nocht o' war. We dinna raise oor voices or oor hands to one anither. And tis no' oor way to hold a grudge. Aye, we too often disagreed amongst oorselves. And we were no' guiltless o' an unkind word now and then, but we judged no' the differences in ithers."

Sighing deeply, she dreamily stared off into space. "Ma brither was ma joy back then. No' a mair handsome lad have I seen. *Och,* and so charmin', he was. Ma sisters and I thought we blessed to have been given a brither so fair o' face. He could melt mornin' dew wi' a glance."

She swallowed convulsively, then went on, "His charm was his downfall, though. And ma clans'. Ma kingdom's.

"I keep wonderin', Winston, how it all came to end as it did. How could ma brither have forgotten oor ways? I had often heard ma parents talk o' the changes in him since his first meetin' wi' Lady Lindsay, and how her husband's wrath would one day touch us all. I was no' concerned wi' anythin' but ma brither's happiness. He was different than maist o' us. Different in how he viewed life, and wha' he wanted for his future.

"Once, he returned from Lady Lindsay's bed in such a snit, he hardly seemed like ma brither atall. His hands were clenched and when I asked him wha' was wrong, he shook one o' them at me. I'd never seen fury as I saw in his eyes tha' night. I've never understood wha' could have induced him to feel such anger tha' he would want to vent it on someone else." She sighed deeply, wistfully. "At least I didna understand till meetin' ye."

Winston jerked in surprise and released a terse laugh. Her gaze crept around to pensively regard him.

"So . . . it amuses ye to rile me, does it? Would I be mair o' a womon if I slapped ye in the face? Would such an act mak me mair *human* in your eyes?"

Scowling, he admitted, "No."

"Then why provoke me?"

"I don't know."

Nodding, she gazed off in the direction of the oak again. "Ye will never accept no' knowin', will ye?"

"Wha' *exactly* are you referrin' to?"

"Ye know *exactly* wha'," she said peevishly, casting him a harried look.

"You spoke o' parents," he said, his gaze dropping to the vicinity of her midriff. "Were you hatched?"

Flabbergasted by the question, she drew back, her eyes wide in disbelief. "Hatched? *Hatched?*" She shimmied and released a groan of frustration. "Ye . . . ye are beyond provokin' me!"

"Am I?" he asked with a wry grin.

"Ye have nae concept o' nature or magic, do ye?" she sputtered, her beautiful eyes snapping, her shoulders held tautly back. "Ye only accept wha' ye deem *normal*, but I be mair *normal* than the likes o' *ye!*"

"I have a belly button," he said airily. "An inny."

"Inny, sminny! Ye have an *inny* brain, too, but I wouldna be braggin' if I were ye!"

"Explain an inny brain." Although he said this with humor, his eyes were narrowed on her.

"Inny bein' *wee* and closed off!"

He nodded obligingly.

"When we clans are blessed wi' wee ones, tis from the purest love," she huffed, her chin angled up in defiance.

"Nae, we dinna come from the womb o' one anither, but from the womb o' MoNae's magic. Spouses must be pure o' heart to be blessed wi' children, and *ma* parents' love produced seventeen!"

"There are *seventeen* o' you?" He glanced heavenward. "That's so comfortin' to know."

When he looked at her, he was chagrined to see tears welling up in her eyes. He'd gone too far, this time, and he didn't know how to rectify the hurt emanating from her trembling form.

"Were seventeen. I be all that's left, so your dark soul can rest."

"Deliah—"

"Nae. Speak no' a lie and I'll respect ye in your prejudice." She swallowed and its sound echoed in his ears. "I mistakenly believed I was where I should be. Here. Wi' ye. Offerin' to ye wha' I could never offer to nae ither. But I canna bring light into a soul as dark as yours. I canna fill the emptiness in ye, because ye *desire* tha' emptiness mair'n ye desire aught in life. Ye embrace it too fiercely, ma dour Scotsmon. I love ye nae less, but I canna bear mair scars on ma heart."

She held up her right hand, palm raised, level to his chin. Winston stared at the slender, graceful fingers and fought back an urge to encompass them within his own. He knew she didn't expect him to touch her. Why the hand was extended, though, he couldn't fathom.

"Ye believe I have cast a spell on ye."

He looked into the palm and for a split second saw a starburst of blue light flare up and vanish. Dizziness washed through him momentarily.

"I've nae spells over ye. I have nocht but love, but love is no' aneuch to win ye.

"I canna leave Baird land. To do so would deny me wha' little connection I have left wi' ma past. And withou' ma past, ma memories o' ma family and ma clan, I am nocht but a dead twig waitin' for the earth to reclaim me."

She slowly lowered the hand, her bleak expression making her eyes seem too large for her face.

"I told ye I was fond o' poetry. There were times I compelled Lachlan to sit in his library and read aloud. O' all I have heard, one in particular comes to mind. Tis called *A Promise*. I know no' its author, but tis why I was gladdened when I thought I saw a faery ring by the old oak this eve.

> *"He who tills the faeries' green*
> *Nae luck again shall have.*
> *An' he who spills the faeries' ring*
> *Betide him want and wae.*
> *But who goes by the faery ring*
> *Nae dule nor pine shall see;*
> *An' he who cleans the faery ring*
> *An easy daith shall dee.*

"I sought answers in the believin' o' a faery ring, but found none. Ye are like tha', too, Winston. But I canna believe in wha' canna be. I can only live and hope tha' ma remainin' years be no' too long, and tha' ma death be easy and ma return to the earth, fruitful.

"So in sayin' this, I promise ye I will no' approach ye. I will no' seek ye to ease ma loneliness. And I will no' seek ye to pleasure. Ye want freedom from the world? Ye have it, Winston. Wi' ma blessin', go on till your end, denyin' wha' could have been—*should* have been—atween us. Find ye your peace in solitude if ye can. Find ye love in wee, fleetin' draughts. I be done wi' ye, Winston. As done as be the hope I once held in ma heart for ye."

Here she was giving him the out he'd wanted from their relationship, but for some inexplicable reason, it frightened him. He suddenly felt as if he'd lost the most precious thing in his life. And had lost a vital part of himself. A little voice in his mind told him to reverse what had just transpired. There was still time to undo the wrongs. Still time to open himself up to the promise of a future filled with love and joy. But that voice wasn't strong enough or persistent enough to win over his instinctual fears, which mostly germinated from his belief that he didn't deserve love. That he didn't deserve *her*. No matter that she wasn't human. No matter how great the mysteries or how great the speculations of her origin. He loved her. The rightness of being with her should overpower everything else. But it didn't. After such a long, convoluted journey through life, he had but one small bridge left to cross, and he couldn't bring himself to take even one step in its direction.

Unable to say anything, he lifted the hatch and descended into darkness, closing the doorway behind him.

His intention had been to return to his room and meditate until he was able to sleep. Instead, he found himself descending to the first-floor landing with a hankering for a cup of coffee. He was about to turn right when an impression triggered his awareness. Mouth grimly set and his eyebrows drawn down in a scowl, he hastened to the library, where he found Lachlan sprawled out on the sofa. An empty bottle of Scotch was on its side on the floor, a short distance from Lachlan's limp hand. Winston picked up the bottle, shook his head while eyeing it, then placed it on one of the end tables. The fire in the hearth was burning low. After restoking it, he covered Lachlan with the knitted afghan draped on the back of the sofa, then headed out of the room.

Again an impression changed his direction. A vivid psychic print of Alby slipping out the front doors and into the night.

*   *   *

Alby tried to close his mouth to stop the cold air from burning his lungs, but he was desperate to scream, and couldn't. His little chubby legs worked against the snow to bring him around the side of the house, this journey taking far longer than when he had gone to the rear of the property.

He'd been afraid to go outside alone after spying the boogeyman from his bedroom window, but more afraid of his brothers' teasing if he hadn't checked to see if their traps had worked yet. Being the youngest wasn't easy. He didn't like being afraid all the time. Didn't like Kevin calling him a chicken, or Kahl always telling him he was such a baby. But if the boogeyman *had* been trapped, and Alby had found him, then his brothers would have to be proud of him. They would have to quit picking on him!

Alby stumbled and fell face first into a soft pile of snow. The coldness stung his skin, and he was so desperate to cry, he nearly couldn't get back onto his feet. Only a growl of a voice from behind him gave him the stamina to flee.

"You little *bastard!*"

His arms stiffly swinging at his sides, Alby ran. Ran in hobbled steps, his fear-filled eyes enormous and focused on nothingness. Terror gripped him, its hold squeezing his heart and cutting off his breath. He resembled a lost penguin scrambling for freedom.

Beyond his snow-crusted blinking eyelashes, he saw someone emerge from the front of the house. The distance seemed very great to him, and for a moment, he faltered in his run, believing the boogeyman had somehow beaten him to the front doors.

"Al—by!"

The shout took a moment to register in his brain. Winston. Winston was calling him. Calling him from the stoop.

The boogeyman was in big trouble now.

Although it felt to Alby that he was running like the wind, in reality, he was sluggishly making his way through the deep snow.

"Alby?" Then Winston was running toward him and sobs were hiccupping from Alby's raw throat. "Alby!"

A cry wrenched from him when he was unexpectedly jerked into the air, the front of his zipped jacket painfully tight against his throat. He was shaken in midair and his ears filled with the liquid-sounding rage of what he knew now was the boogeyman. The boogeyman had him by the back of the coat. Shaking him furiously. Cursing him in sounds that were more animal than people.

"You're dead, you bloody little brat!"

Alby didn't doubt the boogeyman's words. He couldn't move. He couldn't scream. He couldn't breathe.

As the night grew ever darker, he wondered if Lachlan and Beth had been this scared when they had died.

Chapter Twelve

Winston couldn't believe his eyes when he first spied Alby some fifty yards away. He'd nearly missed the snow-clad boy against the white backdrop. For a moment, Winston thought to let Alby make his way back to the house, then realized he was struggling to walk. Winston cast off in a semblance of a run, but stopped when he saw a large, dark shape emerge from seemingly out of nowhere and lift Alby off his feet. Outrage finally doused Winston's shock and he lit into another run. The packed snow was like ice beneath his hard-soled shoes, and maintaining his balance was precarious at best. He didn't consider who the adult might be who was roughly handling the boy, only knew that whoever it was, was going to learn a harsh lesson at the end of Winston's fist when he caught up with him. Granted, he was ticked off with the boy for venturing out-side alone at night, but he would never think about laying a hand on him, let alone shaking him like a rabid dog with a kitten locked in its jaws.

Thirty feet of reaching the man, a glint of steel flashed through the air. Winston came to a skidding stop, his hands held out at his sides, his face frozen in a mask of stark terror. At first he could only focus on the long serrated blade jutting past a black handle gripped in a black gloved hand. The deadly point was leveled at Winston, while the man's other hand held Alby out to one side as if the boy were featherlight. Then Winston's gaze zoomed in on pale eyes, the malevolence in them accentuated by the black knit mask hiding the rest of his face. Reality slammed home in Winston's faltering mind.

The *Phantom.* Alive. Alive and threatening *Alby's* life.

Now Winston could see the boy straining to look at him, and the terrified expression on the boy's face nearly lost Winston what little control he had left.

"Leave him be," Winston demanded of the Phantom, cautiously closing some of the distance. "Put him down, or so help me, I'll kill you wi' ma bare hands!"

A smile of such evil gleamed in the Phantom's eyes, Winston thought for sure he had further endangered Alby's life. But then Alby was released. He fell to the ground in a small heap, where he remained motionless. Winston's gaze pinged from the boy to the Phantom as he repeatedly clenched his hands at his sides.

"I've thought abou' our first meetin'," said the Phantom, his words surprisingly clear despite the knitted wool across his mouth. "The great Detective Connery." He laughed. "The soon to be *late* great, wouldn't you say?"

The Cockney accent was as chilling to Winston as the night air. "It seems your death was grossly exaggerated."

The Phantom shrugged. "You make it so easy," he chuckled. "Tell me, you arrogant pup, do you bleed as bloody red as *normal* people?"

Winston nibbled on the inside of his lower lip and brazened two more steps in the other man's direction. "Redder than you."

"Tha' sounds like a challenge."

"Aye. Mon to mon. You and me. Step away from the boy. There's no need to risk hurtin' him."

The Phantom glanced down at Alby, who was groggily sitting up, then narrowed his eyes on Winston. "I guess it would really tear you up to see the little bastard bleed to death before dyin' yourself, wouldn't it?"

Rage heated Winston's blood. "No' even you are *tha'* sick."

"Oh, I am. I *am*," he said gleefully.

A wail ejected from the Phantom's throat when Alby's teeth sank into the calf of his leg. Instinctively, he kicked out, sending the boy tumbling away, then readied his six-inch blade to receive the man charging at him.

Not since her escape from the root in the cellar, had Deliah felt so cold. Even if she were standing on the tower in the midst of a summer's heat, she would feel as if her blood had turned to rivers of ice. She had spoken of Winston's emptiness, when her own was far worse to fill. She'd once known the love and security of family and clan. Nevermore. Without Winston, her dreams were as adrift as a dried leaf in the wind.

Suddenly she felt more tired than she believed possible. Her chest was heavy with sorrow, her heart a hollow ache.

"I so love ye," she said tearfully into the night.

She started to push away from the wall when she heard Winston's voice call out for Alby. A weary smile touched her lips. The boys were always into or doing something they shouldn't. She had checked in on them before going to the oak. Kevin and Kahl were fast asleep, but Alby was wide-eyed lying atop his bed and, when she asked if he needed company, he refused and said he wanted to think.

Think. What could a three-year-old have to think about that would prompt such a frown on his brow?

A stranger's outcry dashed her reverie and she scanned the front yard to find its cause. The rooflines blocked most of her view, but then she saw two adults struggling on the ground, and a much smaller figure crawling away from them.

Winston?

Another cry was heard, but this one was unmistakably Winston's, and the anguish it carried in the night, alarmed her.

With a swiftness born of instinct, she untied the robe and let it fall to the floor, then pulled down the elastic edging on the back of her nightgown, nearly to her waist. She was first conscious of the buds forming on her back, then of intense, almost searing tingling as the buds opened and her wings unfurled. When they were full and she had flexed them to test their flight-worthiness, she leaped atop the crenellations and cast off.

Air currents helped her to soar downward. She saw the two men break apart. One lashed out with a long-bladed knife and the other fell back clutching his chest. Then the first figure, who was dressed entirely in black, lunged atop the other—Winston, she realized with terrifying clarity.

With the agility and speed of an eagle, she flew off toward the oak by the main road, where she quickly gathered twigs she broke off from one of the laden branches. She sliced through the air back toward the men, and hovered but a moment to analyze the situation.

Winston had just bucked his assailant off him and was attempting to scramble away, crabbing meager inches on his feet and hands. The assailant stood. Moonlight glinted off the polished blade, which he held raised but downward in a threatening manner. Alby scurried to Winston's side, intermittently weeping and shouting at the boogeyman to leave them alone.

For what she planned to do, Deliah needed more space between man and boy, and the stranger. She swooped downward, cutting a path close to the man in black. He cried out in surprise, then lashed out with the knife, missing her right wing by a harrowing margin. Again she dive-bombed him. She caught him on the chest with her bare heels, sending him reeling backward for several feet before he fell on his butt, cursing and snarling threats.

Hovering mere inches above the ground, she blew on the twigs clutched in her hands. Blue mist spilled past her lips and sprinkled the twigs. Then she tossed them on the ground midway between the stranger who was getting to his feet, and her self-appointed charges on the ground behind her.

The instant the twigs hit the ground, countless branches rose from the slender segments. They rapidly entwined as they grew upward and outward, forming an eight-foot-wide, seven-foot-high wall, cutting off the stranger's access.

For several moments, he attempted to breach the barrier, slashing the branches with his knife and gurgling with rage at the futility of his actions. When he finally ran off beyond the carriage house, Deliah's thundering heart began to slow. She lowered her feet to the ground and turned.

The sight which greeted her nearly gave her flight, but she refused to hide anymore.

Alby's eyes were wide with awe as he peered up at her from Winston's side. Winston's expression, on the other hand, pained her. There was also awe in the depths of his eyes, but also horror and disgust etched into his face. As much as she had tried to imagine his reaction to her true form, this was worse than her grimmest musings.

"Are ye hurt, Alby?"

He rapidly shook his head.

"Winston?"

"He's bleeding bad," Alby choked, turning his gaze to the red stain spreading across Winston's chest. "He got cut by the boogeyman."

Deliah knelt to Winston's left. He was on his back, teetering on the elbows propping him up. His eyes were wide, staring at her through rapidly blinking eyelids. His mouth was agape, his face gaunt and pale.

"Winston, can ye tell me how hurt ye be?"

His head barely moved in a negative response.

"Alby, are ye steady enough to run ahead to the house. I'll need help wi' Winston."

Gulping, Alby nodded. He regarded the seemingly vast distance to the front doors, then briefly eyed the wall of branches. "I'll get Uncle Roan," he said and, scrambling to his feet, waddled off toward the house.

Winston watched him for several moments, but returned his gaze to Deliah when she began to unbutton his wool shirt. He heard her gasp, then looked down to see that his chest was covered in blood.

"Ye will need a fast packin'," she said breathlessly, meeting his gaze. "Can ye walk?"

He nodded, but when he attempted to move, he fell completely on his back.

"Nae time to test your legs," she said, and slipped her arms beneath his back and behind his knees. "I canna walk ye to the house, but I can fly wi' ye."

Hoarse breaths came from Winston when she lifted him into her arms and cast off as if he didn't weigh a third of his actual weight. Freezing air buffeted them during the brief flight, and he found he had to watch the doors, not her, if he wanted to keep his stomach from spilling its contents.

She lit upon the stoop with the grace of a butterfly. "Can ye open the door?"

Numb, he reached out, turned the knob, then pushed open one side of the doors. Walking, she carried him through the greenhouse, the strain of her burden evident on her features. But strain couldn't diminish her determination to get him out of the cold. One of the inner doors was left open and she stepped through it and into the main hall.

"Put me down," he demanded shakily. "I'll be damned if I'm seen bein' carried like a child."

With a grunt, she eased him to his feet and helped him to prop himself against the wall.

"Sweet Jesus," murmured a voice behind her.

She turned to find Lachlan standing in the doorway of the library, a blank expression on his face, and a dull look in his bloodshot eyes.

"This Scotch has a maist promisin' kick," he muttered in a slur, then fell hard on his buttocks. He sat with his legs spread, his arms limp at his sides, and his head bobbing on a neck too weak to hold it up. A moment later, he keeled over backward and lay in unconscious oblivion.

Frowning in disapproval, Deliah tore her gaze from him and met Winston's scowling perusal.

"Aye, I be a fay. A faery. One disparagin' word from ye, Winston Ian Connery, and I'll turn ye into a nubby green toad!"

"Wha' the?"

The voice came from Roan, who had just stepped onto the first floor landing. His shock at seeing Deliah's wings outweighed Alby's story of a boogeyman wounding Winston.

Deliah bristled beneath what she felt was unwarranted fascination with her wings. Rearing back her shoulders, she haughtily demanded, "Carry him to his room. I must fetch the makings for a healin' patch."

Giving a brusque, disbelieving shake of his head, Roan maneuvered until he had Winston's left arm firmly across his broad shoulders.

"I can walk!" Winston shouted furiously, stopping his host from lifting him into his arms. "Wi' some help, I can walk!"

"Help you have," Roan murmured, his gaze transfixed on Deliah's face.

"I'll no' tak long," she said. Her wings pressing together at her back, she ran back into the night.

Twice Winston nearly passed out before finding himself reclining on the welcomed comfort of his mattress.

"Wha' happened?" Roan probed, drawing one of the blankets up to Winston's waist. "How did you get cut?"

"The Phantom. He was assaultin' Alby. Tried to stop him."

Roan leveled a look of horror on Winston. "You said he was dead."

"I was wrong." Winston groaned when pain radiated from his chest wound to all other parts of his body. "The bastard got away."

"Deliah?"

"Stopped him from finishin' his work on us," Winston wheezed. He wanted to probe the area of his chest he knew was lacerated, but he was afraid he would discover the wound was fatal. Instead, he went on, "You saw? You saw the wings on her back?"

"Aye, and I'll wager I've never see a mair peculiar sight in ma life."

"A faery," Winston murmured, his eyelids closing halfway as he resisted an urge to sleep. "I would have never guessed. Never in ma wildest fantasies thought such a thing could be possible. A faery. . . ."

Laura entered the room, her eyes sleep-laden and bloodshot. "What's going on?"

Beth dashed into the room, appearing fully awake, but alarmed. She joined Laura and Roan at the bedside and grimaced when she saw Winston's chest. "What happened?"

"Faeries," Winston murmured.

"You know?" Beth asked incredulously.

"What?" asked Laura, puzzled by the strange interaction.

"Deliah," said Roan softly. "She has wings."

"Right," Laura said wryly, then frowned when his serious expression remained. She glanced at Winston. "Did Deliah do this to you?"

"See! See! I told you so!" Alby blustered as he led his sleepy brothers into the room and to Winston's bed. Pointing all the while to Winston's chest, he added, "And the boogeyman whipped out a sword and slashed him *wide* open!"

"Alby," Winston groaned, trying to make light of his predicament. "It was a knife, no' a sword."

"It was *big* as a sword," Alby insisted.

Laura turned a bit green after sitting alongside Winston and inspecting the gaping wound. It was nearly three inches long and ran aslant the lower part of his right pectoral. "We need to get him to a hospital."

"I agree," said Roan, unable to take his gaze off the wound. "But the cars are iced in. I can run to the Lauders and hope to hell they have a phone."

"Run to the neighbors?" Beth asked incredulously. "Even cutting across the fields, which are buried in deep snow, will take forever."

"We need help!"

"I'll be fine," said Winston, then grimaced when he attempted to move. His skin had a gray pallor and his eyes were underscored with dark circles. "We've got to get to a phone and contact the local police. The Phantom won't go far. Durin' our struggle, I caught segments o' his thoughts. He's after Laura." Winston observed Laura's shocked look and gripped one of her hands. "We won't let him near you. I promise you, Laura, I'll take the bastard ou' if it's the last thing I do."

"No' in your condition." Roan clapped a hand on the back of his neck and sighed wearily. "It's too late to mak it to Shortby's and use his phone. You need a doctor and we need help wi' this Phantom. Damn me! I should have at least gotten a cellular phone."

"Don't," Beth said kindly, placing a hand on Roan's shoulder. "In this house, there is no such thing as being prepared." She glanced at the boys and managed a smile. "It's a little late for you three to be up, isn't it?"

"Nope," Kahl said, straining to see Winston's bloodied chest more closely. "We're wide awake now."

"It's time for—" Laura began, but gasped when something flew into the room and headed for the bed. Roan and Beth stepped back, startled and in awe of the four-inch wonder hovering at the left side of the bed. There was no mistaking it was a shrunken Deliah, only a Deliah with translucent wings fluttering at her back. She held something in her tiny hands, but it was too small for anyone to make out. With her head, she gestured for Roan and Beth and the boys to move back more. When they did, she dipped back her head and closed her eyes, as if going into a moment of intense concentration. Then, as she released a long breath, she grew before their eyes until she was again five-foot-six inches tall. The wings remained intact, opalescent shimmers of blue and green. A pale silver web-work of veins were now clearly defined, and pulsed with her heart rate.

"What a babe!" Kevin exclaimed appreciatively.

The adults ignored him, too fascinated by her appearance to be distracted. Deliah's hair, nightgown, face and arms, had smears of dirt and small clumps of snow.

"Twas difficult to reach one o' the roots," Deliah said as she sat alongside Winston. Her wings lightly fluttered, but she didn't appear to notice them. Nor did she seem aware of the wary look in Winston's eyes. Her concentration was focused on a gnarled root sitting atop her left palm. "The snow be verra deep by the oak." Now she looked into Winston's pale eyes and her features took on the bleak look of a woman disillusioned with life. "Swallow your disgust o' me," she rasped chidingly, her voice hollow, defensive. "Ye must focus on the magic for it to work. I canna do this alone."

Glancing at Beth, she mildly ordered, "We be in need of a wet, warm towel. While I summon the magic, I ask ye to clean around the wound."

"Forget it," Winston bit out.

Deliah eyed him impatiently. "I can conjure up vines to hold ye down. Dinna mock ma abilities, Winston. I be stressed and nervous as it is, and need ma wits abou' me to carry this through."

"You're not usin' magic on me!"

"Winston," Beth chided.

Deliah stiffly drew back her shoulders, her look daring him to further defy her. "Ye *would* mak a fine toad, ma friend. Now, do I proceed wi' the healin' or ventin' ma frustration in a mair imaginative manner?"

For a moment, Winston glared at her, then grumbled, "Get on wi' it."

Deliah shifted her gaze to the root. She placed her right hand atop the left, enclosing the root between her warming skin. In a low, singsong voice, she chanted:

"Root o' life, ma heart does hold,
Grant me the healin' o' ma clan's creed.
Root o' magic, ma heart does hold,
To help me undo anither's deed.
Root o' love and honor, ma heart does hold,
Tak from me ma healin' seed.
Root o' compassion, ma heart does hold,
From earth to palm to one in need."

Beth returned to Winston's side. With half an eye on the blue glow pulsing between Deliah's hands, she dabbed away the blood on his chest, now and then offering him an encouraging smile. He was tense and intermittently staring at Deliah's hands in something akin to horror and disgust. His hands remained balled at his sides and his breathing was labored. Perspiration beaded his ashen face although the room was chilly.

Deliah's eyes appeared glassy as they locked with his. He could see the sickly tension in his face reflected in her enigmatic orbs, and a shuddering breath spilled past his lips before he could suppress it. His gaze lowered to her hands. A blue glow was visible, seeming to emanate from her skin rather than the root. She rotated her hands, so the right one was now on the bottom. Her left hand moved to lap, while the other, the cupped palm of which now supported a blue claylike mass, moved toward his chest. Hot liquid shot up into his throat and he swallowed reflexly as his eyes widened on the bizarre poultice. It thrummed with the rhythm of a heart. He could hear its beat in his ears, its cadence matching the erratic drumming of his own heart.

As she dipped her hand over the wound—a motion he felt he was witnessing in slow motion—he tried not to let his burgeoning panic surface. Even as a child, he'd never believed in anything remotely fanciful. Santa Claus. The

Easter Bunny. Monsters hiding in closets or shadows. For as far back as he could remember, reality was nightmare enough, the stuff that kept him awake at night as a young boy, trembling beneath his bedcovers. The reality laid open in his mind since his birth was usually more fantastic than anything anyone's imagination could produce. He'd experienced abstract insanity from external psychic emissions. He'd experienced labor and birth. Death. Every level of physical and mental existence known to the human condition. At least he thought he had.

Her gaze eerily unwavering in its intense focus on his eyes, she lowered the mashed root to his wound. At first he felt only its coldness and its fibrous texture against his fevered flesh. He grimaced, then cast the fay a pleading glance. A hint of a smile played across her lips. Her right hand remained canopying the root. The glow remained, although it appeared to be gradually dimming.

She repeated the chant, her zephyrous voice mesmerizing, seeping into the darkest reaches of his mind and creating a dawn of tranquility to fill him. He felt himself relaxing. The mattress beneath him seemed like a cradling cloud.

Hot tingling seized his wound. He gasped and would have yanked away her hand and the mass, but his limbs were both weighted and buoyant, unwilling to move no matter how great his frantic need. Burning liquid seemed to pass through his opened flesh. He heard Beth cry, "It's hurting him! Deliah, stop!" But Deliah only stared at him in her trancelike state. He was wont to ask her to stop as well, but he couldn't bring himself to speak.

Moments later, the searing sensations waned to pleasant tingling. His wound itched and he squirmed and wished he could scratch the area to relieve the annoyance. He noticed the blue glow was barely visible. As it waned, the tingling waned, until no glow was seen, or sensation remained. With a deep breath he believed was her way of purging herself of the spell's grip, Deliah lifted her right hand. Gasps rang out from the others in the room. The air stirred with an unseen force. Winston gawked down at the smooth, unmarred flesh covering his chest. The root mash was gone, nothing at all remaining to verify it had existed. He was conscious of the mattress' solidity beneath him. Of the wholeness of his body. Of feeling physically energized and mentally nurtured.

"My God," Laura whispered, a hand lifting to her throat.

The fingertips of Deliah's right hand moved down Winston's chest. Delightful chills passed beneath her sensuous trail and he found himself breathless and sexually aroused. To hide the latter, he rolled onto his side and eased into a sitting position. Surprisingly, he wasn't lightheaded. He had no after-effects of the stabbing ordeal or the spell she'd woven over him.

"Are ye well again, Winston?" Deliah asked softly.

To his chagrin, even her voice triggered his libido. If not for the others, he knew without a doubt he would have Deliah, burying himself so deeply in her, they would be one inseparable entity. A fierce shudder passed through him. Clenching his teeth, he rose to his feet and sucked in a breath. By the time he faced the others, he managed a semblance of a smile and, to camouflage his discomfort with his straining erection, quipped, "All I need now is a nip o' Scotch, and I'll be as good as new."

"Scotch," Deliah said dispassionately, then rolled her eyes. To the others, she said over her shoulder, "He be a Scotsmon, true aneuch."

Lachlan moaned low and opened his eyelids to mere slits. Not only was his mouth painfully dry, but he was positive something had crawled onto his tongue and died.

A persistent ache hammered at his temples and between his eyes. To say he was fraught with aches would be an understatement. Dying hadn't made him feel this miserable.

Despite his body's scream to the contrary, he cranked himself into a sitting position and swung his booted feet to the floor. The room was softly lit in a reddish glow, and was so cold, the air nipped at his covered skin.

Getting up from the sofa like a man racked with arthritis, he crossed his arms and rubbed them in a futile attempt to elicit warmth through friction. Countless insects buzzed through the layers of gauze inside his skull, and his bloodshot eyes stung as he tried to focus on the doorway across from him. He was quite sure the portal was tilting this way then that, unwilling to admit he had drunk more than a safe measure of his beloved Scotch.

He released a long belch and grimaced when his taste buds were again assaulted by foulness.

He grumbled in Gaelic, then wheezed, "Beth'll mair'n whack me if she sees me like this. *Och!* Lannie, you fool, wha' have you done?"

Intermittently experiencing spasms of shivers, he ambled into the hall and headed in the direction of the kitchen. Strong black coffee and something solid in his stomach was his only hope of redeeming his misuse of his corporeal existence. He was cross that it had taken Scotch to get him to face the internal wars he'd been battling since his return. How *bloody* ridiculous it was not to praise the miracle, rather than wallow in shallow fears of his own making. He was a *father!* And proud as Braussaw he should be, but, alas, rebirth—he'd reasoned while steeping his insides with Scotch—had forsaken his brain.

He passed the staircase and was intending to go down the secondary hall to the kitchen when a slight clinking gave him pause. The door to the parlor was slightly ajar.

A thin strip of orange light was visible through the opening. Ordinarily, Lachlan would have ignored the moving about, thinking it was someone else in the household looking to satisfy a hunger pang or thirst. But goose bumps broke out on his skin, and a vivid red warning light was flashing in front of his mind's eye. *Intruder* echoed in his head.

Inexplicably acute of mind and sight, he eased open the door and peered into the room. He saw nothing unusual, then noticed the dining room door was also ajar. Soundlessly crossing the room, he pushed open this door and poked his head into the dining room. Another sound drew his attention to the sideboard against the wall to his left. Some twenty feet away, he saw a dark-clothed figure searching through the silverware drawers, a flashlight in the left hand.

Fierce outrage awakened in Lachlan's gut and swiftly spread throughout him. The gaslights in the room had been turned down, but he saw enough to verify someone was robbing him of his precious belongings.

Unhampered by the hangover, which moments ago had been nearly debilitating, he charged into the room. For an instant he was blinded by the glare of the flashlight which had swung around and was trained on his face. He surged forward, anger supplanting logic. The intruder released a grunt when Lachlan rammed him and they both toppled to the floor. The edge of the flashlight rim came home against the side of Lachlan's skull, prompting bursts of light to explode behind his eyelids. Undaunted, Lachlan's fists pummeled the struggling stranger. Grunts and cries rang out from both men.

The stranger managed to buck Lachlan off him and scrambled to his feet. He lit into a run for the door. Before he reached half the distance, Lachlan lifted and tossed something from the sideboard, striking the intruder so forcefully in the back, he pitched forward and struck the floor with the length of him. A shattering sound followed, then Lachlan's growled Gaelic curses.

Dimly, Lachlan was conscious of pounding somewhere in the house. Its echoes harshly reverberated through the walls, like a great deafening bell ringing out to forewarn him of impending danger. But his rage had but one focus.

As the intruder groggily attempted to get to his knees, Lachlan again tackled him. They rolled across the floor, fists sailing and curses abounding.

The mysterious pounding grew more frantic.

"Lachlan!"

The infamous ghost reborn ignored the feminine cry and took advantage of the stranger's momentary distraction when the lights in the room turned up. He drove his fist into the knit-covered face, connecting with the man's jawline. The covered head snapped back, the back of the man's skull cracking against the polished wood floor. Panting, Lachlan lowered his head and squeezed his eyes against the light smarting them. He ached worse than before, and his heart was pounding so hard, pain radiated through his chest.

Faraway voices fell on his ears. From his position astride the unconscious man, he stared at the masked features.

"Lachlan, be ye harmed?"

Releasing a pented breath, he turned and rolled to one side and sat on the floor, facing the general direction of the voice.

"Lachlan?"

"*Haud yer wheesht!*" he barked, clamping his hands over his ears. "A mon canna think around here!"

He'd squinted up to deal the woman a scolding look when the sight of her shocked him insensible. For a moment he could only stare at her, his dark eyes wide, his face ashen and taut. Then, "Sweet Jesus!" he squealed.

He saw her flinch back, her wings fluttering in a manner indicating distress.

"Deliah!" Winston shouted, running into the room. He paused but a moment to assess the others in the room, then dealt the woman a harried look that chilled Lachlan.

"We've company," he informed tightly. "Police at the front door. I suggest you—"

A scream rent the air.

Chapter Thirteen

"Retract your wings!" Winston ordered Deliah, then hopped forward before Lachlan could react and hauled the stranger to his feet. The man was gearing up to release another shrill scream, his horrified pale gaze riveted on Deliah as if she sported horns and glowing red eyes.

Raised voices approached with the sounds of multiple footfalls. Enraged himself, Winston clutched the stranger's collar, his fingers aching to curl around the man's throat and crush his windpipe. He didn't look behind him to see if Deliah had obeyed him. He couldn't look at Lachlan as the man shakily rose to his feet. He could do nothing more than stare into the pale gray eyes of the stranger he believed to be the Phantom.

"Sonofabitch," Winston growled, giving the man a sound shake.

His fevered brain noted drool escaping the man's thick, parted lips. He grimaced contemptuously and gave him another harsh jerk.

"Release him!" ordered a deep voice.

Winston clenched his teeth painfully as he fought against the vileness of his own need to end the man's life. Memories of the forty-seven victims stampeded his mind, calling up every gory detail of their suffering, and the victims' tortured last thoughts before dying. His hands encircled the man's thick neck and he pressed his thumbs against his windpipe. Still, the Phantom remained limp, his insane gaze locked on Deliah. Winston didn't realize he was quaking with rage, or that his arms were being seized by two uniformed men. Breathing laboriously through his flared nostrils, he applied more pressure.

Then a voice penetrated his murderous haze. "Winston, release him! He be done wi' his thievin'!"

Thieving . . . thieving . . . thieving . . . ?

The word echoed discordantly inside his head, disorienting him. He found himself jerked back and his left arm twisted behind him.

Then Lachlan demanded in Winston's defense, "Release him!"

·"As soon as I know wha' the bloody hell is goin' on here!" another stranger barked.

"She has wings!" the man in black cried, then laughed hysterically. "She has 'em hidden 'neath her nightdress! Check! Check and you'll see!"

"Weel," the second officer laughed without mirth, "if it isn't Robbie Donnely in the flesh." He reached out and pulled off the ski mask. A thick mass of steel gray hair tumbled free about the man's head and a gold ring in the left ear became visible. "Aye, Donnely, you slime. Had a busy night, tonight, did you?"

Winston shucked free of the hold on his arm and walked to where he saw a black sack lying on the floor by one of the chairs. Crouching, he spilled the contents onto the floor.

"Wha' have we here?" asked the officer who'd held Winston, his tone dryly humorous.

Silver and gold artifacts ranging from jewelry to figurines lay upon the floor. One piece didn't fit with the accumulation. It was a large serrated knife with smears of blood on the steel blade.

"Don't touch anythin'," ordered the officer, passing Winston a warning look. "We've been efter this bastard for months."

"This is a ruse," said Winston, standing and glaring at the intruder. "Earlier, he attempted to kill me."

"Tha' so?" the restraining officer murmured, also standing and eyeing Donnely.

"I found the friggin' thing!" Donnely wailed. "Ou' in the snow!"

The second officer who had manacled Donnely, frowned at his partner. "Should I call for backup? The car's a fair walk and the ground is so slick."

"We dinna have a phone," said Lachlan, pale now that his adrenaline had slowed.

"What's going on?" Beth burst into the room and looked horrified when her assessing gaze found Lachlan. Rushing to him, she tenderly touched his bruised face and bleeding lower lip. "What happened to you?" she asked, desperation lending her tone a raspy edge. Her gaze followed Lachlan's to the stranger, then returned to search Lachlan's face.

"I heard someone in here and found him goin' through the sideboard," Lachlan said, glaring at the stranger. Then his gaze drifted to something on the floor near the wall by the door. A pinched sound escaped him and, leaving Beth to stare at him in bewilderment, he stopped and retrieved some of the shattered crystal segments scattered on the floor. When he stood and faced the others, he held out some of them on a leveled palm. He looked like a man who had lost someone dear to his heart. A man devastated beyond endurance.

"Twas ma great-grandmither's cherished paperweight," he choked, an accusing, tear-brimmed glare targeting the man in black. "I didna realize wha' I was throwin' at you to stop your escape." Clenching the hand, the segments biting into his flesh, he shook it at the man. "Tis worth mair'n your sorry hide!"

"Calm down," demanded the first officer, a man older than his partner by a good decade. His cold-chapped cheeks were round, his blue eyes as crisp as the night air. "Sir, what's your name?" he asked while removing a pad and pen from an inside pocket of his coat.

"Lachlan Baird."

Winston felt a stab of panic and locked eyes with the laird, who also realized his mistake. Roan, standing by the fireplace, stepped forward and cast Winston and Lachlan a conspiratorial look, letting them know he, too, was aware of Lachlan's lack of foresight. However, it wasn't until the officer completed jotting down Lachlan's name, suspicion crept into his features. He leveled a dour look of impatience on Lachlan, then released a snort.

"Lachlan Baird, is it? Weel, tha' wouldn't be the name o' the infamous ghost who supposedly haunts this house now, is it?"

"Aye," said Lachlan, his shoulders squared defiantly.

"Are you a descendent?"

"Och, mon, I was murdered afore I had a family o' ma own!"

Lachlan's outburst brought upon the room an unnerving silence and stillness. Even Robbie Donnely was as frozen as a statue, his skin the color of sun-bleached bone.

Lachlan glanced at the deadpan expressions staring his way.

"Dammit, Lannie, wha' have you done?" Roan grumbled, raking his fingers through his hair.

"So," the older officer said, "you're the ghost, are you? Is tha' wha' you're sayin'?"

"I'm no' a ghost," Lachlan murmured. His opened his hand to reveal blood-coated segments of crystal. "Anymair. I'm back to stay."

The older officer bobbed his head humorously. "You're a fine-lookin' man for someone—wha'?—a hundred and fifty years auld or so. Have you been imbibin', sir?"

Lachlan gulped and guiltily met Beth's worried gaze. "Aye, sir, I have, but I'm sober aneuch."

Beth went to Lachlan's side, linking one arm through his in a protective manner. She tried to smile at the older officer, but her effort fell short. "He's been bruised and battered. Surely this questioning can wait."

The officer poised his pen above the pad and asked with mock civility, "You must be Beth Stables."

Deciding it prudent not to correct his use of her last name, she nodded, then widened her eyes in horrified regret.

Grumbling beneath his breath, the older officer lowered his hands and released a breath of annoyance. "You know, before I left ma darlin' wife this eve, I told her I had a queer feelin' in ma bones it was goin' to be a crazy night. Imagine ma surprise when I just begin ma shift and get a call tha' your neighbors, the Lauders, have been robbed, and the robber was seen headin' for Kist—beg your pardon—Baird house."

"Officer," Winston prompted, coming to stand in front of the man.

"Clare," he said dully, eyeing Winston impatiently. "Bruce Clare. And your name, sir?"

"Winston Connery. I was formerly wi' the Shields

Agency. I believe you and I met while I was in town last Christmas.''

Recognition gleamed in the man's eyes. "I remember now. You were efter the Phantom, if I'm no' mistaken."

Winston nodded and glanced at Robert Donnely. "Him."

"Him?" After a moment's shock, the officer laughed. "Much as I would love to collar the Phantom, Mr. Connery, this here *bloody* fool is na mair than a thief. And a bad thief at tha'. He's spent mair time in oor jail than in his own home. Easy enough to check the dates, but I can tell you he's na serial killer."

Winston's chest became tight. He didn't know if it stemmed from relief or disappointment. "He came at me wi' tha' knife," he said, pointing to where it lay amidst the stolen treasures.

"We'll fill ou' a report, Mr. Connery, tha' you can be sure. Is it true there's no phone here?"

Winston nodded in confirmation.

The older officer heaved a breath of resignation. "We couldn't get up the drive." He glanced at the thief and scowled. "Guess we'll just have to haul his royal highness here down to the road."

"You didn't search *that* one for her wings!" Donnely cried, jerking his head in Deliah's direction.

The older officer stepped around Winston and comically glanced over the young woman's graceful form. "You're lovely enough to be an angel, miss," he smiled, then cast Donnely a look of exasperation. "You must have really conked your head. Aiken, haul him ou' o' here and wait at the end o' the hall. I'll be wi' you, shortly. Donnely—" He gripped the man's left ear as he started past him, and gave it a painful tug. "—behave. I'm no' in the mood for histrionics. Understand?"

"She does have wings," Donnely said with a glower. "Huge wings like a butterfly!"

"The only butterflies in this room are in your mind," Bruce Clare said, then fell silent while his partner led Donnely into the hall. He waited until Donnely was out of earshot before speaking to the anxious group remaining in the room. "We have enough to hold him for trial, but I'll be expectin' a *detailed* report from each of you." He gathered the evidence into the sack and lifted it. "It'll be a while before your items are returned. You must be patient. We work as fast as we can."

"We appreciate your timeliness," said Winston.

"Nothin' timely abou' oor arrival, 'cept to spare Donnely's life, it seems." Bruce Clare released a weary chuff. "Where were you wounded, Mr. Connery? From what's on the knife—"

"He merely nicked ma shoulder," Winston said on a rushed breath, his right hand going up to cover the area hidden behind his borrowed blue wool jersey.

"Are you in need o' a doctor?"

"No . . . thank you. Deliah patched me up," he said lamely, knowing the officer could see the telltale flush heating his cheeks.

Stepping to one side, Officer Bruce Clare confronted the seemingly timid Deliah. "Are you Deliah?"

She nodded.

"Wha' is your last name, miss?"

She blankly looked to Winston, then met the officer's shrewd gaze and said, "I be just Deliah."

"One o' those fad things her parents went through," Roan piped up, grinning inanely, his face also flushed. "Na last name, tha' is."

Clare nodded as if not believing a word of what was being said. "Okay, folks. We'll-ah, rehash all this at anither time when you all are in better frames o' mind. Meanwhile, lock your doors and have a good night.''

No one moved or spoke until the officers and Donnely had left the house. Then it was Lachlan who broke through the silence, slapping his unwounded palm to his brow.

"Och! O' all the bloody stupidity! Wha' was I thinkin'?''

"Only the truth," Roan sighed miserably. "Damn me, but I didn't help matters, either, did I? This day has been a helluva experience.''

"I could have sworn he was the Phantom," Winston murmured, now sickened that he'd nearly strangled a somewhat innocent man. Thieving and murder were very different crimes. He recalled the conversation he'd had with the man outside, and disparagingly wondered if he hadn't imagined the interchange because it somehow didn't fit right in his mind now. People sometimes held mental conversations with themselves, then later believed someone else had spoken the ''other's'' words aloud. It had never happened to him before, though. And yet it was possible he'd charged at the man fully expecting just such a conversation to ensue. For four years, the Phantom had been a very real demon in Winston's mind.

Something nagged at his conscience, but its meaning was too nebulous for him to grasp. He felt drained and cloaked with self-loathing.

"Winston, are ye weel o' mind?" Deliah asked softly. "Ye be as white as a cloud.''

"I be nuts!" he spat, angry at himself yet mocking her speech mannerism. "I need a drink.''

"I'll second tha'," muttered Roan, and fell into step behind Winston as he headed toward the parlor door.

"Aye," said Lachlan. Brushing the crystal shards from his palm, he followed the men across the parlor and into the hall.

Pique heightened the color in Deliah's cheeks as she

looked at Beth, who was pale and staring at the doorway through a bleak, haunted expression.

"Beth, are ye feelin' jaggy?"

The woman's dark blue eyes swung to solemnly regard Deliah. A moment passed before she shook her head. "I think I'm just tired of men, Deliah. It must be nice to feel so damn detached from responsibility."

Saddened by Beth's sorrow, she placed a consoling hand on the woman's shoulder. "Twas wrong o' me to defend Lachlan to ye. There is nae excuse for his behavior. Nor the ithers."

"Welcome to the world of the male mentality," Beth sighed.

"Aye, they be prideful, but this is no' *their* world. Have ye ever heard o' a *faither* nature?"

Despite the heaviness of her heart, Beth chuckled. "No."

"And twill never be, I can promise ye."

Beth nodded, then said, "It's about time to feed the babies."

"Can I somehow help ye? Rock one while ye nurse the ither?" Deliah asked excitedly.

With a smile of appreciation, Beth shook her head. "I'll manage. I'd like to be alone with them. I hope you don't think I'm being too selfish."

"Nae. Were they mine, I'd be wantin' mair than a wee time alone wi' them. But if ye need me, I'll come."

Deliah stiffened reflexively when Beth's arms circled her neck. The hug was brief, but satisfying.

"Thank you. Oh, and Deliah?" A mischievous grin formed on Beth's mouth. "I personally love your wings. Only next time they're out, flutter them in Winston's face. He could use a *wee* nudge in the sense of humor department."

Deliah blushed. "Night, Beth."

"You, too."

Deliah walked Beth to the door to the hall then, for a time, leaned against the jamb, her thoughts adrift, her gaze staring into nothingness. It had been an unusually unusual day, and she couldn't shake the feeling it was going to be a long night. She could hear the men toasting one another, then the clinks of their glasses—a ritual she considered puzzling. But then most things humans regarded as customs, struck her to be silly rituals. Still, she wanted to be considered one of them. Had yearned for decade after decade after long decade to be among them. Talk their talk and walk their walk. Dress and eat and view the world from their perspectives.

It wasn't easy.

She returned to the dining room and resignedly gathered all the fragments of the crystal paperweight into her left palm. She passed her right hand over the shards, her face expressionless, her demeanor one of uncharacteristic detachment. A brief starbust of blue light detonated amidst the pieces, then magically the paperweight was again intact, its prisms capturing the warm glow of the gaslight fixtures on the walls. She returned the artifact to the sideboard. Her shoulders somewhat sagging, her spirit in a limbo of sadness she couldn't shake, she went into the secondary hall and entered the room she knew the men were in.

They were behind the counter, their expressions showing their vexation with her intrusion. Bracing herself against their foul moods, she closed the door behind her and crossed her arms against her chest like a schoolmarm on the warpath.

"Weel," she huffed with a defiant tilt of her chin, "you three be a sorry sight."

"Go away," Winston grumbled, then tipped his tumbler to his lips and finished off his Scotch. Smacking his lips, he held out the glass for Lachlan to refill, which the laird did with a tad too much eagerness, Deliah thought. "Fly away," Winston grinned, and winked at her before taking a hearty swig of his Scotch. He winced again, shook himself, then released a burp that made Deliah wince. To her chagrin, his drinking partners laughed.

"Wha' grand, strappin' men ye be," she said, her temper surfacing and lending an edge to her tone. "Brave. Trustworthy. Real *champs.*" Her right hand flitted to her mouth. Giggling in a way that suspiciously rang of mockery, she lowered the hand and added, "Pardon me. I meant *chumps.* Vacuous in the head chumps be each and every one o' ye."

Setting down his tumbler with just enough force to tell her he wasn't pleased with her insult, Winston straightened away from the bar and glowered at her. "This is a *mon's* sanctuary. We only permit the *non*-naggin' females to come in, and you aren't even remotely in tha' category. So go away, Deliah. We've earned the right to enjoy a little peace and quiet."

"Earned it, have ye? Ha! Ye, Winston Ian Connery, wi' your projected boogeymen and your damnable moods, are a pain in ma wee arse!"

Lachlan's flute fell from his hand as he leveled a deadpan look on her. "*Bahookie,* lass! Tis no' fittin' for a womon to—"

In the blink of an eye, Deliah pulled down the back of her nightgown, sprouted her wings and leapt atop the counter. Her wings furiously batted the air as she placed her hands on her hips and bent over with a scowl darkening her face.

"But I be no' a womon, be I?" she asked heatedly, a tremor in her tone. "I be a fay. A faery. A-a *freak* to humans, nae? So wha' care I if I say bahookie or *arse.* The latter feels far grander rollin' off ma tongue!"

Stunned, Roan and Lachlan had stepped back at the

beginning of her tirade, while Winston shook his lowered head.

"Naggin' females, are we?" With the tip of her bare toes, she kicked the half-emptied bottle of Scotch into the air, then swatted it behind her with the back of her left hand. The bottle smashed against the wall next to the portrait of the spooning bench.

Lachlan's face grew dark and stormy. *"Och!* You canna treat ma Scotch wi' such disrespect! Tis no' . . . respectful!"

"Ye be a coward, Lachlan Baird! Ye have mair respect for a bottle than your womon and babes!" she charged. "And *ye,* Roan!" She straightened and furiously pointed an isolated finger at him. "Ye shame ma belief in ye!"

"Now wait one damn—"

"Haud yer wheesht!" she cried, mimicking Lachlan, the ferocity in her voice stunning Roan. "Ye are weak like Lachlan. Turnin' to *Scotch* to warm ye, and no' the hearth o' your soul!"

"That's enough," Winston warned in a low growl. His eyes rolled up and dealt her a scowl, but she was too angry to stop now. It was as if the words had been bottled up in her for so long, she couldn't staunch their flow. She didn't want to stop them, not when her insides were so afire and boiling up like lava into her throat.

"Aneuch? Do ye know wha' I see when I look at ye now, Winston Ian Connery?"

He sighed wearily. "I'm sure you're abou' to tell me."

"Aye. *Aye,* I'll tell ye! I see nights withou' stars, days withou' suns, and futures withou' hope. I see a mon who be mair at home walkin' in the grayness o' atween life, than walkin' wi' his fellow mon in the harsh light o' reality."

Tears sprang to her eyes, but she still couldn't stop. "I see a dark aura around ye and it bears nae energy. Ye are burnin' ou' as surely as a wee stick match, but ye are too blind and too stubborn to see ye are soon to be but an ash in the wind!"

"Take a deep breath and quiet down," Winston said softly, although his eyes blazed, condemned her for exposing what he refused to accept as truth.

"Ye would grandly like tha', wouldna ye?" she huffed, her wings shuffling irritably. "Weel, ye poor, poor mon, I be no' the *quiet* wee mouse ye wish I were! I be *nocht* but a tiresome Faerie princess, wi' too much to say and mair than ma fair share o' intelligence." She snapped her fingers in his face. "And have I mentioned I have mair power in ma wee dainty pinky than the lot o' ye thegither! How demasculatin' tha' must be for your egos!"

Planting her hands again on her hips, she proudly squared her shoulders. "I will no' weep for ye, Winston Ian Connery. I will no' ache for ye. *And* I will no' dress like a human to please ye!"

Winston's eyes widened with incredulity when she bent and began to lift the hemline of her nightgown.

"I hear the carriage house callin'," Lachlan sputtered, mortified, his eyes downcast.

"*Och*, Lachlan," she crooned, pausing to issue him a smirk of a smile. "Have ye nae wish to see I have nae inny? Nae navel atall?"

With a guttural growl, Winston threw his arms around her legs. Deliah squealed in surprise and jerked upright when he trapped her legs between his solid chest and the steel-like band of his arms. She whipped the air with her wings, then stilled them, realizing she could do them serious damage were she to wrench free and fly into the ceiling.

Roan released a whoosh of breath and followed Lachlan to the door. "I think you two need to talk," Roan muttered. "Shout if you need us."

"Cowards," Winston grumbled, glaring after them.

As soon as the door closed behind them, he looked up

into Deliah's beet-red face. "I'll let you go if you promise to cool your temper, lass. No' until."

The fire was gone from her. Now she wanted to weep, but pride dammed the tears. "I promise."

Winston glanced at the space behind the bar. Concerned she would somehow hit her wings on the counter or the racks of liquor behind him, he carried her around the counter and placed her on her feet in front of the spooning bench. Then, with a long suffering sigh, he folded his arms against his chest and arched one censorious eyebrow.

"So, there *is* a fire in your bonnet," he said dryly.

Moments ago, she had been brimming with words and indignation, and determined to make him see just how ridiculous was his attitude. But now there was no fight left in her, not even the smallest flicker of a flame. "I've nae mair to say to ye," she said wearily.

Winston was quick to note the way her wings drooped somewhat behind her. Her eyes were downcast, and he could detect a slight quivering in her chin. "Deliah." He sighed again, but this time it bespoke of his own weariness. "I was frightened *for* you in the dining room. I wasn't angry at you."

She regarded him petulantly. "Frightened why?"

"It was bad enough tha' thief saw you like this. The officers? Haven't we had enough to cope wi' in this house?"

"Do ye tak me for a complete fool?" she asked softly.

"No' a complete one."

She turned away from him and stepped to the counter, where she braced her elbows and lowered her chin onto her upturned palms. "Ye freed me and shackled me in one grand swoop, Winston," she said despondently.

A thought occurred to him and his face lit up with realization. "Before, when you said you hid in the oak from Lord Sutherland's magic, you were talkin' about the roots, weren't you?"

Without looking at him, she said irritably, "O' course in the roots. Tis where we slumbered durin' the fall and winter." She spared him a frown, then returned her chin to her palms. "Did ye think I meant I hid in the branches? I have mair sense than tha'."

With a wry grin, Winston chuckled. "O' course I thought you meant in the branches. So, you hid in the roots. Then wha'?"

"I slumbered." Straightening up, she placed her palms on the counter and absently stared at the wall across from her. "At first, when I awakened, I thought it was a wee rest I'd had. No' wee atall. The makin' o' the foundation o' this house is wha' awoke me. By then, it was too late for me to escape. We canna pass through solid objects. I created the grayness to save ma sanity. When Lachlan died, it was there I brought his spirit. I was desperate lonely—although . . . he never did speak to me. I dinna think he knew I was there, but at least I could watch over him and pretend we were clan."

"*You* created the fourth dimension?"

She turned her head just enough to look at him. "Aye, twas ma doin'. It was the only way I could move abou' the house. But a shadow I was.

"Eventually," she went on in a small voice, "some humans discovered it wi' their minds. Like ye. Ye were but a lad when ye first found the realm and sought answers from me. So ye see, Winston, I've been aware o' ye for a verra long time. But it wasna till ye came here tha' I knew I loved ye. For all the good it has done me."

"You said you are a princess."

Now she turned completely to face him, her sadness dulling her eyes. "I had fifteen older sisters. There was never any chance I would one day rule Faerie. When ma brither was born, he became the chosen heir. Males ruled if available, but we females created the laws."

"So you really have no family, no clan."

She glanced off to one side. "There are ither kingdoms around the world, but I would never be but a visitor among them." Her eyes misty with tears, she met Winston's frown of unease. "Blue was the first winter fay to be born to Faerie. She never hibernated durin' the cold months. When we would awaken in the spring, she would tell us stories o' how grand the winter world was. How snow glistened like stars. How icicles hung from branches like crystal dirks. How different the kingdom looked when cloaked in such whiteness. I used to think I could imagine all she told us. Least be I thought I had till I touched and smelled and witnessed it for maself. Ma sisters never had the chance to experience fall and winter. Ma brither . . . weel, he ventured through the passage often aneuch and seldom slumbered among us, but I dinna think he really appreciated anythin' in this world but Lady Lindsay."

"I'm sorry for you," he said softly.

She stiffened. "Dinna pity me."

"No. It's no' pity, Deliah. I know how it feels to be alone and different."

"Do ye?" she asked in a cryptic tone. "Ye created your world, Winston. Mine was stolen from me by evil magic. Ma family and clan was swiped from the earth as easily as your hand can brush away dust from a piece o' furniture. Granted, your parents did no' show their love for ye as did mine, but I wouldna let them taint ma soul were they like yours."

"That's easy to say."

"Nae. No' easy atall. Ye have hurt me mair than I thought possible. And I have fallen to temper because o' it. But ye canna change wha' or who am I, Winston, nae matter your anger or your disgust wi' me. Ye canna slay ma love for ye. Ye can only mak me realize tha' there is nae magic grand aneuch to mak ye love me back."

"Deliah, I'm no' angry or disgusted wi' you."

"Ye have a maist peculiar way o' showin' it, Winston Ian Connery."

A crooked grin tugged at one side of his mouth at her use of his full name again. Whenever she spoke it, delightful chills seemed to swirl around his heart. And because he was feeling lighthearted after his harrowing experiences earlier, he said without thought, "It's *peculiar* knowin' I've fallen in love wi' a fay."

No sooner were the words passed his lips, he jerked back in surprise. Deliah's eyes widened and a delicate pink glow spread across her cheeks, while Winston's turned hot with chagrin.

"Wha' did ye say?" she asked breathlessly, her hands coming up as if to touch his chest, but poising in midair.

Bewilderment, panic and awkwardness flashed across his features and he shifted nervously on his feet. "It was a slip o' the tongue," he grumbled, unable to look into her eyes.

"Mair like a slip o' your heart," she beamed, her wings fluttering rapidly. "Winston, do ye love me?"

Tightness gripped his throat as he forced himself to look her straight in the eye. He felt suddenly claustrophobic. Beads of perspiration broke out on his brow and above his upper lip. He knew he was trembling but couldn't stop.

Her right hand tenderly lit upon his left cheek and it was nearly his undoing.

"Winston, knowin' ye love me is all I need. Knowin' there is a place for me in one verra wee part o' your heart is all I need to keep me happy.

"I know ye be a mon wi' dreams o' family in his future. I canna give ye children. To ma knowin', oor love could be as deep and as pure as a new-formed loch, but it wouldna be aneuch to cross oor worlds and provide a wee one o' oor own.

"One day, ye will find tha' human womon who will give

ye all ye ever desired, and I do pray ye will find her soon. Lovin' ye does no' entitle me to own ye. Does no' entitle me to deny ye the gift o' offspring. I only ask tha' your heart accept ma love and grant me the peace o' knowin' I helped to heal your soul, if even a wee.''

Winston pulled her into his arms and captured her mouth in a passionate kiss. He cast off his doubts and insecurities for a time and basked in the glorious sensations the smell and feel of her awarded him. Her body conformed to his, molding with his with such rightness, he believed they were one inseparable force. His hands explored the softness of her hair, the curve at the base of her spine and the firm roundness of her buttocks. All the while her arms remained tightly fastened about his middle, clinging to him as if she planned to never let go.

He went with an impulse and gingerly brushed the backs of the fingers of his right hand against one of her wings. She drew back her head, a gasp escaping her parted lips. She stared into his eyes with wonder, her face aglow and more beautiful than he'd ever seen it. It left him breathless and giddy at the same time, and he stroked the wing once more. This time she closed her eyes and gave a sweet moan of ecstasy.

"Does it feel good when I touch your wings?''

He actually didn't need to ask, for the answer had already been given him. But he nonetheless had voiced the query, and was glad he had when she replied, "A'maist as good as havin' ye inside me,'' she breathed, gazing into his eyes with passion and such love, his heart skipped a beat. "Winston, may I lie wi' ye, tonight?''

Again his heart began to hammer wildly behind his breast. "Only lie wi' me?'' he teased.

A humorous, chiding gleam sparkled in her eyes. "Nae, ma handsome Scotsman. I'll have ye in me. I'll pleasure ye till the sun winks over the horizon, then till dusk readies the cloak o' night. And I promise ye, Winston, ye will never regret the havin' o' me. When the time comes for us to part, ye will walk away wi' nae hurt or guilt in your heart.''

Winston wanted to swoop her up into his arms and carry her to his bedroom, but instead, he kissed her with the longing that had been festering inside him for what seemed an eternity. He didn't want her to think he was merely after her body. A quick fix to the libido had never been his style. But the sweetness and soft texture of her mouth carried him away. His hands began to draw up her night-gown, the tension in his fingers to touch her private place, maddening. But when he'd gotten the hemline to her hips, there came a hard rap on the door. He released Deliah immediately, and she jumped back and dropped her hem-line to her ankles as the door slowly opened.

''Winston?''

It was Roan. Deliah blushed and Winston scowled.

''Wha', Roan?''

The door opened enough for Roan to step onto the threshold. He appeared ill-at-ease to interrupt the couple, but forced a small smile and stated, ''Lannie and I decided to try to mak it to Shortby's. Interested in joinin' us?''

Winston glanced at the dial of his watch. It was not quite eleven. ''When does it close?''

''Three in the morn. We just need to get away from the house for a time,'' said Roan.

Winston glanced at Deliah. He was surprised to see she had retracted her wings. Wariness shadowed her face, and her eyes searched his with a question he didn't want to answer.

''I'll join you,'' he said to Roan, although his head remained turned and his gaze riveted on Deliah. The light went out of her eyes at his words, and her expression became instantly guarded. Sorrow wafted from her and he absorbed it despite his reluctance. At this time, he didn't want to explain to her that joining the men at Shortby's would give him the chance to discuss his situation with them. A chance to sort through his choices. What she didn't know—and he blocked from his mind—was that if he did make love to her again, there would never be anyone *but* her in his life. Children or no, he would commit only to her.

For a reason he couldn't begin to explain even to himself, he wanted Roan and Lachlan's approval.

"Are you sure?" Roan asked hesitantly.

Winston nodded and faced Roan. "Wi' three o' us, we should be able to get ma car onto the road."

"Beats walkin' to town." Roan dipped his head and smiled a bit nervously at Deliah. "We'll watch over him."

Winston turned to Deliah and, although she stiffened and turned her face aside, telling him she didn't want to be touched, he kissed her tenderly on the cheek. "We'll talk when I return."

There was a hardness in her eyes when she again looked at him, one that surprised and unnerved him. Without another word, he followed Roan into the hall. Deliah trailed behind them, her shoulders sagging, her movements lethargic. Lachlan was waiting in the hall by the parlor door, a full-length coat lending the illusion that he was taller and broader than he actually was. He smiled broadly when he saw Deliah and held out the crystal paperweight.

"Thank you, lass," he said cheerily. "It means a lot to—"

A spark of what looked like blue electricity manifested inside the crystal and it exploded with a soft *fssst* into a thousand segments. Lachlan's leveled palm was not injured, but the diamondlike fragments were scattered everywhere on the floor.

Three pairs of eyes stared at her in disbelief, while Deliah remained unmoved by her actions. Lachlan's expression crumbled to one of disappointment, and he murmured something in Gaelic the others couldn't understand.

"I'll sweep this up," said Roan, brushing past Deliah and heading into the kitchen.

Winston ran upstairs to fetch his coat. Lachlan stared at Deliah for a time, as if trying to understand her motive for destroying one of his treasures.

She had none. She didn't understand what had happened, only knew that she had released the burst of energy and was guilty of shattering the piece.

Within minutes, the crystal was swept up and tossed in the trash can in the kitchen, Winston returned downstairs with his coat and gloves on, and Lachlan had sufficiently recovered and was eager to leave the house. They left by way of the kitchen door, which faced the street where Winston had parked. Deliah waited in the hall until she heard the kitchen door close, then went out on the stoop and forlornly watched the men brazen a precarious path down the hillside to the road. For an undeterminable time she observed them brush off the car and scrape the windows free of snow and ice once Winston had gotten the engine to turn over. Then, with the shovel Roan had brought along, they alternated shoveling and rocking and pushing the car, shoveling and rocking and pushing until, at last, the vehicle was out of its winter bed and on the road. One of them released a howl of glee. Then they were all inside the car and driving off toward Crossmichael. When Deliah could no longer see the tail lights, she burst into uncontrollable tears.

"Deliah?"

Laura stepped aside and Deliah dashed into the kitchen, her weeping so painful, she couldn't speak. When Laura soothingly drew her into her arms, Deliah wept against the woman's shoulder, great, shuddering sobs racking her chilled form.

"What happened?"

After a moment, Deliah managed, "They be gone."

"Who?" Gripping Deliah's upper arms, Laura held her back to see her face. "Who, Deliah?"

"Winston, Lachlan, and Roan."

"Gone where?"

"Someplace called Shortby's."

Sucking in a shuddering breath, Deliah walked to the small table against the wall and sat in one of the two chairs. "We were goin' to mak love. Then Roan asked him to join him and Lachlan. He didna even hesitate, Laura."

Her face pale and taut, Laura angrily tapped a foot on the floor. "Shortby's, huh? Roan didn't even have the decency to tell me he was going out."

"Decency?" Deliah said bitterly. "There be nae decency in how we be treated. I bear ma heart and soul, only to be put off by the prospect o' mair drink."

"They were drinking before they left?"

"Aye. In the ither room wi' the bottles o' drink."

"The bar?"

Deliah nodded.

"What in hell is so appealing about *Scotch?*" Laura cried with frustration.

"Tis a monly thing, they believe. A bondin' ritual." Deliah sighed, miserable. "Tis foul tastin' and burned ma insides."

"Don't tell me they had *you* drinking with them?"

"Nae. I snucked a taste some time ago. Laura?"

"What?"

"Have we nae recourse? How does a human female deal wi' this kind o' hurtin'?"

"We get even," Laura said heatedly.

Beth entered the kitchen in time to see Laura place a

large silver tray on the table. Deliah, sitting at the chair nearest the windows, looked up and gestured for Beth to join them. Laura pulled out a third chair from the corner and placed it at the table, then sat as Beth seated herself between the two women.

"I was going to come up and invite you to join our tea party," said Laura.

Three cups, three spoons, a tall silver teapot, creamer and a bowl of sugar were atop the tray. There was also a bowl of warm brownies with chunks of walnuts visible in the rich chocolate treats.

"I have to pass," Beth said woefully, her mouth watering for both the tea and the brownies.

"Not even a little tea and a nibble of brownie?"

"Laura, it'll give the babies gas."

Laura wrinkled her nose. "Is there something else I can get you?"

"No, thanks." Beth yawned and excused herself. "I need to turn in soon. These two-to-three hour feedings are draining me. I can't remember what sleep is."

"How old are babies before they start sleeping all night?" Laura asked.

"I have no idea."

"I canna help, either," Deliah murmured.

"Deliah, is something wrong?"

Deliah managed a smile for Beth, but before she could respond, Laura filled Beth in on what had happened. When Beth heard that the men had taken off to Shortby's, she closed her eyes for a moment and clenched her teeth.

"I swear the boys are less trouble than our men," said Laura, fuming. She filled two of the cups with steaming tea and passed one to Deliah. "Dammit, we were almost *robbed* tonight! So much for our gallant protectors worrying about us being alone in the house."

"Was Lachlan drunk when they left?" Beth asked Deliah quietly.

"Glowin' a wee, but no' drunked."

Beth gulped painfully. "I don't know what to do, anymore. I'm tired and I'm fed up. But it's not like I can just pack up the twins and leave, is it? I have no identity, no money, and no place to go."

"You're right," said Laura. "You are in a bad position. Hell's bells, aren't we a threesome. I'm the reincarnation of a murderess. You're just back from the dead." Laura sighed deeply as her gaze settled on Deliah. "And you're a faery."

Hearing it all said aloud, Beth laughed. "God, how bizarre can we get!"

"The Three Weirdateers," Laura said wryly.

"Hmm." Beth fell thoughtfully silent for a time. "I just don't know what to do, but I can't stay here. This is Lachlan's house, and yours and Roan's home. I don't belong."

"I do," said Deliah in a husky tone. "This house is built on wha' remains o' ma clan's kingdom, and I'll no' leave."

"The three of us are staying," Laura said with a frown. "We have as much right to be here as any of the men. I can't . . . I can't believe they just took off to have themselves a good ol' time, and left us here to wait for them like dutiful, subservient little wives."

"Tis cold to us they be," said Deliah.

The room fell silent for a time. Then the grandfather clock on the second floor could be heard bringing in the midnight hour. Pensively, the women listened until the last chime echoed through the house, then Beth released a sigh of such desolation, Laura and Deliah focused their attention on her.

"I just want Lachlan back," she said softly, mistily staring off into space. "We went through so much to get where we were. Everything seems so out of place now."

Laura nodded. "He certainly isn't adjusting to fatherhood, is he," she stated, staring into the remains of the cup cradled in her hands. "I guess I'm a helluva one to talk." She gave a nervous chuff. "When I realized I was going to be raising the boys, I panicked. I felt as if someone had snatched away my life and handed me something alien and confining. Now, I can't imagine what my life would be like without them."

Unexpectedly, Deliah burst into tears. She lowered her face into her hands and had herself a good cry before pulling herself together. Breaths hitching, shivers coursing through her, she lifted her head and hastily wiped away the moisture on her face with her hands. "I dinna know wha' be wrong wi' me," she managed, her voice hoarse and shaky. "Either I want to cry or ma temper is on the wing."

Beth chuckled. "On the wing. I like that."

New tears sprang to Deliah's eyes, but she made a valiant bid to smile through them. "I be so confused, lately. I keep thinkin' about ma clan, ma family. Especially ma brither. I so miss him. And I keep thinkin' he would know how I should deal wi' Winston. But I canna ask him, can I?" A new rush of tears streamed down her cheeks. "They all be lost to me, and I dinna like how lonely be ma days and nights. Tis no' fair the heart should feel such pain."

"Oh, hon," Beth consoled, "it won't always be like this. Relationships are never easy. All your problems will work themselves out."

"She's right," Laura said. "Roan and I have had our ups and down. But the ups outweigh the downs, and always will. Love is never painless, Deliah. And you do have family. Here, with us."

"I cry too easily these days," Deliah sniffed, then flashed a smile capable of warming the coldest winter's night. Heaving a fortifying breath, she straightened her shoulders. "I know Winston loves me. As much as his moods frustrate me, I wouldna have him change to please me." She sighed again. "I have so much to learn abou' humanness, it be scary."

"With the exception of evoking magic and sprouting wings, you're as human as we are," said Beth.

"Ye be too kind, Beth."

"Again, Beth is right," Laura piped up, smiling warmly at her companions. She lifted her teacup for a toast. Deliah raised hers, and Beth poured a little tea into the cup that had been reserved for her use. "To the Three Weirdateers! May we conquer every hurdle life tosses at us!"

"Here, here!"

"Aye!"

To Beth and Deliah's dismay, Deliah broke into wretched sobs.

Frowning, Laura said, "If Winston walked through that door right now, I swear I would knock him upside the head with a frying pan."

To the women's further bewilderment, Deliah began to laugh. And she laughed and laughed, the sound not quite ringing true of mirth, but she couldn't seem to stop.

"It's going to be a long night," Laura sighed.

Chapter Fourteen

Practically falling out of the back passenger side of Winston's Audi, Lachlan raised his arms above his head and released a whoop of glee that reverberated through the star-canopied night. Winston and Roan continued to laugh at the laird's enthusiasm at riding in a "motor vehicle", the latter brushing tears from his cheeks as he unfolded from the front passenger seat. From the get-go, Lachlan had loved every glide, slide, stop, and go throughout the drive into town. He'd even marveled at the heater, which actually hadn't begun to blow warm air until a few minutes before pulling into Shortby's car park.

"I want ta drive across all o' Scotland!" Lachlan roared joyously, turning in place, his arms still raised. "Across the whole bloody world—"

His voice hitched when his feet went out from under him and he slammed to the icy ground on his left side. Even this struck him funny and, rolling to a spread-eagle position on his back, he laughed until its throes formed a painful stitch in his side.

"Och, he's lost his mind," Roan laughed. With him taking Lachlan's left hand and Winston the right, they hauled him to his feet. "Steady auld mon," Roan cautioned.

"Dinna call me *auld,*" Lachlan wheezed, then burst into another round of laughter.

By the time the three men arrived at the front door of the establishment, they'd calmed somewhat. Leading the way, Roan opened the door and directed his companions toward the bar counter. Nine patrons were enjoying the cozy warmth of the interior, three of whom were embroiled in a game of darts. All eyes, including those of Silas MacCormick, the owner and bartender who was behind the counter, turned on the trio.

"Silas, ma mon," Roan said merrily, "how the bloody hell have you been?"

"No' as good as you, it seems," said Silas, his blue eyes crinkled in a smile of greeting. He nodded to Winston. "Mr. Connery. Pleasure to see you again."

Winston smiled in return and sat to Roan's left on one of the stools. Both men glanced at Lachlan, whose face was aglow with wonder as he scanned the large room and took in every detail from the country decor to the watchful patrons.

"Sweet Jesus, tis all so much to absorb," Lachlan said jubilantly. He shrugged out of his heavy coat and finally sat to Winston's left, a ludicrously wide grin offered to the bartender as he laid his coat across his lap.

Comically, his white eyebrows arched, Silas looked at Roan and gave a slight nod in Lachlan's direction. "Now here's a character," the old man grinned. His gaze swerved to regard Lachlan's full-sleeved shirt. "Would you be on your way to a masquerade, sir?"

Lachlan smacked his chest with an open palm, then flung his arms out wide. "I live in a masquerade, ma good mon, and I've a wicked thirst. I'll have a pint o' bitter, if you please."

"Comin' right up. Roan . . . Mr. Connery?"

"Winston, please."

The old man scrunched up his face thoughtfully. "I dinna think we carry tha' brand."

To Roan and Winston's embarrassment, Lachlan burst out laughing and slapped the tiled countertop.

"He's got housebound fever," Roan grinned sheepishly at Silas. "I'll have a dark ale."

"Make tha' two," said Winston.

Lachlan's gaze settled on a wicker bowl filled with salted, twisted objects. He contemplated them for a time before lifting one to his mouth. Again he hesitated, then bit into it. He crunched slowly, frowning, fully concentrating on the flavor. Then a grin spread across his face. "Wha' are these?"

"You've never had a pretzel?" Silas asked, then chuffed as he placed a ceramic tankard in front of Lachlan. "Where are you from?"

"Baird House," Lachlan said without thinking, and popped the rest of the pretzel into his mouth.

Winston and Roan were quick to note the deadpan expression that fell across Silas' wrinkled face. Clearing his throat, Roan said, "Don't ask, Silas. I don't think you could handle the answer."

Silas filled two more tankards and placed them in front of Roan and Winston. Winston lifted his immediately and took a long swallow of the tepid brew, then worked his mouth around the tangy aftermath clinging to his tongue.

"So Roan," Silas grinned, leaning his elbows on the counter, "how goes your love life?"

"Couldn't be happier."

"That's an irksome statement," Silas sighed and straightened up from the counter. "When am I goin' to get to meet this womon? I'm beginnin' to think she's one o' tha' cursed place's ghosts." He laughed, but it was cut short when he noticed the intensity in Lachlan's dark eyes.

Over the brim of his tankard, Lachlan said huskily, "Baird House is no' cursed. Tis a far grander place than any in all o' Dumfries and Galloway."

"Lannie," Roan chided in a low growl and a strained smile, "drink your bitter and be quiet."

The ruddy coloring in Silas' cheeks paled. Winston watched the man, scanning him, and realized Silas' suspicions, which the man too quickly dismissed, were close to the truth of Lachlan's identity. But he also glimpsed that the man was too afraid of saying anything more about Baird House, which was a relief. All they needed was more trouble. If word ever got out that Lachlan Baird and his American lady had not only been returned from the dead, but had parented twins. . . .

Pushing the thought from his mind, he observed Silas walk to the far end of the counter, where a man in his mid-thirties parked himself on the end stool. He had short, dark, curly hair and wore silver-toned wire-rimmed glasses. A dark wool coat was draped over one arm, and what looked like a camera case dangled from a wide strap on his left shoulder. Winston reached out and briefly scanned the man. He seemed amicable enough, but it disturbed Winston that the man was concerned with finishing an article that was due by eight in the morning.

"Lachlan," Winston said, keeping his voice low, "you have to be careful o' wha' you say."

"Aye, aye," Lachlan grumbled, then downed the rest of his bitter. "But tis hard to no' speak ma mind."

"Learn. Quickly," Roan quipped. "Keep your mouth filled wi' your drink or the pretzels."

"I think I can managed tha'," Lachlan grinned.

A minute or two passed in silence, then Lachlan said to Winston, "You should have stayed wi' your lass."

Taken aback by the comment, Winston retaliated, "And you shouldn't be denyin' your womon and your children."

Roan groaned and placed down his tankard. Leaning to, he dealt his companions a harried look. "Did we come here to talk abou' oor women or to unwind?"

"Deliah," Winston muttered, staring straight ahead.

Lachlan grimaced. "Beth."

Roan rolled his eyes and released a breath through pursed lips. "Aye. Laura." He signaled for Silas to refill their tankards. When this was done, he took several sips, frowning thoughtfully. "I've been feelin' neglected. And in tha', I'm guilty o' ma fair share o' neglectin' as well."

"Why neglected?" asked Lachlan.

"Why?" Roan released a low laugh that held no mirth. "She spends every spare minute wi' the lads and *your* babes, that's why? Women have this thing abou'—"

Roan choked on the words. His face drained of color, then became flushed as he stared into the contents of his tankard. Winston, having unwittingly glimpsed the train of Roan's thoughts, put in, "Your ex was given custody o' your son. Roan, you did wha' you could. You had no way o' knowin' the fire would happen."

"I agree," said Lachlan, his head bent to better see Roan's profile. "Roan, na mon could love his son mair'n you."

"I wasn't there for him," Roan said, his voice quivering with emotion. "I was a part-time faither and, damn me, I'm the same wi' Laura's nephews. I don't know why, but I'm afraid to let anyone get too close." He sighed, swigged down another gulp of his dark ale, then set the tankard down a bit unsteadily. "I love those lads. God knows, I'd be lost withou' them." He looked at his companions "But

I can't seem to give ma *all* to them. Or to Laura. I always have to hold back a part o' maself."

Lachlan's shoulders moved in a feeble shrug. "Roan, if tis only a part o' yourself I've seen you dishin' ou', then you're a bigger mon than me. I *have* given ma all and, I can tell you, it has been sadly lackin' in somethin'."

A wry grin formed on Winston's mouth as he held up his tankard, then clinked it first to Roan's, then Lachlan's. "Weel, ma friends, at least your women are *human,*" he said in a tone just loud enough for them to hear.

Lachlan chuckled, while Roan grinned, then said, "I don't know, Winston. I think her wings are verra sexy."

"Tell me, gentlemen," Winston continued, "wha' would you do in ma shoes?"

"Probably break ma fool neck," Lachlan said.

Winston frowned at his response. "How so?"

Lachlan leaned back and glanced at Winston's shoes. "They're flimsy footwear."

Roan moaned in mock pain.

Winston grinned. "Seriously, would *you* have a problem wi' a winged wonder?"

"Weel . . ." Lachlan scratched the back of his head, grinning dubiously. ". . . I wouldna turn ma back on her. She's a fine lass, Winston."

"Tha' she is," agreed Roan, lifting his tankard and taking another swallow, then lowering it to the counter. "As a matter o' fact, we are all three fortunate men. The flames o' oor hearts are beautiful, intelligent and—okay, wings *would* give me a wee problem," he added humorously.

"*Och,* Roan, Deliah is as delicate as a butterfly!" Lachlan exclaimed.

"Aye, and possibly as flighty as one," Roan countered humorously. "Flitter here . . . flitter there."

"Flitter your brain," Lachlan muttered.

"All right," Winston cut in, casting each man an exasperated look. "Sorry I asked."

Leaning to, Roan winked at Lachlan, then clapped Winston on the back. "Just razzin' you, Winston. In truth, I think you're a bloody fool to even question your love for her."

"To *three* bloody fools," said Lachlan.

Three tankards clinked in the toast.

"How are you men doin'?" asked Silas from the end of the counter. "Needin' anither refill?"

Collecting his companions' responses with a glance, Roan said, "Na. We're fine, for now." Then he muttered out the left side of his mouth, "The women will skin us alive if we go home pissed."

"I dinna care for tha' expression," said Lachlan. "Pissed. Sounds like I've wet maself. Now *fuddled,* there's the proper word for bein' in your cups."

Winston chuckled and shook his head. "Drunk works fine for me."

Lachlan repeated the word, emphasizing the roll of the *R.* "Fuddled," he insisted, then raised his right hand and gestured for Silas, who came right away.

"Anither bitter?"

Lachlan shook his head. "Have you a fuddlin' cup?"

Silas' smile faded. "A wha'?"

"A fuddlin' cup," Lachlan repeated with a hint of impatience. "You know . . . from which to get *fuddled,* mon!"

With a bewildered shrug, Silas returned to the end of the counter. Roan released what sounded like a strangled laugh.

"Wha' is a fuddlin' cup?" Winston asked, laughter brightening his eyes.

Exasperated with their ignorance, Lachlan polished off his bitter before explaining. "'Tis a drinkin' vessel resemblin' three wee rounded urns stuck thegither. You fill it wi' Scotch, rum—whatever—pass it to someone, and tell them they have to finish one o' the urns as a gesture of friendship. The gimmick is, the insides of the urns are opened ta one anither. The drinker ends up havin' three times as much as expected, and gets fuddled—drunk or pissed, whatever you want ta call it. I canna believe you've never been properly fuddled."

"Weel," Roan sighed, theatrically serious, "but I have ridden in a steel bird. A fair exchange, I think."

Lachlan passed Roan a scowl. "I know wha' a plane is. I've seen them in the skies. But you canna compare one o' *those* to the pleasure o' finishin' off a fuddlin' cup."

"Flyin' fuddled sounds appealing to me," said Roan.

"Here, here," Winston agreed.

"Flyin' fuddled," Lachlan murmured thoughtfully, then bobbed his head appreciatively. "Fuddled would be the only way I'd get in one o' those contraptions."

"Wha' do we have here?" mocked a loud voice from behind the men. Roan was the only one to recognize Arnald Markey's gravelly voice. He was one of the men Roan had brawled with before Christmas Eve. "Well, if it isn't the lord of Kist House!"

"Kiss off," Roan grumbled, keeping his back to the man. He passed a warning glance to Winston and Lachlan not to take the man's bait.

"Ah, Lord Ingliss, forgive this intrusion," Markey blustered, his voice raised to attract the attention of everyone in the pub. "I was just wonderin' wha' possessed you to come amongst we peons? Aren't you afraid oor *commonness* might rub off on you?"

Roan pointedly sipped his ale. Winston clenched his teeth and stared straight ahead. Lachlan, however, turned on the stool and grinned wickedly into the man's pasty face.

"Tell me, sir," Lachlan began, his tone light, his mood

seemingly cheery, "is it you wha' smells so ripe, or are you carryin' somethin' dead in one o' yer pockets?"

Roan gulped and grimaced. Winston, too, knew what was coming.

Markey pressed his face closer to Lachlan and sneered, exposing crooked lower teeth and a missing tooth in the upper center. "I don't believe I have the displeasure o' knowin' your name, *sir.*"

"Lachlan Baird."

"Oh ... shit," Roan groaned.

Winston ran a hand down his face.

Markey straightened, his expression one of comical bewilderment. Two other men, larger in height and girth, left their chairs and came to flank him.

"Lachlan Baird?" Markey said with uncertainty. "Are you related to tha' deil from Kist House?"

"Lannie," Roan warned, but Lachlan nonetheless slipped to his feet and laid his coat across the stool. He was nearly a head taller than Markey, and a good two inches taller than the man's edgy cohorts.

"You could say tha'," Lachlan said with a strained grin.

"I could, could I?" Markey muttered, then inhaled with a snort and squared his unimpressive shoulders as his gaze raked over Lachlan's outdated mode of dress. "Fancy yourself a buccaneer, do you?"

Lachlan continued to grin.

Markey's nostrils flared. "Carry a sword up yer ass, do you?"

Roan whirled on his stool and got to his feet. "Don't start wha' you can't finish," he warned the burly threesome.

"Efter tha' last beatin' you took, Ingliss, I would think you'd watch your smart mouth," sneered McKenna, the redheaded man with the beard, who was standing to Markey's right.

"Are you talkin' abou' tha' love tap you gave me, McKenna?" Roan taunted.

With a loud sigh, Winston rose to stand between his companions. He wasn't a man who usually looked for a fight, but he knew it was coming and decided to face it head-on with Roan and Lachlan.

"Love tap?" McKenna spat, a sardonic grin contorting his face. His dark eyes narrowed on Winston, then he pursed his lips and kissed the air as he turned his attention on Lachlan. "You are a pretty boy." His companions laughed, stoking his egotistical penchant to fight. "So we have us a likeness o' the infamous ghost hisself. But you're just anither loser, aren't you, pretty boy?"

"No' in ma place!" Silas cried angrily from behind the counter. "The last brawl cost me a pretty penny!"

The third instigator, a man in his early forties named Willy Canabra, cupped his crotch and cooed, "Which one o' you *boys* would like to come back to ma table and sit on ma lap for a spell?"

Lachlan cast his companions an airy glance, then leveled a mischievous grin on Canabra. "Weel now, laddie, tis a temptin' offer, but I have somethin' a wee different in mind."

Canabra snorted. "I don't use tongue on the first date."

"Lachlan," Winston warned, having scanned the man's thoughts. "They're no' worth the trouble it'll bring down on oor heads."

Lachlan's broad shoulders moved in a lighthearted shrug. "I'm just bondin' wi' these gentlemen, Winston. Dinna get your breeches in a knot."

Canabra lewdly raked Lachlan over from head to toe. Then, exposing what remained of the teeth he'd lost in his last round with Roan, he issued in a mock feminine tone, "I like a mon who doesn't let fashion dictate his wardrobe. But I think a bit o' ruffle around the neck, though, is needed. Don't you agree, Mr. Baird?"

"Aye, a ruffle or two," Markey chortled.

The redhead grimaced, obviously uncomfortable with the direction the taunting had taken.

Markey brazened a step toward Lachlan. Roan was about to cut the man off, but Lachlan whipped up his left arm in a gesture for Roan to stand back and not interfere. This amused Markey and he chuckled deeply, his eyes gleaming with malevolence.

"Have you cleavage hidin' behind your stays?" Markey jabbed. "For tha' matter, have you balls, mon?"

Markey released a shrill cry when Lachlan swiftly gripped the man's crotch with his right hand and the front of the man's red plaid shirt with the left. As Silas careened around the end of the counter, and Roan and Winston were in the process of grabbing Lachlan's arms, the former ghost of Baird House hoisted Markey off his feet as if he were but a piece of luggage, and tossed him. Markey flew atop one of the round tables and crashed with it to the floor.

A camera flashed repeatedly as all hell broke loose.

The Audi skidded sideways across the steep incline of the driveway. It would have nose-dived into the ravine if not for a low wall of ice high-centering the vehicle, leaving the front wheels dangling in the air. Roaring with laughter, Lachlan fell out the open driver's door and into a heap on the ground. Winston gingerly climbed from the back seat, while Roan, shocky and overly conscious of his churning stomach, unfolded himself from the front passenger seat. Once he was standing, he sucked in a breath to steady himself. Cold air hit his lungs and helped to ease his queasiness.

"You're a bloody lunatic!" Winston gasped, glaring at

Lachlan. He braced himself against the side of his car and watched Lachlan struggle to his feet. Twice Lachlan stood and twice he fell, still laughing, still lost to its weakening throes.

Roan walked around the back of the car and hauled Lachlan to his feet. "Quiet down, mon! You're loud enough to wake the dead!"

Roan's unconscious choice of words only restoked Lachlan's mirth and he howled with laughter. His feet were unsteady beneath him. All that kept him afoot was Roan and Winston positioning themselves to each side of him and gripping his arms.

"Wi' any luck, the women will be asleep," Roan grunted, matching Winston's cautious steps as they guided Lachlan across the slick ground. "Ma head can't tak a scoldin'."

Winston remained silent and stewing in his own juices. It had been reckless of him to allow Lachlan to drive. They were fortunate they'd made it back to the estate in one piece. But the roads had been clear of drivers and the laird persistent, and Winston just drunk enough and roughed up enough not to care until that moment the car had nearly plunged into the ravine.

A zephyrous caress swept through Winston's skull and brought him to an abrupt halt. He ignored Lachlan and Roan falling to the ground when he spun around. His intense gaze swept the snowscape. He thought he glimpsed a glowing green ring near the base of the oak, but it vanished in the blink of an eye, leaving him unsure whether he'd actually seen anything. Then he believed he could hear faint voices. The words were indecipherable, minute tickling bursts against his eardrums.

"Wha' is it?" Roan asked irritably, again on his feet and again holding up Lachlan, who was quiet except for his labored breathing.

"Nothin'," replied Winston, attributing the phenomena

to too much ale and the punches he'd received at Shortby's. "We better get inside before we freeze to death ou' here."

"I think ma testicles are already frozen to ma legs," Lachlan groaned.

"Charmin' image," said Roan.

Silently, cautiously, the threesome made their way across the private road. It was Roan's suggestion they cut through the rhododendron hedge instead of following the driveway to the carriage house, a short cut, he reasoned, that would save them a good five minutes. And right now, five minutes seemed an awfully long time to subject themselves to the bitter cold of the night.

However, cutting through the hedge proved to be a mistake.

Winston was the first to feel something catch him across the shins. Something taut and unyielding. He toppled forward, dragging the others with him, and plunging them all into what at first seemed to be a very large, tenacious spider's web. The more they struggled, the more entangled they each became. Curses in Scottish, Gaelic and English rang through the night. Arms and legs flailed against the restraints. Roan managed to crawl beyond the hedge before the webbing further tightened. He hit the ground and released another stream of expletives.

To add to their consternation, shrill boyish cries rent the air as they were repeatedly assaulted with hard objects.

"Take that!" a familiar voice shouted. "We ain't scared of you!"

"Kevin!" Roan gasped, in time to spare himself from what could have been a serious blow to the head with a child's wooden baseball bat.

Silence weighted the night for several moments until, "Uncle Roan?" a voice squeaked.

"Kevin," Roan panted, "wha' is goin' on!"

"We thought you were the boogeyman," said Kahl.

"Sweet Jesus," Lachlan moaned.

"Wha' are we caught up in?" asked Roan angrily.

"Our trap," said Kevin. "It worked pretty good, huh?"

"We got 'em all over out here," Alby boasted.

Trussed up on his side, Winston ordered, "Cut us free."

"We can't," said Kahl. He shrugged his small shoulders. "We're not allowed to touch scissors or knives."

"Get somethin'!" Roan bellowed.

"Okay, okay!"

Kevin's footfalls plodded in the direction of the house.

"Where did you get this rope?" Roan asked Kahl, glaring up at the boy through the damp hair clinging to his face.

"It ain't rope. It's yarn. We tied it all together."

"Yarn. . . ." Roan's voice drifted off as incredulity settled inside his brain "From the missin' sweaters?"

"Sure," said Kahl. "It was for a good cause. We couldn't let the boogeyman—"

"There is no boogeyman!" Roan thundered, jerking his body within the cocooning yarn.

"Yes sa!" Alby shouted. "He grabbed me, remember?"

"That was a thief," said Winston. "He was only after some o' the treasures in the house."

"Aye," agreed Lachlan. "But the police took him away."

The boys fell silent.

Soon, another sound was heard. The distinct sound of large wings flapping in the air

Winston tightly closed his eyes and clenched his teeth against a groan.

"Lads," he heard Deliah say in a firm tone, "return to the house. We'll be along, shortly."

"But—"

"Kevin, do as ye be told."

The boys headed for the house and Deliah knelt first beside Roan. As she cut away the taut strands of yarn, she scolded, "Ye be fortunate the household be awake, leastwise, we would have found us *three* frozen corpses come morn!"

Holding his tongue against a retort, Roan busied himself with yanking away the strands while she cut Lachlan's bonds, then Winston's. As they finished unwrapping themselves and got to their feet, she stood back with her hands on hips, her wings fluttering in a cadence of unmistakable pique.

"Fine example ye three be settin' for the young ones! Tary no'. Beth and Laura are fraught wi' worry."

With this said, she cast off and flew back to the house, leaving the men to regroup.

"If I know ma Beth—and I do—she's mair likely fraught wi' anger," Lachlan said grimly.

"Shit," Winston muttered.

They headed toward the house, side by side, silent and looking like three men who were expecting to face the guillotine. Some fifteen feet from the front doors, Winston said, "Wait," and pointed to something between the main and carriage houses. Although but a silhouette, a tall, broad tree was clearly visible. A tree where Deliah had tossed the broken oak twigs to create a wall between the thief, Winston and Alby.

"I'll be damned," Roan murmured, his gaze measuring the tree to be at least twelve feet tall.

"Shall we have a closer look?" asked Winston.

Lachlan somberly shook his head. "Best we face the music and be done wi' it."

They entered the house, Lachlan leading the way, with Roan following and Winston tagging along with his hands buried in his pockets. The hallway was vacant and so was the library. Moments later, they found the women waiting for them in the parlor. The air was thick with hostility. The boys sat on the larger sofa, squirming, their gazes lowered guiltily. Of the women, Laura appeared the angriest. High color stained her cheeks and her vibrant green eyes raked over them. She approached the men, stopping several feet in front of them, her heated gaze narrowing in response to their split lips and bruised and bloodied faces.

"You," she began, pointing at Winston, "got the boys all worked up with your nonsense about boogeymen! I just found out they've been sneaking outside every night and using yarn to make a trap for your killer!"

"I'm sorry."

"Is that all you have to say?" she asked furiously.

Winston looked at the boys, who were now staring at him through lowered eyelashes. "The Phantom was in ma mind. There's no one here ou' to hurt anyone."

The boys exchanged conspiratorial looks and mumbled amongst themselves.

Laura released a breath of vexation, then threw her hands up. "We've all been suffering a little cabin fever, but isn't it just swell you *men* can take off on a whim and have yourselves a fun time."

"Laura—"

"Shut up, Roan. I'm so damn angry right now. . . ." She drew in a breath to calm herself. "You think *Scotch* and *beer* are the answer to all your problems, don't you?"

"Na. Laura—"

"Well, I hope it keeps you warm at night, because I sure as hell won't."

Lachlan's face darkened with a scowl as he stepped forward. "You're bein' too harsh. We went ou' for a few drinks! We came back, dinna we?"

"How magnanimous of you," Beth said from her position at the back of the sofa. "And it's obvious you got into a brawl."

"One o' the patrons insulted ma monhood," Lachlan blustered.

Beth came around the sofa and positioned herself next to Laura. Deliah, meanwhile, remained a few feet away, crouched in front of the hearth and warming her hands before the fire. Her wings were retracted, her hair cloaking her slender form.

"We were wrong to leave the house," Winston said wearily, his gaze on Deliah, his heart in his throat.

"Wrong?" Lachlan exclaimed. "Tis a mon's right to—"

"Shut up," Beth warned in a furious, low tone. "Right now your *monhood* is in serious question, so shut the hell up before I do something you will sorely regret."

Lachlan opened his mouth, then clamped it shut with a scowl.

"Do you think scaring the boys to the point they feel they have to invent *traps* humorous?" Laura asked Roan.

"O' course no'." Roan held out his hands in a pleading gesture. "Damn me, Laura, I'm sorrier than I can say. It won't happen again. I swear on Aggie's—"

"You're damn right it won't," Laura bit out, cutting him off with both her words and a slice of her right hand through the air. "I don't know you anymore, Roan. I can't even stand the sight of you, right now."

"Laura," Lachlan rasped, then his gaze fell on Beth's flashing eyes and he held back what he wanted to say.

"I love you, Laura," Roan said softly. "I want to marry you."

"You bastard," she choked, tears brimming her eyes. "I'm not *that* gullible, Roan. And I don't believe any of you really know what you want. It can't be us."

"Laura—"

"No, Roan." She drew in a deep breath and eased back her shoulders. "I don't want to hear another word from you tonight. In fact, I think it would be best if the three of you moved into the carriage house for a time.''

"Tis cold ou' there," Deliah said, rising to her feet.

Laura spared her a glance, then shook her head. "There's the wood stove, and plenty of sleeping bags and blankets in the storage in the back." She met Roan's wilted gaze and released a ragged breath. "We all need to get our priorities in order, and decide what the next step is. A separation for a while can't make matters any worse than they already are."

Roan glumly nodded. "All right."

"They be injured," Deliah said in a small voice.

Winston met her gaze and offered her a tremulous smile. It astounded him she was concerned for their welfare when he'd treated her so badly. To ease her mind, he said, "Just a few cuts and bruises. Nothin' serious. We'll be fine."

Deliah lowered her head and turned her right side to him, blocking his view of her face. He didn't need to scan her to realize that she was on the verge of tears, and it tore him up inside to know he alone was responsible for her misery. He considered apologizing, but then thought any attempt he might make would probably just make their situation more strained.

He glanced at Lachlan and saw that he was staring at Beth with a look that bespoke of his regret and profound sorrow. But he knew Lachlan's pride was overruling his need to tell Beth how much he loved her, and he knew Beth was not in a frame of mind to listen to him even if he managed to break the silence between them.

A choked sound escaped Kahl and Winston cut his gaze to the boys. They were not taking the pending separation between the men and women very well, and he wished he had it within him to comfort them. But he didn't. He could no more open his arms or heart to them, than he could to Deliah.

Indeed, Roan, Lachlan and he had made a helluva mess out of their relationships with their women.

"We'll mak sure the house is locked up and leave," Roan said, staring at his feet. "If you need anythin'—"

"We won't," said Laura curtly, although a tremor was heard in her tone. "We can lock up, ourselves."

Nodding, Roan gave her a long look, then headed out of the room. Lachlan and Winston followed him back into the night. They were between the house and the new oak when the sound of the outer doors being bolted stopped them in their tracks. Each looked back in poignant silence, then proceeded to the carriage house.

Chapter Fifteen

Winston's legs grew heavier and heavier with each step he took through the corridor of light. It was an endless effulgence, with narrow walls of infinite blackness. A place with no sound or scent, and one in which he couldn't even feel solidity beneath his feet. One portion of his mind concentrated on the possibility of falling through the nothingness beneath him, while another strained to see an end to his journey, and yet another harbored fear of what might lurk in the blackness to each side of him. He was alone and isolated from everything remotely familiar to him. And he was afraid he would never return to the people he had come to regard as family.

A zephyrous voice wove its way through the passage. "I will love ye forever, ma dour Scotsman."

Deliah! He tried to shout her name, but no sound passed his lips. Desperate to connect with reality, he reached out with his mind, imploring, *Find me, Deliah! Show me the way back!*

He waited. And waited. And waited. But she never responded. Not verbally. Not telepathically. Not even permitting him a sense of her presence. He now felt more abandoned, more isolated, and more desperate to emerge from this place.

Deliah, I need you! Don't leave me now. Show me the way back to you!

Why should she, though? He'd done everything within his power to shun her, to hurt her, to make *her* cut his heartstrings and spare him from confronting the demons of his inability to commit to love.

Begetters. Who are you? Wha' do you want from me?

Be . . . ye. Be . . . ye. Be . . . ye.

The words tauntingly echoed in his mind.

Deliah!

He was suddenly standing outside the carriage house. Glorious sunlight bathed the land and his heart leapt behind his breast at the sight of the new oak. It stood twenty feet tall, the broad trunk comprised of many smaller trees plaited into one mass. The canopy of branches was laden with vibrant green leaves, through which he glimpsed several peafowl staring down at him. Birds chirped merrily, flitting around the perimeter of the branches. Butterflies were in abundance, colorfully fluttering among wildflowers and ground cover of variegated green, red, and white, scattered around the tree and beyond its outstretched limbs.

A misty, transparent form appeared near the oak. Deliah. Glittering silver strips of material draped from her shoulders and hung the length of her hair. She danced on tiptoe with the grace of a ballerina, twirling and pirouetting, her arms arched above her head and her radiant face lifted to the overhead branches as if in homage. She hummed a tune which further gladdened his heart, her voice hauntingly sweet and beckoning. Her wings graced her like a shimmering cloak swept back by a hearty wind.

Too soon, she melted into the landscape and he experienced a sharp pang of loss. He closed his eyes and willed her back, but when he looked, she remained gone.

He gasped when time and space unexpectedly swept past him, thrusting him through what seemed like forward movement. He came to an abrupt stop and found himself standing within a very different place, this one semi-dark, lit only by a solitary lantern atop a trestle-legged table. There were opened cans, emptied wrappers, and bags strewn about the cement floor. On the table, cold, partially used black candles stood in makeshift tin holders, forming lines to each side of a jeweled dirk. The blade gleamed eerily and he could make out a Celtic knotwork border surrounding a strip of runescript down its center length. The handle was black with raised intricate silver patterns snaking around the jewels. He recognized the dirk. He'd once seen it embedded in Laura's chest not so long ago.

He sucked in a breath and regretted it immediately. The air was stale and reeked of perspiration and an assortment of foods.

Pork rinds. The taste filled his mouth, and yet he had never eaten one.

The room was approximately twelve feet by twelve feet, dank and cold and as quiet as a tomb. Three feet away was a planked door with a hook latch. It was engaged. Beyond the door, he could hear the approach of a slow gait, attired feet scuffing across the floor. Panic gripped him as he watched the hook slowly lift itself from the loop. Lift and lift until it was standing straight up and then became motionless. Then the door began to creak open.

Winston's eyes flew open. Breathing heavily through his nostrils, he stared into darkness, confused and frightened and inwardly struggling to get a fix on his whereabouts. Then he heard—

Snoring.

He almost laughed his relief was so great. Lachlan was snoring on the cot some fifteen feet away. It wasn't as dark as he'd first thought, for now that his eyes had adjusted, he could make out Roan's sleeping bag on the dirt floor a short distance away, and the lump within it that was Roan. Winston was safe and snug within one of his own, ten feet from the still warmth-giving wood stove.

Closing his eyes, he shifted slightly within the thick downy softness of his—hopefully—temporary bed.

Deliah. He hoped if he thought about her hard enough, then when he fell back to sleep, she would return and visit him in his dreams.

When Winston awoke the next morning, it was to moans induced from aching flesh and muscles, and stiff joints. His own grumbled laments joined in as he peeled himself out of his sleeping bag. Apparently, they hadn't fared all that well from the brawl at Shortby's. It had just taken time for their bodies to protest.

In turn, the men went out the back door and relieved themselves, then grouped in front of the stove which Roan had fired up immediately after awakening. They each sat atop empty crates, elbows braced on their upper legs, and working their mouths against the dryness and foul tastes coating their tongues. After a time, they coyly glanced at one another. Then Roan grumbled, "I need coffee. Lots and lots and lots o' strong coffee."

"I wouldna mind a hot bath and a shave," said Lachlan, running his left palm across the coarse stubble along his jawline.

Winston sniffed and grumpily eyed Lachlan. "I wouldn't mind if you had a bath, either."

"Ha . . . ha."

Roan briskly rubbed his hands up and down his face, then made a feeble attempt to run his fingers through his unruly hair. "Coffee, a hot bath, a shave, and Laura to warm ma bones. No' too much for a mon to ask, is it?"

Winston released a cynical chuckle. "Only if you have a death wish. I don't think the ladies have had enough time to cool down."

"I can guarantee you, Beth will be het for some time," Lachlan said with a grimace. "No' tha' I can blame her." He looked askance at his companions and grinned. "But we had us a grand time at Shortby's, na?"

"Grand?" Winston asked indignantly. "Fists slammin' into ma face is no' *ma* idea o' a good time."

Roan shrugged. "Actually, those goons got the worst o' it. Canabra looked like a bloated tomato when I got through wi' him. Felt bloody good, it did. He has always irked the bejesus ou' o' me."

Despite his split lower lip, Winston laughed. "Wha' was the redhead's name?"

"McKenna," said Roan.

"Ah, MacKenna. Abou' two minutes into the brawl, he knew he'd taken on more than he could handle. Canabra and Markey didn't have the good sense to know when to call it quits."

"Aye," Lachlan said wistfully. He glanced at his swollen, raw knuckles with a look of pride. "I wouldna mind facin' off wi' tha' Markey again. Dinna think he'll be urinatin' straight for some time."

Roan and Winston laughed.

"Course," Lachlan sighed, squirming on his crate, "tha' bootin' I got ta ma ass will have me crappin' crooked for a week o' Sundays."

Winston choked on his laughter, and Roan swiped aside a tear of laughter which had fallen onto his cheek.

"Damn," Roan chortled, then heaved a breath to get himself under control. "I don't think we should go to Shortby's anytime soon. Silas was madder than I've ever seen him."

"We paid for the damage," said Winston.

"Aye, but—"

A rap on the front door brought the men to their feet. Roan dashed ahead and threw open the door. Leaning beyond the threshold, he spied Laura heading toward the house, then glanced down and saw a large picnic basket in front of his feet. With a shake of his head, he lifted the basket, then closed the door and returned to the men in front of the hot stove. Adequate morning light streamed in from the window to the left of the stove. Seating himself back on his crate, he placed the basket on his lap and lifted the lid.

"Laura's no' too angry," he said cheerily, holding up a large thermos for the others to see. He handed it to Winston, then removed three cups and passed them to Lachlan. "We have a frying pan, spatula, six eggs, and a sliced section o' ham." He continued to rummage, then, "Some nicely diced potatoes and a tub o' butter. Plastic dishes. Spoons, knives, and forks." He looked up and frowned. "Na pepper or salt, though. Hmm. At least we won't starve."

"I designate you the cook," said Lachlan to Roan.

"Why me?"

"I'll cook," Winston sighed, "after I have a cup o' coffee."

An hour later, their stomachs full and the thermos emptied, they lethargically stared at the potbellied stove. Roan burped. Lachlan scratched the back of his head. Winston breathed deeply and lowered his eyelids half-mast.

"Now wha' do we do?" Winston asked.

"I'm for a bit mair sleep," said Roan, and yawned.

"I need ta burn off some steam," Lachlan murmured, then stretched and released an eye-watering yawn of his own.

"Why is it every time one o' us breathes, this place reeks like a brewery?" Winston asked.

"Have to breathe," Roan quipped.

Lachlan's eyes took on a mischievous gleam. "There was a time. . . ."

"Don't get me laughin' again," warned Roan with a chuckle. He sobered and used his right thumbnail to unwedge a piece of ham from between two of his lower teeth. "We could shovel out the driveway. I noticed some broken limbs on the rhododendron hedge, and the hand-carts could use reloadin' wi' wood and kindle. I'm sure there's plenty to do to keep us ou' o' trouble."

"Aye," said Lachlan, "and we should shovel the snow-drifts away from the house. Dinna need water gettin' into the cellar."

Lachlan noticed Winston's frown and asked, "Wha' are you thinkin' abou'?"

"The dirk," he replied.

Lachlan's eyebrows shot up and he glanced at Roan. "Are we talkin' abou' the infamous MacLachlan dirk? The one wha' done me in and nearly killed Laura?"

Winston nodded, his gaze intently searching Lachlan's bemused features. "I was dreamin' abou' it last night. Why did you call it the 'MacLachlan dirk'?"

"Ma maternal grandfaither gave it to me. Ma mither hailed from the MacLachlan clan. Both sides o' her family were MacLachlan bred and true for as far back as the clan's beginnings. Her faither wasna happy when she mairrit a Baird, although, he was good to ma brithers and me.

Grandfaither was a gruff old bugger, he was, and wi' the whitest hair I have ever seen on a mon.

"For some reason, he really took to me when I was verra young. When I was abou' nine, he told me I had the knowin'. To this day, I still dinna know wha' he meant by tha'. He took me fishin' and huntin' maist weekends, up till abou' the time I was twenty, and many a time we camped beneath the stars and he would tell me stories o' oor family history." He chuckled and went on, "Maist frightened the hell ou' o' me. Apparently, oor wee part o' the clan was fraught wi' mair'n its share o' strange characters. One o' *his* brithers believed hisself to be a *werewolf*, and he wasna the maist peculiar o' the lot, either."

Roan grinned through a grimace, while Winston smiled and shook his head.

"Anyway," Lachlan went on, "the MacLachlan dirk was originally found by ma grandfaither's great-great-great uncle, Broc. Rightfully, it should have been passed down ta ma oldest brither, Patrick, bu' ma grandfaither said I had the *knowin'* and I was to protect it."

"Protect it from wha'?" asked Roan.

Lachlan shrugged. "Grandfaither wasna always good abou' explainin' details."

"Considerin' how it was used to kill you and nearly killed Laura, I would think the dirk needs protectin' *against*," said Winston.

Lachlan shivered. "Perhaps."

"Are the gems real?" asked Winston.

"Aye. In all, three emeralds and three sapphires on one side, and five rubies on the ither. There were originally six rubies. I dinna know when the one came lost. Long afore I received the dirk."

Winston gave a low whistle, then, "Do you know wha' the runescript reads?"

"Na. Do you?"

Winston grinned ruefully. "No. I was just curious. Do you know where it is now?"

"Last I saw it was when I removed it from Laura and placed it on the ground next to me."

Roan frowned. "Come to think o' it, I haven't seen it since. I never even gave it anither thought efter tha' night."

"Winston," Lachlan began hesitantly, "do you know somethin' you're no' sayin'?"

Winston released a laugh and held up his hands. "No. Like I said, I dreamt abou' it and was merely curious. Actually, it was only a fragment o' the dream I had."

"So, nocht to worry abou' the bloody thing then?"

"Lachlan, I swear I'm no' hidin' anythin' from you."

A gust of breath ejected from Lachlan. "Thank God. To be truthful—wi' na disrespect for Grandfaither's trust in me—I wouldna care if I never saw it again."

"I'll second tha'," said Roan and rose to his feet. He stretched his arms, then the small of his back as he walked to the door. Opening it and stepping just beyond the threshold, he filled his lungs with fresh air.

Winston finished repacking the basket, while Lachlan positioned the crates against the wall perpendicular to the stove wall. Carrying the basket, Winston followed Lachlan outside to where Roan now stood by the new oak, inspecting the trunk.

"Have a look," said Roan, running his right hand over the rough bark. "It's grown since last night."

That wasn't all Winston noticed. "Is it ma imagination, or is the temperature over fifty and the snow and ice meltin'?"

"Spring has arrived," Roan grinned.

Lachlan surveyed the landscape. "Aye, so it has. Overnight, na less. It'll tak a while to melt all this, though."

"Look," Roan said pointing to one of the branches.

"Buds. This tree wasn't even here two days ago. And have you ever seen a trunk like this? It's incredible."

Winston tipped back his head and regarded the highest branches. With the exception that the leaves hadn't come out yet, the oak looked as it had in his dream.

"Magical, Deliah would say," Winston murmured, then glanced down at the basket. "I'm goin' to try to get into the kitchen. I want to empty this and clean up the dishes and utensils."

Lachlan passed Roan a hopeful look, then swung his gaze to Winston. "It wouldna hurt if you *happened* across one o' the women and mentioned how sorry we are."

"Laura and Beth are mair likely to watch their tempers around you," said Roan. "You bein' oor guest and all. And Deliah was mair concerned for oor well-bein' than she was angry."

Winston arched an eyebrow. "Have Beth or Laura ever threatened to turn either o' *you* into a nubby toad?"

"She couldn't." Roan shrugged. "She wouldn't." Comical doubt masked his face as he asked, "Would she?"

"Until you see me return in the flesh, watch where you step," Winston said dryly. With an airy salute, he headed toward the house.

Lachlan murmured, "Brave mon."

"Or foolish."

The two men locked gazes a moment, then Lachlan laughed.

Winston's stomach was in knots by the time he reached the far side of the house. He peered through the small panes of the door's window and saw no one in the kitchen. The knob turned in his hand and the door opened.

"Hel—lo," he called as he stepped through the doorway.

The room's stillness made him uneasy, but he closed the door behind him and placed the basket on the island centered in the room. Breakfast odors scented the air and the thirty-five by twenty foot room was warm, suggesting the oven had been used.

"Fresh scones or muffins," he said to himself. "Maybe even a loaf o' bread." He whistled softly as he unloaded the basket onto the oak counter. The throwaway items he gathered and tossed in a tall rubber trash can next to the double sinks. The tub of butter he carried to the far end of the room, where he opened a door to what appeared to be a large closet. Inside was the refrigerator, an ornate wooden piece standing five feet tall and four feet wide. He placed the tub on the second perforated shelf, then glanced down to see the ice block had dwindled to the size of a block of cheese. Closing the door, he removed a deep pan from beneath the refrigerator, something he'd seen Roan do during their baking session. He emptied the water into one of the sinks, returned the tray to its slot, then went to a wall hook next to the door and grabbed the ice tongs. Again as he'd seen Roan do, he went outside to a low wooden chest situated to the right of the stoop. Lifting the top and securing it open with an attached metal rod, he saw three blocks of ice remained, each wrapped in heavy brown paper. Roan had explained how, in the cold weather, the iceman delivered seven blocks of ice every Friday to last a week, while delivering one every morning during the hot weather. With no electricity, it was the only way to keep perishable objects cold.

Winston lowered the block to the ground, closed the top of the lid, then hoisted the ice and carried it into the kitchen. He placed it inside the bottom of the refrigerator, alongside the remains of the last block. With this done, he returned to the basket and transferred the used plates, pans, and utensils to the left sink.

Although the piping system was designed to allow lit fireplaces to heat portions of water for baths and washing at the sinks, the kitchen water had to be heated on the stove to do dishes. Winston was reaching for one of the larger kettles hanging from cast-iron hooks over the island, when he noticed Deliah standing at the doorway to the dining room. He froze in place, his heartbeat throbbing in his throat.

Winston lowered his arms and swallowed hard. She looked more like a teenager at the moment than a woman of her centuries. A baggy red knit jersey hung to her thighs, the long sleeves pushed halfway up her forearms. Cream colored stirrup pants, also loose-fitting, covered her to her bare feet.

Seeming a great deal more at ease than what Winston felt, she took the basket and placed it inside one of the bottom compartments of the massive oak sideboard across the island from him. Her hair was arranged in a single thick braid, which swung against her back with her movements.

Winston frowned when his mind dumped all thought, and he glanced about the room trying to collect himself. From the corner of his eye he saw Deliah walk toward him. She stopped at the end of the island, seven feet away, watching him through an unreadable expression. Still a greeting refused to formulate, so it was his intention to walk out the door until he unwittingly lowered his gaze. Again he found himself paralyzed, staring fixedly at the swell of her breasts and the erect nipples clearly defined through the jersey. Seconds ticked by before she spoke, and her tone was so casual and matter-of-fact, he found himself all the more baffled.

"I canna bring maself to wear the bindin' undergarments.

"Last night," she went on, "Laura asked why female fays have breasts if we dinna give birth and nurse oor wee ones. I explained how we reproduce, and how we are born mair as wha' ye call a toddler, and tha' we are indeed nursed on breast milk for the first two years. Efter tha' stage, we transform to oor middlin' phase, which is a far longer equivalency to wha' ye call your teen years."

Winston finally forced himself to look into her eyes and heard himself gulp. The heat of a blush stole across his cheeks and perspiration broke out on his brow.

"I'm sure the question o' ma breasts would have crossed your mind, sooner or later."

"Umm. . . ."

"Are ye comfortable, Winston?" she asked softly. "In the carriage house?"

He nodded and swallowed hard again. His palms itched and he flexed his fingers in a bid to relieve the irritation.

"May I approach ye?"

The question took him aback. "I wish you would."

Without hesitation, she closed the distance and stood within half an arm's reach. Her gaze solemnly inspected his split and swollen lower lip, the small cut on his right cheek, and the dark red blotch on his left jaw that was transforming into a bruise.

"Are ye in pain?"

"No' really. It's just a bit uncomfortable."

She wrinkled her nose expressively. "Male fays dinna sprout hair on their faces."

"I need to shave."

She searched his eyes with unnerving calm. "I can heal ye if ye allow me."

"Another root job?"

She grinned mischievously. "Nae, but I will need to touch ye."

The idea of that so appealed to Winston, his head reeled. "If it's no' too much trouble."

She studied him for a moment longer, then lifted her hands and placed them on his shoulders as she positioned herself against him. Winston was sure she could hear his heart pounding. Sure she knew just how much he wanted her. Standing on tiptoe, she pressed her lips to the cut on his cheek. He felt moisture against the area, then a tingling sensation that burrowed deeply into the wound. When next she targeted his marred jaw, she was hesitant and he sensed she didn't like the prickly feel of his stubble. Again he felt moisture and the same sensation seep into the layers of his skin. She settled on her heels for a time, inspecting his lower lip. Then, to his surprise, she pursed her lips and he saw a foamy dab of spit emerge from the tiny opening. He nearly flinched when she deposited it on the laceration, but then she lingered this time, and he felt her lips tenderly move against the wound. The tingling was more intense, bordering uncomfortable, when suddenly it vanished. When she settled back this time, he sucked in the injured section and ran his tongue along the surface. It was smooth. Neither cut nor swollen.

With a low, shaky laugh he said, "First time I've been grateful to be spat on. Thank you."

She nodded.

"Have you been outside this mornin'. It actually feels like spring has finally arrived."

To his chagrin, Deliah's eyes filled with tears and she turned her back to him.

"Did I say somethin' wrong?"

She shook her head, but he could tell by the taut posture of her shoulders she was upset.

Heaving a sigh, he glanced about then asked, "Have you seen the new oak?"

"I be aware o' it."

Her voice held such despair, Winston instinctively turned her around and pulled her into his arms. She didn't struggle, but buried her face into his right shoulder and gripped the front of his shirt. Her body shook with sobs for a brief time, then he heard her draw in ragged breaths as if attempting to rein in her emotions.

"Talk to me, Deliah," he whispered, stroking the back of her head. "Why are you so unhappy?"

A disparaging sound escaped her before she lifted her head. She didn't look up and her fingers loosened their hold, instead, lightly plucking at the material as if keeping her hands busy offered her fortification.

"I canna think o' spring withou' achin' for ma family. Tis oor maist cherished season. When we celebrate renewal wi' song and dance and await the arrival o' the young ones."

Winston kissed her on the brow, then propped up her chin with the side of an index finger. Tears still glistened in her eyes as she timidly met his probing gaze.

"Tis all lost, Winston."

"No' all. You're here."

A hitching breath spilled past her lips. "Alone, I canna nurture the land."

Winston smiled. "There are gardeners tha' help in tha' department."

"Aye," she said dully. "They can weed. They can plant. They can grow wha' they sow in the earth. But nae one but a fay can nuture the magic o' the earth. It be the magic wha' prevents blight. Magic wha' keeps leaves from turnin' brown afore their time, and flowers in full bloom throughou' their true phase.

"MoNae relies on us, Winston, to protect her realm. I canna do it alone."

"Deliah—"

Winston sucked in a breath when the dining room door opened and Laura stopped short at the threshold. Her eyes were red and swollen, her face gaunt and pale. Feeling that he had to say something, he managed a strained, "Thank you for breakfast. I came in to return the basket."

Several moments passed in tense silence, during which Deliah's gaze pinged between him and Laura.

"I'll have your lunch ready around noon," she said dispassionately, her solemn gaze watching Deliah.

"I better go," Winston said.

"Laura, canna he stay?" Deliah pleaded.

Winston's lips parted to speak, but Laura cut him off. "Winston, stay if you want. I'm not angry at you. I had no right to take out my frustration on you, last night."

"You were definitely within your rights," he said by way of apology. He looked down into Deliah's glowing face and felt a sharp pang of remorse. "Deliah, I can't. No' as long as Roan and Lachlan are on the outs."

Sorrow crept across her features. "They must mak their own peace. Winston, ye and I need to talk. Please, stay wi' me."

A breath shuddered from Winston and he rolled his eyes heavenward for a moment before looking deeply into hers. "It wouldn't be right if I stayed here."

Unable to stop himself, he crushed her to him and kissed her hard, passionately, then as abruptly released her and walked to the door. Opening it, he glanced back at her, knowing he looked as bleak and as miserable as did she, but unable to justify to himself why he should be forgiven and not Roan and Lachlan.

"I'm sorry," was all he could say. He hurried out the door, closing it behind him.

What began as a beautiful spring day, now struck him as gray and dismal, as dismal as the ache in his heart.

Chapter Sixteen

A bitter taste filled Winston's mouth as he lethargically ambled in the direction of the carriage house, his hands in his pants pockets and his head held low. Deliah's face, lined and shadowed with disappointment and sorrow, occupied the scope of his mindscreen. He repeatedly told himself he should turn around and finish what he'd begun in the kitchen. He had come so close to opening up his heart to her, to confessing how miserable he was away from her, to vowing a *commitment* to love her for the duration of his life, and beyond. In retrospect, he'd become a pro at evasiveness. An excuse always presented itself whenever he found himself in a situation that threatened to make him *feel* anything above and beyond what was required to complete each job. In leaving her this time, he came to the sickening realization that he had been responsible for his family's attitude toward him. Even as a young boy, he had emotionally cut them off, choosing the companion-ship of his psychic world to them. Little wonder they couldn't relate to him. How did any *normal* parent hope to breach the depths of the mental walls he'd constructed? His parents weren't perfect, but whose were? The fact they couldn't find it within themselves to give up their chosen way of life for a child like him, didn't make them selfish or cold or even bad parents. They'd done for him as well as they felt they could. Their emotional abandonment had stemmed from years of frustration and disappointment. His mother couldn't have another child. *He* was it. He'd never scanned his parents and now knew why. It wasn't *their* failings he had been afraid to view, but his own.

He had never cried as a child. Never had a favorite toy. A favorite program or song. He'd always been a passionate reader, but the reason didn't lie in the stories themselves, but in the fact that he could take the mindways and see the authors actually creating their works. Psychometry not only made it easy for him to know their every thought and mood during the productions, but granted him vivid images as if the process of completing the book was a movie playing across his mindscreen. He knew everything about the author, including the creative mindset that formulated each storyline and every character. By the time he was thirteen, he could pick up an author's book and delve into their current thoughts and routines. Clairvoyance. His talents had made it so simple to avoid his own reality and to live through the lives of others.

By the time he reached the new oak, he picked up on the fact that Roan and Lachlan were not in the carriage house. He stopped and released a breath of vexation. Turning his head, he spied the men at the rhododendron hedge and headed in their direction. The air was chilly but tolerable in his shirt, and the snow was already turning to mush.

"Got to admire their ingenuity," he heard Lachlan laugh.

Winston stopped a few feet from their position. They

were crouched and unraveling the yarn from amongst the branches. Already a sizeable pile was on the ground between them.

"If you say so," Roan grumbled. He jerked on a strand of dark green yarn and fell on his butt when it snapped free of its entangled mass. He laughed, then released a sound that resembled a choked sob. "Damn me, that's cold!" he exclaimed, scrambling to his feet and inspecting the soaked seat of his pants.

"Too much coffee," Lachlan quipped, his dark eyes filled with laughter.

"Or too little bladder control," said Winston.

Both men looked at him. Lachlan straightened up, then massaged the back of his thighs as he asked Winston, "How did it go?" Lachlan flashed a grin, adding, "You're no' a nubby toad, so either you didna see Deliah, or she's feelin' the spirit o' spring."

Winston struggled to appear at ease, but he noted Roan watching him through slightly narrowed eyes. A brief scan told him Roan could see through his tenuous facade, and it made him feel all the more vulnerable, a slave to his fledgling emotions.

"I saw her," he said, forcing a smile, but unable to keep from glancing at Roan and measuring his assessing perusal. "She's no' happy wi' the situation, but she's no' upset wi' me."

"Good," said Lachlan.

Roan nodded, a hand plucking at the soaked material clinging to his backside.

"I saw Laura, too." Roan glanced off to one side and Winston went on, "She looked as though she'd been cryin' and hadn't slept."

"Damn me," Roan murmured.

"Wha' o' Beth?"

"I didn't see her, Lachlan."

Lachlan solemnly nodded as his gaze bleakly regarded the house. Winston abruptly threw his shields up to spare himself absorbing the others' grim moods. He was melancholy enough. A compelling urge to run back to the house shuddered through him. Resisting it taxed his ability to appear in control and, to bide time until he settle himself into a comfortable phase of apathy, he stepped beyond Roan, crouched and started to unravel another section of yarn. Several moments passed before Lachlan asked, "Wha' are you doin' ou' here wi' us, laddie?"

The dry humor in the man's tone elicited a chuff of laughter from Winston, but he sobered when he looked up and found both men eyeing him through frowns. They reminded Winston of a set of bookends. Side by side. Arms folded against their chests. Eyebrows drawn down over piercing eyes.

Standing, Winston again slid his hands into the side pockets of his pants. "What's goin' on?"

"You tell us," said Roan, his tone gruff.

"Aye," Lachlan said, his frown turning into a scowl. "I thought we friends, Winston."

Winston thought better of scanning them, instead, offering a light shrug. "We are."

"Ah. I see." Roan sounded flip, peeved. "*You* may be the psychic one, but Lannie and I consider oourselves to be fair judges o' character."

Winston started to lower his mind shield. He couldn't understand what was bothering the others, and he wasn't in the mood to play guessing games. But as he was about to reach out and scan them, Lachlan stepped forward and shook a finger at him.

"Na, laddie. One to one, mon to mon, why are you wastin' your time ou' here wi' us?"

Anger erupted inside Winston, so abruptly and unexpectedly, he spoke without benefit of auditing his thoughts.

"I'm askin' maself the same question!" He pointed toward the main house. "There's a womon in there who asked me to remain wi' her. But for some bloody *misplaced* sense o' loyalty to both o' you, I'm here gettin' lip instead o' lovin' from her!"

Winston trod a circle while he collected the bits of anger he'd been harboring for the past two weeks, and when he squarely faced Roan and Lachlan, his cheeks reddened and he could feel his temples throbbing with an erratic pulse. "Will one o' you *please* explain to me why you cherish pride above the love and respect o' your women? Can you? Can you climb down from your testosterone high long enough to *think* o' how the women must be feelin' abou' oor conduct?" He laughed like a man on the verge of a breakdown, and threw his hands up to emphasize the depths of his pique. "*We* caused this. They've more spine than the lot o' us, and I bloody weel don't like *ma* part in their sufferin'!"

The men stared at Winston for a long pregnant moment, then Lachlan shifted a heated gaze to Roan and asked, "What's a *testosterone* high?"

Chagrined, Roan made a face. "It's a mon thing. I think."

His expression changing to one of wry amusement, Lachlan swerved his eyes to Winston. "So, tis loyalty to friendship wha' wrenched you from Deliah's side, eh?" He clicked his tongue with a shake of his head. "Shame on you, Winston. I'm an *auld* mon and Roan here, weel, he's a proud *Ingliss*. No' the best o' excuses, but we've no' your education nor your worldliness. Friendship is grand, laddie, but na substitute for the love o' a womon."

"Did you insult me?" Roan asked Lachlan, bewildered.

"Aye." Lachlan's shrewd gaze remained fixed on Winston. "I insulted us both. For a good cause."

Roan snorted but didn't otherwise respond.

Running a hand across his mouth, Winston heaved a sigh to calm himself. "I'm sorry. It was ma choice to leave, and I used you both as an excuse to avoid—"

"Facin' the truth o' bein' in love," completed Lachlan sagely.

"We're ou' here to give *oor* women the time to cool off," said Roan. "Deliah doesn't have Laura and Beth's short tempers. You're no' foolin' anyone but yourself, Winston. You can smile and put on the airs o' a mon wi' no' a trouble on his mind, but your eyes always betray you."

Emotions rose and clogged Winston's throat, making it impossible for him to speak. He turned to face the house and folded his arms across his middle. Shortly, Roan and Lachlan stood to each side of him, their hands clasped behind them and their gazes fixed on the house. Again it struck Winston how alike were the two men. More like close brothers than men who had once been enemies. Even their heartbeats were synchronized. Most peculiar.

"If I thought Laura was ready to talk to me, I'd be cozyin' up wi' her in oor bed and bringin' in oor own kind o' spring gladness."

"Aye," Lachlan sighed. "I'd be doin' ma grovelin' for forgiveness right proud, then spendin' the day remindin' her why she fell in love with me in the first place." He turned his head and somberly regarded Winston's profile. "But Beth isna ready or I would have heard from her. If nocht else—" He surveyed the house with unmistakable longing. "—I would have seen her watchin' me from one o' the windows. For her to mak herself unseen and unheard, tis a *deep* hurt ma actions have dealt her. I'm no' only takin' this time to let her temper wane, but to find the courage to face her."

Roan lowered his head and poked the ground with the toe of his right shoe. "We're responsible for draggin' you into this mess." He looked up and met Winston's gaze. "Don't let oor stupidity keep you from Deliah."

"I went to Shortby's willingly," said Winston, disheartened. He sighed and closed his eyes for a second. When he opened them, he looked heavenward as he spoke. "I've never allowed maself to have friends. It's been . . ." He smiled almost shyly as he lowered his gaze to the ground in front of his feet. ". . . an experience. One I don't want to end."

He walked six paces, then turned and faced Roan and Lachlan. "I owe you both a great deal. Ma sanity, for one. I don't want you to think I'm ungrateful, but I love Deliah, and I no' only should be wi' her, I *need* to be wi' her."

A broad grin spread across his companions' faces.

"Laddie," Lachlan said out the side of his mouth, "that's wha' we've been tryin' to tell you."

"You're wastin' time," Roan said with an exaggerated sigh and a sparkle in his eyes.

His heart pounding wildly, Winston bobbed his head. "I'll come by to see you later." He started to back up. "Much later." His facial muscles broke out in a grin and he felt ecstatically buoyant, as if spring had awakened the darkest corners of his mind and heart. "Don't let Beth and Laura wait too long."

"If things aren't resolved by tonight," said Roan, "I plan to storm the house in the morn."

Lachlan shivered and cast Roan a harried look. "Ma exact thoughts. *Fegs*, mon, I think we're spendin' too much time thegither."

With a laugh, Winston turned and lit into a semblance of a run, moving as quickly as the still-slick ground would allow. He didn't look back but kept his focus on the house. As he made his way to the kitchen door, he tried to imagine Deliah's reaction to his return. How could he have been so stupid to leave her again? Where had he found the strength to walk out of the kitchen, knowing everything he wanted and needed in life was right there, watching over him?

He bound into the kitchen, startling Beth. She looked up from the sinks, her face pale, her eyes wide.

"Sorry," he said breathlessly, closing the door. He faced her, knowing he looked ridiculously giddy, but not caring. "I need to see Deliah."

"I believe she's in her room."

"Thank you." He started to run for the dining room door, but stopped short of reaching it. "Beth?"

She looked at him a bit warily from over her shoulder.

"I know it's no' ma place—"

"Then don't," she said coldly, and returned to washing the dishes in the sink.

Winston heaved a ragged breath. "I have to. Please."

For a moment he thought she would keep her back to him, but then she reached for the dish towel on the hook to the left of the sink, and turned while drying her hands. She was in her nightgown and robe, her light brown, curly hair tousled, her eyes underscored with shadows. "Get it off your chest," she said dully.

Again his throat felt blocked. Clearing the psychological sensation, he shifted nervously, then said, "I know there's no excuse for the way Roan, Lachlan, and I have been actin'." He cleared his throat. "This is more difficult than I thought."

"If you're about to plead Lachlan's case, I'm not interested."

The words finally formulated, and he gushed, "Beth, it's his love for you tha' frightens him."

"That's ridiculous. Dammit, Winston, I didn't think anyone could hurt me the way he has! I'll be damned if I let him get away with this!"

"I don't blame you. I don't! But it wouldn't hurt you

so deeply if you didn't love him, Beth. All I'm suggestin' is tha' when he approaches you, listen to wha' he has to say."

Tears rose in her eyes as she trembled against the anger pushing for release. "Before or after I run him through with one of his swords?"

A choked laugh escaped Winston before he could suppress it. "Before, I hope. I'm sorry I upset you."

She turned back to the sink. "Worry about Deliah. Winston?"

"Wha'?"

She didn't look his way, but said in a small voice, "She's really having a hard time dealing with all the uproar around here. Don't say or do anything to make her feel any worse than she does."

"Unless she's averse to acceptin' ma proposal, I hope to mak her verra happy."

She whirled at this, her paleness vanishing beneath a glow of joy. "She thinks. . . ."

"Wha'?"

A hand lifting to rest at the base of her throat, Beth replied, "I shouldn't have said anything."

"Beth, please tell me."

She nodded. "She thinks she isn't worthy of you or a life among us. Winston, she loves you so much."

He smiled from the very core of his being. "I know, and I've been a perfect ass."

"No one's perfect," she quipped, and he blushed. "Thank you for telling me."

"Are you superstitious, Beth?"

"Why?"

"Because I'm going to beg you to keep your fingers crossed for me."

Beth chuckled. "I will. May I mention this to Laura?"

"Only if you think she'll cross her fingers, too."

"I can pretty much guarantee it," Beth said, breathless with excitement. Her eyes shone and her carriage bespoke of renewed energy she hadn't felt for some time. "It'll be nice to have something cheery to focus on."

On impulse, Winston walked around the island and planted a kiss on Beth's cheek. She straightened in surprise, her eyes wide, while Winston backed away, heat surging up his face. "Spring fever," he said, grinning uncontrollably, then he ran from the kitchen and through the dining room.

Deliah's bedroom was on the second floor, next to the tower passage. He paused at the door, the hand about to rap frozen in midair as a shiver of nervousness worked its way through his system. Although he didn't doubt her love for him, or his for her, he couldn't help but remember the devastation he'd read in her eyes when he'd left her in the kitchen. How far could even a fay be pushed before they emotionally shut down? Would she shun him to protect herself? Shun him to make him experience the depths of sorrow she'd endured because of him?

Suddenly he was terrified to cross the threshold and face her. Terrified that in the short time since they'd last spoken, she had hardened her heart against him.

His palms clammy, Winston turned the knob, opened the door, and boldly walked into the room. He saw her immediately, kneeling in front of one of the open windows, her arms folded on the windowsill and her chin resting atop them. Quietly closing the door, he walked across the room. His nerve endings crackled. He felt both hot and cold. Both elongated windows were wide open and the hearth was cold. The room was chilly but not uncomfortable, the air fresh and redolent of spring. Faint floral scents teased his nostrils, scents he knew she somehow exuded.

He stopped close to her, standing off to her right. She was staring unseeingly across the back of the property, lost in a realm of despair he could only begin to imagine. She had unbraided her hair and it fell down her back and pooled on the floor behind her like a carpet of satin. If he lived with her a thousand years, he told himself he would never tire of its sheen and length and texture. It wasn't within him to ever see her as anything less than miraculous and beautiful and enchanting. He'd come too close to letting her slip from his life.

"Deliah," he rasped, his hands knotted at his sides.

She turned her head and looked up at him, but her dreamy expression told him she didn't believe he was actually there. He waited an excruciatingly tense moment, then sank to his knees next to her. The glassiness in her eyes began to wane and her eyebrows twitched as if trying to form a frown. An entanglement of wariness and desperation crept across the delicate structure of her features. Her shoulders shifted. Tensed. He could hear her shallow breathing. Almost swear he could hear the rapid palpitation of her heart.

A timorous smile appeared on Winston's face as he reached out and tenderly touched her jawline. She blinked and her facial muscles made a bid to smile, not quite succeeding. He stroked the soft ridge with the backs of his fingers. She closed her eyes and released a wistful sigh, its sound circling his heart and sending a delightful chill through his system.

"Do you have any idea just how beautiful you are?" he asked in a soft yet husky tone.

"Do ye?" she countered. A genuine smile lit her eyes as she settled back on her heels, her gaze searching his face as if to recommit every line and plane to her memory. "I be surprised to see ye. Why are ye here?"

In response, Winston cupped her nape and simultaneously leaned toward while drawing her closer. He saw her eyelashes lower in a flutter of motion as he brushed his mouth across her lips in a feathery kiss. Then she sighed, her breath as soft and as sweet as spring itself. Winston was about to ease back when she gripped the front of his shirt and pulled him onto his knees and against her. Twisting around, she flung her arms around his neck and kissed him passionately, her fingers intermittently kneading his scalp and trenching through the thick straight strands of his hair. They were both on their knees, flush against each other, Winston's right arm bracing her lower back, his left hand cupping the back of her head. A cool breeze swept through the window and frolicked around them, but their fevered skin was oblivious to its presence.

Desire as hot as lava rose behind Winston's chest, rose until he thought his brain would erupt from his skull. He broke the kiss, untangled her arms from about his neck, then sat back hard on his butt on the floor. His vision was blurred for a moment. When it cleared, he saw her watching him with grim expectancy and knew she believed he was going to run from her again. Shaking his head a bit dazedly, he lifted a hand toward her.

"Deliah, I need a bath and a shave."

"Why?"

An abrupt laugh coughed from him. "Because I reek, and my stubble is irritatin' your skin. I can see chafed areas around your mouth."

"I dinna care. Ye could sprout a forest on your face, Winston, and I wouldna care a wit."

Breathing heavily, Winston forced himself onto his feet, his gaze never straying from the foreboding shadowing her eyes. Once he was steady on his feet, he drew in a fortifying breath and squared his shoulders. "I *do* care a wit, lass. I'll be damned if I mak love to you smellin' like a brewery. I won't be long, I promise." She lowered her eyes, then her head, and he prompted, "Deliah?"

Her head remained dipped.

In a bid to rally his waning courage, Winston glanced about the room, vaguely appreciating its green and beige tones and the heavy, dark stained furniture with its elaborate cherub carvings. Embroidered floral drapes and sheers covered the windows, and a matching quilt covered the bed. The Persian rug centered on the hardwood floor was forest green, gold, and black. The room was the perfect setting for her. Cherubs and flowers. Springtime and winged wonders.

"I've decided to return to work soon," he said matter-of-factly, staring down at her bent head. "It'll mean I'll be travelin' at times, and no' always home wi' ma wife. I'm a difficult enough mon to love, and ma work won't mak it any easier. Trackin' serial killers tends to darken ma mood. I usually suffer aftermath depressions when I've been in the field, and I'm no' fit to be around anyone. Hopefully, knowin' I have a lovin', carin' wife waitin' for me will alter tha' cycle."

He released a gush of breath and went on, "I guess I'm tellin' you this because I don't want you to commit to marriage withou' knowin' wha' to expect given the worst case scenario. I'm thirty-six years old and I've gone this long withou' a social life, no' to mention one o' anythin' remotely intimate. When I marry, it'll be for life. She has to be verra sure I'm wha' she wants. Tha' I'm worth the trouble to love on a long term basis. I can be a broodin', chauvinistic, miserable, intense jerk at times, and tend to isolate maself when I've a lot on ma mind. I'm no' good at voicin' ma feelings because, quite frankly, I didn't know I had any until recently.

"All in all, I can't think o' a good reason why any womon would tolerate someone like me, let alone commit to marriage. But I won't settle for anythin' less."

Nervous because she refused to look at him, and wound up because the more he talked, the more he realized what a pathetic prize he was for any woman, he forged on. "I expect the womon I marry to remain at home. Tis a mon's place to provide, and tha' I can. I speak ma mind and don't have the temperament to put up wi' a quarrelsome womon, so in tha', I expect her to obey ma wishes. I like properly cooked food and prefer to read the news in solitude. And I believe a mon should be privy to mak love to his wife *anywhere* and *anytime* the mood strikes him."

Winston bobbed his head in closure and abruptly headed for the door. He opened it and looked back at her. She hadn't moved, and her hair curtained her profile.

"Deliah, if your door is locked when I return, I'll have your answer. If it isn't, I'll warn you now, there will be no turnin' back."

For what seemed a long time after he had closed the door behind him, Deliah remained motionless. His every word echoed hollowly through her mind, confusing her all the more as seconds became minutes. She hadn't slept all night and told herself she was so muddled because of that. But then it dawned on her that everything he'd said hadn't made sense, because. . . .

Lifting and turning her face toward the window, she closed her eyes as a breeze caressed her skin. She forced herself to clear her mind and breathe in deeply, as if to cleanse herself completely of the darker emotions she had experienced since her escape from the root. When she was calm and in control, she thought back on every conversation she'd had with Winston. He had always perplexed her, even long ago when he was a boy, and she had encountered his mind in the fourth dimension. She hadn't known then that he would one day come to Baird House. That he would one day free her. That he would one day bring into her life equal portions of happiness and sorrow, pleasure and pain. When she recalled his speech of minutes ago, she found herself again bewildered. Why would he speak of what he expected of a wife, to her? Hadn't she promised him she would never prevent him from finding the woman who would give him the love and family he deserved? Hadn't she only asked that she be allowed to love him, be his lover, until the time came when he had to leave her?

Getting to her feet, she walked around the room, her thoughts far removed from her actions, from her location. After a time, she stared at the crystal doorknob, frowning.

Why would she lock the door? Even if she did, what possible answer could that signify?

"All in all, I can't think o' a good reason why any womon would tolerate someone like me, let alone commit to marriage."

"Weel," she huffed, her hands on her hips, "how did you expect me to respond, when I be no' a womon, but a female fay. Damn ye, Winston Ian Connery, wha' were ye tryin' to tell me? Tha' ye already found a womon ye want to marry? When, pray tell? Between the time ye kissed me in the kitchen and ye kissed me here?

"Och, you pestin' mon! Why do I let ye confuse me like this?"

"I speak ma mind and don't have the temperament to put up wi' a quarrelsome womon."

"Ha! A quarrelsome womon be exactly wha' ye need! And privy to mak love anywhere and at anytime a *mon's* right, is it?" She shook furiously, her graceful hands balled at her sides. "Weel, twould be a *kindness* were *men* designed to mak love durin' the tides o' a *womon's* needs. Twould have been mair'n once ye would have been in *ma* bed, I guarantee!"

She walked to the foot of the bed and gripped the decorative molding along its surface. "Deliah, ye were better off afore ye left the root. Time to stop thinkin' wi' your heart!"

A mischievous grin turned up the corners of her mouth

and she arched an eyebrow. "Ye worry abou' chafin' ma face, but no' ma heart. Winston, ye have ma ire up and I dinna like the direction o' ma thoughts, for I can see ye as a nubby toad upon ma palm, croakin' your croaks and puffin' up your wee chest. And would I be cruel aneuch, Winston Ian Connery, to lay ye upon one o' these fine pillows and mak ye listen to me nag ye from dusk till dawn? Aye. I think I could."

She folded her arms against her middle and grinned scoffingly. "Better yet, why no' *three* toads upon ma pillow?"

Her anger deflated so unexpectedly, tears welled up in her eyes and her chin quivered.

"Damn ye, Winston. I wish—"

At the sound of the door opening, she spun around. At the same instant she saw Winston at the threshold, her world went topsy-turvy. For a terrifying moment, she felt herself falling, then clinging to solidity as the whirling inside her head waned.

"What's wrong, Deliah?" she heard Winston ask, the concern in his tone resparking her anger. "Are you dizzy? Do you need to lie down?"

A fey tingling sensation swept through her but she nonetheless found the strength to push him back and walk several paces in the direction of the windows. She felt oddly numb and disoriented, but her anger gave her roots by which to anchor and stabilize herself.

"Deliah?"

Turning with controlled slowness, she fought to present a calm facade, but knew by his probing gaze that he suspected she was upset.

"The door was unlocked."

She thought the statement as confusing as everything else about the man, and said irritably, "So?"

He frowned. "Do you want me to leave?"

It was on the tip of her tongue to tell him to run before she did turn him into a nubby toad, but she glanced him over and found herself quieting again. He was barefoot. Beltless dark slacks. A white shirt, of which the cuffs were unbuttoned and the front left open, revealing his muscular chest and midsection. He was clean shaven, his wet hair combed back, and his eyes greener than usual.

Deliah's mouth went dry as longing stirred deep inside her, taunting her as it had so often the past weeks. She wanted to tell him off as a means of unburdening her heart, but she couldn't initiate the internal fires it would require to do it properly. Instead, she murmured, "I hope ye will be happy."

He seemed surprised and thrust his hands in his pockets. "I hope we *both* are happy." He glanced at the windows. "Mind if I close them? It's ch—"

He bit back the word when with a flick of her right hand, the windows slid shut.

"Thank you."

She nodded.

Seconds of silence ticked by. Winston rocked on his feet while Deliah observed him through hooded eyes.

"So how am I to tak this, Deliah?"

"Tak wha'?"

"The door was unlocked, but I can't say you look too happy to see me."

"Aye."

A comical frown masked his face. "Aye wha'? Will you or won't you, Deliah? I realize it's within your rights to mak me squirm, but it's damn uncomfortable no' knowin' your answer."

"Weel, all I can say is your wife will have her measure o' work handlin' ye, she will. Wha' wi' ye bein' a broodin', chauvinistic, miserable, intense jerk at times."

With a low, cynical laugh, Winston walked around her

and stopped in front of the left window. His back to her, he said, "I guess I shouldn't begrudge you evenin' the score."

"I have nae score to settle, but I be o' a mind to have a few words wi' ye."

Turning, he arched a brow and nodded that she should go on.

"Weel," she sighed, straightening her shoulders and slightly tilting up her chin, "Far be it a *fay* should settle for less than *she* deserves. Twould no' be ma nature to let *any* mon dictate when I should feel the need to mak love, and when to and no' to speak ma mind. Furthermair, a *fair* provider would hire a cook to compensate for his cherished wife's lack thereo', and such provider would *never* sit alone readin' a musty paper while his wife be somewhere else missin' him."

With an airy shrug, Winston said, "All doable."

"Do-a-ble?"

He nodded. "Go on."

She thought his mood very strange and wished she understood what it was he expected from her. "I ask ye, Winston, do ye love this wife to be?"

Without hesitation, he replied, "More than I believed I could ever love anyone."

Deliah painfully swallowed and lowered her gaze. "Then I beg ye be kind to her."

When silence followed, she looked up to find him frowning at her. Then his expression cleared and his bearing took on an air of haughtiness that further bewildered her.

"Kind, eh?" He closed the distance between them and removed his hands from his pockets. "Kinder than I've been to you?"

Her head jerked back and she gasped, "I pray so!"

To her surprise, he laughed as his bright eyes scanned her face. "You know, Deliah, when I left this room a while ago, I promised maself I wouldn't scan you for your answer. And I didn't. And I wouldn't have now if you weren't actin' so peculiar."

"Tis be a *fay* thing, this peculiar," she said airily, although unease twittered in the pit of her stomach.

"Have you any idea why I'm here?" he asked teasingly.

"To torment me, nae doubt."

"You're goin' to mak me do it, aren't you?"

Weary and frustrated, she asked, "Do wha'?"

He lowered himself to one knee. "Get down on a knee." He took her left hand and kissed the ring finger. "Tak your hand and asked for it in marriage."

Deliah blinked down at him. "Ma hand?"

"I would prefer *all* o' you."

"Me?"

"Will you marry me?"

"Me?" she croaked, trying to retain her reasoning despite the buzzing in her head.

"Who did you think I was talkin' abou'?"

"No' . . . me."

His arms went around her thighs and he lifted her as he stood. Then he loosened his hold just enough to let her slide against him until her feet were again on the floor. Heat washed through Deliah and she found herself breathlessly staring into a face glowing with love and such devotion, she wondered if *he* had somehow cast a spell on her.

Laughingly, he chided, "You remembered 'broodin', chauvinistic, miserable, intense jerk at times', but no' when I said I didn't want *you* to commit to marriage withou' knowin' wha' to expect when I'm at ma worst?"

She thought this over, then blushed. "The worst case scenario. Aye. I do now."

"And?"

"Winston, I canna give ye children, and I canna cook!"

His kissed one corner of her mouth. "You are all the family I need. As for cookin'." He released a laugh and gave her an affectionate squeeze. "Like you said, we can always hire someone." He took in a deep breath and released it slowly while he soberly caressed her face with his gaze. When he spoke again, his words were deep and husky, quivering with emotion. "I've been such a fool, Deliah. I vow, if you marry me, I'll do everythin' I can to mak you happy."

Tears of joy spilled down Deliah's radiant face. "Lovin' me is aneuch." She reached up and framed his face with her trembling hands. "Ye be ma lover, ma hopes, ma dreams, and ma life, Winston Ian Connery. I vow to serve ye proper wi' ma heart, ma mind, and ma spirit."

Now tears formed in his eyes and a tremulous smile quirked on his lips. "Are you sayin' *yes,* Deliah?"

"O' course, ma dour Scotsmon. I will marry ye."

Winston wound his arms tighter about her and nuzzled the left side of his face to hers. Deliah wrapped her arms around his neck and clung to him, glorying in the feel of his hard body molded against her. Their hearts beat as one in a symphony of profound love and joy.

"God, how I love you!" he gasped, then laughed a bit unsteadily, drew back and looked deeply into her eyes. "How anythin' so . . ." He brushed the back of a hand down her cheek and hitched a breath. ". . . perfect could want me!"

"Want?" she countered softly. "Winston, ye be ma sun and moon, ma breath and ma pulse. Wantin' be no' the measure, but the necessity. Withou' love, life be but fallow land, existin' yet uncultivated. Withou' *ye,* ma heart would be barren and have nae hope o' nurturin' ma spirit. *Want* ye, Winston? I *need* ye!"

Winston kissed her then, passionately, deeply. Deliah didn't need to unfurl her wings for she soared on wings of love, within an infinite blueness of happiness. Whatever life brought them now, she knew they would face it together. Darkness would never again find a place to hide, and sorrow would never touch them long enough to even blemish their lives.

By the time Winston ended the kiss, Deliah was deliriously content. She dreamily peered into his handsome face and mutely thanked the fates for delivering her into his arms. "Winston, mak love to me."

"Wouldn't you rather wait until we're officially Mr. and Mrs. Winston Ian Connery?"

Although his tone was almost playful, she detected a serious note as well. She studied his features for a few seconds more. When she spoke, her words were but a whisper. "Oor spirits were wed when first ye kissed me. Wait, ye ask?" She smiled impishly, then nipped his chin. "On ma word, Winston, I'll perish from achin' if ye dinna join wi' me now."

In response, Winston lifted her into his arms and carried her to the bed, where he stood for a time staring into her face as if incredulous he'd truly been granted fortune's favor.

"You have no doubts?"

Deliah laughed. "*Och,* ye be a pestin' mon, ma Winston!"

Smiling from the depths of his enlightened soul, he lowered her to the bed.

We hope you've enjoyed LOVE EVERLASTIN', the third book in Mickee Madden's wonderful series that began with EVERLASTIN' and DUSK BEFORE DAWN. In June of 1999, the magic will continue with HOPE EVERLASTIN'. Here's taste of what's in store for Lachlan and Beth . . .

HOPE EVERLASTIN'
By
Mickee Madden

Barefoot and wearing only her torn nightgown, Beth dashed into the night. She was soaked before she rounded the house, and numb by the time she reached the woods. Nonetheless, she hastened along the path to the field.

She slowed her pace when she was close enough to see that he was on his knees in front of her headstone, his fingertips toughing the engraved lettering on the granite.

"When there is too much to forgive, wha' does tha' leave a mon to do?" he said in a low, husky voice. "I canna live without you, Beth, nor can I die. I've na way to know how to mak up for the wrongs."

Beth waited a few moments until thoughts of snuggling beside him in a warm bed gave her the courage to break the silence.

"March 23rd, 1843—" His head shot up and his dark eyes looked at her as if he were seeing a ghost. "—a heartless bride took her husband's life and had her lover wall his body up in the tower.

"On March 23rd, 1995," she forced herself to go on, "another heartless lover drove this same man into the cold of a rainy night."

She stepped closer to the stone and gripped it. A breath lodged in her throat when Lachlan slowly rose to his feet, still staring at her as though disbelieving she were real.

"Are you hoping to die of pneumonia out here, is that it?" she asked. "Well it just won't do, Lachlan. I can't allow you to deny your children their father."

He stepped around the headstone, his boots making sucking sounds in the mud as he cam closer to her. He didn't say a word.

Beth cast a forlorn look toward the mansion. She was cold and tired, and her stomach was tied in knots. The twins would be waking at any time to be fed. And Lachlan was making her squirm. Waiting for her to say what he wanted to hear, not her feeble attempt to skirt around an outright apology.

"I'm sorry," she finally said in a small voice.

"Sorry for wha'?" he asked, his deep voice husky.

Furious, she open-handedly whacked him on the chest and sputtered, "For ever coming to this *damn* country—" She gasped, then straightened back her shoulders and looked into his eyes with what she hoped was a semblance of remorse. "For hitting you. Okay . . . for hitting you *and* running off at the mouth."

She released a shuddering breath. "Damn you, Lachlan, you make me crazy, sometimes! I told you I want you in my life. What more do you want to hear? That I want you in m-my bed?" She sucked in a breath to calm her nerves "Okay. O . . . kay, I do. Want you in my bed, I mean."

Expressionless, Lachlan ran a hand over the top of his sodden hair. "Are you sayin' you want me back in *ma* bed, lass, or in *any* bed *wi'* you?"

A strangled chuff of laughter escaped her before she gripped the remains of the front of his shirt. Lifting on tiptoes immersed in mud, she calmly stated, "If you don't kiss me now, I'm going to bury you where you stand."